CASTLE GAY

NOTE

The earlier doings of Dougal, Jaikie, and Mr. Dickson McCunn will be found in a novel entitled *Huntingtower*.

J. B.

CASTLE GAY

BY

JOHN BUCHAN

THOMAS NELSON AND SONS, Ltd.
LONDON, EDINBURGH, NEW YORK
TORONTO, AND PARIS

*First printed July 1930. Reprinted July, August,
October, November 1930.
First printed in this edition, September 1932.*

CONTENTS

CASTLE GAY

CHAPTER I

TELLS OF A RUGBY THREE-QUARTER

MR. DICKSON McCUNN laid down the newspaper, took his spectacles from his nose, and polished them with a blue-and-white spotted handkerchief.

" It will be a great match," he observed to his wife. " I wish I was there to see. These Kangaroos must be a fearsome lot." Then he smiled reflectively. " Our laddies are not turning out so bad, Mamma. Here's Jaikie, and him not yet twenty, and he has his name blazing in the papers as if he was a Cabinet Minister."

Mrs. McCunn, a placid lady of a comfortable figure, knitted steadily. She did not share her husband's enthusiasms.

" I know fine," she said, " that Jaikie will be coming back with a bandaged head and his arm in a sling. Rugby in my opinion is not a game for Christians. It's fair savagery."

" Hoots, toots ! It's a grand ploy for young folk. You must pay a price for fame, you know.

Besides, Jaikie hasn't got hurt this long time back. He's learning caution as he grows older, or maybe he's getting better at the job. You mind when he was at the school we used to have the doctor to him every second Saturday night. . . . He was always a terrible bold laddie, and when he was getting dangerous his eyes used to run with tears. He's quit of that habit now, but they tell me that when he's real excited he turns as white as paper. Well, well! we've all got our queer ways. Here's a biography of him and the other players. What's this it says ? "

Mr. McCunn resumed his spectacles.

" Here it is. ' J. Galt, born in Glasgow. Educated at the Western Academy and St. Mark's College, Cambridge . . . played last year against Oxford in the victorious Cambridge fifteen, when he scored three tries. . . . This is his first International . . . equally distinguished in defence and attack. . . . Perhaps the most unpredictable of wing three-quarters now playing. . . .' Oh, and here's another bit in ' Gossip about the Teams.' " He removed his spectacles and laughed heartily. " That's good. It calls him a ' scholar and a gentleman.' That's what they always say about University players. Well, I'll warrant he's as good a gentleman as any, though he comes out of a back street in the Gorbals. I'm not so sure about the scholar. But he can always do anything he sets his mind to, and he's a worse glutton for books than me. No man can tell what may happen to Jaikie yet. . . . We can take credit for these

laddies of ours, for they're all in the way of doing
well for themselves, but there's just the two of them
that I feel are like our own bairns. Just Jaikie
and Dougal—and goodness knows what will be the
end of that red-headed Dougal. Jaikie's a douce
body, but there's a determined daftness about
Dougal. I wish he wasn't so taken up with his
misguided politics."

" I hope they'll not miss their train," said the
lady. " Supper's at eight, and they should be here
by seven-thirty, unless Jaikie's in the hospital."

" No fear," was the cheerful answer. " More
likely some of the Kangaroos will be there. We
should get a telegram about the match by six
o'clock."

So after tea, while his wife departed on some
domestic task, Mr. McCunn took his ease with a
pipe in a wicker chair on the little terrace which
looked seaward. He had found the hermitage for
which he had long sought, and was well content
with it. The six years which had passed since he
forsook the city of Glasgow and became a country-
man had done little to alter his appearance. The
hair had indeed gone completely from the top of
his head, and what was left was greying, but there
were few lines on his smooth, ruddy face, and the
pale eyes had still the innocence and ardour of youth.
His figure had improved, for country exercise and
a sparer diet had checked the movement towards
rotundity. When not engaged in some active enterprise, it was his habit to wear a tailed coat and
trousers of tweed, a garb which from his boyish

recollection he thought proper for a country laird,
but which to the ordinary observer suggested a
bookmaker. Gradually, a little self-consciously, he
had acquired what he considered to be the habits
of the class. He walked in his garden with a spud;
his capacious pockets contained a pruning knife
and twine; he could talk quite learnedly of crops
and stock, and, though he never shouldered a gun,
of the prospects of game; and a fat spaniel was
rarely absent from his heels.

The home he had chosen was on the spur of a
Carrick moor, with the sea to the west, and to
south and east a distant prospect of the blue
Galloway hills. After much thought he had rejected the various country houses which were open
to his purchase; he felt it necessary to erect his
own sanctuary, conformable to his modest but
peculiar tastes. A farm of some five hundred
acres had been bought, most of it pasture-fields
fenced by dry-stone dykes, but with a considerable
stretch of broom and heather, and one big plantation of larch. Much of this he let off, but he
retained a hundred acres where he and his grieve
could make disastrous essays in agriculture. The
old farm-house had been a whitewashed edifice of
eight rooms, with ample outbuildings, and this he
had converted into a commodious dwelling, with
half a dozen spare bedrooms, and a large chamber
which was at once library, smoking-room, and
business-room. I do not defend Mr. McCunn's
taste, for he had a memory stored with bad prece-
dents. He hankered after little pepper-box turrets,

which he thought the badge of ancientry, and in internal decoration he had an unhallowed longing for mahogany panelling, like a ship's saloon. Also he doted on his vast sweep of gravel. Yet he had on the whole made a pleasing thing of Blaweary (it was the name which had first taken his fancy), for he stuck to harled and whitewashed walls, and he had a passion for green turf, so that, beyond the odious gravel, the lawns swept to the meadows unbroken by formal flower-beds. These lawns were his special hobby. " There's not a yard of turf about the place," he would say, " that's not as well kept as a putting-green."

The owner from his wicker chair looked over the said lawns to a rough pasture where his cows were at graze, and then beyond a patch of yellowing bracken to the tops of a fir plantation. After that the ground fell more steeply, so that the tree-tops were silhouetted against the distant blue of the sea. It was mid-October, but the air was as balmy as June, and only the earlier dusk told of the declining year. Mr. McCunn was under strict domestic orders not to sit out of doors after sunset, but he had dropped asleep and the twilight was falling when he was roused by a maid with a telegram.

In his excitement he could not find his spectacles. He tore open the envelope and thrust the pink form into the maid's face. " Read it, lassie—read it," he cried, forgetting the decorum of the master of a household.

" Coming seven-thirty," the girl read primly.

" Match won by single point." Mr. McCunn upset his chair, and ran, whooping, in search of his wife.

The historian must return upon his tracks in order to tell of the great event thus baldly announced. That year the Antipodes had dispatched to Britain such a constellation of Rugby stars that the hearts of the home enthusiasts became as water, and their joints were loosened. For years they had known and suffered from the quality of those tall young men from the South, whom the sun had toughened and tautened—their superb physique, their resourcefulness, their uncanny combination. Hitherto, while the fame of one or two players had reached these shores, the teams had been in the main a batch of dark horses, and there had been no exact knowledge to set a bar to hope. But now Australia had gathered herself together for a mighty effort, and had sent to the field a fifteen most of whose members were known only too well. She had collected her sons wherever they were to be found. Four had already played for British Universities ; three had won a formidable repute in international matches in which their country of ultimate origin had entitled them to play. What club, county, or nation could resist so well equipped an enemy ? And, as luck decided, it fell to Scotland, which had been having a series of disastrous seasons, to take the first shock.

That ancient land seemed for the moment to have forgotten her prowess. She could produce a strong, hard-working, and effective pack, but her great three-quarter line had gone, and she had lost the scrum-half who the year before had been her chief support. Most of her fifteen were new to an international game, and had never played together. The danger lay in the enemy halves and three-quarters. The Kangaroos had two halves possessed of miraculous hands and a perfect knowledge of the game. They might be trusted to get the ball to their three-quarters, who were reputed the most formidable combination that ever played on turf. On the left wing was the mighty Charvill, an Oxford Blue and an English International; on the right Martineau, who had won fame on the cinder-track as well as on the football-field. The centres were two cunning brothers, Clauson by name, who played in a unison like Siamese twins. Against such a four Scotland could scrape up only a quartet of possibles, men of promise but not yet of performance. The hosts of Tuscany seemed strong out of all proportion to the puny defenders of Rome. And as the Scottish right-wing three-quarter, to frustrate the terrible Charvill, stood the tiny figure of J. Galt, Cambridge University, five foot six inches in height and slim as a wagtail.

To the crowd of sixty thousand and more that waited for the teams to enter the field there was vouchsafed one slender comfort. The weather, which at Blaweary was clear and sunny, was abominable in the Scottish midlands. It had rained all the preceding night, and it was hoped that the ground might be soft, inclining to mud

—mud dear to the heart of our islanders but hateful
to men accustomed to the firm soil of the South.

The game began in a light drizzle, and for Scotland it began disastrously. The first scrimmage
was in the centre of the ground, and the ball came
out to the Kangaroo scrum-half, who sent it to his
stand-off. From him it went to Clauson, and then
to Martineau, who ran round his opposing wing,
dodged the Scottish full-back, and scored a try,
which was converted. After five minutes the
Kangaroos led by five points.

Presently the Scottish forwards woke up, and
there was a spell of stubborn defence. The Scottish
full-back had a long shot at goal from a free kick,
and missed, but for the rest most of the play was in
the Scottish twenty-five. The Scottish pack strove
their hardest, but they did no more than hold their
opponents. Then once more came a quick heel out,
which went to one of the Clausons, a smart cut-
through, a try secured between the posts and easily
converted. The score was now ten points to nil.

Depression settled upon the crowd as dark as
the weather, which had stopped raining but had
developed into a sour *haar*. Followed a period
of constant kicking into touch, a dull game which
the Kangaroos were supposed to eschew. Just
before half-time there was a thin ray of comfort.
The Scottish left-wing three-quarter, one Smail,
a Borderer, intercepted a Kangaroo pass and
reached the enemy twenty-five before he was
brought down from behind by Martineau's marvellous sprinting. He had been within sight of success,

and half-time came with a faint hope that there was still a chance of averting a runaway defeat.

The second half began with three points to Scotland, secured from a penalty kick. Also the Scottish forwards seemed to have got a new lease of life. They carried the game well into the enemy territory, dribbling irresistibly in their loose rushes, and hooking and heeling in the grand manner from the scrums. The white uniforms of the Kangaroos were now plentifully soiled, and the dark blue of the Scots made them look the less bedraggled side. All but J. Galt. His duty had been that of desperate defence conducted with a resolute ferocity, and he had suffered in it. His jersey was half torn off his back, and his shorts were in ribbons : he limped heavily, and his small face looked as if it had been ground into the mud of his native land. He felt dull and stupid, as if he had been slightly concussed. His gift had hitherto been for invisibility ; his fame had been made as a will-o'-the-wisp ; now he seemed to be cast for the part of that Arnold von Winkelried who drew all the spears to his bosom.

The ball was now coming out to the Scottish halves, but they mishandled it. It seemed impossible to get their three-quarters going. The ball either went loose, or was intercepted, or the holder was promptly tackled, and whenever there seemed a chance of a run there was always either a forward pass or a knock-on. At this period of the game the Scottish forwards were carrying everything on their shoulders, and their backs seemed hopeless.

Any moment, too, might see the deadly echelon of the Kangaroo three-quarters ripple down the field.

And then came one of those sudden gifts of fortune which make Rugby an image of life. The ball came out from a heel in a scrum not far from the Kangaroo twenty-five, and went to the Kangaroo stand-off half. He dropped it, and, before he could recover, it was gathered by the Scottish stand-off. He sent it to Smail, who passed back to the Scottish left-centre, one Morrison, an Academical from Oxford who had hitherto been pretty much of a passenger. Morrison had the good luck to have a clear avenue before him, and he had a gift of pace. Dodging the Kangaroo full-back with a neat swerve, he scored in the corner of the goalline amid a pandemonium of cheers. The try was miraculously converted, and the score stood at ten points to eight, with fifteen minutes to play.

Now began an epic struggle, not the least dramatic in the history of the game since a century ago the Rugby schoolboy William Webb Ellis first " took the ball in his arms and ran with it." The Kangaroos had no mind to let victory slip from their grasp, and, working like one man, they set themselves to assure it. For a little their magnificent three-quarter line seemed to have dropped out of the picture, but now most theatrically it returned to it. From a scrimmage in the Kangaroo half of the field, the ball went to their stand-off and from him to Martineau. At the moment the Scottish players were badly placed, for their three-quarters were standing wide in order to overlap the faster

enemy line. It was a perfect occasion for one of Martineau's deadly runs. He was, however, well tackled by Morrison and passed back to his scrum-half, who kicked ahead towards the left wing to Charvill. The latter gathered the ball at top-speed, and went racing down the touch-line with nothing before him but the Scottish right-wing three-quarter. It seemed a certain score, and there fell on the spectators a sudden hush. That small figure, not hitherto renowned for pace, could never match the Australian's long, loping, deadly stride.

Had Jaikie had six more inches of height he would have failed. But a resolute small man who tackles low is the hardest defence to get round. Jaikie hurled himself at Charvill, and was handed off by a mighty palm. But he staggered back in the direction of his own goal, and there was just one fraction of a second for him to make another attempt. This time he succeeded. Charvill's great figure seemed to dive forward on the top of his tiny assailant, and the ball rolled into touch. For a minute, while the heavens echoed with the shouting, Jaikie lay on the ground bruised and winded. Then he got up, shook himself, like a heroic, bedraggled sparrow, and hobbled back to his place.

There were still five minutes before the whistle, and these minutes were that electric testing time, when one side is intent to consolidate a victory and the other resolute to avert too crushing a defeat. Scotland had never hoped to win ; she had already done far better than her expectations, and she gathered herself together for a mighty effort to hold what she had gained. Her hopes lay still in her forwards. Her backs had far surpassed their form, but they were now almost at their last gasp.

But in one of them there was a touch of that genius which can triumph over fatigue. Jaikie had never in his life played so gruelling a game. He was accustomed to being maltreated, but now he seemed to have been pounded and smothered and kicked and flung about till he doubted whether he had a single bone undamaged. His whole body was one huge ache. Only the brain under his thatch of hair was still working well. . . . The Kangaroo pack had gone down field with a mighty rush, and there was a scrum close to the Scottish twenty-five. The ball went out cleanly to one of the Clausons, but it was now very greasy, and the light was bad, and he missed his catch. More, he stumbled after it and fell, for he had had a punishing game. Jaikie on the wing suddenly saw his chance. He darted in and gathered the ball, dodging Clauson's weary tackle. There was no other man of his side at hand to take a pass, but there seemed just a slender chance for a cut-through. He himself of course would be downed by Charvill, but there was a fraction of a hope, if he could gain a dozen yards, that he might be able to pass to Smail, who was not so closely marked.

His first obstacle was the Kangaroo scrum-half, who had come across the field. To him he adroitly sold the dummy, and ran towards the right touch-line, since there was no sign of Smail. He had little hope of success, for it must be only a question of seconds before he was brought down. . He did not hear the roar from the spectators as he appeared in the open, for he was thinking of Charvill waiting for his revenge, and he was conscious that his heart was behaving violently quite outside its proper place. But he was also conscious that in some mysterious way he had got a second wind, and that his body seemed a trifle less leaden.

He was now past the half-way line, a little distance ahead of one of the Clausons, with no colleague near him, and with Charvill racing to intercept him. For one of Jaikie's inches there could be no hand-off, but he had learned in his extreme youth certain arts not commonly familiar to Rugby players. He was a most cunning dodger. To the yelling crowd he appeared to be aiming at a direct collision with the Kangaroo left-wing. But just as it looked as if a two-seater must meet a Rolls-Royce head-on at full speed, the two-seater swerved and Jaikie wriggled somehow below Charvill's arm. Then sixty thousand people stood up, waving caps and umbrellas and shouting like lunatics, for Charvill was prone on the ground, and Jaikie was stolidly cantering on.

He was now at the twenty-five line, and the Kangaroo full-back awaited him. This was a small man, very little taller than Jaikie, but immensely broad and solid, and a superlative place-kick. A different physique would have easily stopped the runner, now at the very limits of his strength, but the Kangaroo was too slow in his tackle to meet Jaikie's swerve.

He retained indeed in his massive fist a considerable part of Jaikie's jersey, but the half-naked wearer managed to stumble on just ahead of him, and secured a try in the extreme corner. There he lay with his nose in the mud, utterly breathless, but obscurely happy. He was still dazed and panting when a minute later the whistle blew, and a noise like the Last Trump told him that by a single point he had won the match for his country.

There was a long table below the Grand Stand, a table reserved for the Press. On it might have been observed a wild figure with red hair dancing a war dance of triumph. Presently the table collapsed under him, and the rending of timber and the recriminations of journalists were added to the apocalyptic din.

At eight o'clock sharp a party of four sat down to supper at Blaweary. The McCunns did not dine in the evening, for Dickson declared that dinner was a stiff, unfriendly repast, associated in his mind with the genteel in cities. He clung to the fashions of his youth—ate a large meal at one o'clock, and a heavy tea about half-past four, and had supper at eight from October to May, and in the long summer days whenever he chose to come indoors. Mrs. McCunn had grumbled at first, having dim social aspirations, but it was useless to resist her husband's stout conservatism. For the evening meal she was in the habit of arraying herself in black silk and many ornaments, and Dickson on occasions of ceremony was persuaded to put on a dinner jacket; but to-night he had declined to change, on the ground that the guests were only Dougal and Jaikie.

There were candles on the table in the pleasant dining-room, and one large lamp on the sideboard. Dickson had been stubborn about electric light, holding that a faint odour of paraffin was part of the amenities of a country house. A bright fire crackled on the hearth, for the October evenings at Blaweary were chilly.

The host was in the best of humours. " Here's the kind of food for hungry folk. Ham and eggs —and a bit of the salmon I catched yesterday ! Did you hear that I fell in, and Adam had to gaff me before he gaffed the fish ? Everything except the loaf is our own providing—the eggs are our hens', the ham's my own rearing and curing, the salmon is my catching, and the scones are Mamma's baking. There's a bottle of champagne to drink Jaikie's health. Man, Jaikie, it's an extraordinary thing you've taken so little hurt. We were expecting to see you a complete lameter, with your head in bandages."

Jaikie laughed. " I was in more danger from the crowd at the end than from the Kangaroos. It's Dougal that's lame. He fell through the reporters' table."

He spoke with the slight sing-song which is ineradicable in one born in the west of Scotland, but otherwise he spoke pure English, for he had an imitative ear and unconsciously acquired the speech of a new environment. One did not think of Jaikie as short, but as slight, for he was admir-

ably proportioned and balanced. His hair was soft
and light and unruly, and the small wedge of face
beneath the thatch had an air of curious refinement
and delicacy, almost of wistfulness. This was partly
due to a neat pointed chin and a cherubic mouth,
but chiefly to large grey eyes which were as appeal-
ing as a spaniel's. He was the incarnation of
gentleness, with a hint of pathos, so the old ladies
longed to mother him, and fools occasionally despised
him—to their undoing. He had the look of one
continually surprised at life, and a little lost in it.
To-night his face from much contact with mother
earth had something of the blue, battered appearance
of a pugilist's, so that he seemed to be a cherub, but
a damaged cherub, who had been violently ejected
from his celestial home.

The fourth at the table, Dougal Crombie, made a
strong contrast to Jaikie's elegance. The aforetime
chieftain of the Gorbals Die-hards had grown into a
powerful young man, about five feet ten inches in
height, with massive shoulders and a fist like a black-
smith's. Adolescence had revised the dispropor-
tions of boyhood. His head no longer appeared to
be too big for his body ; it was massive, not monstrous. The fiery red of his hair had toned down to
a deeper shade. The art of the dentist had repaired
the irregularities of his teeth. His features were
rugged but not unpleasing. But the eyes remained
the same, grey-green, deep-set, sullen, smouldering
with a fierce vitality. To a stranger there was something about him which held the fancy, as if a door
had been opened into the past. Even so must have

looked some Pictish warrior, who brewed heather-
ale, and was beaten back from Hadrian's Wall ;
even so some Highland cateran who fired the barns
of the Lennox ; even so many a saturnine judge of
Session and heavy-handed Border laird. Dougal
in appearance was what our grandfathers called a
" Gothic survival." His manner to the world was
apt to be assertive and cynical ; he seemed to be
everlastingly in a hurry, and apt to jostle others off
the footpath. It was unpleasant, many found, to
argue with him, for his eye expressed a surly contempt ; but they were wrong—it was only interest.
Dougal was absorbed in life, and since his absorption
was fiercer than other people's, it was misunderstood.
Therefore he had few friends ; but to those few—
the McCunns, Jaikie, and perhaps two others—he
was attached with a dog-like fidelity. With them
he was at his ease and no longer *farouche* ; he talked
less, and would smile happily to himself, as if their
presence made him content. They gave him the
only home life he had ever known.

Mr. McCunn spoke of those who had years before
acknowledged Dougal's sway.

" You'll want to have the last news," he said.
" Bill's getting on grand in Australia. He's on
his own wee farm in what they call a group settle-
ment, and his last letter says that he's gotten all
the roots grubbed up and is starting his first plough-
ing, and that he's doing fine with his hens and his
dairy cows. That's the kind of job for Bill—there
was always more muscle than brains in him, but

there's a heap of common sense. . . . Napoleon's
in a bank in Montreal—went there from the London
office last July. He'll rise in the world no doubt,
for he has a great head for figures. Peter Paterson
is just coming out for a doctor, and he has lifted a
tremendous bursary—I don't mind the name of it,
but it will see him through his last year in the hos-
pitals. Who would have said that Peter would
turn out scientific, and him such a through-other
laddie ? . . . But Thomas Yownie is the big surprise. Thomas, you mind, was all for being a pirate.
Well, he'll soon be a minister. He had aye a grand
voice, and they tell me his sermons would wile the
birds from the trees. . . . That's the lot, except for
you and Jaikie. Man, as Chief Die-hard, I'm proud
of my command."

Dickson beamed on them affectionately, and they
listened with a show of interest, but they did not
share his paternal pride. Youth at twenty is full
of hard patches. Already to the two young men
the world of six years ago and its denizens had
become hazy. They were remotely interested in
the fates of their old comrades, but no more. The
day would come when they would dwell sentiment-
ally on the past : now they thought chiefly of the
present, of the future, and of themselves.

" And how are you getting on yourself, Dougal ? "
Dickson asked. " We read your things in the paper,
and we whiles read about you. I see you're running
for Parliament."

" I'm running, but I won't get in. Not yet."

" Man, I wish you were on a better side. You've

got into an ill nest. I was reading this very morning a speech by yon Tombs—he's one of your big men, isn't he?—blazing away about the sins of the boorjoysee. That's just Mamma and me."

"It's not you. And Tombs, anyway, is a trumpery body. I have no use for the intellectual on the make, for there's nothing in him but vanity. But see here, Mr. McCunn. The common people of this land are coming to their own nowadays. I know what they need and I know what they're thinking, for I come out of them myself. They want interpreting and they want guiding. Is it not right that a man like me should take a hand in it?"

Dickson looked wise. "Yes, if you keep your head. But you know fine, Dougal, that those who set out to lead the mob are apt to end by following. You're in a kittle trade, my man. And how do you manage to reconcile your views with your profession? You've got a good job with the Craw papers. You'll be aspiring some day to edit one of them. But what does Mr. Craw say to your politics?"

The speaker's eye had a twinkle in it, but Dougal's face, hitherto as urbane as its rugged features permitted, suddenly became grim.

"Craw!" he cried. "Yon's the worst fatted calf of them all. Yon's the old wife. There's no bigger humbug walking on God's earth to-day than Thomas Carlyle Craw. I take his wages, because I give good value for them. I can make up a paper with any man, and I've a knack of descriptive writing. But thank God! I've nothing to do with

his shoddy politics. I put nothing of myself into
his rotten papers. I keep that for the *Outward*
every second Saturday."

" You do," said Dickson dryly. " I've been reading some queer things there. What ails you at
what you call ' modern Scotland ' ? By your way
of it we've sold our souls to the English and the
Irish."

" So we have." Dougal had relapsed again into
comparative meekness. It was as if he felt that
what he had to say was not in keeping with a firelit
room and a bountiful table. He had the air of being
a repository of dark things which were not yet ready
for the light.

" Anyway, Scotland did fine the day. It's time
to drink Jaikie's health."

This ceremony over, Dickson remained with his
glass uplifted.

" We'll drink to your good health, Dougal, and
pray Heaven, as the Bible says, to keep your feet
from falling. It would be a sad day for your friends
if you were to end in jyle. . . . And now I want
to hear what you two are proposing to do with
yourselves. You say you have a week's holiday,
and it's a fortnight before Jaikie goes back to
Cambridge."

" We're going into the Canonry," said Jaikie.

" Well, it's a fine countryside, the Canonry.
Many a grand day I've had on its hill burns. But
it's too late for the fishing. . . . I see from the
papers that there's a by-election on now. Is Dougal
going to sow tares by the roadside ? "

"He would like to," said Jaikie, "but he won't be allowed. We'll keep to the hills, and our head-quarters will be the Back House of the Garroch. It's an old haunt of ours."

"Fine I know it. Many a time when I've been fishing Loch Garroch I've gone in there for my tea. What's the wife's name now? Catterick? Ay, it was Catterick, and her man came from Sanquhar way. We'll get out a map after supper and you'll show me your road. The next best thing to tramping the hills yourself is to plan out another man's travels. There's grand hills round the Garroch—the Muneraw and the Yirnie and the Calmarton and the Caldron. . . . Stop a minute. Doesn't Mr. Craw bide somewhere in the Canonry? Are you going to give him a call in, Dougal?"

"That's a long way down Glen Callowa," said Jaikie. "We mean to keep to the high tops. If the weather holds, there's nothing to beat a Canonry October."

"You're a pair of desperate characters," said Dickson jocosely. "You're going to a place which is thrang with a by-election, and for ordinary you'll not keep Dougal away from politics any more than a tyke from an ash-bucket. But you say you're not heeding the election. It's the high hills for you—but it's past the time for fishing, and young legs like yours will cover every top in a couple of days. I wish you mayna get into mischief. I'm afraid of Dougal with his daftness. He'll be for starting a new Jacobite rebellion. 'Kenmure's on and awa', Willie.'"

Mr. McCunn whistled a stave of the song. His spirits were soaring.

"Well, I'll be at hand to bail you out. . . . And remember that I'm old, but not dead-old. If you set up the Standard on Garroch side, send me word and I'll on with my boots and join you."

CHAPTER II

INTRODUCES A GREAT MAN IN ADVERSITY

FIFTY-EIGHT years before the date of this tale a child was born in the school-house of the landward parish of Kilmaclavers in the kingdom of Fife. The schoolmaster was one Campbell Craw, who at the age of forty-five had espoused the widow of the provost of the adjacent seaport of Partankirk, a lady his junior by a single summer. Mr. Craw was a Scots dominie of the old style, capable of sending boys direct to the middle class of Humanity at St. Andrews, one who esteemed his profession, and wore in the presence of his fellows an almost episcopal dignity. He was recognized in the parish and far beyond it as a " deep student," and when questions of debate were referred to his arbitrament, he would give his verdict with a weight of polysyllables which at once awed and convinced his hearers. The natural suspicion which might have attached to such profundity was countered by the fact that Mr. Craw was an elder of the Free Kirk and in politics a sound Gladstonian. His wife was a kindred spirit, but in her, religion of a kind took the place of philosophy. She was a noted connoisseur of sermons, who would travel miles to hear some select preacher, and her voice had acquired something of the pulpit monotone. Her world was the Church, in which she hoped that her solitary child would some day be a polished pillar.

The infant was baptized by the name of Thomas Carlyle, after the sage whom his father chiefly venerated; Mrs. Craw had graciously resigned her own preference, which was Robert Rainy, after the leader of her communion. Never was a son the object of higher expectations or more deeply pondered plans. He had come to them unexpectedly; the late Provost of Partankirk had left no offspring; he was at once the child of their old age, and the sole hope of their house. Both parents agreed that he must be a minister, and he spent his early years in an atmosphere of dedication. Some day he would be a great man, and the episodes of his youth must be such as would impress the readers of his ultimate biography. Every letter he wrote was treasured by a fond mother. Each New Year's Day his father presented him with a lengthy epistle, in the style of an evangelical Lord Chesterfield, which put on record the schoolmaster's more recent reflections on life: a copy was carefully filed for the future biographer. His studies were minutely regulated. At five, though he was still shaky in English grammar, he had mastered the Greek alphabet. At eight he had begun Hebrew. At nine he had read *Paradise Lost*, Young's *Night Thoughts*, and most of Mr. Robert Pollok's *Course of Time*. At eleven he had himself, to his parents' delight, begun the first canto of an epic on the subject of Eternity.

It was the way to produce a complete prig, but

somehow Thomas Carlyle was not the ordinary prig. For one thing, he was clearly not born for high scholastic attainments. There was a chronic inaccuracy in him which vexed his father's soul. He was made to dabble in many branches of learning, but he seemed incapable of exact proficiency in any. When he had finished with the school of Kilmaclavers, he attended for two years the famous academy of Partankirk, which had many times won the first place in the college bursaries. But he was never head boy, or near it, and the bursary which he ultimately won (at Edinburgh) was only a small one, fitted to his place of twenty-seventh in the list. But he was noted for his mental activity. He read everything he could lay his hand on, and remembered a good deal of it. He was highly susceptible to new ideas, which he frequently misunderstood. At first he was unpopular among his contemporaries, because of his incapacity for any game and his disinclination to use his fists, but in each circle he entered he won his way eventually to tolerance if not to popularity. For he was fruitful of notions; he could tell his illiterate comrades wonderful things which he had picked up from his voracious reading ; he could suggest magnificent schemes, though in carrying them out he was at the best a campfollower.

At the age of twenty we find Thomas Carlyle Craw in the last year of his Edinburgh arts course, designing to migrate presently to a theological college. His career has not been distinguished, though he has won a fifth prize in the English

Literature class and a medal for an essay on his namesake. But he has been active in undergraduate journalism, and has contributed many pieces to the evening papers. Also he has continued his miscellaneous reading, and is widely if inaccurately informed on every current topic. His chief regret is that he is a miserable public speaker, his few efforts having been attended by instant failure, and this is making him lukewarm about a ministerial career. His true weapon, he feels, is the pen, not the tongue. Otherwise he is happy, for he is never bored—and pleasantly discontented, for he is devouringly ambitious. In two things his upbringing has left an abiding mark. The aura of dedication hangs over him; he regards himself as predestined to be a great man, though he is still doubtful about the kind of greatness to be attained. Also father and mother have combined to give him a serious view of life. He does not belie his name, for the sage of Ecclefechan has bequeathed him some rags of his mantle. He must always be generalizing, seeking for principles, philosophizing; he loves a formula rather than a fact: he is heavily weighted with unction; rhetoric is in every fibre. He has a mission to teach the world, and, as he walks the pavements, his head is full of profound aphorisms or moving perorations—not the least being the obituary which some day men will write of him. One phrase in it will be, " He was the Moses who led the people across the desert to the Promised Land "; but what the Promised Land was to be like he would have been puzzled to say.

That winter he suffered his first calamity. For Campbell Craw fell ill of pneumonia and died, and a month later Euphemia, his wife, followed him to Kilmaclavers churchyard. Thomas Carlyle was left alone in the world, for his nearest relative was a cousin in Manitoba whom he had never seen. He was an affectionate soul and mourned his parents sincerely ; when his grief dulled a little he wrote a short biography of them, " A Father and a Mother in Israel," which appeared in the *Partankirk Advertiser* and was justly admired. He was left now to his own resources, to shape his life without the tender admonitions of the school-house. Long and solemnly he perpended the question of the ministry. It had been his parents' choice for him, he had been " dedicated " to it, he could not lightly forsake it. But his manifest lack of preaching endowments— he had a weak, high-pitched voice and an extreme nervousness—convinced him that common sense must prevail over filial piety. He discussed the matter with the minister of Kilmaclavers, who approved. " There's more ways of preaching than in a pulpit," was that sage's verdict.

So Thomas decided upon letters. His parents had bequeathed him nearly three thousand pounds, he had no debts, he was accustomed to live sparingly ; on such a foundation it seemed to him that he could safely build the first storey of what should one day be a towering edifice. After taking an undistinguished degree, he migrated to London, according to the secular fashion of ambitious Scottish youth.

His first enterprises were failures. The serious

monthlies would have none of his portentous
treatises on the conduct of life, and the *Times*
brusquely refused a set of articles on current politics,
in the writing of which he had almost wept at his
own eloquence.   But he found a niche in a popular
religious weekly, where, under the signature of
" Simon the Tanner," he commented upon books
and movements and personalities.

Soon that niche became a roomy pulpit, from
which every week he fulminated, argued, and senti-
mentalized with immense acceptation.   His columns
became the most popular feature of that popular
journal.   He knew nothing accurately about any
subject in the world, but he could clothe his ignorance in pontifical vestments and give his confusion
the accents of authority.   He had a remarkable flair
for discerning and elaborating the tiny quantum of
popular knowledge on any matter.   Above all, he
was interesting and aggressively practical.   He took
the hand of the half-educated and made them believe
that he was leading them to the inner courts of
wisdom.   Every flicker of public emotion was fanned
by him into a respectable little flame.   He could be
fiercely sarcastic in the manner of his namesake, he
could wallow in the last banalities of sentiment, he
could even be jocose and kittenish, but he knew his
audience and never for a moment lost touch with it.
" Helpful " was the epithet most commonly applied
to him.   He was there to encourage and assist, and
his answers to correspondents began to fill a large
space in his chosen journal.

So at the age of twenty-four Thomas was making

a good income, and was beginning to be much in request by uplift societies. He resolutely refused to appear in public : he was too wise to let his halting utterance weaken the impression of his facile pen. But a noble discontent was his, and he marshalled his forces for another advance. Generations on his mother's side of small traders in Partankirk had given him considerable business acumen, and he realized that the way to fortune did not lie in writing for other men. He must own the paper which had its vogue from his talents, and draw to himself the whole profits of exploiting the public taste. Looking about him, he decided that there was room for a weekly journal at a popular price, which would make its appeal to the huge class of the aspiring half-baked, then being turned out by free education. They were not ardent politicians ; they were not scholars ; they were homely, simple folk, who wanted a little politics, a little science, a little religion, set to a domestic tune. So he broke with his employers, and, greatly daring, started his own penny weekly. He had considerably added to his little fortune, for he had no extravagant tastes, and he had made many friends in the circles of prosperous nonconformity. There was a spice of the gambler in Thomas, for every penny he possessed or could borrow he put into the new venture.

The *Centre-Forward* was a success from the first. The name was a stroke of genius ; being drawn from the popular sport of football, it was intelligible to every one, and it sounded a new slogan. The paper would be in the van of progressive thought, but also

in the centre of the road, contemptuous alike of
right-hand reaction and left-hand revolution. It
appeared at that happy time in the 'nineties, when
the world was comfortable, mildly progressive, and
very willing to be amused by toys. And Thomas
was an adroit editor. He invented ingenious competitions, and offered prizes of a magnitude hitherto
unknown in British journalism. He discovered
three new poets—poetry was for the moment in
fashion—and two new and now completely forgotten humorists, and he made each reader share
in the discovery and feel that he too was playing
the part of a modest Mæcenas. He exposed abuses
with a trenchant pen, when his lawyers had convinced him that he was on safe legal ground. Weekly
he addressed the world, under his own signature, on
every conceivable topic and with an air of lofty
brotherhood, so that the humblest subscriber felt
that the editor was his friend. The name of Thomas
Carlyle Craw might be lightly regarded by superfine
critics, but by some hundreds of thousands of plain
Britons it was extolled and venerated.

Thomas proved an acute man of business. The
Centre-Forward was never allowed to languish for
lack of novelties ; it grew in size, improved in
paper and type, carried a great weight of advertise-
ments, and presently became a pioneer in cheap
pictures. Every detail of its manufacture and dis-
tribution, in which it struck out many new lines, he
personally supervised. Also it became the parent
of several offspring. It was the time when the
gardening craze was beginning in England, and the

Country-Dweller was founded, a sumptuously produced monthly which made a feature of its illustra-
tions. This did no more than pay its way, but a
children's halfpenny paper made a big hit, and an
unctuous and snobbish penny weekly for the home
made a bigger. He acquired also several trade
journals, and put them on a paying basis.

When the South African War broke out Thomas
was a wealthy man, piling up revenue yearly, for
he still lived in two rooms in Marylebone and spent
nothing on himself. The war more than doubled his
profits. In the *Centre-Forward* he had long been a
moderate exponent of the new imperialism, and his
own series of articles " The Romance of Empire "
had had a large sale when issued as a book. Now
he became a fervent patriot. He exposed abuses
in the conduct of the campaign—always on the best
legal advice—he had much to say about inefficient
generals, he appeared before the world as the soldiers'
friend. The result was a new paper, *Mother England*,
price one penny, which was the *Centre-Forward*
adapted to lower strata of democracy—a little
slangy and vulgar, deliberately sensational, but
eminently sound at heart. Once a month Thomas
Carlyle Craw compelled the motley array of its
subscribers to view the world from his own lofty
watch-tower.

Fortune treated him kindly. After the war came
the Liberal revival, and he saw his chance. His
politics now acquired a party character, and he
became the chief Free Trade trumpet in the generally
Protectionist orchestra of the Press. Once again he

took a bold step, for he started a new halfpenny daily. For the better part of a year it hovered on the brink of failure, and the profits on Thomas's other publications went into its devouring maw. Then, suddenly, it turned the corner, and raced up the slope to the pinnacle of public favour. The *View* fed an appetite the existence of which Thomas alone had divined. It was bright and fresh and admirably put together ; large sums were spent on special correspondence ; its picture pages were the best of their kind ; every brand of notable, at high fees, enlivened its pages. But above all it was a paper for the home and the home-maker, and the female sex became its faithful votaries. Much of this success was due to Thomas himself. He made himself the centre of the paper and the exponent of its policy. Once a week, in the *View*, as in the *Centre-Forward*, he summarized the problems of immediate interest and delivered his weighty judgments.

He was compelled to change his simple habits of life. He was compelled, indeed, elaborately to seek seclusion. There was no other alternative for one who had no gift of utterance and had hitherto gone little into society. With hundreds daily clamouring for interviews, demanding his help in cash or influence, urging policies and persons upon his notice, he must needs flee to sanctuary. In the palatial offices which he built in the neighbourhood of Fleet Street he had a modest flat, where he occasionally passed a night behind a barbed-wire entanglement of secretaries. But for the rest he had no known abode, though here I am privileged to

Mr. Pickwick. A cigar, a begonia, a new scent, and a fashionable hotel in the Evallonian capital were named in his honour.

Such at the date of this tale was the position of Thomas Carlyle Craw in the world of affairs. He was an illustrious figure, and a self-satisfied, though scarcely a happy man. For he suffered from a curious dread which the scientific call *agoraphobia*. A master of publicity, he shrank from it in person. This was partly policy. He had the acumen to see that retirement was his chief asset ; he was the prophet speaking from within the shrine, a voice which would lose its awfulness if it were associated too closely with human lineaments. But there was also timidity, a shrinking of the flesh. He had accustomed himself for thirty years to live in a shell, and he had a molluscan dread of venturing outside it. A lion on paper, he suspected that he would be a rabbit in personal intercourse. He realized that his vanity would receive cruel wounds, that rough hands would paw his prophetic mantle. How could he meet a rampant socialist or a republican Evallonian face to face ? The thought sent a shiver down his spine. . . .

So his sensitiveness became a disease, and he guarded his seclusion with a vestal jealousy. He had accumulated a personal staff of highly paid watch-dogs, whose business was not only the direction of the gigantic Craw Press but the guardianship of the shrine consecrated to its master. There was his principal secretary, Freddy Barbon, the son of a bankrupt Irish peer, who combined the duties of grand vizier and major-domo. There was his general manager, Archibald Bamff, who had been with him since the early days of the *Centre-Forward*. There was Sigismund Allins, an elegant young man who went much into society, and acted, unknown to the world, as his chief's main intelligence-officer. There was Bannister, half valet, half butler, and Miss Elena Cazenove, a spinster of forty-five and the most efficient of stenographers. With the exception of Bamff, this entourage attended his steps—but never together, lest people should talk. Like the police in a Royal procession, they preceded or followed his actual movements and made straight the path for him. Among them he ruled as a mild tyrant, arbitrary but not unkindly. If the world of men had to be kept at a distance lest it should upset his poise and wound his vanity, he had created a little world which could be, so to speak, his own personality writ large.

It is the foible of a Scot that he can never cut the bonds which bind him to his own country. Thomas had happy recollections of his childhood on the bleak shores of Fife, and a large stock of national piety. He knew in his inmost heart that he would rather win the approval of Kilmaclavers and Partankirk than the plaudits of Europe. This affection had taken practical form. He had decided that his principal hermitage must be north of the Twood. Fife and the East coast were too much of a home in the country for his purpose, the Highlands were too remote from London, so he settled upon the south-west corner, the district known as the

Canonry, as at once secluded and accessible. He had no wish to cumber himself with land, for Thomas desired material possessions as little as he desired titles ; so he leased from Lord Rhynns (whose wife's health and declining fortune compelled him to spend most of the year abroad) the ancient demesne of Castle Gay. The place, it will be remembered, lies in the loveliest part of the glen of the Callowa, in the parish of Knockraw, adjoining the village of Starr, and some five miles from the town of Port-away, which is on the main line to London. A high wall surrounds a wild park of a thousand acres, in the heart of which stands a grey stone castle, for whose keep Bruces and Comyns and Macdowalls contended seven centuries ago. In its cincture of blue mountains it has the air of a place at once fortified and forgotten, and here Thomas found that secure retirement so needful for one who had taken upon himself the direction of the major problems of the globe. The road up the glen led nowhere, the fishing was his own, and no tourist disturbed the shining stretches of the Callowa, the hamlet of Starr had less than fifty inhabitants, and the folk of the Canonry were not the type to pry into the affairs of eminence in retreat. To the countryside he was only the Castle tenant—" yin Craw, a newspaper body frae England." They did not read his weekly pronouncements, preferring older and stronger fare.

But at the date of this tale a thorn had fixed itself in Thomas's pillow. Politics had broken in upon his moorland peace. There was a by-election

in the Canonry, an important by-election, for it was
regarded as a test of the popularity of the Government's new agricultural policy. The Canonry in
its seaward fringe is highly farmed, and its uplands
are famous pasture ; its people, traditionally Liberal, have always been looked upon as possessing
the toughest core of northern common sense.   How
would such a region regard a scheme which was
a violent departure from the historic attitude of
Britain towards the British farmer ?   The matter
was hotly canvassed, and since a General Election
was not far distant, this contest became the cynosure
of political eyes.   Every paper sent a special correspondent, and the candidates found their halting
utterances lavishly reported. The Canonry woke
up one morning to find itself " news."

Thomas did not like it. He resented this publicity at his doorstep.   His own press was instructed
to deal with the subject in obscure paragraphs, but
he could not control his rivals.   He was in terror
lest he should be somehow brought into the limelight—a bogus interview, perhaps ; such things had
happened—there were endless chances of impairing
his carefully constructed dignity.   He decided that
it would be wiser if he left the place till after the
declaration of the poll. The necessity gave him
acute annoyance, for he loved the soft bright October
weather at Castle Gay better than any other season
of the year. The thought of his suite at Aix—
taken in the name of Mr. Frederick Barbon—offered
him no consolation.

But first he must visit Glasgow to arrange with

his builders for some reforms in the water supply, which, with the assent of Lord Rhynns, he proposed to have installed in his absence. Therefore, on the evening of the Kangaroo match already described, his discreet and potent figure might have been seen on the platform of Kirkmichael as he returned from the western metropolis. It was his habit to be met there by a car, so as to avoid the tedium of changing trains and the publicity of Portaway station.

Now, as it chanced, there was another election in process. The students of the western capital were engaged in choosing their Lord Rector. On this occasion there was a straight contest ; no freak candidates, nationalist, sectarian, or intellectual, obscured the issue. The Conservative nominee was a prominent member of the Cabinet, the Liberal the leader of the Old Guard of that faith. Enthusiasm waxed high, and violence was not absent—the violence without bitterness which is the happy mark of Scottish rectorial contests. Already there had been many fantastic doings. The Conservative headquarters were decorated by night with Liberal red paint, prints which set the law of libel at nought were sold in the streets, songs of a surprising ribaldry were composed to the discredit of the opposing candidates. No undergraduate protagonist had a single physical, mental, or moral oddity which went unadvertised. One distinguished triumph the Liberals had won. A lanky Conservative leader had been kidnapped, dressed in a child's shorts, blouse, socks, and beribboned sailor hat, and attached by padlocked

chains to the college railings, where, like a culprit
in the stocks, for a solid hour he had made sport
for the populace. Such an indignity could not go
unavenged, and the Conservatives were out for
blood.

The foremost of the Liberal leaders was a man,
older than the majority of students, who, having
forsaken the law, was now pursuing a belated
medical course. It is sufficient to say that his
name was Linklater, for he does not come into this
story. The important thing about him for us is his
appearance. He looked older than his thirty-two
years, and was of a comfortable figure, almost wholly
bald, with a round face, tightly compressed lips, high
cheek-bones, and large tortoise-shell spectacles. It
was his habit to wear a soft black hat of the kind
which is fashionable among statesmen, anarchists,
and young careerists. In all these respects he was
the image of Thomas Carlyle Craw. His parental
abode was Kirkmichael, where his father was a
Baptist minister.

On the evening in question Thomas strode to the
door of the Kirkmichael booking-office, and to his
surprise found that his car was not there. It was
a drizzling evening, the same weather which that
day had graced the Kangaroo match. The weather
had been fine when he left Castle Gay in the morning,
but he had brought a light raincoat with which he
now invested his comfortable person. There were
no porters about, and in the dingy station yard
there was no vehicle except an antique Ford.

His eye was on the entrance to the yard, where

he expected to see any moment the headlights of his car in the wet dusk, when he suddenly found his arms seized. At the same moment a scarf was thrown over his head which stopped all utterance. . . . About what happened next he was never quite clear, but he felt himself swung by strong arms into the ancient Ford. Through the folds of the scarf he heard its protesting start. He tried to scream, he tried to struggle, but voice and movement were forbidden him. . . .

He became a prey to the most devastating fear. Who were his assailants ? Bolshevists, anarchists, Evallonian Republicans, the minions of a rival press ? Or was it the American group which had offered him two days ago by cable ten millions for his properties ? . . . Whither was he bound ? A motor launch on the coast, some den in a city slum ? . . .

After an hour's self-torture he found the scarf switched from his head. He was in a car with five large young men in waterproofs, each with a muffler covering the lower part of his face. The rain had ceased, and they seemed to be climbing high up on to the starlit moors. He had a whiff of wet bracken and heather.

He found his voice, and with what resolution he could muster he demanded to know the reason of the outrage and the goal of his journey.

" It's all right, Linklater," said one of them. " You'll know soon enough."

They called him Linklater ! The whole thing was a blunder. His incognito was preserved. The habit of a lifetime held, and he protested no more.

CHAPTER III

THE BACK HOUSE OF THE GARROCH

THE road to the springs of the Garroch water, a stream which never descends to the lowlands but runs its whole course in the heart of mossy hills, is for the motorist a matter of wide and devious circuits. It approaches its goal circumspectly, with an air of cautious reconnaissance. But the foot-traveller has an easier access. He can take the cart-road which runs through the heather of the Clachlands glen and across the intervening hills by the Nick of the Threshes. Beyond that he will look into the amphitheatre of the Garroch, with the loch of that name dark under the shadow of the Caldron, and the stream twining in silver links through the moss, and the white ribbon of highway, on which wheeled vehicles may move, ending in the yard of a moorland cottage.

The Blaweary car had carried Jaikie and Dougal swiftly over the first fifteen miles of their journey. At about three o'clock of the October afternoon they had reached the last green cup where the Clachlands has its source, and were leisurely climbing the hill towards the Nick. Both had ancient knapsacks on their shoulders, but it was their only point of resem-

blance. Dougal was clad in a new suit of rough
tweed knickerbockers which did not fit him well ;
he had become very hot and carried his jacket on
his arm, and he had no hat. Jaikie was in old
flannels, for he abominated heavy raiment, and,
being always more or less in training, his slender
figure looked pleasantly cool and trim. Sometimes
they sauntered, sometimes they strode, and now
and then they halted, when Dougal had something
to say. For Dougal was in the first stage of holiday, when to his closest friend he had to unburden
himself of six months' store of conversation. It
was as inevitable as the heat and discomfort which
must attend the first day's walk, before his body
rid itself of its sedentary heaviness. Jaikie spoke
little ; his fate in life was to be a listener.

It is unfair to eavesdrop on the babble of youth
when its flow has been long pent up. Dougal's ran
like Ariel over land and sea, with excursions into the
upper air. He had recovered his only confidant,
and did not mean to spare him. Sometimes he
touched upon his daily task—its languors and difficulties, the harassments of the trivial, the profound
stupidity of the middle-aged. He defended hotly
his politics, and drew so many fine distinctions
between his creed and those of all other men, that
it appeared that his party was in the loyal, compact,
and portable form of his single self. Then ensued
torrential confessions of faith and audacious ambi-
tion. He was not splashing—he was swimming
with a clean stroke to a clear goal. With his pen
and voice he was making his power felt, and in time

the world would listen to him. His message?
There followed a statement of ideals which was
nobly eclectic. Dougal was at once nationalist and
internationalist, humanitarian and man of iron,
realist and poet.

They were now in the Nick of the Threshes,
where, in a pad of green lawn between two heathery
steeps, a well bubbled among mosses. The thirsty
idealist flung himself on the ground and drank deep.
He rose with his forelock dripping.

"I sometimes think you are slipping away from
me, Jaikie," he said. "You've changed a lot in
the last two years. . . . You live in a different
kind of world from me, and every year you're
getting less and less of a Scotsman. . . . And I've
a notion, when I pour out my news to you and
haver about myself, that you're criticizing me all
the time in your own mind. Am I not right?
You're terribly polite, and you never say much, but
I can feel you're laughing at me. Kindly, maybe,
but laughing all the same. You're saying to yourself, ' Dougal gets dafter every day. He's no better
than a savage.' "

Jaikie regarded the flushed and bedewed countenance of his friend, and the smile that broadened
over his small face was not critical.

"I often think you daft, Dougal. But then I
like daftness."

"Anyway, you've none of it yourself. You're
the wisest man I ever met. That's where you and
I differ. I'm always burning or freezing, and you
keep a nice, average, normal temperature. I take

desperate likes and dislikes. You've something good
to say about the worst scallywag, and, if you haven't,
you hold your tongue. I'm all for flinging my cap
over the moon, while you keep yours snug on your
head. No. No "—he quelled an anticipated protest. " It's the same in your football. It was like
that yesterday afternoon. You never run your head
against a stone wall. You wait till you see your
chance, and then you're on to it like forked lightning,
but you're determined not to waste one atom of
your strength."

" That's surely Scots enough," said Jaikie, laughing. " I'm economical."

" No, it's not Scots. We're not an economical
race. I don't know what half-wit invented that
libel. We spend ourselves—we've always spent ourselves—on unprofitable causes. What's the phrase
—*perfervidum ingenium* ? There's not much of the
perfervid about you, Jaikie."

" No ? " said the other, politely interrogatory.

" No. You've all the pluck in creation, but it's
the considering kind. You remember how Alan
Breck defined his own courage—' Just great penetration and knowledge of affairs.' That's yours.
. . . Not that you haven't got the other kind too.
David Balfour's kind—' auld, cauld, dour, deidly
courage.' "

" I've no courage," said Jaikie. " I'm nearly
always in a funk."

" Aye, that's how you would put it. You've
picked up the English trick of understatement—
what they call *meiosis* in the grammar books. I

doubt you and me are very unlike. You'll not catch me understating. I want to shout both my vices and my virtues on the house-tops. . . . If I dislike a man I want to hit him on the head, while you'd be wondering if the fault wasn't in yourself. . . . If I want a thing changed I must drive at it like a young bull. If I think there's dirty work going on I'm for starting a revolution. . . . You don't seem to care very much about anything, and you're too fond of playing the devil's advocate. There was a time . . ."

"I don't think I've changed," said Jaikie. "I'm a slow fellow, and I'm so desperately interested in things that I feel my way cautiously. You see, I like so much that I haven't a great deal of time for hating. I'm not a crusader like you, Dougal."

"I'm a poor sort of crusader," said Dougal ruefully. "I get into a tearing passion about something I know very little about, and when I learn more my passion ebbs away. But still I've a good hearty stock of dislikes and they keep me from boredom. That's the difference between us. I'm for breaking a man's head, and I probably end by shaking hands. You begin by shaking hands. . . . All the same, God help the man or woman or creed or party that you make up your slow mind to dislike. . . . I'm going to make a stir in the world, but I know that I'll never be formidable. I'm not so sure about you."

"I don't want to be formidable."

"And that's maybe just the reason why you will be—some day. But I'm serious, Jaikie. It's a sad business if two ancient friends like you and me are starting to walk on different sides of the road. Our tracks are beginning to diverge, and, though we're still side by side, in ten years we may be miles apart. . . . You're not the good Scotsman you used to be. Here am I driving myself mad with the sight of my native land running down the brae—the cities filling up with Irish, the countryside losing its folk, our law and our letters and our language as decrepit as an old wife. Damn it, man, in another half-century there will be nothing left, and we'll be a mere disconsidered province of England. . . . But you never bother your head about it. Indeed, I think you've gone over to the English. What was it I heard you saying to Mr. McCunn last night ?— that the English had the most political genius of any people because they had the most humour ? "

" Well, it's true," Jaikie answered. " But every day I spend out of Scotland I like it better. When I've nothing else to do I run over in my mind the places I love best—mostly in the Canonry—and when I get a sniff of wood smoke it makes me sick with longing for peat reek. Do you think I could forget that ? "

Jaikie pointed to the scene which was now spread before them, for they had emerged from the Nick of the Threshes and were beginning the long descent to the Garroch. The October afternoon was warm and windless, and not a wisp of cloud broke the level blue of the sky. Such weather in July would have meant that the distances were dim, but on this autumn day, which had begun with frost, there was a

crystalline sharpness of outline in the remotest hills.
The mountains huddled around the amphitheatre,
the round bald forehead of the Yirnie, the twin peaks
of the Caldron which hid a tarn in their corrie, the
steel-grey fortress of the Calmarton, the vast menacing bulk of the Muneraw. On the far horizon the
blue of the sky seemed to fade into white, and a hill
shoulder which rose in one of the gaps had an air of
infinite distance.   The bog in the valley was a mosaic
of colours like an Eastern carpet, and the Garroch
water twined through it like some fantastic pictured
stream in a missal.   A glimpse could be had of Loch
Garroch, dark as ink in the shadow of the Caldron.
There were many sounds, the tinkle of falling burns
far below, a faint calling of sheep, an occasional note
of a bird.   Yet the place had an overmastering
silence, a quiet distilled of the blue heavens and the
primeval desert.   In that loneliness lay the tale of
ages since the world's birth, the song of life and
death as uttered by wild living things since the rocks
first had form.

The two did not speak for a little.   They had seen
that which touched in both some deep elemental
spring of desire.

Down on the level of the moss, where the green
track wound among the haggs, Dougal found his
tongue.

"I would like your advice, Jaikie," he said,
"about a point of conduct. It's not precisely a
moral question, but it's a matter of good taste.
I'm drawing a big salary from the Craw firm, and
I believe I give good value for it. But all the time

I'm despising my job, and despising the paper I help to make up, and despising myself. Thank God, I've nothing to do with policy, but I ask myself if I'm justified in taking money from a thing that turns my stomach."

"But you're no more responsible for the paper than the head of the case-room that sets the type. You're a technical expert."

"That's the answer I've been giving myself, but I'm not sure that it's sound. It's quite true that my leaving Craw's would make no difference—they'd get as good a man next day at a lower wage—maybe at the same wage, for I will say that for them, they're not skinflints. But it's a bad thing to work at something you can't respect. I'm condescending on my job, and that's ruin for a man's soul."

"I see very little harm in the Craw papers," said Jaikie. "They're silly, but they're decent enough."

"Decent!" Dougal cried. "That's just what they are not. They're the most indecent publications on God's earth. They're not vicious, if that's what you mean. They would be more decent if they had a touch of blackguardism. They pander to everything that's shoddy and slushy and third-rate in human nature. Their politics are an opiate to prevent folk thinking. Their endless stunts, their competitions and insurances and country-holiday schemes—that's the ordinary dodge to get up their circulation, so as to raise their advertisement prices. I don't mind that, for it's just common business. It's their uplift, their infernal uplift, that makes my spine cold. Oh, Lord! There's not a vulgar instinct, not a half-baked silliness, in the whole nation that they don't dig out and print in leaded type. And above all, there's the man Craw ! ''

" Did you ever meet him ? '' Jaikie asked.

" Never. Who has ? They tell me he has a house somewhere in the Canonry, when he gets tired of his apartments in foreign hotels. But I study Craw. I'm a specialist in Craw. I've four big press-cutting books at home full of Craw. Here's some of the latest.''

Dougal dived into a pocket and produced a batch of newspaper cuttings.

" They're mostly about Evallonia. I don't worry about that. If Craw wants to be a king-maker he must fight it out with his Evallonians. . . . But listen to some of the other titles. ' Mr. Craw's Advice to Youth ! ' ' Mr. Craw on the Modern Drama.'—He must have sat in the darkness at the back of a box, for he'd never show up in the stalls.— ' Mr. Craw on Modern Marriage.'—A fine lot he knows about it !—' Mr. Craw warns the Trade Unions.'—The devil he does !—' Mr. Craw on the Greatness of England.' ' Mr. Craw's Open Letter to the President of the U.S.A.' Will nobody give the body a flea in his ear ? . . . I could write a book about Craw. He's perpetually denouncing, but always with a hopeful smirk. I've discovered his formula. ' This is the best of all possible worlds, and everything in it is a necessary evil.' He wants to be half tonic and half sedative, but for me he's just a plain emetic.''

Dougal waved the cuttings like a flag.

" The man is impregnable, for he never reads any paper but his own, and he has himself guarded like a gun-factory. But I've a notion that some day I'll get him face to face. Some day I'll have the chance of telling him just what I think of him, and what every honest man——"

Jaikie by a dexterous twitch got possession of the cuttings, crumpled them into a ball, dropped it in a patch of peat, and ground it down with his heel.

" What's that you've done ? " Dougal cried angrily. " You've spoiled my Craw collection."

" Better that than spoiling our holiday. Look here, Dougal, my lad. For a week you've got to put Craw and all his works out of your head. We are back in an older and pleasanter world, and I won't have it wrecked by your filthy journalism. . . ."

For the better part of five minutes there was a rough-and-tumble on the green moor-road, from which Jaikie ultimately escaped and fled. When peace was made the two found themselves at a gate in a dry-stone dyke.

" Thank God," said Dougal. " Here is the Back House at last. I want my tea."

Their track led them into a little yard behind the cottage, and they made their way to the front, where the slender highway which ascended the valley of the Garroch came to an end in a space of hill gravel before the door. The house was something more than a cottage, for fifty years ago it had been the residence of a prosperous sheep-farmer, before the fashion of " led " farms had spread over

the upland glens. It was of two storeys and had a
little wing at right angles, the corner between being
filled with a huge bush of white roses. The roof was
slated, the granite walls had been newly whitewashed, and were painted with the last glories of
the tropæolum. A grove of scarlet-berried rowans
flanked one end, beyond which lay the walled garden
of potatoes and gooseberry bushes, varied with
golden-rod and late-flowering phloxes. At the other
end were the thatched outhouses and the walls of a
sheepfold, where the apparatus for boiling tar rose
like a miniature gallows above the dipping trough.
The place slept in a sunny peace. There was a hum
of bees from the garden, a slow contented clucking
of hens, the echo of a plashing stream descending the
steeps of the Caldron, but the undertones made by
these sounds were engulfed in the dominant silence.
The scent of the moorlands, compounded of miles of
stone and heather and winds sharp and pure as the
sea, made a masterful background from which it was
possible to pick out homelier odours—peat-reek,
sheep, the smell of cooking food. To ear, eye, and
nostril the place sent a message of intimate and
delicate comfort.

The noise of their feet on the gravel brought some
one in haste to the door. It was a woman of between
forty and fifty, built like a heroine of the Sagas, deep-
bosomed, massive, straight as a grenadier. Her
broad comely face was brown like a berry, and the
dark eyes and hair told of gipsy blood in her ancestry.
Her arms were bare, for she had been making butter,
and her skirts were kilted, revealing a bright-coloured

petticoat, so that she had the air of a Highland warrior.

But in place of the boisterous welcome which Jaikie had expected, her greeting was laughter. She stood in the doorway and shook. Then she held up a hand to enjoin silence, and marched the two travellers to the garden gate out of earshot of the house.

" Did you get my postcard, Mrs. Catterick ? " Jaikie asked, when they had come to a standstill under a rowan tree.

" Aye, I got your postcaird, and I'm blithe to see ye baith. But ye come at an unco time. I've gotten anither visitor."

" We don't want to inconvenience you," Jaikie began. " We can easily go down the water to the Mains of Garroch. The herd there will take us in."

" Ye'll dae nae siccan thing. It will never be said that Tibby Catterick turned twae auld freends frae her door, and there's beds to spare for ye baith. . . . But ye come at an unco time and ye find me at an unco job. I'm a jyler."

" A what ? "

" A jyler. I've a man inbye, and I'm under bond no to let him stir a fit frae the Back House till the morn's morn. . . . I'll tell ye the gospel truth. My guid-brither's son—him that's comin' out for a minister—is at the college, and the morn the students are electin' what they ca' a Rector. Weel, Erchie's a stirrin' lad and takes muckle ado wi' their politics. It seems that there was a man on the ither side that they wanted to get oot o' the road—it was fair eneugh, for he had pitten some terrible affronts on Erchie. So what maun the daft laddie dae but kidnap him? How it was done I canna tell, but he brocht him here late last nicht in a cawr, and pit me on my aith no to let him leave the place for thirty 'oors. . . . So you see I'm turned jyler." Mrs. Catterick again shook with silent merriment.

" Have you got him indoors now? "

" He's ben the hoose in the best room. I kinnled a fire for him, for he's a cauldrife body. What's he like? Oh, a fosy wee man wi' a bald heid and terrible braw claithes. Ye wad say he was ower auld to be a student, but Erchie says it takes a lang time to get through as a doctor. Linklater, they ca' him."

" Has he given you any trouble? " Dougal asked anxiously. He seemed to long to assist in the task of gaoler.

" No him. My man's awa wi' the crocks to Gledmouth, and, as ye ken, we hae nae weans, but I could manage twa o' him my lane. But he never offered to resist. Just ate his supper as if he was in his ain hoose, and spak nae word except to say that he likit my scones. I lent him ane o' John's sarks for a nicht-gown, and this mornin' he shaved himsel' wi' John's razor. He's a quiet, saft-spoken wee body, but there's nae crack in him. He speaks wi' a kind o' English tongue and he ca's me Madam. I doot that deil Erchie maun be in the wrang o' it, but kin's kin and I maun tak' the wyte o' his cantrips."

Again Jaikie became apologetic and proposed withdrawal, and again his proposal was rejected.

" Ye can bide here fine," said Mrs. Catterick, " now that ye ken the truth. I couldna tell it ye at the door-cheek, for ye were just forenent his windy. . . . Ye'll hae your meat wi' me in the kitchen, and ye can hae the twa beds in the loft. . . . Ye'd better no gang near Linklater, for he maybe wadna like folk to ken o' this performance—nor Erchie neither. He has never stirred frae his room this day, and he's spak no word except to speir what place he was in and how far it was frae Glen Callowa. . . . Now I think o't, that was a queer thing to speir, for Erchie said he brocht him frae Kirkmichael. . . . Oh, and he was wantin' to send a telegram, but I tell't him there was nae office within saxteen miles and the post wadna be up the water till the morn. . . . I'm just wonderin' how he'll get off the morn, for he hasna the buits for walkin'. Ye never saw sic snod, wee, pappymashy things on a man's feet. But there's twa bicycles, yin o' John's and yin that belongs to the young herd at the west hirsel. Wi' yin o' them he'll maybe manage down the road. . . . But there's nae sense in crossin' brigs till ye come to them. I've been thrang wi' the kirnin', but the butter's come, and the kettle's on the boil. Your tea will be ready as sune as ye've gotten your faces washed."

Half an hour later Jaikie and Dougal sat in the kitchen, staying a hearty hunger with farles of oat-cake and new-baked scones, and a healthier thirst with immense cups of strong-brewed tea. Their

5

hostess, now garbed somewhat more decorously, presided at the table. She apologized for the delay.

" I had to gie Linklater his tea. He's gettin' terrible restless, puir man. He's been tryin' to read the books in the best room, but he canna fix his mind, and he's aye writin' telegrams. He kens ye're here, and speired whae ye were, and I telled him twa young lads that were trampin' the country. I could see that he was feared o' ye, and nae wonder. It would be sair on a decent body if folk heard that he had been kidnapped by a deil like Erchie. I tried to set his mind at rest about the morn, and telled him about John's bicycle."

But the meal was not the jovial affair which Jaikie remembered of old. Mrs. Catterick was pre-occupied, and did not expand, as was her custom, in hilarious gossip. This new task of gaoler lay heavy on her shoulders. She seemed always to be listening for sounds from the farther part of the house. Twice she left the table and tiptoed along the passage to listen at the door.

" He's awfu' restless," she reported. " He's walkin' aboot the floor like a hen on a het girdle. I wish he mayna loss his reason. Dod, I'll warm Erchie's lugs for this ploy when I get a haud o' him. Sic a job to saddle on a decent wumman ! "

Then for a little there was peace, for a question of Jaikie's led their hostess to an account of the great April storm of that year.

" Thirty and three o' the hill lambs deid in ae nicht. . . . John was oot in the snaw for nineteen 'oors and I never looked to see him mair. Puir

man, when he cam' in at last he couldna eat—just
a dram o' whisky in het milk—and he sleepit a round
o' the clock. . . . I had fires in ilka room and lambs
afore them in a' the blankets I possessed. . . . Ay,
and it was waur when the snaw went and the floods
cam'. The moss was like a sea, and the Caldron
was streikit wi' roarin' burns. We never saw the
post for a week, and every brig atween here and
Portaway gaed doun to the Solway. . . . Wheesht!"

She broke off and listened. A faint cry of
" Madam " came from the other end of the house.

" It's him. It's Linklater. ' Madam ' he ca's me.
Keep us a' ! "

She hurried from the kitchen, shutting the door
carefully behind her.

When she returned it was with a solemn face.

" He's wonderin' if ane o' you lads wad take a
telegram for him to the office. He's terrible set
on't. ' Madam,' he says wi' his Englishy voice,
' I assure you it's a matter of the first importance.' "

" Nonsense," said Dougal. " Sixteen miles after
a long day's tramp ! He can easily wait till the
morning. Besides, the office would be closed before
we got there."

" Ay, but hearken." Mrs. Catterick's voice was
hushed in awe. " He offers twenty punds to the
man that will dae his will. He's gotten the notes
in his pooch."

" Now where on earth," said Dougal, " did a
medical student get twenty pounds ? "

" He's no like a student. The mair I look at
him the better I see that he's nane o' the rough clan

that Erchie rins wi'. He's ane that's been used wi'
his comforts. And he's aulder than I thocht—an
aulder man than John. I wadna say but that
blagyird Erchie has kidnapped a Lord Provost, and
whaur will we a' be then ? "

" We had better interview him," said Dougal.
" It's a shame to let him fret himself."

" Ane at a time," advised Mrs. Catterick, " for
he's as skeery as a cowt. You gang, Dougal. Ye
ken the ways o' the college lads."

Dougal departed, and the two left behind fell
silent. Mrs. Catterick's instinct for the dramatic
had been roused, and she kept her eye on the door,
through which the envoy would return, as if it had
been the curtain of a stage play. Even Jaikie's
placidity was stirred.

" This is a funny business, Mrs. Catterick," he
said. " Dougal and I come here for peace, and we
find the Back House of the Garroch turned into a
robbers' den. The Canonry is becoming a stirring
place. You've an election on, too."

" So I was hearin', and the post brings us papers
about it. John maun try and vote, if he can get
an orra day atween the sales. He votit last time,
honest man, but we never heard richt whae got in.
We're ower far up the glens for poalitics. Wheesht!
Is that Dougal ? "

It was not. He did not return for nearly half
an hour, and when he came it was to put his head
inside the door and violently beckon Jaikie. He
led him out of doors to the corner of the garden, and
then turned on him a face so excited and portentous

that the appropriate utterance should have been a
shout.   He did not shout ; he whispered hoarsely :
   " Do you mind our talk coming up the road ? . . .
Providence has taken me at my word. . . . Who do
you think is sitting ben the house ?   It's the man
Craw ! "

CHAPTER IV

THE RECONNAISSANCE OF CASTLE GAY

THE westering sun was lighting up the homely furniture of Mrs. Catterick's best room—the sheepskins on the floor, the framed photographs decorated with strings of curlews' eggs on the walls—when Dougal and Jaikie entered the presence of the great man. Mr. Craw was not at the moment an impressive figure. The schoolmaster's son of Kilmaclavers had been so long habituated to the attentions of an assiduous valet that he had found some difficulty in making his own toilet. His scanty hair was in disorder, and his spruce blue suit had attracted a good deal of whitewash from the walls of his narrow bedroom. Also he had lost what novelists call his poise. He sat in a horsehair-covered arm-chair drawn up at a table, and strove to look as if he had command of the situation, but his eye was uncertain and his fingers drummed nervously.

" This is Mr. Galt, sir," said Dougal, adding, " of St. Mark's College, Cambridge."

Mr. Craw nodded.

" Your friend is to be trusted ? " and his wavering eyes sought Jaikie. What he saw cannot have greatly reassured him, for Jaikie was struggling with a strong inclination to laugh.

"I have need to be careful," he said, fixing his gaze upon a photograph of the late Queen Victoria, and picking his words. "I find myself, through no fault of my own, in a very delicate position. I have been the subject of an outrage on the part of—of some young men of whom I know nothing. I do not blame them. I have been myself a student of a Scottish University. . . . But it is unfortunate— most unfortunate. It was apparently a case of mistaken identity. Happily I was not recognized. . . . I am a figure of some note in the world. You will understand that I do not wish to have my name associated with an undergraduate—'rag,' I think, is the word."

His two hearers nodded gravely. They were bound to respect such patent unhappiness.

"Mr.—I beg your pardon—Crombie?—has told me that he is employed on one of my papers. Therefore I have a right to call upon his assistance. He informs me that I can also count on your goodwill and discretion, sir," and he inclined his head towards Jaikie. "It is imperative that this foolish affair should never be known to the public. I have been successful in life, and therefore I have rivals. I have taken a strong stand in public affairs, and therefore I have enemies. My position, as you are no doubt aware, is one of authority, and I do not wish my usefulness to be impaired by becoming the centre of a ridiculous tale."

Mr. Craw was losing his nervousness and growing fluent. He felt that these two young men were of his own household, and he spoke to them as he

would have addressed Freddy Barbon, or Sigismund
Allins, or Archibald Bamff, or Bannister, his butler,
or that efficient spinster Miss Elena Cazenove.

"I don't think you need be afraid, sir," said
Dougal. "The students who kidnapped you will
have discovered their mistake as soon as they saw
the real Linklater going about this morning. They
won't have a notion who was kidnapped, and they
won't want to inquire. You may be sure that they
will lie very low about the whole business. What
is to hinder you sending a wire to Castle Gay to
have a car up here to-morrow, and go back to your
own house as if nothing had happened? Mrs.
Catterick doesn't know you from Adam, and you
may trust Jaikie and me to hold our tongues."

"Unfortunately the situation is not so simple."
Mr. Craw blinked his eyes, as if to shut out an unpleasing picture, and his hands began to flutter
again. "At this moment there is a by-election in
the Canonry—a spectacular by-election. . . . The
place is full of journalists—special correspondents—
from the London papers. They were anxious to
drag me into the election, but I have consistently
refused. I cannot embroil myself in local politics.
Indeed, I intended to go abroad, for this inroad
upon my rural peace is in the highest degree dis-
tasteful. . . . You may be very certain that these
journalists are at this moment nosing about Castle
Gay. Now, my household must have been alarmed
when I did not return last night. I have a discreet
staff, but they were bound to set inquiries on foot.
They must have telephoned to Glasgow, and they

may even have consulted the police.   Some rumours
must have got abroad, and the approaches to my
house will be watched.   If one of these journalists
learns that I am here—the telegraph office in these
country parts is a centre of gossip—he will follow up
the trail.   He will interview the woman of this cottage, he will wire to Glasgow, and presently the
whole ridiculous business will be disclosed, and there
will be inch headlines in every paper except my
own."

" There's something in that," said Dougal.   " I
know the ways of those London journalists, and
they're a dour crop to shift.   What's your plan,
sir ? "

" I have written a letter."   He produced one of
Mrs. Catterick's disgraceful sheets of notepaper on
which her disgraceful pen had done violence to Mr.
Craw's neat commercial hand.   " I want this put
into the hand of my private secretary, Mr. Barbon,
at once.   Every hour's delay increases the danger."

" Would it not be best," Dougal suggested, " if
you got on to one of the bicycles—there are two
in the outhouse, Mrs. Catterick says—and I escorted
you to Castle Gay this very night.   It's only about
twenty miles."

" I have never ridden a bicycle in my life," said
Mr. Craw coldly.   " My plan is the only one, I fear.
I am entitled to call upon you to help me."

It was Jaikie who answered.   The first day's walk
in the hills was always an intoxication to him, and
Mrs. Catterick's tea had banished every trace of
fatigue.

" It's a grand night, Dougal," he said, " and there's a moon. I'll be home before midnight. There's nothing I would like better than a ride down Garroch to the Callowa. I know the road as well as my own name."

" We'll go together," said Dougal firmly. " I'm feeling fresher than when I started. . . . What are your instructions, sir ? "

" You will deliver this letter direct into Mr. Barbon's hands. I have asked him to send a car in this direction to-morrow before midday, and I will walk down the glen to meet it. It will wait for me a mile or so from this house. . . . You need not say how I came here. I am not in the habit of explaining my doings to my staff."

Mr. Craw enclosed his letter in a shameful envelope and addressed it. His movements were brisker now and he had recovered his self-possession. " I shall not forget this, Mr. Crombie," he said benignly. " You are fortunate in being able to do me a service."

Dougal and Jaikie betook themselves to the outhouse to examine the bicycles of John Catterick and the herd of the west hirsel.

" I eat the man's bread," said the former, " so I am bound to help him, but God forbid that I should ever want to accept his favours. It's unbelievable that we should spend the first night of our holiday trying to save the face of Craw. . . . Did you ever see such an image ? He's more preposterous even than I thought. But there's a decency in all things, and if Craw's bones are to be picked it will be me that has the picking of them, and not those London corbies."

But this truculence did not represent Dougal's true mind, which presently became apparent to his companion as they bumped their way among the heather bushes and flood-gravel which composed the upper part of the Garroch road. He was undeniably excited. He was a subaltern officer in a great army, and now he had been brought face to face with the general-in-chief. However ill he might think of that general, there was romance in the sudden juxtaposition, something to set the heart beating and to fire the fancy. Dougal regarded Mr. Craw much as a stalwart republican might look on a legitimate but ineffectual monarch ; yet the stoutest republican is not proof against an innocent snobbery and will hurry to a street corner to see the monarch pass. Moreover, this general-in-chief was in difficulties ; his immediate comfort depended upon the humble subaltern. So Dougal was in an excited mood and inclined to babble. He was determined to do his best for his chief, but he tried to salve his self-respect by a critical aloofness.

" What do you think of the great Craw ? " he asked Jaikie.

" He seems a pleasant fellow," was the answer.

" Oh, he's soft-spoken enough. He has the good manners of one accustomed to having his own way. But, man, to hear him talk was just like hearing a grandfather-clock ticking. He's one mass of artifice."

Dougal proceeded to a dissection of Mr. Craw's

mind which caused him considerable satisfaction. He proved beyond question that the great man had no brains of his own, but was only an echo, a repository for other men's ideas. "A cistern, not a spring," was his conclusion. But he was a little dashed by Jaikie, who listened patiently to the analysis, and then remarked that he was talking rubbish.

"If a man does as much in the world as Craw, and makes himself as important, it's nonsense to say he has no brains. He must have plenty, though they may not be the kind you like. You know very well, Dougal, that you're mightily pleased to have the chance of doing the great man a favour. And maybe rather flattered."

The other did not reply for a moment. "Perhaps I am," he said at length. "We're all snobs in a way—all but you. You're the only true democrat I know. What's the phrase—'Fellow to a beggar and brother to a king, if he be found worthy'? It's no credit to you—it's just the way you're made."

After that it was impossible to get a word out of Jaikie, and even Dougal drifted by way of monosyllables into silence, for the place and the hour had their overmastering enchantments. There was no evening mist, and in the twilight every hill stood out clean-cut in a purple monochrome. Soon the road skirted the shores of the Lower Loch Garroch, twining among small thickets of birch and hazel, with the dark water on its right lapping ghostly shingle. Presently the glen narrowed and the Garroch grumbled to itself in deep linns, appearing

now and then on some rock-shelf in a broad pool
which caught the last amethyst light of day. There
had been no lamps attached to the bicycles of John
Catterick and the herd of the west hirsel, so the
travellers must needs move circumspectly. And
then the hills fell back, the glen became a valley,
and the Garroch ran free in wild meadows of rush
and bracken.

The road continued downstream to the junction
with the Callowa not far from the town of Portaway.
But to reach Castle Gay it was necessary to break
off and take the hill-road on the left, which crossed
the containing ridge and debouched in the upper part
of Glen Callowa. The two riders dismounted, and
walked the road which wound from one grassy howe
to another till they reached the low saddle called the
Pad o' the Slack, and looked down upon a broader
vale. Not that they had any prospect from it—for
it was now very dark, the deep autumn darkness
which precedes moonrise ; but they had an instinct
that there was freer space before them. They remounted their bicycles, and cautiously descended a
road with many awkward angles and hairpin bends,
till they found themselves among trees, and suddenly
came on to a metalled highway.

" Keep to the right," Jaikie directed. " We're
not more than two miles from the Castle gates."

The place had the unmistakable character of a
demesne. Even in the gloom it had an air of being
well cared for, and the moon, which now began to
send a shiver of light through the darkness, revealed
a high wall on the left—no dry-stone dyke but a

masoned wall with a coping. The woods, too, were
not the scrub of the hills, but well-grown timber
trees and plantations of fir. Then the wall fell back,
there were two big patches of greensward protected
by chains and white stones, and between them a
sweep of gravel, a castellated lodge, and vast gates
like a portcullis. The Lord Rhynns of three generations ago had been unhappily affected by the Gothic
Revival.

" Here's the place," said Dougal. " It's a mighty
shell for such a weé body as Craw."

The gates were locked. There was a huge bell
pendant from one of the pillars and this Jaikie rang.
It echoed voluminously in the stillness, but there was
no sign of life in the lodge. He rang again and yet
again, making the night hideous, while Dougal hammered at the massive ironwork of the gate.

" They're all dead or drunk," the latter said.
" I'm positive there's folk in the lodge. I saw a bit
of a light in the upper window. What for will they
not open ? "

Jaikie had abandoned the bell and was peering
through the ironwork.

" Dougal," he whispered excitedly, " look here.
This gate is not meant to open. Look what's behind
it. It's a barricade. There's two big logs jammed
between the posts. The thing would keep a Tank
out. Whoever is in there is terrified of something."

" There's somebody in the lodge watching us.
I'm certain of that. What do they mean by be-
having as if they were besieged ? I don't like it,
Jaikie. There's something here we don't under-

stand—and Craw doesn't understand. How can
they expect to defend as big a space as a park ?
Any active man could get over the wall."

" Maybe they want to keep out motors. . . .
Well, we needn't waste time here. That letter has
got to be delivered, and there's more roads than the
main road."

" Is there another entrance ? "

" Yes. This is the main one, but there's a second
lodge a mile beyond Starr—that's the village—on
the Knockraw road. But we needn't worry about
that. We can leave our bicycles, and get into the
park at the Callowa bridge."

They remounted and resumed their course along
the highway. One or two cottages were passed,
which showed no sign of life, since the folk of these
parts rise early and go early to bed. But in an
open space a light was visible from a larger house
on the slope to the right. Then came a descent and
the noise of a rapid stream.

The bicycles were shoved under a hawthorn bush,
and Jaikie clambered on to the extreme edge of the
bridge parapet.

" We can do it," he reported. " A hand traverse
for a yard or two and then a ten-foot drop. There's
bracken below, so it will be soft falling."

Five minutes later the two were emerging from
a bracken covert on to the lawn-like turf which
fringed the Callowa. The moon was now well up
in the sky, and they could see before them the
famous wild park of Castle Gay. The guide-books
relate that in it are both red deer and fallow deer,

and in one part a few of the ancient Caledonian wild
cattle.   But these denizens must have been asleep,
for as Jaikie and Dougal followed the river they saw
nothing but an occasional rabbit and a belated heron.
They kept to the stream side, for Jaikie had once
studied the ordnance map and remembered that the
Castle was close to the water.

The place was so magical that one of the two
forgot his errand.   It was a cup among high hills,
but, seen in that light, the hills were dwarfed, and
Jaikie with a start realized that the comb of mountain, which seemed little more than an adjacent
hillock, must be a ridge of the great Muneraw, twenty
miles distant.   The patches of wood were black as ink
against the pale mystery of the moonlit sward.   The
river was dark too, except where a shallow reflected
the moon.   The silence was broken only by the small
noises of wild animals, the ripple of the stream, and
an occasional splash of a running salmon.

Then, as they topped a slope, the house lay
before them.   It stood on its own little plateau,
with the ground falling from it towards the park
and the stream, and behind it the fir-clad Castle
Hill.   The moon turned it into ivory, so that it had
the air of some precious Chinese carving on a jade
stand.   In such a setting it looked tiny, and one had
to measure it with the neighbouring landscape to
realize that it was a considerable pile.   But if it did
not awe by its size, it ravished the eyes with its per-
fection.   Whatever may have been crude and ugly
in it, the jerry-building of our ancestors, the demented reconstruction of our fathers, was mellowed

by night into a classic grace. Jaikie began to whistle softly with pure delight, for he had seen a vision.

The practical Dougal had his mind on business. "It's past eleven o'clock, and it looks as if they were all in their beds. I don't see a light. There'll be gardens to get through before we reach the door. We'd better look out for dogs too. The folk here seem a bit jumpy in their nerves."

But it was no dog that obstructed them. Since they had come in sight of their goal they had moved with circumspection, and, being trained of old to the game, were as noiseless as ferrets. They had left the wilder part of the park, had crossed a piece of meadowland from which an aftermath of hay had lately been taken, and could already see beyond a ha-ha the terraces of a formal garden. But while they guarded against sound, their eyes were too much on their destination to be wary about the foreground.

So it befell that they crossed the ha-ha at the very point where a gentleman was taking his ease. Dougal fell over him, and the two travellers found themselves looking at the startled face of a small man in knickerbockers.

His pipe had dropped from his mouth. Jaikie picked it up and presented it to him. "I beg your pardon, sir," he said, "I hope you're not hurt." In the depths of the ha-ha there was shadow, and Jaikie took the victim of Dougal's haste for some one on the Castle staff.

"What are you doing here?" The man's air

6

was at once apologetic and defiant. There was
that in his tone which implied that he might in turn
be asked his business, that he had no prescriptive
right to be sitting smoking in that ha-ha at midnight.

So Jaikie answered : " Just the same as you.
Taking the air and admiring the view."

The little man was recovering himself.

" You gave me quite a start when you jumped
on the top of me. I thought it was one of the
gamekeepers after a poacher." He began to fill his
pipe. " More by token, who are you ? "

" Oh, we're a couple of undergraduates seeing the
world. We wanted a look at the Castle, and there's
not much you can see from the highroad, so we got
in at the bridge and came up the stream. . . . We're
strangers here. There's an inn at Starr, isn't there ?
What sort of a place is it ? "

" Nothing to write home about," was the answer.
" You'd better go on to Portaway. . . . So you're
undergraduates ? I thought that maybe you were
of my own profession, and I was going to be a bit
jealous. I'm on the staff of the *Live Wire*."

Dougal's hand surreptitiously found Jaikie's wrist
and held it tight.

" I suppose you're up here to cover the by-
election," he observed, in a voice which he strove
to keep flat and uninterested.

" By-election be hanged ! That was my original
job, but I'm on to far bigger business. Do you
know who lives in that house ? "

Two heads were mendaciously shaken.

" The great Craw ! Thomas Carlyle Craw ! The man that owns all the uplift papers. If you've never heard of Craw, Oxford's more of a mausoleum than I thought."

" We're Cambridge," said Jaikie, " and of course, we've heard of Craw. What about him ? "

" Simply that he's the mystery man of journalism. You hear of him but you never see him. He's a kind of Delphic oracle that never shows his face. The *Wire* doesn't care a hoot for by-elections, but it cares a whole lot about Craw. He's our big rival, and we love him as much as a cat loves water. He's a go-getter, is Craw. There's a deep commercial purpose behind all his sanctimonious bilge, and he knows how to rake in the shekels. His circulation figures are steadily beating ours by at least ten per cent. He has made himself the idol of his public, and till we pull off the prophet's mantle and knock out some of the sawdust, he has us licked all the time. But it's the deuce and all to get at him, for the blighter is as shy as a wood nymph. So, when this election started, my chief says to me : ' Here's our chance at last,' he says. ' Off you go, Tibbets, and draw the badger. Get him into the limelight somehow. Show him up for the almighty fool he is. Publicity about Craw,' he says, ' any kind of publicity that will take the gilt off the image. It's the chance of your life ! ' "

" Any luck ? " Dougal asked casually.

Mr. Tibbets's voice became solemn. " I believe," he said, " that I am on the edge of the world's biggest scoop. I discovered in half a day that we could never get Craw to mix himself up in an election. He knows too much. He isn't going to have the *Wire* and a dozen other papers printing his halting utterances verbatim in leaded type, and making nice, friendly comments. . . . No, that cock won't fight. But I've found a better. D'you know what will be the main headline in to-morrow's *Wire*? It will be '*Mysterious Disappearance of Mr. Craw—Household Distracted*.'—And by God, it will be true—every word of it. The man's lost."

"How do you mean?"

"Just lost. He never came back last night."

"Why should he? He has probably offed it abroad—to give the election a miss."

"Not a bit of it. He meant to go abroad to-morrow, and all the arrangements were made—I found out that from standing a drink to his second chauffeur. But he was expected back last night, and his car was meeting him at Kirkmichael. He never appeared. He has a staff like Buckingham Palace, and they were on the telephone all evening to Glasgow. It seems he left Glasgow right enough. . . . I got that from the chauffeur fellow, who's new and not so damned secretive as the rest. So I went to Kirkmichael this morning on a motor-bike, and the ticket collector remembered Craw coming off the Glasgow train. He disappeared into the void somewhere between here and Kirkmichael at some time after 7.15 last night. Take my word for it, a judgment has fallen upon Craw."

"Aren't you presuming too much?" Jaikie asked. "He may have changed his mind and be coming back to-morrow—or be back now—or he's wiring his servants to meet him somewhere. Then you and the *Wire* will look rather foolish."

"It's a risk, no doubt, but it's worth taking. And if you had seen his secretary's face you wouldn't think it much of a risk. I never saw a chap so scared as that secretary man. He started off this afternoon in a sports-model at eighty miles an hour, and was back an hour later as if he had seen his father's ghost. . . . What's more, this place is in a state of siege. They wouldn't let me in at the lodge gates. I made a long detour and got in by the back premises, and blessed if I hadn't to run for my life ! . . . Don't tell me. The people in that house are terrified of something, and Craw isn't there, and they don't know why Craw isn't there. . . . That's the mystery I'm out to solve, and I'll get to the bottom of it or my name isn't Albert Tibbets."

"I don't quite see the point," said Jaikie. "If you got him on a platform you might make capital out of his foolishness. But if some accident has happened to him, you can't make capital out of a man's misfortunes."

"We can out of Craw's. Don't you see we can crack the shell of mystery ? We can make him *news*—like any shop-girl who runs away from home or city gent that loses his memory. We can upset his blasted dignity."

Dougal got up. "We'll leave you to your midnight reveries, Mr. Tibbets. We're for bed. Where are your headquarters ? "

"Portaway is my base. But my post at present

is in and around this park. I'm accustomed to roughing it."

" Well, good-night, and good luck to you."

The two retraced their steps down the stream.

" This letter will have to wait till the morn's morn," said Dougal. " Craw was right. It hasn't taken long for the opposition Press to get after him. It's our business, Jaikie my man, to make the *Wire* the laughing-stock of British journalism. . . . Not that Tibbets isn't a dangerous fellow. Pray heaven he doesn't get on the track of the students' rag, for that's just the kind of yarn he wants. . . . They say that dog doesn't eat dog, but I swear before I've done with him to chew yon tyke's ear. . . . I'm beginning to think very kindly of Craw."

CHAPTER V

INTRODUCES A LADY

JAIKIE was roused next morning in his little room in the Westwater Arms by Dougal sitting down heavily on his toes. He was a sound sleeper, and was apt to return but slowly to a waking world. Yet even to his confused perceptions the state of the light seemed to mark an hour considerably later than that of seven a.m., which had been the appointed time. He reached for his watch and saw that it was nearly nine o'clock.

" You never called me," he explained apologetically.

" I did not, but I've been up since six myself. I've been thinking hard. Jaikie, there's more in this business than meets the eye. I've lain awake half the night considering it. But first I had to act. We can't let the *Wire's* stuff go uncontradicted. So I bicycled into Portaway and called up the office on the telephone. I caught Tavish just as he was going out to his breakfast. I had to take risks, so I said I was speaking from Castle Gay on Mr. Craw's behalf. . . . Tavish must have wondered what I was doing there. . . . I said that Mr. Craw had left for the Continent yesterday and would be away some weeks, and that an announcement to that effect was to appear in all the Craw papers."

" Did he raise any objection ? "

" I thought he would, for this is the first time that Craw has advertised his movements, and I was prepared with the most circumstantial lies. But I didn't need to lie, for he took it like a lamb. Indeed, it was piper's news I was giving him, for he had had the same instructions already. What do you think of that ? "

" He got them from Barbon the secretary ? "

" Not a bit of it. He had had no word from Castle Gay. He got them yesterday afternoon from London. Now, who sent them ? "

" The London office."

" I don't believe it. Bamff, the General Manager, is away in Canada over the new paper contracts. Don't tell me that Craw instructed London to make the announcement before he was bagged by the students. It isn't his way. . . . There's somebody else at work on this job, somebody that wants to have it believed that Craw is out of the country."

Jaikie shook a sceptical head.

" You were always too ingenious, Dougal. You've got Craw on the brain, and are determined to find melodrama. . . . Order my breakfast like a good chap. I'll be down in twenty minutes."

Jaikie bathed in the ancient contrivance of wood and tin, which was all that the inn provided, and was busy shaving when Dougal returned. The latter sat himself resolutely on the bed.

" The sooner we're at the Castle the better," he

trespassers, and there will be an awful row if Mac-killop catches you."

" We're not," said Dougal. " We're carrying a letter from Mr. Craw to Mr. Barbon. I have it in my pocket."

" Is that true ? " The eyes were sceptical, but also startled.

For answer Dougal drew the missive from his inner pocket. " There it is : ' The Honourable Frederick Barbon.' Look for yourself ! "

The girl peered down at the superscription. The degraded envelope of Mrs. Catterick's did not per-haps carry conviction, but something in the two faces below persuaded her of their honesty. With a swift movement she wriggled out of the crutch, caught a bough with both hands, and dropped lightly to the ground. With two deft kicks she repelled the attentions of Tactful and Pensive, and stood before the travellers, smoothing down her short skirt. She was about Jaikie's height, very slim and straight, and her interrogation was that of a general to his staff.

" You come from Mr. Craw ? "

" Yes."

" When did you leave him ? "

" Last night."

" Glory be ! Let's sit down. There's no hurry, and we must move very carefully. For I may as well let you know that the Devil has got into this place. Yes. The Devil. I don't quite know what form he has taken, but he's rampant in Castle Gay. I came here this morning to prospect, for I feel in a way responsible. You see it belongs to my father, and Mr. Craw's our tenant. My name is Alison Westwater."

" Same name as the pub in Starr ? " asked Dougal, who liked to connect his knowledge organically.

She nodded. " The Westwater Arms. Yes, that's my family. I live at the Mains with my aunt, while Papa and Mamma are on the Continent. I wouldn't go. I said, ' You can't expect me after a filthy summer in London to go ramping about France wearing tidy clothes and meeting the same idiotic people.' I had a year at school in Paris, and that gave me all the France I want in this life. I said, ' Castle Gay's my home, though you've chosen to let it to a funny little man, and I'm not going to miss my whack of Scotland.' So I hopped it here at the end of July, and I've been having a pretty peaceful time ever since. You see, all the outdoor people are *our* people, and Mr. Craw has been very nice about it and lets me fish in the Callowa and all the lochs, and treat the place as if he wasn't there."

" Do you know Mr. Craw well ? " Dougal asked.

" I have seen him three times and talked to him once—when Aunt Harriet took me to tea with him. I thought him rather a dear, but quite helpless. Talks just like a book, and doesn't appear to understand much of what you say to him. I suppose he is very clever, but he seems to want a lot of looking after. You never saw such a staff. There's a solemn butler called Bannister. I believe Bannister washes Mr. Craw's face and tucks him up in bed. . . . There's the type-writing woman by the name of

Cazenove with a sharp nose and horn spectacles, who never takes her eyes off him, and is always presenting him with papers to read. It's slavery of some kind, but whether she's his slave or he's her slave I don't know. I had to break a plate at tea, just to remind myself that there was such a thing as liberty. . . . Then there is Mr. Allins, a very glossy young man. You've probably come across him, for he goes about a lot. Mr. Allins fancies himself the perfect man of the world and a great charmer. I think if you met him you would say he wasn't quite a gentleman." She smiled confidentially at the two, as if she assumed that their standards must coincide with hers.

" Mr. Barbon ? " Dougal asked.

" And of course there's Freddy. There's nothing wrong with Freddy in that way. He's some sort of cousin of ours. Freddy is the chief of the staff and has everything on his shoulders. He is very kind and very anxious, poor dear, and now the crash has come ! Not to put too fine a point on it, for the last twenty-four hours Freddy has gone clean off his head. . . ."

She stopped at an exclamation from Jaikie. He had one of those small field-glasses which are adapted for a single eye, with which he had been examining the approaches to the castle.

" Tibbets can't have had much of a breakfast," he announced. " I see him sitting in that trench place."

" Who is Tibbets ? " she demanded.

" He's a journalist on the *Live Wire*, one of

Mr. Craw's rivals. We ran into him late last night, and that's why we couldn't deliver the letter."

"Little beast! That's the first of Freddy's anxieties. This place has been besieged by journalists for a week, all trying to get at Mr. Craw. . . . Then the night before last Mr. Craw did not come home. *You* know where he is, but Freddy doesn't, so that's the second of his troubles. Somehow the fact of Mr. Craw's disappearance has leaked out, and the journalists have got hold of it, and yesterday it almost came to keeping them off with a gun. . . . And out of the sky dropped the last straw."

She paused dramatically.

"I don't know the truth about it, for I haven't seen Freddy since yesterday morning. I think he must have had a letter, for he rushed to the Mains and left a message for Aunt Harriet that she was on no account to let any stranger into the house or speak to anybody or give any information. He can't have meant the journalists only, for we knew all about them. . . . After that, just after luncheon, while I was out for a walk, I saw a big car arrive with three men in it. It tried to get in at the West Lodge, but Jameson—that's the lodge-keeper—wouldn't open the gate. I thought that odd, but when I went riding in the evening I couldn't get in at the West Lodge either. They had jammed trunks of trees across. That means that Freddy is rattled out of his senses. He thinks he is besieged. Is there any word for that but lunacy? I can understand his being worried about the journalists and Mr. Craw not coming home. But this! Isn't it what they call persecution-mania ? I'm sorry about it, for I like Freddy."

" The man's black afraid of something," said Dougal, " but maybe he has cause. Maybe it's something new—something we know nothing about."

The girl nodded. " It looks like it. Meantime, where is Mr. Craw ? It's your turn to take up the tale."

" He's at the Back House of the Garroch, waiting for Barbon to send a car to fetch him."

Miss Westwater whistled. " Now how on earth did he get there ? I know the place. It's on our land. I remember the shepherd's wife. A big, handsome, gipsy-looking woman, isn't she ? "

Dougal briefly but dramatically told the story of the rape of Mr. Craw. The girl listened with open eyes and an astonishment which left no room for laughter.

" Marvellous ! " was her comment. " Simply marvellous ! That it should happen to Mr. Craw of all people ! I love those students. . . . What, by the way, are you ? You haven't told me."

" Jaikie here is an undergraduate—Cambridge."

" Beastly place ! I'm sorry, but my sympathies are all with Oxford."

" And I'm a journalist by trade. I'm on one of the Craw papers. I've no sort of admiration for Craw, but of course I'm on his side in this row. The question is——"

Jaikie, who had been busy with his glass, suddenly clutched the speaker by the hair and forced him down. He had no need to perform the same

office for Miss Westwater, for at his first movement
she had flung herself on her face. The three were
on a small eminence of turf with thick bracken before and behind them, and in this they lay crouched.

" What is it ? " Dougal whispered.

" There's a man in the hollow," said Jaikie.
" He's up to no good, for he's keeping well in cover.
Wait here, and I'll stalk him."

He wriggled into the fern, and it was a quarter
of an hour before he returned to report. " It's a
man, and he's wearing a queer kind of knicker-
bocker suit. He hasn't the look of a journalist.
He has some notion of keeping cover, for I could
get no more than a glimpse of him. He's trying to
get to the house, so we'll hope he'll tumble over
Tibbets in the ditch, as Dougal and I did last
night."

" The plot thickens ! " The girl's eyes were
bright with excitement. " He's probably one of
the strangers who came in the car. . . . The question is, what is to be done next ? Mr. Craw is at
the Back House of the Garroch, twenty miles away,
and no one knows it but us three. We have to get
him home without the unfriendly journalists knowing about it."

" We have also to get him out of the country,"
said Dougal. " There was some nonsense in the
Wire this morning about his being lost, but all the
Craw papers will announce that he has left for the
Continent. . . . But the first thing is to get him
home. We'd better be thinking about delivering
that letter, Jaikie."

" Wait a moment," said the girl. " How are you going to deliver the letter ? Freddy won't let you near him, even though you say you come from Mr. Craw. He'll consider it a *ruse de guerre*, and small blame to him. I don't know what journalists look like as a class, but I suppose you bear the mark of your profession."

" True. But maybe he wouldn't suspect Jaikie."

" He'll suspect any one. He has journalists on the brain just now."

" But he'd recognize the handwriting."

" Perhaps, if the letter got to him. But it won't.
. . . Besides, that man in the ha-ha—what do you call him—Tibbets ?—will see you. And the other man who is crawling down there. All the approaches to the house on this side are as bare as a billiard table. At present you two are dark horses. The enemy doesn't connect you with Mr. Craw, and that's very important, for you are the clue to Mr. Craw's whereabouts. We mustn't give that card away. We don't want Tibbets on your track, for it leads direct to the Back House of the Garroch."

" That's common sense," said Dougal with conviction. " What's your plan, then ? "

The girl sat hunched in the fern, with her chin on one hand, and her eyes on the house and its terraces, where the gardeners were busy with the plots as if nothing could mar its modish tranquillity.

" It's all very exciting and very difficult. We three are the only people in the world who can do anything to help. Somehow we must get hold of Freddy Barbon and pool our knowledge. I'm begin-

ning to think that he may not be really off his head
—only legitimately anxious. What about getting
him to come to the Mains ? I could send a message
by Middlemas—that's our butler—he wouldn't suspect him. Also we could get Aunt Harriet's advice.
She can be very wise when she wants to. And——"

She broke off.

" Mother of Moses ! " she cried, invoking a saint
not known to the Calendar. " I quite forgot.
There's an Australian coming to stay. He's arriving
in time for luncheon. He should be a tower of
strength. His name is Charvill—Robin Charvill.
He's at Oxford and a famous football player. He
played in the international match two days ago."

" I saw him," said Jaikie.

" He's marvellous, isn't he ? "

" Marvellous."

" Well, we can count him in. That makes four
of us—five if we include Aunt Harriet. A pretty
useful support for the distraught Freddy ! The next
thing to do is to get you inconspicuously to the Mains.
I'll show you the best way."

Dougal, who had been knitting his brows, suddenly
gave a shout.

" What like was the man you stalked down
there ? " he demanded of Jaikie.

" I didn't see much of him. He was wearing
queer clothes—tight breeches and a belt round his
waist."

" Foreign-looking ? "

" Perhaps."

He turned to the girl.

" And the men you saw yesterday in the car ?
Were they foreigners ? "

She considered. " They didn't look quite English. One had a short black beard. I remember
that one had a long pale face."

" I've got it," Dougal cried. " No wonder
Barbon's scared. It's the Evallonian Republicans !
They're after Craw ! "

CHAPTER VI

THE TROUBLES OF A PRIVATE SECRETARY

THE pleasant dwelling, known as the Mains of Starr, or more commonly the Mains, stands on a shelf of hillside above the highway, with a fine prospect over the park of Castle Gay to the rolling heathy uplands which form the grouse-moor of Knockraw. From it indeed had shone that light which Jaikie and Dougal had observed the previous night after they left the barricaded lodge. It is low and whitewashed; it has a rounded front like the poop of a three-decker; its gables are crow-stepped; its air is resolutely of the past.

As such it was a fitting house for its present occupant. In every family there are members who act as guardians of its records and repositories of its traditions. Their sole distinction is their family connection, and they take good care that the world shall not forget it. In Scotland they are usually high-nosed maiden ladies, and such a spinsterhood might well have seemed to be the destiny of Harriet Westwater. But, on a visit to Egypt one winter, she had met and espoused a colonel of Sappers, called Brisbane-Brown, and for a happy decade had followed the drum in his company. He rose to be a major-general before he died of pneumonia (the result of a bitter day in an Irish snipe-bog), and left her a well-dowered widow.

The marriage had been a success, but the change of name had been meaningless, for the lady did not cease to be a Westwater. It used to be the fashion in Scotland for a married woman to retain her maiden name even on her tombstone, and this custom she had always followed in spirit. The Brisbane-Browns gave her no genealogical satisfaction. They were Browns from nowhere, who for five generations had served in the military forces of the Crown and had spent most of their lives abroad. The " Brisbane " was not a link with the ancient Scottish house of that ilk ; the General's father had been born in the capital of Queensland, and the word had been retained in the family's nomenclature to distinguish it from innumerable other Browns. As wife and widow she remained a Westwater, and the centre of her world was Castle Gay.

Her brother, Lord Rhynns, did not share her creed, for increasing financial embarrassments had made him a harsh realist ; but, though acutely aware of his imperfections, she felt for him, as head of the family, the reverence with which the devout regard a Prince of the Church. Her pretty invalidish sister-in-law—a type which she would normally have regarded with contempt—shared in the same glamour. But it was for their only child, Alison, that her family loyalty burned most fiercely. That summer, at immense discomfort to herself, she had chaperoned the girl in her first London season.

Her house was Alison's home, and she strove to
bring her up in conformity with the fashions of her
own childhood.   She signally failed, but she did not
repine, for behind her tartness lay a large, tolerant
humour, which gave her an odd kinship with youth.
The girl's slanginess and tom-boyishness were proofs
of spirit—a Westwater characteristic ; her youthful
intolerance was not unpleasing to a laudator of the
past ; her passionate love of Castle Gay was a variant
of her own clannishness.   After the experience of a
modern season she thanked her Maker that her niece
was not one of the lisping mannequins who flutter
between London night-clubs and the sands of Deau-
ville or the Lido.

To the tenant of the Castle she was well disposed.
She knew nothing of him except that he was a
newspaper magnate and very rich, but he paid her
brother a large rent, and did not, like too many
tenants nowadays, fill the house with noisy underbred parties, or outrage the sense of decency of the
estate servants.   She respected Mr. Craw for his
rigid seclusion.   On the occasion of her solitary visit
to him she had been a little shocked by the luxury
of his establishment, till she reflected that a millionaire must spend his money on something, and
that three footmen and a horde of secretaries were
on the whole innocent extravagances.   But indeed
Mr. Craw and the world for which he stood scarcely
came within the orbit of her thoughts.   She was no
more interested in him than in the family affairs of
the Portaway grocer who supplied her with pro-
visions.

Politics she cared nothing for, except in so far as they affected the families which she had known all her life. When there was a chance of Cousin Georgie Whitehaven's second boy being given a post in the Ministry, she was much excited, but she would have been puzzled to name two other members of that Ministry, and of its policy she knew nothing at all. She read and re-read the books which she had loved from of old, and very occasionally a new work, generally a biography, which was well spoken of by her friends. She had never heard of Marcel Proust, but she could have passed a stiff examination in Shakespeare, Jane Austen, and Walter Scott. Morris and Burne-Jones had once enchained her youthful fancy ; she could repeat a good deal of the more decorous parts of Swinburne ; she found little merit in recent painting, except in one or two of Sargent's portraits. Her only musician was Beethoven, but she was a learned connoisseur of Scottish airs.

In her small way she was a notable administrator. The Edinburgh firm of Writers to the Signet who managed her affairs had cause to respect her acumen. Her banker knew her as a shrewd judge of investments. The household at the Mains ran with a clockwork precision, and all the servants, from the butler, Middlemas, to the kitchenmaid, were conscious of her guiding hand. Out of doors an ancient gardener and a boy from the village wrought under her supervision, for she was a keen horticulturist, and won prizes at all the local flower shows for her sweet-peas and cauliflowers. She had given up her carriage, and refused to have a motor-car ; but she drove two fat lazy ponies in a phaeton, and occasionally a well-bred grey gelding in a high dog-cart. The older folk in the countryside liked to see her pass. She was their one link with a vanished world which they now and then recalled with regret.

Mrs. Brisbane-Brown was a relic, but only the unthinking would have called her a snob. For snobbishness implies some sense of insecurity, and she was perfectly secure. She was a specialist, a specialist in kindred. Much has been made in history and fiction of the younger son, but we are apt to forget the younger daughters—the inconspicuous gentlewomen who cling loyally to the skirts of their families, since their birth is their chief title to consideration, and labour to preserve many ancient trifling things which the world to-day holds in small esteem. Mrs. Brisbane-Brown loved all that had continuance, and strove to rivet the weakening links. She kept in touch with the remotest members of her own house, and, being an indefatigable letter-writer, she constituted herself a *trait d'union* for a whole chain of allied families. She was a benevolent aunt to a motley of nephews and nieces who were not nephews and nieces by any recognized table of affinity, and a cousin to many whose cousinship was remote even by Scottish standards. This passion for kinship she carried far beyond her own class. She knew every ascendant and descendant and collateral among the farmers and cottagers of the countryside. Newcomers she regarded with suspicion, unless they could link

themselves on to some of the Hislops and Blairs
and Macmichaels whom she knew to be as long
descended as the Westwaters themselves. Her
aristocracy was wholly of race ; it had nothing to
do with position or wealth ; it was a creed belated,
no doubt, and reactionary, but it was not vulgar.

Jaikie and Dougal made a stealthy exit from the
park by the gate in the wall which Alison unlocked
for them. Then, with a promise to appear at the
Mains for luncheon at one o'clock, they sought the
inn at Starr, where they had left their knapsacks,
recovering on the road their bicycles from the hazel
covert. They said little to each other, for both their
minds were full of a new and surprising experience.
Dougal was profoundly occupied with the Craw
problem, and his own interpretation of its latest
developments. Now and then he would mutter to
himself, " It's the Evallonians all right. Poor old
Craw has pulled the string of the shower-bath this
time." Jaikie, it must be confessed, was thinking
chiefly of Alison. He wished he was like Charvill,
and could call her cousin.

As they made their way to the Mains they encountered Tibbets on his motor-bicycle, a dishevelled
figure, rather gummy about the eyes. He dismounted to greet them.

" Any luck ? " Dougal asked.

He shook his head. " Not yet. I'll have to try
other tactics. I'm off to Portaway to get to-day's
Wire. And you ? "

" We're continuing our travels. The *Wire* will

keep us informed about your doings, no doubt. Good-bye."

Tibbets was off with a trail of dust and petrol fumes. Dougal watched him disappear round a corner.

" Lucky he doesn't know yet what a chance he has. God help Craw if Tibbets once gets on to the Evallonians ! "

With this pious thought they entered the gate of the Mains, and pushed their bicycles up the steep avenue of sycamores and horse-chestnuts. The leaves were yellowing with the morning frosts, and the fallen nuts crackled under the wheels, but, when they reached the lawn, plots and borders had still a summer glory of flowers. Great banks of Michael-mas daisies made a glow like an autumn sunset, and multi-coloured dahlias stood stiffly like grenadiers on parade. The two followed Middlemas through the shadowy hall with a certain nervousness. It seemed odd to be going to luncheon in a strange house at the invitation of a girl whom they had seen that morning for the first time.

They were five minutes late owing to Tibbets, and the mistress of the house was a precisian in punctuality. Consequently they were ushered into the dining-room, where the meal had already begun. It was a shy business, for Alison did not know their names. She waved a friendly hand. " These are my friends, Aunt Hatty," she began, when she was interrupted by a tall young man who made a third at the table.

" Great Scot ! " he cried, after one stare at Jaikie.

" It's Galt ! Whoever would have thought of seeing you here ! " And he seized Jaikie's hand in a massive fist. " You're entertaining a first-rate celebrity, Aunt Harriet. This is the famous John Galt, the greatest Rugby three-quarter playing to-day. I'm bound to say that in self-defence, for he did me in most nobly on Wednesday."

The lady at the head of the table extended a gracious hand. " I am very glad to see you, Mr. Galt. You bear a name which is famous for other things than football. Was it a kinsman who gave us the *Annals of the Parish* ? "

Jaikie, a little confused, said no, and presented Dougal, who was met with a similar genealogical probing. " I used to know Crombies in Kincardine. One commanded a battalion of the Gordons when I was in India. You remind me of him in your colouring."

These startling recognitions had the effect of putting Dougal more at his ease. He felt that he and Jaikie were being pleasantly absorbed into an unfamiliar atmosphere. Jaikie on the contrary was made slightly unhappy, the more so as the girl beside whom he sat turned on him reproachful eyes.

" You ought to have told me you played in the match," she said, "when I spoke about Cousin Robin. I might have made an awful *gaffe*."

" We were talking about more solemn things than football," he replied ; adding, " I thought Mr. Barbon would be here."

" He is coming at three. Such a time we had

getting hold of him ! They wouldn't let Middlemas in—he only managed it through one of our
maids who's engaged to the second footman. . . .
But we mustn't talk about it now. My aunt forbids
disagreeable topics at lunch, just as she won't let
Tactful and Pensive into the dining-room."

Mrs. Brisbane-Brown had strong views about the
kind of talk which aids digestion. It must not
be argumentative, and it must not be agitating.
It was best, she thought, when it was mildly remi-
niscent. But her reminiscences were not mildly
phrased ; as a rule they pointed with some acerbity
the contrast between a dignified past and an un-
worthy present. She had been brought up in the
school of straight backs, and she sat as erect as a
life-guardsman. A stiff net collar held her head
high, a head neat and poised like that of a superior
bird of prey. She had the same small high-bridged
nose as her niece, and that, combined with a slight
droop at the corners of her mouth, gave her an air
of severity which was redeemed by her bright,
humorous brown eyes. Her voice was high and
toneless, and, when she was displeased, of a peculiar
detached, insulting flatness, but this again was
atoned for by a very pleasant, ready, girlish laugh.
Mrs. Brisbane-Brown was a good example of the
art of ageing gracefully. Her complexion, always
a little high-coloured from being much out of doors,
would have done credit to a woman of twenty-five ;
her figure had the trimness of youth ; but the fine
wrinkles about her eyes and the streak of grey in
her hair told of the passage of time. She looked her

fifty-seven years; but she looked what fifty-seven should be at its happiest.

The dining-room was of a piece with its mistress. It was full of pictures, most of them copies of the Rhynns family portraits, done by herself, and one fine Canaletto which she had inherited from her mother. There was a Rhynns with long love-locks and armour, a Rhynns in periwig and lace, a Rhynns in a high-collared coat and cravat, and the original Sir Andrew Westwater, who had acquired Castle Gay by a marriage with the Macdowall heiress, and who looked every inch the ruffian he was. There were prints, too, those mellow mezzotints which are the usual overflow of a great house. The room was sombre and yet cosy, a place that commemorated the past and yet was apt for the present. The arrogant sheen of the mahogany table, which mirrored the old silver and the great bowl of sunflowers (the Westwater crest), seemed to Dougal to typify all that he publicly protested against and secretly respected.

The hostess was cross-examining Mr. Charvill about his knowledge of Scotland, which, it appeared, was confined to one visit to a Highland shooting lodge.

"Then you know nothing about us at all," she declared firmly. "Scotland is the Lowlands. Here we have a civilization of our own, just as good as England, but quite different. The Highlands are a sad, depopulated place, full of midges and kilted haberdashers. I know your Highland lodges—my husband had an unfortunate craze for stalking—

gehennas of pitch-pine and deer's hair—not a bed fit to sleep in, and nothing for the unfortunate women to do but stump in hobnails between the showers along boggy roads !"

Charvill laughed. " I admit I was wet most of the time, but it was glorious fun. I never in my life had so much hard exercise."

" You can walk ? "

" A bit. I was brought up pretty well on horse-back, but since I came to England I have learned to use my legs."

" Then you are a fortunate young man. I cannot think what is to become of the youth of to-day. I was staying at Glenavelin last year, and the young men when they went to fish motored the half-mile to the river. My cousin had a wire from a friend who had taken Machray forest, begging him to find somebody over fifty to kill his stags, since his house was full of boys who could not get up the hills. You two," her eyes passed from Dougal to Jaikie, " are on a walking tour. I'm very glad to hear it. That is a rational kind of holiday."

She embarked on stories of the great walkers of a century ago—Barclay of Urie, Horatio Ross, Lord John Kennedy. " My father in his youth once walked from Edinburgh to Castle Gay. He took two days, and he had to carry the little spaniel that accompanied him for the last twenty miles. We don't breed such young men to-day. I daresay they are more discreet and less of an anxiety to their parents, and I know that they don't drink so much. But they are a feeble folk, like the conies.

They never want to fling their caps over the moon. There is a lamentable scarcity of wild oats of the right kind."

" Aunt Harriet," said the girl, " is thinking of the young men she saw at balls this summer."

Mrs. Brisbane-Brown raised her hands. " Did you ever know such a kindergarten ? Pallid infants with vacant faces. It was cruel to ask a girl to waste her time over them."

" You asked *me*, you know, in spite of my protests."

" And rightly, my dear. It is a thing every girl must go through—her form of public-school education. But I sincerely pitied you, my poor child. When I was young and went to balls I danced with interesting people—soldiers, and diplomats, and young politicians. They may have been at the balls this season, but I never saw them. What I did see were hordes upon hordes of children—a sort of *crèche*—vapid boys who were probably still at school or only just beginning the University. What has become of the sound English doctrine that the up-bringing of our male youth should be monastic till at least twenty-one ? We are getting as bad as the Americans with their ghastly co-education."

Jaikie was glad when they rose from table. He had wanted to look at Alison, who sat next him, but that meant turning his head deliberately, and he had been too shy. He wished that, like Dougal, he had sat opposite her. Yet he had been cheered by Mrs. Brisbane-Brown's diatribes. Her condemnation of modern youth excluded by implication the three who lunched with her. She approved of Charvill, of

8

course. Who wouldn't ? Charvill with his frank
kindliness, his height, his orthodox good looks, was
the kind of person Jaikie would have envied, had it
been his nature to envy. But it would appear that
she had also approved of Dougal and himself, and
Jaikie experienced a sudden lift of the heart.

Now he was free to look at Alison, as she stood
very slim and golden in the big sunlit drawing-room.
It was the most beautiful room Jaikie had ever
beheld. The chairs and sofas were covered with a
bright, large-patterned chintz, all roses, parrots, and
hollyhocks ; the carpet was a faded Aubusson,
rescued from a bedroom in Castle Gay ; above the
mantelpiece, in a gilt case, hung a sword of honour
presented to the late General Brisbane-Brown, and
on the polished parts of the floor, which the Aubusson
did not reach, lay various trophies of his marks-
manship. There was a huge white fleecy rug, and
between that and the fire a huge brass fender.
There were vitrines full of coins and medals and
Roman lamps and flint arrows and enamelled snuff-
boxes, and cabinets displaying Worcester china and
Leeds earthenware. On the white walls were cases
of miniatures, and samplers, and two exquisite
framed fans, and a multitude of water-colours, all
the work of Mrs. Brisbane-Brown. There were
views from the terraces of Florentine villas, and
sunsets on the Nile, and dawns over Indian deserts,
and glimpses of a dozen strange lands. The series
was her travel diary, the trophy of her wanderings,
just as a man will mount heads on the walls of his
smoking room. But the best picture was that pre-

sented by the two windows, which showed the wild
woods and hollows of the Castle park below, bright
in the October afternoon, running to the dim purple
of the Knockraw heather.

In this cheerful and gracious room, before Middlemas had finished serving coffee, before Jaikie had
made up his mind whether he preferred Alison in
her present tidiness or in the gipsydom of the
morning, there appeared a figure which effectually
banished its complacent tranquillity.

Mr. Frederick Barbon entered by an open window,
and his clothes and shoes bore the marks of a rough
journey. Yet neither clothes nor figure seemed
adapted for such adventures. Mr. Barbon's appearance was what old-fashioned people would have
called "distinguished." He was very slim and
elegant, and he had that useful colouring which does
not change between the ages of thirty and fifty ; that
is to say, he had prematurely grizzled locks and a
young complexion. His features were classic in
their regularity. Sometimes he looked like a successful actor ; sometimes, when in attendance on
his master, like a very superior footman in mufti
who had not got the powder out of his hair ; but
there were moments when he was taken for an
eminent statesman. It was his nervous blue eyes
which betrayed him, for Mr. Barbon was an anxious
soul. He liked his little comforts, he liked to feel
important and privileged, and he knew only too
well what it was to be a poor gentleman tossed from
dilemma to dilemma by the unsympathetic horns
of destiny. Since the war—when he had held a

commission in the Foot Guards—he had been suc-
cessively, but not successfully, a land-agent (the
property was soon sold), a dealer in motor-cars (the
business went speedily bankrupt), a stockbroker on
half-commission, the manager of a tourist agency,
an advertisement tout, and a highly incompetent
society journalist. From his father, the aged and
penniless Clonkilty, he could expect nothing. Then
in the service of Mr. Craw he had found an undreamed
of haven ; and he was as determined as King Charles
the Second that he would never go wandering again.
Consequently he was always anxious. He was an
admirable private secretary, but he was fussy. The
dread that haunted his dreams was of being hurled
once more into the cold world of economic strife.

He sank wearily into a chair and accepted a cup
of coffee.

" I had to make a detour of nearly three miles,"
he explained, " and come down on this place from
the hill. I daren't stop long either. Where is Mr.
Craw's letter ? "

Dougal presented the missive, which Mr. Barbon
tore open and devoured. A heavy sigh escaped him.

" Lucky I did not get this sooner and act on it,"
he said. " Mr. Craw wants to come back. But the
one place he mustn't come near is Castle Gay."

Dougal, though very hungry and usually a stout
trencherman, had not enjoyed his luncheon. Indeed he had done less than justice to the excellent
food provided. He was acutely aware of being in
an unfamiliar environment, to which he should have
been hostile, but which as a matter of plain fact he

enjoyed with trepidation. Unlike Jaikie he bristled
with class-consciousness. Mrs. Brisbane-Brown's
kindly arrogance, the long-descended air of her
possessions, the atmosphere of privilege so secure
that it need not conceal itself—he was aware of it
with a half-guilty joy. The consequence was that
he was adrift from his moorings, and not well at
ease. He had not spoken at table except in answer
to questions, and he now stood in the drawing-room
like a colt in a flower-garden, not very certain what
to do with his legs.

The sight of the embarrassed Barbon revived
him. Here was something he could understand, a
problem in his own world. Craw might be a fool,
but he belonged to his own totem, and this Barbon
man (of his hostess's world) was clearly unfit to deal
with the web in which his employer had entangled
himself. He found his voice. He gave the company a succinct account of how Mr. Craw had come
to be in the Back House of the Garroch.

" That's all I have to tell. Now you take up
the story. I want to hear everything that happened since Wednesday night, when Mr. Craw did
not come home."

The voice was peremptory, and Mr. Barbon raised
his distinguished eyebrows. Even in his perplexity
he felt bound to resent this tone.

" I'm afraid . . . I . . . I don't quite understand your position, Mr. —— ? "

" My name's Crombie. I'm on one of the Craw
papers. My interest in straightening things out is
the same as yours. So let's pool our knowledge

and be quick about it. You began to get anxious about Mr. Craw at half-past eight on Wednesday, and very anxious about ten. What did you do?"

"We communicated with Glasgow—with Mr. Craw's architect. He had accompanied him to the station and seen him leave by the six-five train. We communicated with Kirkmichael station, and learned that he had arrived there. Then I informed the police—very confidentially of course."

"The journalists got wind of that. They were bound to, since they sit like jackdaws on the steps of the telegraph office. So much for Wednesday. What about yesterday?"

"I had a very anxious day," said Mr. Barbon, passing a weary hand over his forehead and stroking back his thick grizzled hair. "I hadn't a notion what to think or do. Mr. Craw, you must understand, intended to go abroad. He was to have left this morning, catching the London express at Gledmouth. Miss Cazenove and I were to have accompanied him, and all arrangements had been made. It seemed to me that he might have chosen to expedite his departure, though such a thing was very unlike his usual custom. So I got the London office to make inquiries, and ascertained that he had not travelled south. You are aware of Mr. Craw's dislike of publicity. I found myself in a very serious quandary. I had to find out what had become of him. Anything might have happened —an accident, an outrage. And I had to do this without giving any clue to those infernal reporters."

"Practically impossible," said Dougal. "No wonder you were in a bit of a stew. I suppose they were round the house like bees yesterday."

"Like wasps," said Mr. Barbon tragically. "We kept them at arm's length, but they have defeated us." He produced from his pocket and unfolded a copy of a journal. "We have special arrangements at the Castle for an early delivery of newspapers, and this is to-day's *Live Wire*. Observe the headings."

"I know all about that," said Dougal. "We ran across the *Wire* man—Tibbets they call him—and he was fair bursting with his news. But this will only make the *Wire* crowd look foolish if they can't follow it up. That's what we've got to prevent. I took the liberty this morning of speaking to Tavish in Glasgow on the telephone, and authorizing him— I pretended I was speaking for Mr. Craw—to announce that Mr. Craw had left for the Continent. That will give us cover to work behind."

"You might have spared yourself the trouble," said Mr. Barbon, unfolding another news-sheet. "This is to-day's issue of the *View*. It contains that announcement. It was inserted by the London office. Now who authorized it?"

"I heard of that from Tavish. Could it have been Mr. Craw?"

"It was not Mr. Craw. That I can vouch for, unless he sent the authorization after half-past seven on Wednesday evening, which on your story is impossible. It was sent by some person or persons who contrived to impress the London office with

their authority, and who wished to have it believed
that Mr. Craw was out of the country. For their
own purpose. Now, what purpose ? "

" I think I can make a guess," said Dougal
eagerly.

" There is no need of guess-work. It is a matter
of certain and damning knowledge. Mr. Craw left
for Glasgow on Wednesday before his mail arrived.
In that mail there was a registered letter. It was
marked ' most confidential,' and elaborately sealed.
I deal with Mr. Craw's correspondence, but letters
marked in such a way I occasionally leave for him
to open, so I did not touch that letter. Then,
yesterday morning, at the height of my anxieties,
I had a telephone message."

Mr. Barbon paused dramatically. " It was not
from London. It was from Knockraw House, a
place some five miles from here. I knew that
Knockraw had been let for the late autumn, but
I had not heard the name of the tenant. It is the
best grouse-moor in the neighbourhood. The speaker
referred to a confidential letter which he said Mr.
Craw had received on the previous day, and he
added that he and his friends proposed to call upon
Mr. Craw that afternoon at three o'clock. I said
that Mr. Craw was not at home, but the speaker
assured me that Mr. Craw would be at home to him.
I did not dare to say more, but I asked for the
name. It was given me as Casimir—only the one
word. Then I think the speaker rang off.

" I considered it my duty," Mr. Barbon continued, " to open the confidential letter. When I

had read it, I realized that instead of being in the frying-pan we were in the middle of the fire. For that letter was written in the name of the inner circle of the——"

" Evallion Republicans," interjected Dougal, seeking a cheap triumph.

" It was not. It was the Evallonian Monarchists."

" Good God ! " Dougal was genuinely startled, for he saw suddenly a problem with the most dismal implications.

" They said that their plans were approaching maturity, and that they had come to consult with their chief well-wisher. There was an immense amount of high-flown compliment in it after the Evallonian fashion, but there was one thing clear. These people are in deadly earnest. They have taken Knockraw for the purpose, and they have had the assurance to announce to the world Mr. Craw's absence abroad so that they may have him to themselves without interruption. They must have had private information about his movements, and his intention of leaving Scotland. I don't know much about Evallonian politics—they were a personal hobby of Mr. Craw's—but I know enough to realize that the party who wish to upset the republic are pretty desperate fellows. It was not only the certain notoriety of the thing which alarmed me, though that was bad enough. Imagine the play that our rivals would make with the story of Mr. Craw plotting with foreign adventurers to upset a Government with which Britain is in friendly relations ! It was the effect upon Mr. Craw himself.

He hates anything to do with the rough-and-tumble of political life. He is quite unfit to deal with such people. He is a thinker and an inspirer—a seer in a watch-tower, and such men lose their power if they go down into the arena."

This was so manifestly an extract from the table-talk of Mr. Craw that Dougal could not repress a grin.

" You laugh," said Mr. Barbon gloomily, " but there is nothing to laugh at. The fortunes of a great man and a great Press are at this moment on a razor-edge."

" Jaikie," said Dougal in a whisper, " Mr. McCunn was a true prophet. He said we were maybe going to set up the Jacobite standard on Garroch side. There's a risk of another kind of Jacobite standard being set up on Callowa side. It's a colossal joke on the part of Providence."

Mr. Barbon continued his tale.

" I felt utterly helpless. I did not know where Mr. Craw was. I had the threatening hordes of journalists to consider. I had those foreign desperadoes at the gates. They must not be allowed to approach Castle Gay. I had no fear that Casimir and his friends would take the journalists into their confidence, but I was terribly afraid that the journalists would get on to the trail of Casimir. An Eastern European house-party at Knockraw is a pretty obvious mark. . . . I gave orders that no one was to be admitted at either lodge. I went further and had the gates barricaded, in case there was an attempt to force them."

" You lost your head there," said Dougal.   " You were making the journalists a gift."

" Perhaps I did.   But when one thinks of Eastern Europe one thinks of violence.   Look at this letter I received this morning.   Note that it is addressed to me by my full name."

The writer with great simplicity and in perfect English informed the Honourable Frederick Barbon, M.C., that it was quite futile to attempt to deny his friends entrance to Castle Gay, but that they had no wish to embarrass him.   To-morrow at 11 a.m. they would wait upon Mr. Craw, and if they were again refused they would take other means of securing an audience.

Dougal whistled.   " The writer of this knows all about the journalists.   And he knows that Mr. Craw is not at the Castle, but believes that you are hiding him somewhere.   They've a pretty useful intelligence department."

Mrs. Brisbane-Brown, who had listened to Mr. Barbon's recital with composure, now entered the conversation.

" You mustn't let your nerves get the upper hand of you, Freddy.   Try to take things more calmly.   I'm afraid that poor Mr. Craw has himself to thank for this predicament.   Why will newspaper owners meddle with things they don't understand ? Politics should be left to those who make a profession of them.   But we must do our best to help him. Mr. Crombie," she turned to Dougal, whose grim face was heavy with thought, " you look capable. What do you propose ? "

The fire of battle had kindled in Dougal's eyes, and Jaikie saw in them something which he remembered from old days.

" I think," he said, " that we're in for a stiff campaign, and that it must be conducted on two fronts. We must find some way of heading off those Evallonians, and it won't be easy. When a foreigner gets a notion into his head he's apt to turn into a demented crusader. They're all the same—Socialists, Communists, Fascists, Republicans, Monarchists—I daresay Monarchists are the worst, for they've less inside their heads to begin with. . . . And we must do it without giving the journalists a hint of what is happening. We must suppress Tibbets by force, if necessary."

" Perhaps the Evallonians will do that for you," suggested Alison.

" Very likely they will. . . . The second front is wherever Mr. Craw may be. At all costs he must be kept away from here. Now, he can't stay at the Back House of the Garroch. The journalists will very soon be on to the Glasgow students, and they'll hear about the kidnapping, and they'll track him to the Back House. I needn't tell you that it's all up with us if any reporter gets sight of Mr. Craw. I think he had better be smuggled out of the country as quickly as possible."

Mr. Barbon shook his head.

" Impossible ! " he murmured. " I've already thought of that plan and rejected it. The Evallonians will discover it and follow him, and they will find him in a foreign land without friends. I

wonder if you understand that Mr. Craw will be
terrified at the thought of meeting them. Terrified! That is his nature. I think he would prefer
to risk everything and come back here rather than
fall into their hands in another country than his
own. He has always been a little suspicious of
foreigners."

"Very well. He can't come back here, but he
needn't go abroad. He must disappear. Now,
how is that to be managed?"

"Jaikie," he said, after a moment's reflection,
"this is your job. You'll have to take charge of
the Craw front."

Jaikie opened his eyes. He had not been attend-
ing very carefully, for the preoccupations of the
others had allowed him to stare at Alison, and he
had been wondering whether her hair should be
called red or golden. For certain it had no connection with Dougal's. . . . Also, why a jumper
and a short tweed skirt made a girl look so much
more feminine than flowing draperies. . . .

"I don't quite understand," he said.

"It's simple enough. We're going to have some
difficult work on the home front, and the problem
is hopeless if it's complicated by the presence of
Mr. Craw. One of us has to be in constant attendance on him, and keep him buried . . ."

"But where?"

"Anywhere you like, as long as you get him away
from the Back House of the Garroch. He'll not
object. He's not looking for any Evallonians.
You've the whole of Scotland, and England too, to

choose from. Pick your own hidy-hole. He'll not
be difficult to hide, for few people know him by
sight and he looks a commonplace little body. It's
you or me—and better you than me, for you're
easy tempered, and I doubt Mr. Craw and I would
quarrel the first day."

Jaikie caught Alison's eyes and saw in them so
keen a zest for a new, exciting adventure that his
own interest kindled. He would have immensely
preferred to be engaged on the home front, but he
saw the force of Dougal's argument. He had a
sudden vision of himself, tramping muddy roads in
October rain, putting up at third-rate inns, eating
bread and cheese in the heather—and by his side, a
badly scared millionaire, a fugitive leader of the
people. Jaikie rarely laughed aloud, but at the
vision his face broke into a slow smile.

" I'll need a pair of boots," he said, " not for
myself—for Mr. Craw. The things he is wearing
would be knocked to pieces in half a day."

Mr. Barbon, whose dejection had brightened at the
sound of Dougal's crisp mandates, declared that the
boots could be furnished.   He suggested other necessaries, which Jaikie ultimately reduced to a tooth-
brush, a razor, spare shirts, and pyjamas.   A servant
from the Castle would deliver them a mile up the
road.

" You'd better be off," Dougal advised.   " He'll
have been ranging round the Back House these
last four hours like a hyena, and if you don't
hurry we'll have him arriving here on his two
legs. . . . You'll have to give us an address for

letters, for we must have some means of communication."

"Let it be Post Office, Portaway," said Jaikie; and added, in reply to the astonished stare of the other, "Unless there's a reflector above, the best hiding-place is under the light."

CHAPTER VII

BEGINNING OF A GREAT MAN'S EXILE

JAIKIE had not a pleasant journey that autumn afternoon over the ridge that separates Callowa from Garroch and up the latter stream to the dark hills of its source. To begin with, he was wheeling the bicycle which Dougal had ridden, for that compromising object must be restored as soon as possible to its owner; and, since this was no easy business on indifferent roads, he had to walk most of the way. Also, in addition to the pack on his back, he had Dougal's, which contained the parcel duly handed over to him a mile up the road by a Castle Gay servant. . . . But his chief discomfort was spiritual.

From his tenderest years he had been something of a philosopher. It was his quaint and placid reasonableness which had induced Dickson McCunn, when he took in hand the destinies of the Gorbals Die-hards, to receive him into his own household. He had virtually adopted Jaikie because he seemed more broken to domesticity than any of the others. The boy had speedily become at home in his new environment, and with effortless ease had accepted and adapted himself to the successive new worlds which opened to him. He had the gift of living for the moment where troubles were concerned and not anticipating them, but in pleasant things of letting his fancy fly happily ahead. So he accepted docilely his present task, since he was convinced of the reason for it ; Dougal was right—he was the better person of the two to deal with Craw. . . . But the other, the imaginative side of him, was in revolt. That morning he had received an illumination. He had met the most delightful human being he had ever encountered. And now he was banished from her presence.

He was not greatly interested in Craw. Dougal was different ; to Dougal Craw was a figure of mystery and power ; there was romance in the midge controlling the fate of the elephant. To Jaikie he was only a dull, sententious, elderly gentleman, probably with a bad temper, and he was chained to him for an indefinite number of days. It sounded a bleak kind of holiday. . . . But at Castle Gay there were the Evallonians, and Mrs. Brisbane-Brown, and an immense old house now in a state of siege, and Alison's bright eyes, and a stage set for preposterous adventures. The lucky Dougal was there in the front of it, while he was condemned to wander lonely in the wings.

But as the increasing badness of the road made riding impossible, and walking gave him a better chance for reflection, the prospect slowly brightened. It had been a fortunate inspiration of his, the decision to keep Craw hidden in the near neighbourhood. It had been good sense, too, for the best

9

place of concealment was the unexpected. He
would not be far from the main scene of conflict,
and he might even have a chance of a share in it. . . .
Gradually his interest began to wake in the task
itself. After all he had the vital rôle. If a man-
hunt was on foot, he had charge of the quarry. It
was going to be a difficult business, and it might be
exciting. He remembered the glow in Alison's eyes,
and the way she had twined and untwined her
fingers. They were playing in the same game, and
if he succeeded it was her approval he would win.
Craw was of no more interest to him than the ball
in a Rugby match, but he was determined to score
a try with him between the posts.

In this more cheerful mood he arrived at the Back
House about the hour of seven, when the dark had
fallen. Mrs. Catterick met him with an anxious
face and the high lilt of the voice which in her type
is the consequence of anxiety.

" Ye're back ? Blithe I am to see ye. And ye're
your lane ? Dougal's awa' on anither job, says
you ? Eh, man, ye've been sair looked for. The
puir body ben the hoose has been neither to haud nor
to bind. He was a mile doun the road this mornin'
in his pappymashy buits. He didna tak' a bite o'
denner, and sin' syne he's been sittin' glunchin' or
lookin' out o' the windy." Then, in a lowered voice,
" For guid sake, Jaikie, do something, or he'll loss
his reason."

" It's all right, Mrs. Catterick. I've come back
to look after him. Can you put up with us for
another night ? We'll be off to-morrow morning."

"Fine that. John'll no be hame or Monday. Ye'll hae your supper thegither? It's an ill job a jyler's. Erchie will whistle lang ere he sees me at it again."

Jaikie did not at once seek Mr. Craw's presence. He spread his map of the Canonry on the kitchen table and brooded over it. It was only when he knew from the clatter of dishes that the meal was ready in the best room that he sought that chamber.

He found the great man regarding distastefully a large dish of bacon and eggs and a monstrous brown teapot enveloped in a knitted cosy of purple and green. He had found John Catterick's razor too much for him, for he had not shaved that morning, his suit had acquired further whitewash from the walls of his bedroom, and his scanty hair was innocent of the brush. He had the air of one who had not slept well and had much on his mind. The eyes which he turned on Jaikie had the petulance of a sulky child.

"So you've come at last," he grumbled. "Where is Mr. Crombie? Have you brought a car?"

"I came on a bicycle. Dougal—Mr. Crombie—is staying at Castle Gay."

"What on earth do you mean? Did you deliver my letter to Mr. Barbon?"

Jaikie nodded. He felt suddenly rather dashed in spirits. Mr. Craw, untidy and unshaven and as cross as a bear, was not an attractive figure, least of all as a companion for an indefinite future.

"I had better tell you exactly what happened," he said, and he recounted the incidents of the previous evening up to the meeting with Tibbets. " So we decided that it would be wiser not to try to deliver the letter last night."

Mr. Craw's face showed extreme irritation, not unmingled with alarm.

" The insolence of it ! " he declared. " You say the *Wire* man has got the story of my disappearance, and has published it in to-day's issue ? He knows nothing of the cause which brought me here ? "

" Nothing. And he need never know, unless he tracks you to this place. The *Wire* stands a good chance of making a public goat of itself. Dougal telephoned to your Glasgow office, and your own papers published to-day the announcement that you had gone abroad."

Mr. Craw looked relieved. " That was well done. As a matter of fact I had planned to go abroad to-day, though I did not intend to announce it. It has never been my habit to placard my movements like a Court Circular. . . . So far good, Mr. Galt. I shall travel south to-morrow night. But what possessed Barbon not to send the car at once ? I must go back to Castle Gay before I leave, and the sooner the better. My reappearance will spike the guns of my journalistic enemies."

" It would," Jaikie assented. " But there's another difficulty, Mr. Craw. The announcement of your going abroad to-day was not sent to your papers first by Dougal. It was sent by very different people. The day before yesterday, when you were in Glasgow, these same people sent you a letter. Yesterday they telephoned to Mr. Barbon, wanting to see you, and then he opened the letter. Here it is." He presented the missive, whose heavy seals Mr. Barbon had already broken.

Mr. Craw looked at the first page, and then subsided heavily into a chair. He fumbled feverishly for his glasses, and his shaking hand had much ado to fix them on his nose. As he read, his naturally ruddy complexion changed to a clayey white. He finished his reading, and sat staring before him with unseeing eyes, his fingers picking nervously at the sheets of notepaper. Jaikie, convinced that he was about to have a fit, and very much alarmed, poured him out a scalding cup of tea. He drank a mouthful, and spilled some over his waistcoat.

It was a full minute before he recovered a degree of self-possession, but self-possession only made him look more ghastly, for it revealed the perturbation of his mind.

" You have read this ? " he stammered.

" No. But Mr. Barbon told us the contents of it."

" Us ? " he almost screamed.

" Yes. We had a kind of conference on the situation this afternoon. At the Mains. There was Mr. Barbon, and Miss Westwater and her aunt, and Dougal and myself. We made a sort of plan, and that's why I'm here."

Mr. Craw clutched at his dignity, but he could not grasp it. The voice which came from his lips was small, and plaintive, and childish, and, as Jaikie noted, it had lost its precise intonation and had returned to the broad vowels of Kilmaclavers.

" This is a dreadful business. . . . You can't

realize how dreadful. . . . I can't meet these people.
I can't be implicated in this affair. It would mean
absolute ruin to my reputation. . . . Even the fact
of their being in this countryside is terribly compromising. Supposing my enemies got word of it!
They would put the worst construction on it, and
they would make the public believe it. . . . As you
are aware, I have taken a strong line about Evallonian politics—an honest line. I cannot recant my
views without looking a fool. But if I do not recant
my views, the presence of those infernal fools will
make the world believe that I am actually dabbling
in their conspiracies. I, who have kept myself aloof
from the remotest semblance of political intrigue!
Oh, it is too monstrous!"

"I don't think the *Wire* people will get hold of
it very easily," was Jaikie's attempt at comfort.

"Why not?" he snapped.

"Because the Evallonians will prevent it. They
seem determined people, determined to have you to
themselves. Otherwise they wouldn't have got your
papers to announce that you had gone abroad."

This was poor comfort for Mr. Craw. He ejacu-
lated "Good God!" and fell into a painful medi-
tation. It was not only his repute he was thinking
of, but his personal safety. These men had come to
coerce him, and their coercion would not stop at
trifles. I do not know what picture presented itself
to his vision, but it was probably something highly
melodramatic (for he knew nothing at first hand of
foreign peoples)—dark, sinister men, incredibly cunning, with merciless faces and lethal weapons in

every pocket. He groaned aloud. Then a thought
struck him.

"You say they telephoned to Castle Gay," he
asked wildly. "Where are they?"

"They are at Knockraw. They have taken the
place for the autumn. Mr. Barbon, as I told you,
refused to let them in. They seemed to know about
your absence from the Castle, but they believe that
he can put his hand on you if he wants. So they
are going there at eleven o'clock to-morrow morning,
and they say they will take no denial."

"At Knockraw!" It was the cry of a fugitive
who learns that the avenger of blood is in the next
room.

"Yes," said Jaikie. "We've got the Recording
Angel established in our back garden on a strictly
legal tenure. We must face that fact."

Mr. Craw seemed disinclined to face it. He sunk
his face in his hands and miserably hunched his
shoulders. Jaikie observed that the bacon and eggs
were growing cold, but the natural annoyance of a
hungry man was lost in pity for the dejected figure
before him. Here was one who must have remarkable talents—business talents, at any rate, even if
he were not much of a thinker or teacher. He was
accustomed to make men do what he wanted. He
had the gift of impressing millions of people with his
strength and wisdom. He must often have taken
decisions which required nerve and courage. He
had inordinate riches, and to Jaikie, who had not a
penny, the acquisition of great wealth seemed proof
of a rare and mysterious power. Yet here was this

great man, unshaven and unkempt, sunk in childish
despair, because of a situation which to the spectator
himself seemed simple and rather amusing.

Jaikie had a considerable stock of natural piety.
He hated to see human nature, in which he profoundly believed, making a discreditable exhibition
of itself.   Above all he hated to see an old man—
Mr. Craw seemed to him very old, far older than
Dickson McCunn—behaving badly.   He could not
bring himself to admit that age, which brought
success, did not also bring wisdom.   Moreover he
was by nature kindly, and did not like to see a
fellow-being in pain.   So he applied himself to the
duties of comforter.

" Cheer up, Mr. Craw," he said.   " This thing is
not so bad as all that.   There's at least three ways
out of it."

There was no answer, save for a slight straightening
of the shoulders, so Jaikie continued :

" First, you can carry things with a high hand.
Go back to Castle Gay and tell every spying journalist
to go to blazes.   Sit down in your own house and be
master there.   Your position won't suffer.   If the
Wire gets hold of the story of the students' rag, what
does it matter ?   It will be forgotten in two days,
when the next murder or divorce comes along.   Besides, you behaved well in it.   You kept your
temper.   It's not a thing to be ashamed of.   The
folk who'll look foolish will be Tibbets with his bogus
mysteries, and the editor who printed his stuff.   If I
were you I'd put the whole story of your adventure
in your own papers and make a good yarn of it.

Then you'll have people laughing with you, not at you."

Mr. Craw was listening. Jaikie understood him to murmur something about the Evallonians.

"As for the Evallonians," he continued, "I'd meet them. Ask the whole bally lot to luncheon or dinner. Tell them that Evallonia is not your native land, and that you'll take no part in her politics. Surely a man can have his views about a foreign country without being asked to get a gun and fight for it. If they turn nasty, tell them also to go to the devil. This is a free country, and a law-abiding country. There's the police in the last resort. And you could raise a defence force from Castle Gay itself that would make yon foreign bandits look silly. Never mind if the thing gets into the papers. You'll have behaved well, and you'll have reason to be proud of it."

Jaikie spoke in a tone of extreme gentleness and moderation. He was most anxious to convince his hearer of the desirability of this course, for it would remove all his own troubles. He and Dougal would be able with a clear conscience to continue their walking tour, and every minute his distaste was increasing for the prospect of taking the road in Mr. Craw's company.

But that moderation was an error in tactics. Had he spoken harshly, violently, presenting any other course as naked cowardice, it is possible that he might have struck an answering spark from Mr. Craw's temper, and forced him to a declaration from which he could not have retreated. His equable

reasonableness was his undoing. The man sitting
hunched up in the chair considered the proposal,
and his terrors, since they were not over-ridden
by anger, presented it in repulsive colours to his
reason.

" No," he said, " I can't do that. It is not
possible. . . . You do not understand. . . . I am
not an ordinary man. My position is unique. I
have won an influence, which I hold in trust for
great public causes. I dare not impair it by being
mixed up in farce or brawling."

Jaikie recognized the decision as final. He also
inferred from the characteristic stateliness of the
words and the recovered refinement of the accent,
that Mr. Craw was beginning to be himself again.

" Very well," he said briskly. " The second way
is that you go abroad as if nothing had happened.
We can get a car to take you to Gledmouth, and
Mr. Barbon will bring on your baggage. Go anywhere you like abroad, and leave the Evallonians
to beat at the door of an empty house. If their
mission becomes known, it won't do you any harm,
for you'll be able to prove an alibi."

Mr. Craw's consideration of this project was brief,
and his rejection was passionate. Mr. Barbon had
been right in his forecast.

" No, no," he cried, " that is utterly and eternally
impossible. On the Continent of Europe I should
be at their mercy. They are organized in every
capital. Their intelligence service would discover
me—you admit yourself that they know a good
deal about my affairs even in this country. I should

have no protection, for I do not believe in the Continental police."

"What are you afraid of?" Jaikie asked with a touch of irritation. "Kidnapping?"

Mr. Craw assented darkly. "Some kind of violence," he said.

"But," Jaikie argued in a voice which he tried to keep pleasant, "how would that serve their purpose? They don't need you as a hostage. They certainly don't want you as leader of an armed revolution. They want the support of your papers, and the influence which they think you possess with the British Government. You're no use to them except functioning in London."

It was a second mistake in tactics, for Jaikie's words implied some disparagement of Craw the man as contrasted with Craw the newspaper proprietor. There was indignation as well as fear in the reply.

"No. I will not go abroad at such a time. It would be insanity. It would be suicide. You must permit me to judge what is politic in such circumstances. I assure you I do not speak without reflection."

"Very well," said Jaikie, whose spirits had descended to his boots. "You can't go back to Castle Gay. You won't go abroad. You must stay in this country and lie low till the Evallonians clear out."

Mr. Craw said nothing, but by his silence he signified an unwilling assent to this alternative.

"But when?" he asked drearily after a pause. "When will the Evallonians give up their mission? Have we any security for their going within a reasonable time ? You say that they have taken Knockraw for the season. They may stay till Christmas."

" We've left a pretty effective gang behind us to speed their departure."

" Who ? "

" Well, there's Mrs. Brisbane-Brown. I wouldn't like to be opposed to yon woman."

" The tenant of the Mains ? I scarcely know her."

" No, she said that when she met you you looked at her as if she were Lady Godiva. Then there's her niece, Miss Westwater."

" The child I have seen riding in the park ? What can she do ? "

Jaikie smiled. " She might do a lot. And there's your staff at the Castle, Mr. Barbon and the rest. And most important of all, there's Dougal."

Mr. Craw brightened perceptibly at the last name. Dougal was his own henchman, an active member of the great Craw brotherhood. From him he could look for loyal and presumably competent service. Jaikie saw the change in expression, and improved the occasion.

" You don't know Dougal as I know him. He's the most determined fellow on earth. He'll stick at nothing. I'll wager he'll shift the Evallonians, if he has to take to smoke bombs and poison gas. . . . Isn't it about time that we had supper ? I'm famished with hunger."

The bacon and eggs had to be sent back to be heated up, and Mrs. Catterick had to make a fresh brew of tea. Under the cheering influence of the thought of Dougal, Mr. Craw made quite a respectable meal. A cigar would have assisted his comfort, but he had long ago emptied his case, and he was compelled to accept one of Jaikie's cheap Virginian cigarettes. His face remained a little clouded, and he frequently corrugated his brows in thought, but the black despair of half an hour ago had left him.

When the remains of supper had been cleared away he asked to see Jaikie's map, which for some time he studied intently.

"I must reach the railway as soon as possible," he said. "On the other side from Castle Gay, of course. I must try to walk to some place where I can hire a conveyance."

"Where did you think of going?" Jaikie asked.

"London," was the reply. "I can find privacy in the suite in my office."

"Have you considered that that will be watched? These Evallonians, as we know, are careful people who mean business, and they seem to have a pretty useful intelligence system. You will be besieged in your office just as badly as if you were at Castle Gay. And with far more publicity."

Mr. Craw pondered ruefully. "You think so? Perhaps you are right. What about a quiet hotel?"

Jaikie shook his head. "No good. They will find you out. And if you go to Glasgow or Edinburgh or Manchester or Bournemouth it will be the same. It doesn't do to underrate the cleverness of the enemy. If Mr. Craw goes anywhere in these islands as Mr. Craw some hint of it will get out, and they'll be on to it like a knife."

Despair was creeping back into the other's face. "Have you any other course to suggest?" he faltered.

"I propose that you and I go where you're not expected, and that's just in the Canonry. The Evallonians will look for you in Castle Gay and everywhere else except in its immediate neighbourhood. It's darkest under the light, you see. Nobody knows you by sight, and you and I can take a quiet saunter through the Canonry without anybody being the wiser, while Dougal finishes the job at the Castle."

Mr. Craw's face was a blank, and Jaikie hastened to complete his sketch.

"We'll be on a walking tour, the same as Dougal and I proposed, but we'll get out of the hills. An empty countryside like this is too conspicuous. . . . I know the place, and I'll guarantee to keep you well hidden. I've brought Dougal's pack for you. In it there's a suit of pyjamas and a razor and some shirts and things which I got from Mr. Barbon . . ."

Mr. Craw cried out like one in pain.

" . . . And a pair of strong boots," Jaikie concluded soothingly. "I'm glad I remembered that. The boots you have on would be in ribbons the first day on these stony roads."

It was Jaikie's third error in tactics. Mr. Craw had experienced various emotions, including terror, that evening, and now he was filled with a horrified disgust. He had created for himself a padded and cosseted life; he had scaled an eminence of high importance; he had made his daily existence a

ritual every item of which satisfied his self-esteem.
And now this outrageous young man proposed that
he should scrap it all and descend to the pit out of
which thirty years ago he had climbed. Even for
safety the price was far too high. Better the perils
of high politics, where at least he would remain a
figure of consequence. He actually shivered with
repulsion, and his anger gave him a momentary air
of dignity and power.

" I never," he said slowly, " never in my life
listened to anything so preposterous. You suggest
that I—*I*—should join you in wandering like a tramp
through muddy Scottish parishes and sleeping in
mean inns ! . . . To-morrow I shall go to London.
And meantime I am going to bed."

CHAPTER VIII

CASIMIR

MISS ALISON WESTWATER rose early on the following morning, and made her way on foot through the now unbarricaded lodge gates to the Castle. The fateful meeting with the Evallonians, to which she had not been bidden, was at eleven, and before that hour she had much to do.

She was admitted by Bannister. " I don't want to see Mr. Barbon," she said. " I want to talk to you." Bannister, in his morning undress, bowed gravely, and led her into the little room on the left side of the hall where her father used to keep his boots and fishing-rods.

Bannister was not the conventional butler. He was not portly, or sleek, or pompous, or soft-voiced, though he was certainly soft-footed. He was tall and lean, with a stoop which, so far from being servile, was almost condescending. He spoke the most correct English, and was wont to spend his holidays at a good hotel in this or that watering-place, where his well-cut clothes, his quiet air, his wide knowledge of the world, and his somewhat elaborate manners caused him to be taken in the smoking-room for a member of the Diplomatic

Service. He had begun life in a famous training stable at Newmarket, but had been compelled to relinquish the career of a jockey at the age of eighteen owing to the rate at which he grew. Thereafter he had passed through various domestic posts, always in the best houses, till the age of forty-seven found him butler to that respected but ineffective statesman, the Marquis of Oronsay. At the lamented death of his patron he had passed to Mr. Craw, who believed that a man who had managed four different houses for an irascible master with signal success would suit his own more modest requirements. He was right in his judgment. Bannister was a born organizer, and would have made an excellent Quartermaster-General. The household at Castle Gay moved on oiled castors, and Mr. Craw's comfort and dignity and his jealous retirement suffered no jar in Bannister's hands. Mr. Barbon might direct the strategy, but it was the butler who saw to the tactics.

The part suited him exactly, for Bannister was accustomed to generous establishments—*ubi multa supersunt*—and he loved mystery. It was meat and drink to him to be the guardian of a secret, and a master who had to be zealously shielded from the public eye was the master he loved to serve. He had acquired the taste originally from much reading of sensational fiction, and it had been fostered by the circumstances of his life. He had been an entranced repository of many secrets. He knew why the Duke of Mull had not received the Garter ; why the engagement between Sir John Rampole and the

Chicago heiress was broken off—a tale for which
many an American paper would have gladly paid
ten thousand dollars ; almost alone he could have
given a full account of the scandals of the Braddis-
dale marriage ; he could have explained the true
reason for the retirement from the service of the
State of one distinguished Ambassador, and the
inexplicable breakdown in Parliament of a rising
Under-Secretary. His recollections, if divulged,
might have made him the humble Greville of his age.
But they were never divulged—and never would
be. Bannister was confidential, because he enjoyed
keeping a secret more than other men enjoy telling
one. It gave him a sense of mystery and power.

There was only one thing wanting to his satisfaction. He had a profound—and, as he would
have readily admitted, an illogical—liking for the
aristocracy. He wished that his master had accepted a peerage, like other Press magnates ; in his
eyes a new title was better than none at all. For
ancient families with chequered pasts he had a
romantic reverence. He had studied in the county
histories the story of the house of Rhynns, and it
fulfilled his most exacting demands. It pleased him
to dwell in a mansion consecrated by so many misdeeds. He wished that he could meet Lord Rhynns
in the flesh. He respected the household at the
Mains as the one link between himself and the older
nobility. Mrs. Brisbane-Brown was his notion of
what a middle-aged gentlewoman should be ; and
he had admired from afar Alison galloping in the
park. She was like the Ladies Ermyntrude and

Gwendolen of whom he had read long ago, and whom he still cherished as an ideal, in spite of a lifetime of disillusionment. There was a fount of poetry welling somewhere in Bannister's breast.

" I've come to talk to you, Bannister," the girl began, " about the mess we're in. It concerns us all, for as long as Mr. Craw lives in Castle Gay we're bound to help him. As you are aware, he has disappeared. But, as you may have heard, we have a rough notion of where he is. Well, we've got to straighten out things here while he is absent. Hold the fort, you know."

The butler bowed gravely.

" First, there's the foreigners, who are coming here at eleven."

" If I might hazard a suggestion," Bannister interrupted. " Are you certain, Miss, that these foreigners are what they claim to be ? "

" What do you mean ? "

" Is it not possible that they are a gang of international crooks who call themselves Evallonians, knowing Mr. Craw's interest in that country, and wish to effect an entry into the Castle for sinister purposes ? "

" But they have taken Knockraw shooting."

" It might be a blind."

The girl considered. " No," she said emphatically. " That is impossible. You've been reading too many detective stories, Bannister. It would be imbecility for a gang of crooks to take the line they have. It would be giving themselves away hopelessly. . . . These people are all right. They repre-

sent the Evallonian Monarchist party, which may
be silly but is quite respectable. Mr. Barbon knows
all about them. One is Count Casimir Muresco.
Another is Prince Odalisque, or some name like that.
And there's a Professor Something or other, who
Mr. Crombie says has a European reputation for
something. No doubt about it. They're tremendous swells, and we've got to treat them as such.
That's one of the things I came to speak to you
about. We're not going to produce Mr. Craw,
which is what they want, but, till we see our way
clear, we must snow them under with hospitality.
If they are sportsmen, as they pretend to be, they
must have the run of the Callowa, and if Knockraw
is not enough for them we must put the Castle moors
at their disposal. Oh, and the Blae Moss. They're
sure to want to shoot snipe. The grouse is only
found in Britain, but there must be plenty of snipe
in Evallonia. You know that they're all coming to
dine here to-night ? "

" So Mr. Barbon informed me."

" Well, it must be a Belshazzar. That's a family
word of ours for a regular banquet. You must get
the chef to put his best foot forward. Tell him he's
feeding Princes and Ministers and he'll produce
something surprising. I don't suppose he knows
any special Evallonian dishes, so the menu better
have a touch of Scotland. They'll appreciate local
colour. We ought to have a haggis as one of the
entrées, and grouse of course, and Mackillop must
dig a salmon out of the Callowa. I saw a great
brute jumping in the Dirt Pot. . . . Plenty of

flowers, too. I don't know what your cellar is like ? "

" I can vouch for it, Miss. Shall the footmen wear their gala liveries ? Mr. Craw made a point of their possessing them."

" Certainly. . . . We have to make an impression, you see. We can't produce Mr. Craw, but we must impress them with our importance, so that they will take what we tell them as if it came from Mr. Craw. Do you see what I mean ? We want them to go away as soon as possible, but to go away satisfied and comfortable, so that they won't come back again."

" What will be the party at dinner ? "

" The three Evallonians—the Count, and the Prince, and the Herr Professor. You can get the names right from Mr. Barbon. Mr. Barbon and Mr. Crombie, of course, who are staying in the house. My aunt and Mr. Charvill and myself. It's overweighted with men, but we can't help that."

" May I ask one question, Miss ? Mr. Crombie, now. He is not quite what I have been accustomed to. He is a very peremptory gentleman. He has taken it upon himself to give me orders."

" Obey them, Bannister, obey them on your life. Mr. Crombie is one of Mr. Craw's trusted lieutenants. You may consider him the leader of our side. . . . That brings me to the second thing I wanted to say to you. What about the journalists ? "

" We have had a visit from three already this morning." There was a flicker of a smile on the butler's face. " I made a point of interviewing

them myself." He drew three cards from a waistcoat pocket, and exhibited them. They bore the
names of three celebrated newspapers, but the *Wire*
was not among them. "They asked to see Mr.
Craw, and according to my instructions I informed
them that Mr. Craw had gone abroad. They appeared to accept my statement, but showed a desire
to engage me in conversation. All three exhibited
money, which I presume they intended as a bribe.
That, of course, led to their summary dismissal."

"That's all right," the girl declared, "that's plain
sailing. But I don't like Tibbets keeping away. Mr.
Crombie says that he's by far the most dangerous.
Look here, Bannister, this is your very particular
job. You must see that none of these reporters get
into the Castle, and that nobody from the Castle
gossips with them. If they once get on the trail of
the Evallonians we're done. The lodge-keeper has
orders not to admit anybody who looks like a
journalist. I'll get hold of Mackillop and tell him
to clear out anybody found in the policies. He can
pretend they're poachers. I wonder what on earth
Tibbets is up to at this moment?"

Dougal could have provided part of the answer
to that question. The night before, when it was
settled that he should take up his quarters in the
Castle, he had wired to his Glasgow lodgings to
have his dress clothes sent to him by train. That
morning he had been to Portaway station to collect
them, in a car hired from the Westwater Arms,
and in a Portaway street he had run across

Tibbets. The journalist's face did not show, as he had hoped, embarrassment and disappointment. On the contrary, the light of victorious battle was in his eye.

" I thought you were off for good," was his greeting, to which Dougal replied with a story of the breakdown of his bicycle and his compulsory severance from his friend. " I doubt I'll have to give up this expedition," Dougal said. " How are you getting on yourself ? I read your thing in the *Wire* last night."

" Did you see the Craw papers ? They announce that Craw has gone abroad. It was heaven's own luck that they only got that out the same day as my story, and now it's bloody war between us, for our credit is at stake. I wired to my chief, and I've just got his reply. What do you think it is ? Craw never left the country. Places were booked for him in the boat train yesterday in the name of his man Barbon, but he never used them. Our information is certain. That means that Craw's papers are lying. Lying to cover something, and what that something is I'm going to find out before I'm a day older. I'm waiting here for another telegram, and then I'll go up the Callowa to comfort Barbon."

Dougal made an inconspicuous exit from the station, after satisfying himself that Tibbets was not about. He left his suit-case at the Starr Inn, with word that it would be sent for later, for he did not wish to publish his connection with the Castle any sooner than was needful. He entered

the park by the gate in the wall, which he opened
with Alison's key, and had immediately to present
his credentials—a chit signed by Barbon—to a
minion of Mackillop, the head keeper, who was
lurking in a covert. He was admitted to the house
by Bannister at ten minutes to eleven, five minutes
after Alison had left on her quest of Mackillop and
a Callowa salmon.

The party from Knockraw was punctual. Mr.
Barbon and Dougal received them in the library,
a vast apartment on the first floor, lit by six narrow
windows and commanding a view of the terrace
and the windings of the river. The seventh Lord
Rhynns had been a collector, and from the latticed
shelves looked down an imposing array of eighteenth-
century quartos and folios. Various pieces of clas-
sical sculpture occupied black marble pedestals, and
a small, richly carved sarcophagus, of a stone which
looked like old ivory, had a place of honour under
the great Flemish tapestry, which adorned the only
wall free of books. The gilt baroque clock on the
mantelpiece had not finished chiming when Bannister
ushered in the visitors.

They bowed from their hips at the door, and they
bowed again when they were within a yard of
Barbon. One of the three spoke. He was a tall
man with a white face, deep-set brown eyes, and
short curly brown hair. Except for his nose he
would have been theatrically handsome, but his
nose was a pronounced snub. Yet this imperfection
gave to his face a vigour and an attractiveness which
more regular features might have lacked. He looked

amazingly competent and vital. His companions
were a slim, older man with greying hair, and a burly
fellow with spectacles and a black beard. All three
were ceremoniously garbed in morning coats and
white linen and dark ties. Dougal wondered if they
had motored from Knockraw in top hats.

" Permit me to make the necessary introductions,"
said the spokesman. " I am your correspondent,
Count Casimir Muresco. This is Prince Odalchini,
and this is the Herr Doctor Jagon of the University
of Melina. We are the chosen and accredited representatives of the Nationalist Party of Evallonia."

Barbon had dressed himself carefully for the
occasion, and his flawless grey suit made a painful
contrast to Dougal's ill-fitting knickerbockers. He
looked more than ever like an actor who had just
taken his cue in a romantic Victorian comedy.

" My name is Barbon," he said, " Frederick
Barbon. As you are no doubt aware, I am Mr.
Craw's principal confidential secretary."

" You are the second son of Lord Clonkilty, is it
not so ? " said the Prince. " You I have seen once
before—at Monte Carlo."

Barbon bowed. " I am honoured by your recollection. This is Mr. Crombie, one of Mr. Craw's
chief assistants in the management of his newspapers."

The three strangers bowed, and Dougal managed
to incline his stiff neck.

" You wish to see Mr. Craw ? Mr. Craw unfortunately is not at home. But in his absence my
colleague and I are here to do what we can for you."

" You do not know where Mr. Craw is ? " inquired Count Casimir sharply.

" Not at this moment," replied Barbon truthfully. " Mr. Craw is in the habit of going off occasionally on private business."

" That is a misfortune, but it is temporary. Mr. Craw will no doubt return soon. We are in no hurry, for we are at present residents in your beautiful country. You are in Mr. Craw's confidence, and therefore we will speak to you as we would speak to him."

Barbon motioned them to a table, where were five chairs, and ink, pens, and blotting paper set out as for a board meeting. He and Dougal took their seats on one side, and the three Evallonians on the other.

" I will be brief," said Count Casimir. " The movement for the restoration of our country to its ancient rights approaches fruition. I have here the details, which I freely offer to you for your study. The day is not yet fixed, but when the word is given the people of Evallonia as one man will rise on behalf of their Prince. The present misgovernors of our land have no popular following, and no credit except among international Jews."

Mr. Barbon averted his eyes from the maps and papers which the other pushed towards him.

" That is what they call a Putsch, isn't it ? " he said. " They haven't been very successful, you know."

" It is no foolish thing like a Putsch," Count Casimir replied emphatically. " You may call it a *coup d'état*, a bloodless *coup d'état*. We have waited till our cause is so strong in Evallonia that there need be no violence. The hated republic will tumble down at a touch like a rotten branch. We shall take the strictest precautions against regrettable incidents. It will be the sudden uprising of a nation, a thing as irresistible as the tides of the sea."

"You may be right," said Barbon. "Obviously we cannot argue the point with you. But what we want to know is why you come to us. Mr. Craw has nothing to do with Evallonia's domestic affairs."

"Alas!" said Prince Odalchini, "our affairs are no longer domestic. The republic is the creation of the Powers, the circumscription of our territories is the work of the Powers, the detested League of Nations watches us like an elderly and spectacled governess. We shall succeed in our revolution, but we cannot maintain our success unless we can assure ourselves of the neutrality of Europe. That is why we come to Britain. We ask her—how do you say it?—to keep the ring."

"To Britain, perhaps," said Barbon. "But why to Mr. Craw?"

Count Casimir laughed. "You are too modest, my friend. It is the English habit, we know, to reverence historic forms even when the power has gone elsewhere. But we have studied your politics very carefully. The Herr Professor has studied them profoundly. We know that in these days with your universal suffrage the fount of authority is not in King or Cabinet, or even in your Parliament. It lies with the whole mass of your people, and who are their leaders? Not your statesmen, for you have lost your taste for oratory, and no longer attend meetings. It is your newspapers that rule you. What your man in the street reads in his newspaper he believes. What he believes he will make your Parliament believe, and what your Parliament orders your Cabinet must do. Is it not so ? "

Mr. Barbon smiled wearily at this startling version of constitutional practice.

" I think you rather exaggerate the power of the printed word," he said.

Count Casimir waved the objection aside.

" We come to Mr. Craw," he went on. " We say, ' You love Evallonia. You have said it often. You have ten—twenty millions of readers who follow you blindly. You will say to them that Evallonia must be free to choose her own form of government, for that is democracy. You will say that this follows from your British principles of policy and from that Puritan religion in which Britain believes. You will preach it to them like a good priest, and you will tell them that it will be a very great sin if they do not permit to others the freedom which they themselves enjoy. The Prime Minister will wake up one morning and find that he has what you call a popular mandate, which if he does not obey he will cease to be Prime Minister. Then, when the day comes for Evallonia to declare herself, he will speak kind words about Evallonia to France and Italy, and he will tell the League of Nations to go to the devil.' "

" That's all very well," Barbon protested. " But

I don't see how putting Prince John on the throne
will help you to get back your lost territories."

" It will be a first step. When we have once
again a beloved King, Europe will say, ' Beyond
doubt Evallonia is a great and happy nation. She
is too good and happy a nation to be so small.' "

" We speak in the name of democracy," said the
Professor in a booming voice. He spoke at some
length, and developed an intricate argument to show
the true meaning of the word " self-determination."
He dealt largely with history ; he had much to say
of unity of culture as opposed to uniformity of race ;
he touched upon Fascism, Bolshevism, and what he
called " Americanism " ; he made many subtle distinctions, and he concluded with a definition of
modern democracy, of which he said the finest flower
would be an Evallonia reconstituted according to
the ideas of himself and his friends.

Dougal had so far maintained silence, and had
studied the faces of the visitors. All three were
patently honest. Casimir was the practical man,
the schemer, the Cavour of the party. The Prince
might be the prophet, the Mazzini—there was a mild
and immovable fanaticism in his pale eyes. The
Professor was the scholar, who supplied the ammuni-
tion of theory. The man had written a famous book
on the British Constitution and had a European
reputation ; but this was Dougal's pet subject, and
he suddenly hurled himself into the fray.

It would have been well if he had refrained. For
half an hour three bored and mystified auditors were
treated to a harangue on the fundamentals of

politics, in which Dougal's dialectical zeal led him
into so many overstatements that to the scandalized
Barbon he seemed to be talking sheer anarchism.
Happily to the other two, and possibly to the Professor, he was not very intelligible. For just as in
the excitement of debate the Professor lost hold of
his careful English and relapsed into Evallonian
idioms, so Dougal returned to his ancestral language
of Glasgow.

The striking of a single note by the baroque clock
gave Count Casimir a chance of breaking off the
interview. He gathered up his papers.

" We have opened our case," he said graciously.
" We will come again to expand it, and meantime
you will meditate. . . . We dine with you to-night at
eight o'clock ? There will be ladies present ? So ? "

" One word, Count," said Barbon. " We're in-
fernally plagued with journalists. There's a by-
election going on now in the neighbourhood, and
they all want to get hold of Mr. Craw. I needn't
tell you that it would be fatal to your cause if they
got on to your trail—and very annoying to us."

" Have no fear," was the answer. " The official
tenant of Knockraw is Mr. Williams, a Liverpool
merchant. To the world we are three of Mr.
Williams's business associates who are enjoying his
hospitality. All day we shoot at the grouse like
sportsmen. In the evening our own servants wait
upon us, so there are no eavesdroppers."

Mr. Craw had entertained but little in Castle Gay,
but that night his representatives made up for his

remissness. The party from the Mains arrived to find the hall blazing with lights, Bannister with the manner of a Court Chamberlain, and the footmen in the sober splendour of their gala liveries. In the great drawing-room, which had scarcely been used in Alison's recollection, Barbon and Dougal were holding in play three voluble gentlemen with velvet collars to their dress-coats and odd bits of ribbon in their buttonholes. Their presentation to the ladies reminded Alison of the Oath of the Tennis Court or some other high and disposed piece of history, and she with difficulty preserved her gravity. Presently in the dining-room, which was a remnant of the old keep and vaulted like a dungeon, they sat down to a meal which the chef was ever afterwards to refer to as his masterpiece.

The scene was so bright with flowers and silver, so benignly backgrounded by the mellow Westwater portraits, that it cast a spell over the company and made every one content—except Dougal. The Evallonians did not once refer to their mission. They might have been a party of county neighbours, except that their talk was of topics not commonly discussed by Canonry sportsmen. The Prince spoke to Mrs. Brisbane-Brown of her own relations, for he had been a secretary of legation in London and had hunted several seasons with the Cottesmore. The Professor oraculated on letters, with an elephantine deference to his hearers' opinions, withdrawing graciously his first judgment that Shakespeare was conspicuously inferior to Mr. Bernard Shaw when he saw Mrs. Brisbane-Brown's scandalized face. Count

Casimir endeavoured to propitiate Dougal, and
learned from him many things about the Scottish
race which are not printed in the books. All three,
even the Professor, understood the art of social
intercourse, and the critical Alison had to admit to
herself that they did it well. It appeared that the
Prince was a keen fisherman, and Count Casimir an
ardent snipe shot, and the offer of the Callowa and
the Blae Moss was enthusiastically received.

Dougal alone found the evening a failure. He felt
that they were wasting time. Again and again he
tried to lead the talk to the position of the Press
in Britain, in the hope that Mrs. Brisbane-Brown,
with whom the strangers were obviously impressed,
would enlighten them as to its fundamental unim-
portance. But Mrs. Brisbane-Brown refused his
lead. Indeed she did the very opposite, for he
heard her say to the Professor : " We have new
masters to-day. Britain still tolerates her aristocracy as a harmless and rather ornamental pet, but
if it tried to scratch it would be sent to the stables.
Our new masters don't do it badly either. When
my brother lived here this was a shabby old country
house, but Mr. Craw has made it a palace."

" It is the old passion for romance," the Professor
replied. " The sense of power is generally accompanied by a taste for grandeur. *Ubi magnitudo ibi
splendor*. That, I believe, is St. Augustine."

Late that night, in the smoking-room at Knockraw, there was a consultation. " Things go well,"
said Casimir. " We have prepared the way, and

the Craw *entourage* will not be hostile. I do not
like the red-haired youth. He is of the fanatic
student type, and his talk is flatulence. Him I
regard as an enemy. But Barbon is too colourless
and timid to oppose us, and we have won favour,
I think, with the high-nosed old woman and the
pretty girl. They, as representatives of an ancient
house, have doubtless much weight with Craw,
who is of the lesser bourgeoisie. With them in view,
I think it may be well to play our trump card now.
His Royal Highness arrives to-day in London, and
is graciously holding himself at our disposal."

"That thought was in my own mind," said
Prince Odalchini, and the Professor concurred.

At the same hour Dougal at Castle Gay was
holding forth to Barbon. "Things couldn't be
worse," he said. "The dinner was a big mistake.
All that magnificence only increases their belief in
Craw's power. We've got to disillusion them. I
can't do it, for I can see fine that they think me a
Bolshevik. You can't do it, for they believe that
you would do anything for a quiet life, and they
discount your evidence accordingly. What we want
is some real, representative, practical man who would
come down like a sledge-hammer on their notions—
somebody they would be compelled to believe—
somebody that they couldn't help admitting as
typical of the British nation."

"I agree. But where are we to find him without
giving Mr. Craw away?"

"There's one man," said Dougal slowly. "His
name's McCunn—Dickson McCunn—and he lives

about fifty miles from here.   He was a big business
man in Glasgow—but he's retired now.   I never met
his equal for whinstone common sense.   You've
only to look at him to see that what he thinks about
forty million others think also.   He is the incarnate
British spirit.   He's a fine man, too, and you could
trust him with any secret."

"How old ? " Barbon asked.

"A few years older than Craw.   Not unlike him
in appearance.   The morn's Sunday and there's no
train where he lives.   What about sending a car with
a letter from me and bringing him back, if he'll
come ?   I believe he'd do the trick."

Barbon, who was ready to seek any port in the
storm, and was already in the grip of Dougal's fierce
vitality, wearily agreed.   The pleasantness of the
dinner had for a little banished his anxieties, but
these had now returned and he foresaw a sleepless
night.   His thoughts turned naturally to his errant
master.

"I wonder where Mr. Craw is at this moment ? "
he said.

"I wonder too.   But if he's with Jaikie I bet
he's seeing life."

CHAPTER IX

THE FIRST DAY OF THE HEJIRA—THE INN AT WATERMEETING

THE October dawn filled the cup of the Garroch with a pale pure light. There had been no frost in the night, but the heather of the bogs, the hill turf, and the gravel of the road had lost their colour under a drench of dew. The mountains were capped with mist, and the air smelt raw and chilly. Jaikie, who, foreseeing a difficult day, had prepared for it by a swim in the loch and a solid breakfast, found it only tonic. Not so Mr. Craw, who, as he stood before the cottage, shivered, and buttoned up the collar of his raincoat.

Mrs. Catterick scornfully refused payment. " Is it likely ? " she cried. " Ye didna come here o' your ain wull. A body doesna tak' siller for bein' a jyler."

" I will see that you are remunerated in some other way," Mr. Craw said pompously.

He had insisted on wearing his neat boots, which his hostess had described as " pappymashy," and refused those which Jaikie had brought from Castle Gay. Also he made no offer to assume Dougal's pack, with the consequence that Jaikie added it to his own, and presented the appearance of Christian

at the Wicket-gate in some old woodcut from the
Pilgrim's Progress.   Mr. Craw even endued his hands
with a pair of bright wash-leather gloves, and with
his smart Homburg hat and silver-knobbed malacca
looked exactly like a modish elderly gentleman about
to take a morning stroll at a fashionable health
resort.   So incongruous a figure did he present in
that wild trough of the hills, that Mrs. Catterick
cut short her farewells and politely hid her laughter
indoors.

Thus fantastically began the great Hejira.

Mr. Craw was in a bad temper, and such a mood
was new to him, for in his life small berufflements
had been so rare that his ordinary manner was a composed geniality.   Therefore, besides being cross, he
was puzzled, and a little ashamed.   He told himself
that he was being scandalously treated by Fate, and
for the first half-mile hugged his miseries like a sulky
child. . . . Then he remembered that officially he
had never admitted the existence of Fate.   In how
many eloquent articles had he told his readers that
man was the maker of his own fortunes, the captain
of his soul ?   He had preached an optimism secure
against the bludgeonings of Chance ! . . . This
would never do.   He cast about to find an attitude
which he could justify.

He found it in his intention to go straight to
London.   There was vigour and decision in that
act.   He was taking up arms against his sea of
troubles.   As resolutely as he could he shut out
the thought of what might happen when he got
to London—further Evallonian solicitations with a

horrid chance of publicity. London was at any rate familiar ground, unlike this bleak, sodden wilderness. He had never hated anything so much as that moorland cottage where for two days and three nights he had kept weary vigil. Still more did he loathe the present prospect of sour bent, gaping haggs, and mist low on the naked hills.

" How far is it to the nearest railway station ? " he asked the burdened figure at his side.

" It's about twelve miles to Glendonan," Jaikie answered.

" Do you know anything about the trains ? "

" It's a branch line, but there's sure to be an afternoon train to Gledmouth. The night mail stops there about eleven, I think."

Twelve miles ! Mr. Craw felt some sinking of the heart, which was succeeded by a sudden consciousness of manhood. He was doing a bold thing, the kind of thing he had always admired. He had not walked twelve miles since he was a boy, but he would force himself to finish the course, however painful it might be. The sight of the laden Jaikie woke a momentary compunction, but he dared not cumber himself with the second pack. After all he was an elderly man and must husband his strength. He would find some way of making it up to Jaikie.

The road, after leaving the Back House of the Garroch, crossed a low pass between the Caldron and a spur of the great Muneraw, and then, after threading a patch of bog, began to descend the upper glen of a burn, which joined a tributary of the distant Gled. Mr. Craw's modish boots had been tolerable

on the fine sand and gravel of the first mile. They
had become very wet in the tract of bog, where
the heather grew thick in the middle of the road, and
long pools of inky water filled the ruts. But as the
path began its descent they became an abomination.
The surface was cut by frequent rivulets which had
brought down in spate large shoals of gravel. Sometimes it was deep, fine scree, sometimes a rockery of
sharp-pointed stones. The soles of his boots, thin
at the best, and now as sodden as a sponge, were no
protection against the unyielding granite. His feet
were as painful as if he was going barefoot, and
his ankles ached with constant slips and twists.

He was getting warm, too. The morning chill
had gone out of the air, and, though the sky was
still cloudy, there was a faint glow from the hidden
sun. Mr. Craw began by taking off his gloves. Then
he removed his raincoat, and carried it on his arm.
It kept slipping and he trod on its tail, the while he
minced delicately to avoid the sharper stones.

The glen opened and revealed a wide shallow
valley, down which flowed one of the main affluents
of the Gled. The distances were hazy, but there
was a glimpse of stubble fields and fir plantations,
proof that they were within view of the edge of the
moorlands. Mr. Craw, who for some time had been
walking slowly and in evident pain, sat down on the
parapet of the little bridge and lifted his feet from
the tormenting ground.

" How many miles more ? " he asked, and when
told " Seven," he groaned.

Jaikie unbuckled his packs.

"It's nonsense your wearing these idiotic things," he said firmly. "In another hour you'll have lamed yourself for a week." From Dougal's pack he extracted a pair of stout country boots and from his own a pair of woollen socks. "If you don't put these on, I'll have to carry you to Glendonan."

Mr. Craw accepted the articles with relief. He bathed his inflamed and aching feet in the burn, and encased them in Jaikie's homespun. When he stood up he regarded his new accoutrements with disfavour. Shooting boots did not harmonize with his neat blue trousers, and he had a pride in a natty appearance. "I can change back at the station," he observed, and for the first time that day he stepped out with a certain freedom.

His increased comfort made him magnanimous.

"You had better give me the second pack," he volunteered.

"I can manage all right," was Jaikie's answer. "It's still a long road to Glendonan."

Presently, as the track dipped to the levels by the stream side, the surface improved, and Mr. Craw, relieved of his painful bodily preoccupation, and no longer compelled to hop from stone to stone, returned to forecasting the future. To-morrow morning he would be in London. He would go straight to the office, and, the day being Sunday, would have a little time to think things out. Bamff, his manager, was in America. He could not summon Barbon, who had his hands full at Castle Gay. Allins—Allins was on holiday—believed to be in Spain—he might conceivably get hold of Allins.

There were others, too, who could assist him—his
solicitor, Mr. Merkins, of Merkins, Thrawn, & Merkins
—he had no secrets from him. And Lord Wassell,
whom he had recently brought on to the board of
the *View*—Wassell was a resourceful fellow, and
deeply in his debt.

He was slipping into a better humour. It had
been a preposterous adventure—something to laugh
over in the future—*meminisse juvabit*—how did the
tag go ?—he had used it only the other day in
one of his articles. . . . He felt rather hungry—no
doubt the moorland air. He ought to be able to
get a decent dinner in Gledmouth. What about his
berth in the sleeping-car ? It was the time of year
when a good many people were returning from
Scotland. Perhaps he had better wire about it
from Glendonan. . . . And then a thought struck
him, which brought him to a halt and set him
feeling for his pocket-book.

It was Mr. Craw's provident habit always to
carry in his pocket-book a sum of one hundred
pounds in twenty-pound notes as an insurance
against accidents. He opened the pocket-book with
anxiety, and the notes were not there.

He remembered only too well what had happened. The morning he had gone to Glasgow he
had emptied the contents of his pocket-book on
his dressing-table in order to find the card with his
architect's address. He had not restored the notes,
because they made the book too bulky, and he had
proposed to get instead two fifty-pound notes from
Barbon, who kept the household's petty cash. He

had forgotten to do this, and now he had nothing
on his person but the loose change left from his
Glasgow journey. It lay in his hand, and amounted
to twelve shillings, a sixpence, two threepenny bits,
and four pennies.

To a man who for the better part of a lifetime
has taken money for granted and has never had
to give a thought to its importance in the conduct
of life, a sudden shortage comes as a horrid surprise.
He finds it an outrage alike against decency and
dignity. He is flung neck and crop into a world
which he does not comprehend, and his dismay is
hysterical.

" I have no money," he stammered, ignoring the
petty coins in his palm.

Jaikie slid the packs to the ground.

" But you offered Dougal and me twenty pounds
to go to Castle Gay," he protested.

Mr. Craw explained his misadventure. Jaikie
extracted from an inner pocket a skimpy leather
purse, while the other watched his movements with
the eyes of a hungry dog who believes that there is
provender going. He assessed its contents.

" I have two pounds, thirteen and ninepence,"
he announced. " I didn't bring much, for you don't
spend money in the hills, and I knew that Dougal
had plenty."

" That's no earthly use to me," Mr. Craw wailed.

" I don't know. It will buy you a third-class
ticket to London and leave something for our meals
to-day. You're welcome to it."

" But what will you do ? "

"I'll go back to Mrs. Catterick, and then I'll find Dougal. I can wire for some more. I'm pretty hard up just now, but there's a few pounds left in my allowance. You see, *you* can't get any more till you get to London."

Mr. Craw's breast was a maelstrom of confused emotions. He was not without the quality which in Scotland is called "mense," and he was reluctant to take advantage of Jaikie's offer and leave that unfortunate penniless. Moreover, the thought of travelling third-class by night roused his liveliest disgust. Fear, too—for he would be mixed up in the crowd, without protection against the enemies who now beset his path. He shrank like a timid spinster from rough contacts. Almost to be preferred was this howling wilderness to the chances of such sordid travel.

"There's another way," said the helpful Jaikie. He wanted to get rid of his companion, but he was aware that it was his duty, if possible, to detain that companion at his side, and to detain him in the Canonry. The conclave at the Mains had instructed him to keep Mr. Craw hidden, and he had no belief in London as a place of concealment. So, "against interest," as the lawyers say, he propounded an alternative.

"We could stay hereabouts for a couple of days, and I could borrow a bicycle and slip over to Castle Gay and get some money."

Mr. Craw's face cleared a little. He was certain now that the moors of the Canonry were better than a third-class in the London train. He brooded a little and then announced that he favoured the plan.

" Good," said Jaikie. " Well, we needn't go near Glendonan. We'd better strike south and sleep the night at Watermeeting. It's a lonely place, but there's quite a decent little inn, and it's on the road to Gledmouth. To-morrow I'll try to raise a bicycle and get over to Castle Gay, and with luck you may be in London on Monday morning. We needn't hurry, for it's not above ten miles to Watermeeting, and it doesn't matter when we turn up."

" I insist on carrying one of the packs," said Mr. Craw, and, his future having cleared a little, and being conscious of better behaviour, he stepped out with a certain alacrity and ease.

Presently they left the road, which descended into the Gled valley, and took a right-hand turning which zigzagged up the containing ridge and came out on a wide benty moor, once the best black-game country in Scotland, which formed the glacis of the chief range of the hills. A little after midday they lunched beside a spring, and Mr. Craw was moved to commend Mrs. Catterick's scones, which at break-fast he had despised. He accepted one of Jaikie's cigarettes. There was even a little conversation. Jaikie pointed out the main summits among a multi-tude which had now become ominously blue and clear, and Mr. Craw was pleased to show a certain interest in the prospect of the Muneraw, the other side of which, he said, could be seen from the upper windows of Castle Gay. He became almost con-fidential. Landscape, he said, he loved, but with a temperate affection ; his major interest was reserved for humanity. " In these hills there must be some remarkable people. The shepherds, for instance——"

" There's some queer folk in the hills," said Jaikie. " And I doubt there's going to be some queer weather before this day is out. The wind's gone to the south-west, and I don't like the way the mist is coming down on the Black Dod."

He was right in his forecast. About two o'clock there came a sudden sharpness into the air, the hills were blotted out in vapour, and a fine rain descended. The wind rose ; the drizzle became a blast, and then a deluge, the slanting, drenching downfall of October. Jaikie's tattered burberry and Mr. Craw's smart raincoat were soon black with the rain, which soaked the legs of their trousers and trickled behind their upturned collars. To the one this was a common experience, but to the other it was a revelation, for he had not been exposed to weather for many a year. He thought darkly of rheumatism, the twinges he had suffered from two years ago and had gone to Aix to cure. He might get pneumonia—it was a common complaint nowadays—several of his acquaintances had fluffed out like a candle with it—healthy people, too, as healthy as himself. He shivered, and thought he felt a tightness in his chest. " Can we not shelter ? " he asked, casting a woeful eye round the wet periphery of moor.

" It'll last the day," said Jaikie. " We'd better step out, and get under cover as soon as we can. There's no house till Watermeeting."

The thought of Watermeeting did not console

Mr. Craw. A wetting was bad enough, but at the end of it there was no comforting hot bath and warm dry clothes, and the choice between bed and a deep armchair by a fire. They would have to pig it in a moorland inn, where the food would certainly be execrable, and the bed probably damp, and he had no change of raiment. Once again Mr. Craw's mind became almost hysterical. He saw sickness, possibly death, in the near future. His teeth were chattering, and, yes—he was certain he had a pain in his side.

Something loomed up in the haze, and he saw that it was a man with, in front of him, a bedraggled flock of sheep. He was a loutish fellow, much bent in the shoulders, with leggings, which lacked most of the buttons, over his disreputable breeks. By his side padded a big ruffianly collie, and he led by a string a miserable-looking terrier, at which the collie now and then snapped viciously.

The man did not turn as they came abreast. He had a bag slung on his shoulders by a string, from which protruded the nose of a bottle and the sodden end of a newspaper. The peak of his cap hid the upper part of his face ; the lower part was composed of an unshaven chin, a gap-toothed mouth, and a red ferrety nose.

" Ill weather," said Jaikie.

" Hellish," was the answer. A sharp eye stole a sidelong glance and took in Mr. Craw's prosperous but water-logged garments. The terrier sniffed wistfully at Jaikie's leg. Jaikie looked like the kind of person who might do something for him.

" Hae ye a smoke ? " the drover asked. Jaikie

reluctantly parted with a cigarette, which the other
lit by making a shelter of his cap against the wind.
The terrier, in order to avoid the collie, wove its
string round his legs and received a savage kick.

" Where are you bound for ? " Jaikie asked.

" Near by. I've brocht thae sheep frae Cumnock
way." Then, as an overflow of water from the
creases of his cap reached his unwashen neck, he
broke into profanity about the weather, concluding
with a malediction on the unhappy terrier, who
showed signs of again entangling his lead. The dog
seemed to be a cross between wire-haired and
Sealyham, a wretched little fellow with a coat as
thick as a sheep's, a thin piebald face, whiskers
streaked backwards by the wet, and a scared eye.
The drover brought his stick down hard on its hind
quarters, and as it jumped howling away from him
the collie snapped at its head. It was a bad day for
the terrier.

" That's a nice little beast," said Jaikie.

" No bad. Pure-bred Solomon. He's yours if
ye'll pay my price."

" I've no use for a dog. Where did you get
him ? "

" A freend bred him. I'm askin' a couple o' quid.
I brocht him along wi' me to sell. What about the
other yin o' ye ? He'd be the better o' a dug."

Mr. Craw did not look as if such an acquisition
would ease his discomfort. He was glancing nervously at the collie, which had turned on him an
old-fashioned eye. Jaikie quickened his pace, and
began to circumvent the sheep.

"Haud on," said the drover. "I turn up the next road. Gie's your crack till the turn."

But Jaikie had had enough of him, and the last they heard was the whining of the terrier, who had again been maltreated.

"Is that one of the hill shepherds?" Mr. Craw asked.

"Hill shepherd! He's some auction-ring tout from Glasgow. Didn't you recognize the tongue? I'm sorry for that little dog. He stole it, of course. I hope he sells it before he kills it."

The high crown of the moorland now began to fall away into a valley which seemed to be tributary to the Gled. The two were conscious that they were descending, but they had no prospect beyond a yard or two of dripping roadside heather. Already the burns were rising, and tawny rivulets threaded the road, all moving in the direction they were going. Jaikie set a round pace, for he wanted to save his companion from a chill, and Mr. Craw did his best to keep up with it. Sometimes he stopped, put his hand to his side, and gasped—he was looking for the pain which was the precursor of pneumonia. Soon he grew warm, and his breath came short, and there had to be frequent halts to relieve his distress. In this condition of physical wretchedness and the blackest mental gloom Mr. Craw became aware of a roaring of flooded waters and a bridge which spanned a porter-coloured torrent. The sight of that wintry stream combined with the driving rain and the enveloping mist to send a chill almost of terror to Mr. Craw's heart. He was terribly sundered from the warm kindly world which he knew. Even so, from an icy shore, might some lost Arctic explorer have regarded the approach of the Polar night.

"That's the Gryne burn," said Jaikie reverentially. "It's coming down heavy. It joins the Water of Stark out there in the haugh. The inn's not a hundred yards on."

Presently they reached a low building, a little withdrawn from the road, on which a half-obliterated sign announced that one Thomas Johnston was licensed to sell ale and tobacco. Jaikie's memory was of a sunny place visited once in a hot August noon, when he had drunk ginger-beer on the settle by the door, and amid the sleepy clucking of hens and the bleating of sheep had watched the waters of Gryne and Stark beginning their allied journey to the lowlands. Now, as it came into view through the veils of rain, it looked a shabby place, the roughcast of the walls blotched and peeling, the unthatched stacks of bog-hay sagging drunkenly, and a disconsolate up-ended cart with a broken shaft blocking one of the windows. But at any rate here was shelter, and the smell of peat-reek promised a fire.

In the stone-flagged kitchen a woman was sitting beside a table engaged in darning socks—a thinfaced elderly woman with spectacles. The kitchen was warm and comfortable, and, since she had been baking earlier in the day, there was an agreeable odour of food. On the big old-fashioned hearth a bank of peats glowed dully, and sent out fine blue spirals.

The woman looked them over very carefully in response to Jaikie's question.

" Bide the nicht ? I'm sure I dinna ken. My man's lyin'—he rickit his back bringin' hame the peats, and the doctor winna let him up afore the morn. It's a sair business lookin' after him, and the lassie's awa' hame for her sister's mairriage. Ye'll no be wantin' muckle ? "

" That's a bad job for you," said Jaikie sympathetically. " We won't be much trouble. We'd like to get dry, and we want some food, and a bed to sleep in. We're on a walking tour and we'll take the road again first thing in the morning."

" I could maybe manage that. There's just the one room, for the ceiling's doun in the ither, and we canna get the masons out from Gledmouth to set it right. But there's twa beds in it. . . ."

Then spoke Mr. Craw, who had stripped off his raiment and flung it from him, and had edged his way to the warmth of the peats.

" We must have a private room, madam. I presume you have a private sitting-room. Have a fire lit in it as soon as possible."

" Ye're unco partic'lar," was the answer. " What hinders ye to sit in the kitchen ? There's the best room, of course, but there hasna been a fire in the grate since last New Year's Day, and I doot the stirlins have been biggin' in the lum."

" The first thing," said Jaikie firmly, " is to get dry. It's too early to go to bed. If you'll show us our room we'll get these wet things off. I can manage fine in pyjamas, but my friend here is not

so young as me, and he would be the better of something warmer. You couldn't lend him a pair of
breeks, mistress ? And maybe an old coat ? "

Jaikie, when he chose to wheedle, was hard to
resist, and the woman regarded him with favour.
She also regarded Mr. Craw appraisingly. " He's
just about the size o' my man. I daresay I could
find him some auld things o' Tam's. . . . Ye'd
better tak' off your buits here and I'll show ye your
bedroom."

In their wet stocking-soles the travellers followed
their hostess up an uncarpeted staircase to a long
low room, where were two beds and two wash-
stands and little else. The rain drummed on the
roof, and the place smelt as damp as a sea-cave.
She brought a pail of hot water from the kitchen
kettle, and two large rough towels. " I'll be gettin'
your tea ready," she said. " Bring doun your wet
claithes, and I'll hang them in the kitchen."

Jaikie stripped to the skin and towelled himself
violently, but Mr. Craw hung back. He was not
accustomed to baring his body before strangers.
Slowly and warily he divested himself of what
had once been a trim blue suit, the shirt which
was now a limp rag, the elegant silk underclothing.
Then he stood irresolute and shamefaced, while
Jaikie rummaged in the packs and announced glee-
fully that their contents were quite dry. Jaikie
turned to find his companion shivering in the blast
from the small window which he had opened.

" Tuts, man, this will never do," he cried. " You'll
get your death of cold. Rub yourself with the

towel. Hard, man ! You want to get back your circulation.''

But Mr. Craw's efforts were so feeble that Jaikie took the matter in hand. He pummelled and slapped and scrubbed the somewhat obese nudity of his companion, as if he had been grooming a horse. He poured out a share of the hot water from the pail, and made him plunge his head into it.

In the midst of these operations the door was half opened and a bundle of clothes was flung into the room. '' That's the best I can dae for ye,'' said the voice of the hostess.

Jaikie invested Mr. Craw with a wonderful suit of pale blue silk pyjamas, and over them a pair of Mr. Johnston's trousers of well-polished pepper-and-salt homespun, and an ancient black tailed coat which may once have been its owner's garb for Sabbaths and funerals. A strange figure the great man presented as he stumbled down the stairs, for on his feet were silk socks and a pair of soft Russia leather slippers—provided from Castle Gay—while the rest of him was like an elderly tradesman who has relinquished collar and tie in the seclusion of the home. But at any rate he was warm again, and he felt no more premonitions of pneumonia.

Mrs. Johnston met them at the foot of the stairs and indicated a door. '' That's the best room. I've kinnled a fire, but I doot it's no drawin' weel wi' thae stirlins.''

They found themselves in a small room in which for a moment they could see nothing because of the volume of smoke pouring from the newly-lit fire of sticks and peat. The starlings had been malignly active in the chimney. Presently through the haze might be discerned walls yellow with damp, on which hung a number of framed photographs, a mantelpiece adorned with china mugs and a clock out of action, several horsehair-covered chairs, a small, very hard sofa, and a round table decorated with two photograph albums, a book of views of Gledmouth, a workbox, and a blue-glass paraffin lamp.

Jaikie laboured with the poker at the chimney, but the obstruction was beyond him. Blear-eyed and coughing, he turned to find Mr. Craw struggling with a hermetically sealed window.

"We can't stay here," he spluttered. "This room's uninhabitable till the chimney's swept. Let's get back to the kitchen. Tea should be ready by now."

Mrs. Johnston had spread a clean cloth on the kitchen table, and ham and eggs were sizzling on the fire. She smiled grimly when she saw them.

"I thocht ye would be smoored in the best room," she said. "Thae stirlins are a perfect torment. . . . Ay, ye can bide here and welcome. I aye think the kitchen's the nicest bit in the hoose. . . . . There's a feck o' folk on the road the day, for there's been anither man here wantin' lodgin's! I telled him we were fou up, and that he could mak' a bed on the hay in the stable. I didna like the look o' him, but a keeper o' a public daurna refuse a body a meal. He'll hae to get his tea wi' you."

Presently she planted a vast brown teapot on the

table, and dished up the ham and eggs. Then, announcing that she must see to her husband, she left the kitchen.

Jaikie fell like a famished man on the viands, and Mr. Craw, to his own amazement, followed suit. He had always been a small and fastidious eater, liking only very special kinds of food, and his chef had often a difficult task in tempting his capricious appetite. It was years since he had felt really hungry, and he never looked forward to the hour of dinner with the gusto of less fortunate mortals. But the hard walking in the rain, and the rough towelling in the bedroom, had awakened some forgotten instinct. How unlike the crisp shavings of bacon and the snowy puff-balls of eggs to which he was accustomed was this dish swimming in grease! Yet it tasted far better than anything he had eaten for ages. So did the thick oat-cakes and the new scones and the butter and the skim-milk cheese, and the strong tea sent a glow through his body. He had thought that he could tolerate nothing but the best China tea and little of that, and here he was drinking of the coarsest Indian brew. . . . He felt a sense of physical well-being to which he had long been a stranger. This was almost comfort.

The door opened and there entered the man they had met driving sheep. He had taken off his leggings, and his wet trouser ends flapped over his grimy boots. Otherwise he had made no toilet, except to remove his cap from his head and the bag from his shoulder. His lank black hair straggled over his eyes, and the eyes themselves were unpleasant. There must have been something left in the bottle whose nose had protruded from the bag.

He dropped into a chair and dragged it screamingly after him along the kitchen floor till he was within a yard of the table. Then he recognized the others.

" Ye're here," he observed. " Whit was a' your hurry ? Gie's a cup o' tea. I'm no wantin' nae meat."

He was obviously rather drunk. Jaikie handed him a cup of tea, which, having dropped in four lumps of sugar, he drank noisily from the saucer. It steadied him, and he spread a scone thick with butter and jelly and began to wolf it. Mr. Craw regarded him with extreme distaste and a little nervousness.

" Whit about the Solomon terrier ? " he asked. " For twa quid he's yours."

The question was addressed to Mr. Craw, who answered coldly that he was not buying dogs.

" Ay, but ye'll buy this dug."

" Where is it ? " Jaikie asked.

" In the stable wi' the ither yin. Toff doesna like the wee dug, so I've tied them up in separate stalls, or he'd hae it chowed up."

The rest of the meal was given up to efforts on the part of the drover to effect a sale. His price came down to fifteen shillings and a glass of whisky. Questioned by Jaikie as to its pedigree, he embarked on a rambling tale, patently a lie, of a friend who bred Solomons and had presented him with this specimen in payment of a bet. Talk made the

drover thirsty. He refused a second cup of tea and
shouted for the hostess, and when Mrs. Johnston
appeared he ordered a bottle of Bass.

Jaikie, remembering the plans for the morrow,
asked if there was such a thing as a bicycle about
the place, and was told that her man possessed one.
She saw no objection to his borrowing it for half a
day. Jaikie had found favour in her eyes.

The drover drank his beer morosely and called for
another bottle. Mrs. Johnston glanced anxiously at
Jaikie as she fulfilled the order, but Jaikie gave no
sign. Now beer on the top of whisky is bad for the
constitution, especially if little food has accompanied
it, and soon the drover began to show that his case
was no exception. His silence gave place to a
violent garrulity. Thrusting his face close to the
scandalized Mr. Craw, he announced that that
gentleman was gorily well going to buy the Solomon
—that he had accepted the offer and that he would
be sanguinarily glad to see the immediate colour of
his money.

Mr. Craw withdrew his chair, and the other
lurched to his feet and came after him. The profanity of the drover, delivered in a hoarse roar,
brought Mrs. Johnston back in alarm. The seller's
case was far from clear, but it seemed to be his
argument that Mr. Craw had taken delivery of a
pup and was refusing payment. He was working
himself into a fury at what he declared to be a case
of strongly qualified bilk.

" Can ye dae naething wi' him ? " the hostess
wailed to Jaikie.

"I think we've had enough of him," was the answer. Then he lifted up his voice. "Hold on, man. Let's see the dog. We've never had a proper look at it."

But the drover was past caring about the details of the bargain. He was pursuing Mr. Craw, who, he alleged, was in possession of monies rightly due to him, and Mr. Craw was retreating from the fire to the vacant part of the floor where Jaikie stood.

Then suddenly came violent happenings. "Open the door, mistress," cried Jaikie. The drover turned furiously towards the voice, and found himself grabbed from behind and his arms forced back. He was a biggish fellow and managed to shake himself free. There was a vicious look in his eye, and he clutched the bread-knife from the table. Now, Mrs. Johnston's rolling-pin lay on the dresser, and with this Jaikie hit him smartly on the wrist, causing the knife to clatter on the floor. The next second Jaikie's head had butted his antagonist in the wind, and, as he stumbled forward gasping, Jaikie twisted his right arm behind his back and held it in a cruel lock. The man had still an arm loose with which he tried to clutch Jaikie's hair, and, to his own amazement, Mr. Craw found himself gripping this arm, and endeavouring to imitate Jaikie's tactics, the while he hammered with his knee at the drover's hind quarters. The propulsion of the two had its effect. The drover shot out of the kitchen into the rain, and the door was locked by Mrs. Johnston behind him.

" He'll come back," Mr. Craw quavered, repenting of his temerity.

" Not him," said Jaikie, as he tried to smooth his hair. " I know the breed. I know the very Glasgow close he comes out of. There's no fight in that scum. But I'm anxious about the little dog."

The kitchen was tidied up, and the two sat for a while by the peats. Then Mr. Craw professed a desire for bed. Exercise and the recent excitement had made him weary; also he was still nervous about the drover and had a longing for sanctuary. By going to bed he would be retiring into the keep of the fortress.

Jaikie escorted him upstairs, helped him to get out of Mr. Johnston's trousers, borrowed an extra blanket from the hostess, and an earthenware hot bottle which she called a " pig," and saw him tucked up comfortably. Then Jaikie disappeared with the lamp, leaving him to solitude and darkness.

Mr. Craw for a little experienced the first glimmerings of peace which he had known since that fateful hour at Kirkmichael when his Hejira began. He felt restful and secure, and as his body grew warm and relaxed he had even a moment of complacence. . . . He had, unsolicited, helped to eject a ruffian from the inn kitchen. He had laid violent hands upon an enemy. The thing was so novel in his experience that the memory of it sent a curious pleasant little shiver through his frame. He had shown himself ready in a crisis, instant in action. The thinker had proved himself also the doer. He dwelt happily with the thought. . . . Strange waters

surrounded him, but so far his head was above the
waves. Might there not be a purpose in it all, a
high purpose ? All great teachers of mankind had
had to endure some sojourn in the wilderness. He
thought of Mahomet and Buddha, Galileo in prison,
Spinoza grinding spectacles. Sometimes he had
wondered if his life were not too placid for a man
with a mission. These mishaps—temporary, of
course—might prove a stepping-stone from which
to rise to yet higher things.

Then he remembered the face of the drover as
he had last seen him, distorted and malevolent. He
had incurred the enmity of a desperate man. Would
not his violence be terribly repaid ? Even now, as
the drunkenness died in him, his enemy would
be planning his revenge. To-morrow—what of to-
morrow ? Mr. Craw shuddered, and, as the bedroom door opened and a ray of candle-light ran
across the ceiling, he almost cried aloud.

It was only Jaikie, who carried in his arms a
small dog. Its thick fleece, once white, was matted
in dry mud, and the finer hair of its face and legs,
streaked down with wet, gave these parts of it so
preposterous an air of leanness, that it looked like
a dilapidated toy dog which had lost its wheels.
But it appeared to be content. It curled itself at
the foot of Jaikie's bed, and, before beginning its
own toilet, licked his hand.

" I've bought that fellow's dog," Jaikie announced.
" It must have been stolen, but it has come through
a lot of hands. I beat him down to four shillings."

" Were you not afraid ? " gasped Mr. Craw.

"He's practically sober now," Jaikie went on. "You see, he barged into the cart beside the door and got a crack on the head that steadied him. There was nothing to be afraid of except his brute of a collie."

As Jaikie wriggled into bed he leaned forward and patted the head of his purchase. "I'm going to call him Woolworth," he said, "for he's as woolly as a sheep, and he didn't cost much."

CHAPTER X

THE storm blew itself out in the night, and the travellers awoke to a morning of soft lights and clear, rain-washed distances. They awoke also to the pea-hen call of their hostess at the foot of the stairs.

" Megsty me ! " ran the plaint. " D'ye ken what has happened ? The body in the stable is off or I was up, and he's never paid for his supper. . . . Waur nor that ! " (the voice rose to a keen) " He's ta'en yae pair o' the breeks that was dryin' afore the fire. The best pair ! The blue yins ! "

These last words drew Mr. Craw precipitately from his bed. He thrust a scared head out of the bedroom door.

" What do you say, woman ? My trousers ! "

" Ay, your trousers ! Sorrow and disgrace yon blagyird has brocht on this hoose ! Whae wad keep a public ? But we'll set the pollis on him. As soon as my man's up, he'll yoke the gig an' get the pollis."

Jaikie added his voice to the clamour.

" I'll be down in a jiffey, mistress, and I'll go after him on your man's bicycle."

" Ye daurna. He'll kill ye. He's a desperate blagyird."

" Give me my flannel bags," said Jaikie, " and I'll be on the road in ten minutes. He can't be many miles ahead."

But when the two descended to the kitchen—Mr. Craw chastely habited in the trousers of Mr. Johnston —they were met by a wild-eyed hostess and an apple-cheeked servant girl.

" Waur and waur ! " wailed the former. " The scoondrel has stolen Tam's bicycle, and he didna tak' the Glendonan road, but the road to Gledmouth, and that's maistly doun hill. This lassie was bicyclin' back frae her mither's, and at the foot o' the Kirklaw brae she seen something by the road-side. She seen it was a bicycle, and she kent it for Tam's bicycle, and it was a' bashed to bits. The body maun hae run into the brig."

" How far off ? " Jaikie asked.

" The better pairt o' fower miles. Na, ye'll no make up on him. Yon's the soople blagyird, and he'll be hidin' in a Gledmouth close long or ye gat near him. Wae's me for Tam's guid new bicycle that cost ten pund last Martinmas."

" Is it much damaged ? " Jaikie asked the girl.

" Dung a' to smithers," was the answer. " The front wheel's the shape o' a peesweep's egg, and the handle-bars are like a coo's horn."

" Heard ye ever the like ? " Mrs. Johnston lamented. " And the pollis will never get him, and if they did he wad gang to jyle, but he couldna pay the price o' the bicycle. It's an unco blow, for Tam has nae siller to spare."

It is to Mr. Craw's credit that he did not think

only of the bearing of this disaster on his own
affairs.

" I am very sorry for the misfortune," he told
his hostess. " At the moment I am travelling light
and have little money. But I am not without
means, and I will see that you receive the sum of
ten pounds within a week."

He was met by a solemn stare. Certainly with
his borrowed trousers, much stained collar, and
draggled tie (for Jaikie had forgotten to bring from
Castle Gay these minor adornments), he did not
look like a moneyed man. " Thank ye kindly," she
said, but it was obvious that she put no trust in his
promise.

Breakfast was an uncomfortable meal, hurriedly
served, for Mrs. Johnston was busy upstairs, preparing for the emergence of her husband from his
sick-room. Beside Jaikie sat Woolworth, his new
purchase, very hungry, but not yet certain how far
he dared to presume. He pirouetted about on his
lengthy hind legs, and then slapped Jaikie's arm
with an urgent paw. Jaikie prepared for him a
substantial meal of scraps, which was devoured in
a twinkling. " I wonder when that beast last saw
food," he observed.

Then he borrowed an old dishcloth and a piece
of soap, and retired with Woolworth to the pump.
When Mr. Craw joined them the terrier, shivering
violently, and with a face of woe, had been thoroughly scrubbed, and now was having his thick
fleece combed with a gap-toothed instrument which
Jaikie had discovered in the stable. Followed a

drastic dressing down with a broken brush, while Jaikie made the same hissing sounds that had accompanied his towelling of Mr. Craw the previous evening. Jaikie had said no word of plans at breakfast. He seemed to be waiting for his companion to make the first comment on a shattering miscarriage.

" I cannot go to London in these clothes," said Mr. Craw, looking down at the well-worn grey breeks.

Jaikie's eyes left Woolworth and regarded him critically. He was certainly a different figure from the spruce gentleman who, twenty-four hours ago, had left the Back House of the Garroch. He was not aggressively disreputable, but the combination of trousers, blue jacket, and dirty collar made him look like a jobbing carpenter, or a motor mechanic from some provincial garage. The discordant element in the picture was his face, which belied his garb, for it was the face of a man accustomed to deference, mildly arrogant, complacent for all the trouble in his eyes. Such a face never belonged to a mechanic. Jaikie, puzzled to find a name for the apparition, decided that Mr. Craw had become like the kind of man who spoke on Sunday in Hyde Park, a politician from the pavement. He remembered a Communist orator in Glasgow who had had something of the same air.

" I can't get to Castle Gay without a bicycle, and be back in time," was all he said.

" That means postponing still further my journey to London," said Mr. Craw. The curious thing was

that he did not say it dolefully. Something had
changed in him this morning. His tone was resigned, almost philosophic. A sound sleep after a
day of hard exercise had given him a novel sense
of physical well-being. He had just eaten, with a
hearty appetite, a very plain breakfast, at which his
chef would have shuddered. The tonic air of the
upland morning put vigour into his blood. He was
accustomed to start his day with a hot bath, and
emerge from warm rooms with his senses a little
dulled. This morning he had had no bath of any
kind, yet he felt cleaner than usual, and his eyes
and nostrils and ears seemed to be uncommonly
awake. He had good long-distance sight, so he
discarded his spectacles, which for the moment were
useless, and observed with interest the links of the
two flooded streams with some stray cocks of moorland hay bobbing on their current. . . . There were
golden plover whistling on the hill behind the inn;
he heard them with a certain delight in the fitness
of their wild call to that desert. . . . He sniffed the
odour of wet heather and flood water and peat reek
—and something else, homely and pleasant, which
recalled very distant memories. That was, of
course, the smell of cows; he had forgotten that
cows smelt so agreeably.

" Have you anything to propose ? " he asked in
a tone which was quite amiable.

Jaikie looked up sharply, and saw that in his
companion's face which he had not seen before, and
scarcely expected.

" I doubt there's nothing for it but to make our

way round the butt-end of the hills towards Portaway. That will bring us near Castle Gay, and I'll
find a chance to see Dougal and Barbon and get
some money. . . . It's at least twenty-seven miles
to Portaway, but we needn't get there to-night. I
know most of the herds, and we can easily find a
place to stop at when we get tired. It's a grand
day for the hills."

"Very well," said Mr. Craw, and his tone was
rather of contentment than of resignation.

They paid their modest bill, and put a luncheon
of scones and cheese in their packs, one of which
Mr. Craw insisted on shouldering. He reiterated
his promise to pay for the bicycle, and Mrs. Johnston,
assured of his good will if not of his means, shook
his hand. The voice of the convalescent husband
cut short their leave-takings, and their last recollection of the place was a confused noise within, caused
by that husband, with many appeals to his Maker,
beginning a cautious descent of the stairs.

Almost at once they left the Gledmouth highway
and turned up a green loaning, an old drove-road
which zigzagged along the face of a heather hill.
Woolworth at first trotted docilely at Jaikie's heels,
but soon, lured by various luscious scents, he took
to investigating the environs. There was not a cloud
in the sky, and the firmament was the palest blue,
infinitely clear, with a quality of light which made
the lowlands to the south and east seem like some
background in an Italian primitive. There was
little sound but the scrunch of their boots on the

patches of scree, and a great crying of birds, but from very far away came an echo of bells, ringing to kirk in some distant clachan. Except for an occasional summons to Woolworth Jaikie spoke no word, for he was not much given to speech. Mr. Craw, too, was silent. He was thinking his own thoughts.

He was thinking about Death, an odd subject for a shining morning. At the back of his mind he had a great fear of death, against which the consolations were void of that robust philosophy which he preached in public. His fear took a curious shape. He had made for himself a rich environment of money and houses and servants and prestige. So long as he lived he was on a pinnacle above the crowd, secure from all common ills. But when he died he would be no more than a tramp in a ditch. He would be carried out naked from his cosy shelter to lie in the cold earth, and his soul—he believed in the soul—would go shivering into the infinite spaces. Mr. Craw had often rebuked himself for thinking in such materialist terms of the ultimate mystery, but whatever his reason might say, his fancy kept painting the same picture. Stripped cold and bare ! The terror of it haunted him, and sometimes he would lie awake at night and grapple with it. . . . He felt that men who led a hard life, the poor man with famine at his threshold, the sailor on the sea, the soldier in the trench, must think of death with more complacency. They had less to lose, there was less to strip from them before the chilly journeying. . . . Sometimes he had wished that he could be like them.

If he could only endure discomfort and want for a little—only feel that the gap was narrower between his cosseted life and the cold clay and the outer winds ! . . . Now he had a feeling that he was bridging the gap. He was exposed to weather like any tinker, he was enduring fatigue and cold and occasional hunger, and he was almost enjoying it. To this indoor man the outdoor world was revealing itself as something strange and wild and yet with an odd kindness at the heart of it. Dimly there was a revelation at work, not only of Nature but of his own soul.

Jaikie's voice woke him out of his dreams. He had halted, and was pointing to a bird high up in the sky.

" There's a buzzard," he cried. " Listen. You're a great writer, Mr. Craw, but I think that most writers go wrong about birds. How would you describe that sound ? "

" Mewing," was the answer.

" Right. People talk about a buzzard screaming, but it mews like a sick cat. . . . I've heard a kestrel scream, but not a buzzard. Listen to that, too. That's a raven."

A bird was coasting along the hillside, with its mate higher up on a bank of shingle.

" They say a raven croaks. It's sharper than that. It's a bark. . . . Words are good things, if you get them right."

Mr. Craw was interested. Words were his stock in trade, out of which he had won fortune. Was there not capital to be made out of these novel

experiences ? He saw himself writing with a new
realism. He never read criticisms, but he was
aware that he had his critics. Here was a chance
to confound them.

" I thought that you might want to write," Jaikie
went on, " so I brought something in my pack.
Barbon said you had a special kind of envelope in
which you sent your articles, and that these en-
velopes were opened first in the mail at your office.
I got a batch of them from him, and some paper
and pencils. He said you always wrote with a
pencil."

Mr. Craw was touched. He had not expected
such consideration from this taciturn young man.
He was also flattered. This youth realized that his
was an acquisitive and forward-looking mind, which
could turn a harsh experience into a message of
comfort for the world. His brain began to work
happily at the delightful task of composition. He
thought of vivid phrases about weather, homely
idioms heard in the inn, word-pictures of landscapes,
tough shreds of philosophy, and all coloured with a
fine, manly, out-of-doors emotion. There was a new
manner waiting for him. When they sat down to
lunch by a well-head very near the top of the Callowa
watershed, he felt the cheerfulness of one on the
brink of successful creation.

Munching his scones and cheese, he became
talkative.

" You are a young man," he said. " I can remember when I also was twenty. It was a happy
time, full of dreams. It has been my good fortune

to carry those dreams with me throughout my life.
Yes, I think I was not yet twenty when I acquired
my philosophy. The revelation came to me after
reading Thomas Carlyle's 'Characteristics.' Do
you know the essay ? "

Jaikie shook his head. He was an omnivorous
reader, but he had found Carlyle heavy going.

" Ah, well ! That great man is too little read
to-day, but his turn will come again. I learned
from him not to put too high a value upon the mere
intellect. He taught me that the healthy life is the
unconscious life, and that it is in man's dim illogical
instincts that truth often lies. We are suffering
to-day, Mr. Galt, from a surfeit of clever logicians.
But it is the biologist rather than the logician or the
mathematician to whom we should look for guidance.
The infinite power and value of the unreasoned has
always been one of my master principles."

" I know," said Jaikie. He remembered various
articles above Mr. Craw's signature which had ap-
pealed to what he called " the abiding instincts of
the people," and he had wondered at the time how
any man could be so dogmatic about the impon-
derable.

" From that principle," the other went on, " I
deduce my optimism. If we live by reason only
we must often take a dark view of the world and
lose hope. But the irrational instinct is always
hopeful, for it is the instinct to live. You must
have observed the astonishing cheerfulness of the
plain man, when the intellectual despairs. It was
so in the War. Optimism is not a pre-condition of

thought, but it is a pre-condition of life.   Thus mankind, which has the will to continue, ' never turns
its back, but marches breast-forward.' "   He filled
his chest and delivered the full quotation from
Browning.

Jaikie, to whom Browning had always seemed
like a slightly intoxicated parson, shifted uncomfortably.

" I hope you do not affect pessimism," said Mr.
Craw.   " I believe it is often a foolish pose of youth.
Dishonest, too."

" I don't know," was the answer.   " No.   I'm
not a pessimist.   But I haven't been through bad
enough times to justify me in being an optimist.
You want to have been pretty hardly tried before
you have any right to say that the world is good."

" I do not follow."

" I mean that to declare oneself an optimist, without having been down into the pit and come up on
the other side, looks rather like bragging."

" I differ profoundly.   Personal experience is not
the decisive factor.   You have the testimony of the
ages to support your faith."

" Did you ever read *Candide* ? " Jaikie asked.

" No," said Mr. Craw.   " Why ? "

But Jaikie felt that it would take too long to
explain, so he did not answer.

The drove-road meandered up and down glens and
across hill-shoulders till it found itself descending
to the valley of one of the Callowa's principal tribu-
taries, in which ran a road from Gledmouth to

Portaway. The travellers late in the afternoon came to the edge of that road, which on their left might be seen winding down from the low moorish table-land by which it had circumvented the barrier of the high mountains. On their right, a quarter of a mile away, it forked, one branch continuing down the stream to Portaway, twelve miles distant, while the other kept west around a wooded spur of hill.

Mr. Craw squatted luxuriously on a dry bank of heather. He had not a notion where he had got to, but spiritually he was at ease, for he felt once again master of himself. He had stopped forecasting the immediate future, and had his eye on the articles which he was going to write, the fresh accent he would bring to his messages. He sat in a bush like a broody hen, the now shapeless Homburg hat squashed over his head, the image of a ruminating tramp.

Jaikie had gone down to the road fifty yards away, where a stream fell in pools. He was thirsty, since, unlike his companion, he had not drunk copiously of wayside fountains. As he knelt to drink, the noise of an approaching car made him raise his head, and he watched an ancient Ford pass him and take the fork on the left, which was the road to Portaway. It was clearly a hired car, presumably from Gledmouth. In it sat the kind of driver one would expect, a youth with a cap on one side of his brow and an untidy mackintosh. The other occupant was a young man wearing a light grey overcoat and a bowler hat, a young man with a high-coloured face and a small yellow moustache.

It was a lonely place and an unfrequented road, but to his surprise he knew the traveller.

He watched the car swing down the valley towards Portaway, and was busy piecing together certain recollections, when he was recalled to attention by the shouts of Mr. Craw from the hillside. Mr. Craw was in a state of excitement. He ran the fifty yards towards Jaikie with surprising agility.

" Did you see that ? " he puffed. " The man in the car. It's my secretary, Sigismund Allins. I tried to stop him, but I was too late. He was on holiday in Spain, and was not expected back for another fortnight. I can only assume that Barbon has recalled him by wire. What a pity we missed him, for he could have provided us with the money we need. At any rate he could have arranged for sending it and my clothes from Castle Gay without troubling you to go there. . . . I am relieved to think Allins is back. He is a very resourceful man in an emergency."

" You are sure it was he ? "

" Absolutely certain. I had a good look at him as the car passed, but I found my voice too late. I may be trusted to recognize the inmates of my own household."

Jaikie too had recognized the man, though he did not know his name. His memory went back to an evening in Cambridge a year before, when he had dined in what for him was strange company—the Grey Goose Club, a fraternity of rich young men who affected the Turf. It had been the day before the Cambridgeshire, and the talk had been chiefly of Newmarket. Among the guests had been a brisk gentleman who was not an undergraduate, and who had been pointed out to him as a heroic and successful plunger. " He's got the *View* in his pocket," his host had told him, " and that, of course, means that he gets the best tips." He remembered that he had not liked the guest, whose talk sounded to him boastful and indecent. He had set him down as a *faux bonhomme*, noting the cold shiftiness of his light eyes. What was it that Alison had said of Mr. Allins ? " If you met him you would say that he wasn't quite a gentleman." He certainly would go thus far.

The last stage of the day's walk in the purple October dusk was for Mr. Craw a pleasant experience. He was agreeably tired. He was very hungry and had Jaikie's promise of a not too distant meal, and his mind—this was always a factor in his comfort—was working busily. The sight of his secretary had assured him that his proper world could be readily recaptured when he wished, but he was content to dwell a little longer in the new world to which he had been so violently introduced. About six o'clock they reached the shepherd's house of the Black Swire, some eight miles from Portaway, the eastern hirsel on the Knockraw estate. There Jaikie was given an effusive welcome by his old friends, the shepherd and his wife, and, since the house was new and commodious, they had a bedroom far superior to Mrs. Catterick's or that of the Watermeeting inn. Mr. Craw faced without blenching a gigantic supper of the inevitable ham and eggs, and drank three cups of tea. At the meal he condescended affably, and discoursed with the shepherd, who was a stout Radical, on the prospects of the Canonry election. Jaikie had introduced him as a friend from London, and it pleased him to cultivate his anonymity, when by a word he might have set the shepherd staring.

The host and hostess went early to bed, after the fashion of countryfolk, and the two travellers were left alone by the fire. Mr. Craw felt wakeful, so he had out the foolscap from Jaikie's pack, and composed an article which, when it appeared two days later, gave pleasure to several million readers. Its subject was the value of the simple human instincts, too often overlaid by the civilized, the essential wisdom of the plain man. Just as a prophet must sojourn occasionally in the wilderness, so it was right for culture now and then to rub shoulders with simplicity, as Antæus drew his strength from contact with his mother, the Earth.

Jaikie sat by the peats, Woolworth's head against his knee, and brooded. What he had seen that evening had altered his whole outlook. . . . Allins was not bound for Castle Gay. He had not mentioned it to his companion, but the road to Castle Gay was the right fork, and the car had taken the left. It was less than eight miles to Castle Gay by the straight road at the point where they had seen the car, but it was thirteen by Portaway. . . . Why should Allins go to Portaway when he was supposed to be on holiday? He did not believe for one moment that he had been recalled by Barbon, who had spoken of him coldly. He was Mr. Craw's *protégé*, not Barbon's. . . . He must have come from Gledmouth, probably arriving there by the 6.30 train from the south. Why had he chosen that route to Portaway? It was longer than by the coast, and a most indifferent road. But it was lonely, and his only reason must have been that he wanted to be unobserved. ... . Jaikie had a very clear picture of Allins that night at the Grey Goose Club. Was that the sort of fox to be safely domesticated by an innocent like Craw?

The innocent in question was busy at his article, sometimes sucking the end of his pencil, sometimes scribbling with a happy smirk, sometimes staring into the fire. Jaikie, as his eyes dwelt on him, had a sudden conviction about two things. One was that he liked him. The other was that this business was far more complicated than even Dougal realized. It was more than protecting the privacy of a newspaper proprietor and saving his face. There were darker things to be looked for than rival pressmen and persistent Evallonians.

As this conviction became firm in his mind, Jaikie felt an immense access of cheerfulness. There was going to be some fun in the business after all.

CHAPTER XI

THE TROUBLES OF A JOURNALIST

MR. ALBERT TIBBETS, after his meeting with Dougal in Portaway, spent an unprofitable day. He duly received the second wire from his chief, confirming him in his view of the Craw mystery, and urging an instant and unrelenting quest. Fired with these admonitions, he proceeded to Castle Gay to carry out his intention of " comforting Barbon." But he found many difficulties in his path. He was refused admission, as he expected, at both the lodge gates. When, after a good deal of trouble and considerable loss of skin, he twice made his way into the park, he was set upon by the satellites of Mackillop and rudely ejected. The second time, indeed, he received so rough a handling that even his hardy spirit was daunted. He retired to the inn at Starr to write out his notes and perpend the situation.

He was convinced that Mr. Craw had been lost, and that he had not travelled south. But it was possible that by this time he was back at the Castle. In that case it was his business to find out the reason why the Castle itself had been so gravely perturbed. There was a mystery somewhere, and it behoved him, for the credit of his paper, to unriddle it. If he could come on the secret, he might use it to compel an interview with Mr. Craw, which would be a triumph of a high order. But nothing could be done by daylight with those watchful myrmidons. Mr. Tibbets, like other conspirators, waited for the darkness.

He had no particular plans when, fortified by a good dinner, he set out on his motor-bicycle at the hour of half-past seven. Rather aimlessly he made his way to the principal lodge near the Mains, and set himself down opposite it to smoke a pipe and consider his tactics. Almost immediately he was rewarded by a remarkable sight. A big closed car slid up the road and stopped at the lodge. Apparently it was expected, for the gates were at once opened. It passed through, and the bars fell behind it, but not before Mr. Tibbets had had a glimpse of its occupants. He saw that they were men, and one at least was in evening dress, for he caught a glimpse of a white shirt-front.

This was news with a vengeance. This party had come to dine at the Castle—not to stay, for there was no luggage on the car. In time they would return, and it was his business to wait for them and follow them.

For more than three hours he kept his chilly vigil. Nothing passed him on the road except a dog-cart going up the valley, and two farm lads on bicycles. He remembered the other lodge, and had a moment's fear that the visitors might leave by that. Finally, about twenty minutes past eleven, he saw the glow of headlights rising beyond the park walls, the gates

opened, and the car swung into the highway. Mr.
Tibbets, with very stiff limbs but an eager heart,
mounted his machine and followed it.

It was an easy task, for the car travelled slowly,
as if driven by a man not accustomed to the twisting
Canonry roads. It turned to the left before Starr
village and passed the other lodge. Then it climbed
through a mile of fir-woods to an open moor, where
Mr. Tibbets prudently fell some distance behind.
Once again he found himself in tortuous roads
among pasture-fields, and, coming too quickly round
a corner, all but ran into the car, which had halted
at another lodge. He subsided quietly into a ditch,
and watched the car disappear into a dark avenue
of beeches. He noticed that, as at Castle Gay, the
lodge-keeper locked the gates behind it.

Mr. Tibbets's investigations had given him a fair
general idea of the neighbourhood. He recognized
the place as Knockraw, which he understood had
been let to shooting tenants. His ardour for the
quest rose like a rocket. If Craw was still lost, these
people must be mixed up in the business, for the
anxious Barbon would not ask them to dine as a
matter of ordinary hospitality. If Craw had returned, what did he want with the strangers—Craw,
who notoriously never dined out and led a cloistered
life ? Who were they ? Craw was no sportsman,
and could have no interest in sporting neighbours.
. . . Mr. Tibbets had a stout heart, and he determined not to lose the scent. He decided that he
had better prospect the immediate neighbourhood
of Knockraw. He had a vision of a smoking-room

window, perhaps open a little, where he might view the party at close quarters and haply overhear their talk.

He carefully disposed of his bicycle behind a clump of broom and entered the modest demesne of Knockraw. This was easy enough, for only a wire fence separated it from the road. The moon was up by now, the Hunters' Moon shining in a clear sky, and it guided him through the beechwood and a plantation of young spruces to the corner of a walled kitchen garden. Beyond it he saw the rambling whitewashed house, and the square of gravel by the front door. He had run fast and by the shortest road, and as he came in sight of the door the car had only just turned and was making its way to the garage. The household was still awake, for there were half a dozen lit windows.

Mr. Tibbets, still possessed by the idea of a smoking-room window, began a careful circuit of the dwelling. Keeping strictly in cover, he traversed a lawn with flower-beds, an untidy little rose garden, and a kind of maze composed of ill-clipped yews. The windows on this side were all dark. Then, rounding a corner of the house, he found himself on another rough lawn, cut by two gravelled paths and ending in a shrubbery and some outhouses. There was light here, but it was clearly the kitchen and servants' quarters, so he turned on his tracks, and went back to the front door. He was convinced that the living-rooms, if the party had not gone to bed, must be on the other side of the house, where it abutted on the heathery slopes of Knockraw Hill.

This meant a scramble to avoid a dense thicket of rhododendrons, but presently he had passed the corner, and looked down on what was the oldest part of the dwelling. Sure enough there was a lit window—open, too, for the night was mild. He saw an arm draw the curtain, and it was the arm of a man in evening dress.

The sleuth in Mr. Tibbets was now fully roused. There was a ledge to the window which would give him cover, and he crawled down the slope towards it. There was a gap in the curtains, and he was able to peep into the room. He saw the back of one man, and noticed that his dress-coat had a velvet collar; the bearded profile of another; and the hand of a third which held a tumbler. They were talking, but in some foreign tongue which Mr. Tibbets did not understand. Try as he might, he could get no better view. He had raised himself and was peering through the gap, when a movement towards him made him drop flat. A hand shut the windows and fastened the catch. Then he heard a general movement within. The light was put out and the door was closed. The three men had gone to bed.

Bitterly disappointed, Mr. Tibbets got to his feet and decided that there was nothing more to be done for the moment. All he had found out was that the three diners at Castle Gay were foreigners, and that one had a black beard. He had studied the bearded profile so carefully that he thought he should know its owner if he met him again. He remounted the slope, intending to pass the rhododendron clump on its upper side. With a dormant household behind him, as he believed, it is possible that he may have gone carelessly. For as he rounded the rhododendrons he was suddenly challenged by a voice from above.

He yielded to the primeval instinct and ran. But he did not run far. He was making for the highroad and his motor-bicycle, but he travelled barely fifty yards. For something of an incredible swiftness was at his heels, and he found himself caught by the knees so that he pitched head foremost down the slope towards the front door. Dazed and winded, he found the something sitting on his stomach and holding his throat with unpleasing strictness. His attempts to struggle only tightened the constriction, so he gave up the contest.

After that he scarcely knew what happened to him. His captor seemed to have multiplied himself by two or three, and he felt himself being bundled on to men's shoulders. Then he was borne into darkness, into light, into darkness, and again into bright light. When he returned to full possession of his wits, he was in what seemed to be a cellar, with his wrists and ankles tightly corded and nothing to recline on but a cold stone floor.

Count Casimir Muresco, while completing a leisurely Sunday-morning toilet, was interrupted by Jaspar, the butler, a man who in the service of Prince Odalchini had acquired a profound knowledge of many lands and most human conundrums. Jaspar reported that the previous night the two footmen,

who were also from the Prince's Evallonian estates,
having been out late in pursuance of some private
business, had caught a poacher in the garden, and,
according to the best Evallonian traditions, had
trussed him up and deposited him for the night in a
cellar, which was the nearest equivalent they could
find to the princely dungeons.

Casimir was perturbed by the news, for he was
aware that the Evallonian methods were not the
British, and he had no desire to antagonize the
countryside. He announced that at eleven o'clock
he would himself interview the prisoner, and that
in the meantime he should be given breakfast.

The interview, when it took place, effectually
broke up the peace of mind of the Knockraw establishment. For instead of a local poacher, whom
Casimir had intended to dismiss with an admonition
and a tip, the prisoner proved to be a journalist in
a furious temper. Mr. Tibbets had passed a miserable night. The discomfort of his bonds had prevented him from sleeping, and in any case he had
only the hard floor for a couch. The consequence
was that he had spent the night watches in nursing
his wrath, and, having originally been rather scared,
had ended by becoming very angry. Patriotism
added fuel to his fires. He had been grossly maltreated by foreigners, and he was determined to
make his wrongs a second case of Jenkins's Ear, and,
in the words of that perjured mariner, to " commend
his soul to God and his cause to his country." He
was convinced that he had fallen into a den of
miscreants, who were somehow leagued with Craw,

and professional rivalry combined with national pre-
judices and personal grievances to create a mood of
righteous wrath. He had told Jaspar what he
thought of him when the butler had removed his
bonds that morning, and he had in no way been
mollified by a breakfast of hot rolls and excellent
coffee. Consequently, when Casimir appeared at
eleven o'clock, he found himself confronted with the
British Lion.

Casimir had the wit to see the gravity of the
blunder. This was one of the journalists whom at
all costs he must avoid—Barbon and Dougal had
dinned that into him. He was apparently the most
dangerous, for, being a student of the British Press,
Casimir had a lively respect for the power of the
Wire. The fellow had been gravely affronted, and
was in the most truculent temper.

Casimir was a man of action. He relapsed into
broken English. He apologized profusely—he even
wept. The ways of his own land (he did not, of
course, mention Evallonia) were different from Scotland, and his servants had been betrayed unwittingly
into a grievous fault. Not for the gold of Crœsus
would he have been party to an insult to the so-
great British Press. But let Mr. Tibbets picture the
scene—the darkness, the late hour, servants accustomed to predatory and revolutionary peasants,
servants knowing nothing of the free and equal
British traditions. There was room for an innocent
mistake, but he cast ashes on his head that it should
have happened to Mr. Tibbets. Then Casimir's
English began to fail him. He could not explain.

He could not make atonement. Let the resources of the establishment be placed at his guest's disposal. A hot bath ? Then a car would await him, while his bicycle would be retained and sent on to Portaway.

Casimir overflowed with obscure apologies. He conducted Mr. Tibbets himself to a bedroom and prepared his bath. A bed was ready, with pyjamas laid out, and a pleasant fire burning. The journalist began to thaw, for he was very sleepy. He would do as Casimir suggested ; afterwards, he told himself, he would pump these penitent foreigners on the subject of Mr. Craw. He bathed and retired to rest, and, though he did not know it, the bedroom door was locked and the key in Casimir's pocket.

After a consultation with his colleagues Casimir rang up Castle Gay and poured his difficulties into the sympathetic ear of Barbon. There was now no defect in his English. " The man will go away full of suspicion," he said. " I distrust him. He has not forgiven us, and will make journalistic capital out of his adventures. . . . No. He does not know who we are, but he will make inquiries, and he may find out. . . . You say he is the chief journalistic enemy of Mr. Craw. I have a suggestion. He has been trying to enter Castle Gay, and has failed. Let me send him to you. I will say that we cannot express adequately our apologies, but that my good friend Barbon will do that for us. By entering Castle Gay he will be placated. . . . There is no difficulty, for Mr. Craw is not there. You will receive him as an English friend of mine who desires to add his apologies to ours."

Mr. Barbon's response was not encouraging, but Casimir continued to press his case, and at last prevailed. " I don't want to be mixed up in this business," Barbon said, " but Mr. Crombie might manage it. He could talk to him as one journalist to another." Barbon's voice gradually became more cordial. He was beginning to think that such a visit might help with his own problem. If Tibbets came to Castle Gay, and was well received, and saw for himself that the master of the house was absent, he might be choked off his present dangerous course. There was no reason why he should not write a story for his paper about Castle Gay. It would all tend to show that they had nothing to conceal.

Tibbets slept till half-past three. Then he arose, to find shaving things laid out for him and all the necessaries of the toilet. At the first sign of movement Jaspar had been instructed to unlock the bedroom door. Presently came a modest tap, and Casimir appeared with ungrammatical hopes that his guest had slept well. Tibbets was conducted downstairs, where he ate an excellent luncheon, while Casimir entertained him with accounts of the Knockraw sport and questions revealing an abysmal ignorance of British politics. " My car is waiting for you," he said, " to take you wherever you wish to go. But I should be glad if you would permit it to take you first to Castle Gay. I have not been able to express to you our full contrition, but I have asked my friend Mr. Barbon, through whose kind

offices I took this place, to speak for me and say
how little I desire to wound the heart of so eminent
an Englishman. I and my friends are, so to say,
guests in your country, and we would die sooner
than be guilty of a breach of hospitality."

"That's all right, Count," said Tibbets. (His
host had introduced himself as Count Anton Murat-
sky and had hinted at a Styrian domicile.) "We'll
say no more about last night. I can see that it was
a servant's blunder, and, anyway, I had no business
to be wandering about so late close to your house.
I lost my road trying to take a short cut. I'll be
very glad to look in at Castle Gay. I don't know
Mr. Barbon, but I'd be pleased to meet him."

Privately, he exulted. The Fates had done
well by him, and had opened the gates of the Dark
Tower. He would not be worth much if he
couldn't get a good story out of Barbon, whom
he had seen from afar and written down as a nin-
compoop.

He reached Castle Gay in the Knockraw car just
about five o'clock. He was obviously expected, for
Bannister greeted him with a smiling face—" From
Knockraw, sir ? "—and led him upstairs and along
a corridor to the library where the day before the
Evallonian delegates had been received in conference. Mr. Tibbets stared with interest at the
vast apartment, with the latticed book-laden shelves
lining three walls, the classic sculptures, and the
great Flemish tapestry. The room was already
dusky with twilight, but there were lights before
the main fireplace, and a small table set out for

tea. There sat a short elderly gentleman in brown tweeds, who rose at his approach and held out a welcoming hand.

"Come away, Mr. Tibbets," he said, "and have your tea. I'm fair famished for mine."

The journalist had the surprise of a not uneventful life. He had entered the palace for an appointment with a major-domo and instead had been ushered into the Presence. He had never seen Mr. Craw in the flesh, but his features were well known to the world, since weekly his portrait surmounted his articles. Before him beyond doubt was the face that had launched a thousand ships of journalism— the round baldish head, the bland benevolent chin, the high cheek-bones, the shrewdly pursed lips. The familiar horn spectacles were wanting, but they lay beside him on the floor, marking a place in a book. Now that he had Mr. Craw not a yard away from him, he began hurriedly to revise certain opinions he had entertained about that gentleman. This man was not any kind of fool. The blue eyes which met his were very wide awake, and there was decision and humour in every line of that Pickwickian countenance.

His breath stopped short at the thought of his good fortune. To be sure the Craw mystery had proved to be nonsense, and he had been barking loudly up the wrong tree. But that stunt could easily be dropped. What mattered was that he was interviewing Craw—the first man in the history of journalism who had ever done it. He would refuse to be bound over to silence. He had got his

chance, and nothing could prevent him taking it.
. . . But he must walk very warily.

Dickson McCunn had been to church in the
morning, and on returning had found Dougal's
letter awaiting him, brought by a Castle Gay car.
He decided at once to accept the call. The salmon
fishing in his own stream was nearly over, the
weather was fine, and he felt stirring in him a desire
for movement, for enterprise, for new sights and
new faces. This longing always attacked him in
the spring, but it usually came also in the autumn,
just before he snuggled down into the warm domesticity of winter. So he had packed a bag, and
had been landed at Castle Gay a little after four
o'clock, when Barbon had concluded his telephone
conversation with Knockraw.

At once a task had been set him. Dougal declared that he was the man to pacify Tibbets. " I
don't want to appear in the thing, nor Barbon either,
for the chap is an enemy. He won't make anything
of you—just that you're a friend of the family—and
you can pitch him a yarn about the innocent foreigners at Knockraw and how they haven't enough
English to explain their penitence. If he asks you
about yourself you can say you have just arrived on
a visit, and if he starts on Craw you can say you
know nothing about him—that he's away on holiday, and that you're a friend of Barbon's—your
niece married his cousin—any lie you like. You've
got just the kind of manner to soothe Tibbets, and
make him laugh at his troubles and feel rather
ashamed of having made so much fuss."

Dickson lost no time in fulfilling his mission.

"Those poor folk at Knockraw," he said. "They've made an awful mess of it, but a man like you can see for yourself that they meant no harm. The Count's a friend of Mr. Barbon's and a great sportsman, and it seems they haven't any grouse in their own country—I'm not just sure what it is, but it's somewhere near Austria— so they were determined to take a Scotch moor. The mistake was in bringing a lot of wild heathen servants, when they could have got plenty of decent folk here to do their business. The Count was lamenting on the telephone, thinking you'd set the police and the Procurator-fiscal on him or make a rumpus in the newspapers. But I knew you were not that kind of man, and I told him so." Dickson beamed pleasantly on his companion.

But Tibbets scarcely appeared to be listening. "Oh, that business!" he said. "Of course, it was all a mistake, and I'll never say another word about it."

"That's fine!" said Dickson heartily. "I knew you would take it like a sensible fellow. I needn't tell you I've a great admiration for you journalists, and I daresay I often read you in the papers!"

"You read the *Wire*?" asked the startled Tibbets. Mr. Craw was generally supposed to look at no papers but his own.

"Not regularly. But I often pick it up. I like a turn at the *Wire*. You've grand pictures, and a brisk way of putting things. I always say there's

not a livelier paper in this land than the *Wire*.   It
keeps a body from languor."

A small note-book and a pencil had emerged from
Tibbets's pocket. Dickson observed them unperturbed. The man was a journalist and must be
always taking notes.

"Your praise of the *Wire* will give enormous
satisfaction," said Tibbets, and there was almost
a quaver in his voice. He neglected the cup of
tea which had been poured out for him, and sat
gazing at his companion as a hopeful legatee might
gaze at a lawyer engaged in reading a will.

"You only arrived to-day, sir ? " he asked.

"Just an hour ago. I've been in Carrick. A
fine country, Carrick, none better, but the fishing
in my water there is just about over. The Callowa
here goes on for another fortnight. You're not an
angler, Mr. Tibbets ? A pity that, for I might have
got Mr. Barbon to arrange a day on the Callowa
for you."

Tibbets wrote. Mr. Craw as a fisherman was a
new conception, for he was commonly believed to
be apathetic about field sports.

"Would you care to say anything about the
Canonry election, sir ? " he asked deferentially.

Dickson laughed and poured himself out a third
cup of tea. "To tell you the truth," he said, " I
know nothing about it. I'm a poor hand at politics.
I suppose I'm what you call a Tory, but I often get
very thrawn with the Tories. I don't trust the
Socialists, but whiles I think they've a good deal to
say for themselves. The fact is, I'm just a plain

Scotsman and a plain business man. I'm terrible fond of my native country, but in these days it's no much a man like me can do for her. I'm as one born out of due season, Mr. Tibbets. I would have been more use when the job was to hunt the English back over the Cheviots or fight the French. I like straight issues."

"You believe in a business Government, sir ? " Tibbets asked, for this was the *Wire*'s special slogan.

"I believe in the business spirit—giving plain answers to plain questions and finding what's the right job to do and taking off your coat to it. We're all smothered nowadays with fine talk. There's hardly a man in public life with a proper edge to his mind. They keep blazing away about ideals and principles, when all they're seeking is just to win seats at the next election, and meantime folk stand hoasting at the street-corners with no chance of a job. This country, Mr. Tibbets, is suffering from nobility of language and ignobility of practice. There's far too much damned uplift abroad, and far too little common sense. In the old days, when folk stuck closer to the Bible, there was the fear of hell-fire to remind them that faith without works was dead."

Dickson said much more, for it was one of his favourite topics. He expanded on the modern lack of reverence for the things that mattered and the abject veneration for trash. He declared that the public mind had been over-lubricated, that discipline and logic were out of fashion, and that the prophets as a fraternity had taken to prophesying smooth things. He just checked himself in time, remembering where he was, for he almost instanced Mr. Craw as a chief sinner.

Tibbets scribbled busily, gulped down his cup of now lukewarm tea, and rose to go. He had got an interview which was the chief professional triumph of his career. The Knockraw car was still at his disposal. He could be in Portaway in time to write out his story and send it by the mail which reached London at 4.30 a.m. and so catch the later editions of his paper. Meantime he would telephone to his chief and prepare him for the thunderbolt.

He bowed over Dickson's hand. "I am honoured to have met you, sir. I can only hope that it is a privilege which may be repeated."

Dickson sought out Dougal and Barbon in the smoking-room. "Yon's a pleasant-spoken fellow," he said. "I made it all right about Knockraw, and sent him away as crouse as a piper. We had a fine crack, and he wrote down what I said in a wee book. I suppose I've been interviewed, and that's the first time in my life."

A sudden suspicion awoke in Dougal's eye.

"What kind of thing did you give him?" he asked.

Dickson sketched the main lines of his conversation, and Dougal's questions became more peremptory till he had extracted all of Tibbets's interrogatories and Dickson's answers. Then he lay back in his chair and laughed.

"He left in a hurry, you say. No wonder. He

has a story that will keep the *Wire* busy for a fortnight. . . . No, no, you're not to blame. It's my
fault that I never guessed what might happen.
Tibbets is a proud man to-night. He took you for
Craw, and he's got in his pocket the first interview
that Craw ever gave to mortal man. . . . We're in
the soup this time, right enough, for you've made
the body blaspheme every idol he worships."

CHAPTER XII

PORTAWAY—THE GREEN TREE

THE eight miles to Portaway were taken by the travellers at a leisurely pace, so that it was noon before they came in sight of the Canonry's capital. There had been some frost in the night, and, when they started, rime had lain on the stiffened ruts of the road and the wayside grasses. Presently the sun burned it up, and the shorn meadows and berry-laden hedges drowsed under a sky like June. The way, after they had left the Knockraw moors, was mostly through lowlands—fat farms with full stack-yards, and woods loud with the salutes of pheasants. Now and then at a high place they stopped to look back to the blue huddle of the great uplands.

"Castle Gay lies yonder." Jaikie directed his companion's eyes. "Yon's the Castle Hill."

Mr. Craw viewed the prospect with interest. His home had hitherto been for him a place without environment, like a walled suburban paradise where a city man seeks his repose. He had enjoyed its park and gardens, but he had had no thought of their setting. Now he was realizing that it was only a little piece of a vast and delectable country-side. He had come down from bleak hills into

meadows, and by contrast the meadows seemed
a blessed arcady. . . . His mind was filled with
pleasant and fruitful thoughts. The essence of
living lay in its contrasts. The garden redoubled
its charm if it marched with heather ; the wilderness
could be a delight if it came as a relief from a world
too fatted and supine. . . . Did not the secret of
happiness lie in the true consciousness of environment ? Castle Gay was nothing if the thought of
it was confined to its park walls. The mind must
cultivate a wide orbit, an exact orientation, for the
relief from trouble lay in the realization of that
trouble's narrow limits. Optimism, a manly optimism, depended only upon the radius of the en-
circling soul. He had a recollection of Browning :
" *Somewhere in the distance Heaven is blue above
Mountains where sleep the unsunn'd tarns.*" . . . On
this theme he saw some eloquent articles ahead of
him.

He was also feeling very well. Autumn scents
had never come to his nostrils with such aromatic
sharpness. The gold and sulphur and russet of the
woods had never seemed so marvellous a pageant.
He understood that his walks had hitherto, for so
many years, been taken with muffled senses—the
consequence of hot rooms, too frequent meals, too
heavy a sequence of little indoor duties. To-day
he was feeling the joys of a discoverer. Or was it
re-discovery ? By the time they had come to the
beginnings of Portaway he was growing hungry, and
in the narrow street of the Eastgate, as it dropped
to the Callowa bridge, they passed a baker's shop.

He stared at the window and sniffed the odour from
the doorway with an acuteness of recollection which
was almost painful. In the window was a heap
of newly-baked biscuits, the kind called " butter
biscuits," which are still made in old-fashioned
shops in old-fashioned Scots towns. He remembered them in his childhood—how he would flatten
his nose of a Saturday against a baker's window in
Partankirk, when he had spent his weekly penny,
and his soul hungered for these biscuits' delicate
crumbly richness. . . . He must find a way to
return to this shop, and for auld lang syne taste a
butter biscuit again.

Jaikie's mind on that morning walk had been
differently engaged. He was trying to find a clue
through the fog of suspicions which the sight of
Sigismund Allins had roused in him. Allins was
a confidential secretary of Mr. Craw. He was also
a gambler, and a man who bragged of his power with
the Craw Press. Allins was, therefore, in all likeli-
hood a dweller in the vicinity of Queer Street. If he
had money troubles—and what more likely ?—he
would try to use his purchase with Craw to help him
through. But how ? Jaikie had a notion that Mr.
Craw would not be very tolerant towards Allins's
kind of troubles.

Allins had gone off on holiday before the present
crisis began, and was not expected back for another
fortnight. He had obviously nothing to do with
the persecution of Craw by the journalists—there
was no profit for him that way. But what about the
Evallonians ? They had known enough of Craw's

ways and had sufficient power to get his papers to
print the announcement of his going abroad. Barbon
had assumed that they had an efficient intelligence
service. Was it not more likely that they had
bought Allins ? Why should Allins not be—for a
consideration—on their side ?

But in that case why had he returned prematurely
from his holiday ? The wise course, having got his
fee, was to stay away till the Evallonians had done
their business, in order that he might be free from
any charge of complicity. But he had returned
secretly by a roundabout road. He could have gone
direct to Portaway, for the train which had deposited him at Gledmouth stopped also at that
station. He wanted to be in the neighbourhood,
unsuspected, to watch developments. It was a bold
course and a dangerous. There must be some
compelling motive behind it.

Jaikie questioned Mr. Craw about Allins, and got
vague answers, for his companion's thoughts were
on higher things. Allins had been recommended to
him by some business friends ; his people were well
known in the city ; he had been private secretary to
Lord Wassell ; he was a valuable man, because he
went a great deal into society, unlike Barbon, and
could always find out what people were talking
about. He had been with him two years. Yes,
most useful and diplomatic and an excellent linguist.
He had often accompanied him abroad, where he
seemed to know everybody. Did Barbon like him ?
Certainly. They were a happy family, with no
jealousies, for each had his appointed business.

15

Well off? Apparently. He had a substantial salary, but must spend a good deal beyond it. Undoubtedly he had private means. No, Allins had nothing to do with the management of the papers. He was not seriously interested in politics or literature. His study was mankind. Womenkind too, perhaps. It was necessary for one like himself, who had heavy intellectual preoccupations, to provide himself with eyes and ears. "Allins is what you call a man of the world," said Mr. Craw. "Not the highest type of man, perhaps, but for me indispensable."

"I don't think he has gone to Castle Gay," said Jaikie. "I'm certain he is in Portaway. It is very important that he should not see you."

Mr. Craw asked why.

"Because the game would be up if you were recognized in Portaway, and it would be too dangerous for you to be seen speaking to one of your own secretaries. As you are just now, it wouldn't be easy for any one to spot you—principally because no one is expecting you, and there isn't the right atmosphere for recognition. But if you and Allins were seen together, that might give the clue."

Mr. Craw accepted the reasoning. "But I must have money—and clothes," he added.

"I'm going to send a line to Dougal as soon as we get to Portaway."

"And I must post the article I wrote last night."

"There's something else," said Jaikie. "You'll have to be in Portaway for at least twenty-four hours, and your rig won't quite do. It's all right except the jacket, which gives you away. We must get you a ready-made jacket to match Johnston's breeks."

So at a small draper's, almost next door to the baker's shop, a jacket of rough tweed was purchased —what is known to the trade as a " sports " line, suitable for the honest man who plays bowls or golf after his day's work. Mr. Craw was apparently stock-size for this class of jacket, for one was found which fitted him remarkably well. Also two soft collars were purchased for him. Jaikie looked with satisfaction on his handiwork. The raincoat and the hat were now battered by weather out of their former glossiness. Clad in well-worn grey trousers and a jacket of cheap tweed, Mr. Craw was the image of the small tradesman on holiday. Having no reading to do, he had discarded his spectacles, and the sun and wind had given him a healthy colouring. Moreover, he had relapsed a little from his careful speech to the early idiom of Kilmaclavers. He would be a clever man, thought Jaikie, who could identify this homeliness with the awful dignity of him who had sat in Mrs. Catterick's best room.

The town of Portaway lies on both banks of the Callowa, which there leaves its mountain vale and begins its seven miles of winding through salty pastures to the Solway. The old town is mostly on the left shore ; on the right has grown up a suburb of villas and gardens, with one flaring Hydropathic, and a large new Station Hotel, which is the resort of golfers and anglers. The capital of the Canonry is half country market town, half industrial centre, for in the hills to the south-east lie the famous quarries, which employ a large and transient population. Hence the political activities of the constituency centre in the place. The country-side is Tory or Liberal ; among the quarrymen is a big Socialist majority, which its mislikers call Communist. As Jaikie and Mr. Craw descended the Eastgate the posters of all three candidates flaunted in shop windows and on hoardings, and a scarlet rash on a building announced the Labour committee rooms.

In a back street stood the ancient hostelry of the Green Tree, once the fashionable county inn where in autumn the Canonry Club had its dinners, but now the resort only of farmers and the humbler bagman. Jaikie had often slept there on his tramps, and had struck up a friendship with Mrs. Fairweather, its buxom proprietress. To his surprise he found that the election had not congested it, for the politicians preferred the more modern hotels across the bridge. He found rooms without trouble, in one of which was a writing-table, for the itch of composition was upon Mr. Craw. They lunched satisfactorily in an empty coffee-room, and there at a corner table he proceeded to compose a letter. He wrote not to Dougal but to Alison. Dougal might be suspect, and unable to leave the Castle, while Alison was free as the winds. He asked for money and a parcel of Mr. Craw's clothing, but he asked especially for an interview at the Green Tree, fixing for it the hour of 11 a.m. the next day. There were various questions he desired to ask which could only be answered by some one familiar with the Castle *ménage*. It thrilled him to be writing to the girl. He began, " Dear Miss Westwater," and then changed it to " Dear Miss Alison." There had been something friendly and confidential about her eyes which justified the change. His handwriting was vile, and he regarded the address on the envelope with disfavour. It looked like " The Horrible Alison Westwater." He tried to amend it, but only made it worse.

Mr. Craw proposed to remain indoors and write. This intention was so clear that Jaikie thought it unnecessary to bind him down with instructions. So, depositing the deeply offended Woolworth in his bedroom, Jaikie left the inn and posted his letter to Alison and arranged for the dispatch of Mr. Craw's precious article by the afternoon train. Then he crossed the Callowa bridge to the new part of the town. He proposed to make a few private inquiries.

He thought it unlikely that Allins would be at the Station Hotel. It was too public a place, and he might be recognized. But he had stayed there once himself, and, according to his fashion, had been on good terms with the head-porter, so, to make assurance sure, he made it his first port of call. It was as he expected. There was no Sigismund Allins in the register, and no one remotely resembling him staying in the house. The most likely place was the Hydropathic, which had famous electric baths and was visited by an odd assortment of humanity. Thither Jaikie next directed his steps.

The entrance was imposing. He passed a garage

full of cars, and the gigantic porch seemed to be crowded with guests drinking their after-luncheon coffee. He had a vision of a hall heaped with golf clubs and expensive baggage. The porter was a vast functionary in blue and gold, with a severe eye. Jaikie rather nervously entered the hall, conscious that his clothes were not in keeping with its grandeur, and asked a stately lady in the bureau if a Mr. Allins was living in the house. The lady cast a casual eye at a large volume and told him " No."

It was the answer he expected, but he saw that further inquiries were going to be difficult. The porter was too busy and too proud—no chance of establishing confidential relations there. Jaikie emerged from the portals, and finding the Gods unfriendly, decided to appeal to Acheron. He made his way round to the back regions, which had once been stables and coach-houses, and housed now the electric plant and a repairing shop for cars. There was a kind of courtyard, with petrol pumps and water pumps, and at the corner to mark the fairway several white stones, which in old days had been the seat of relaxing ostlers. On two of these sat two men, both in mechanic's overalls, hotly disputing.

A kind fate had led him that way, for, as he sauntered past them he heard the word " Kangaroos " several times repeated. He heard the names of Morrison and Smail and Charvill—he heard his own, joined to a blasphemous epithet which seemed to be meant as commendation. He sidled towards the speakers

" What I say," said one, speaking slowly and
with great emphasis, " is that them that selected
oor team should be drooned like kittens in a bucket.
It wasna representative. I say it wasna representative. If it had been, we micht hae dung yon
Kangaroos a' to hell."

" Ye're awfu' clever, Wulkie. How wad ye hae
seleckit it ? "

" I wad hae left Morrison oot, and I wad hae
played "—here followed sundry names of no interest
to the reader. " And I wad hae played Galt at
stand-off half. It was fair manslaughter pittin' him
at wing three-quarter. He hasna the pace nor the
wecht."

" He's a dam fine wee felly," said the other. " Ye
ken weel he won the match."

" But he'd have won it better at stand-off. Yon
Sneddon was nae mair use than a tattie-bogle. Ye
canna pit Galt higher than I pit him, but the richt
use wasna made o' him. That's why I wad droon
the selectors."

" I think I would let them live a little longer,"
Jaikie interposed. " After all, we won against odds.
Sneddon was better than you think."

" Did ye see the match ? " the man called Wilkie
demanded fiercely.

" Yes," said Jaikie. " And I still feel it in my
bones. You see, I was playing in it."

The two regarded him wildly, and then a light
of recollection awoke in Wilkie's eye. " By God,
it's Galt," he cried. " It's J. Galt." He extended
a dirty palm. " Pit it there. I'm prood to shake

hands wi' ye. Man, the wee laddies in Glesca the
day are worshippin' bits o' your jersey."

"It's an occasion to celebrate wi' a drink," said
the other man solemnly. "But we're baith busy,
and there's nae drink to be had in this dam teetotal
shop. Will ye no meet us in the Briar Bush the
nicht? There's mony a man in this toun wad be
blithe to see J. Galt."

The ice was now broken, and for five minutes
there was a well-informed discussion on the subtler
aspects of Rugby football. Then Jaikie gently in-
sinuated his own purpose. He wanted to find out
who was living in the Hydropathic, and he did not
want to trouble the higher functionaries.

"Nae wonder," said Wilkie. "There's a pentit
Jezebel in yon bewry that wad bite a body's heid
off."

Was there no one, Jaikie asked, no friend of his
friend's inside the building with whom he could have
a friendly talk?

"There's Tam Grierson, the heid-porter," he was
told. "He's a decent body, though he looks like a
bubbly-jock. He'll be comin' off duty for his tea
in ten minutes. He bides at the lodge ayont the
big garage. I'll tak' ye doun and introduce ye.
Tam will be set up to see ye, for he's terrible keen
on fitba'."

So presently Jaikie found himself drinking tea
with the resplendent personage, who had removed
his braided frock-coat for comfort in his own
dwelling. Mr. Grierson off duty was the soul of
friendliness. They spoke of the match, they spoke

of Rugby heroes of old days. They spoke of
Scotland's chances against England. Then Jaikie
introduced the subject of his quest. " There's a
man whose name I'm not very sure about," he said,
" something like Collins or Allen. My friend, with
whom I'm on a walking tour, is anxious to know if
he's staying here." He described in great detail the
appearance of Mr. Allins, his high colour, his pale
eyes, his small yellow moustache.

" Ho ! " said the head-porter. " I ken him fine !
He arrived last night. I don't just mind his name.
He's a foreigner, anyway, though he speaks English.
I heard him jabberin' a foreign langwidge wi' the
others."

" What others ? "

" The other foreigners. There's generally a lot o'
queer folk bidin' in the Hydro, and a lot o' them's
foreigners. But the ones I mean came by the
London mail last night, and your freend arrived
about dinner-time. He seemed to be very thick wi'
them. There's seven o' them a'thegither. Four
has never stirred outbye the day. One gaed off in a
cawr after lunch, and your freend and the other are
down in Portaway. Ye can come back wi' me and
see if ye can get a glisk o' them."

Presently the head-porter resumed his braided
frock-coat, and, accompanied by Jaikie, returned
to the scene of his labours, and incidentally to the
grand manner. Jaikie was directed to an inconspicuous seat at the back of the porch, while the
head-porter directed the activities of boots and
waiters. At first there was a lull. The tea-drinkers

had finished their meal and for the most part gone
indoors, and on the broad sweep of gravel the dusk
descended. The head-porter spared an occasional
moment for conversation, but for the most part
Jaikie was left to himself to smoke cigarettes and
watch the lights spring out in the valley below.

About half-past five the bustle began. The
Hydropathic omnibuses began to roll up and dis-
charge new guests, and they were followed by several
taxi-cabs and one ancient four-wheeler. " It's the
train frae the south," he was informed by Grierson,
who was at once swept into a whirl of busyness.
His barrack-room voice—he had once been a ser-
geant in the K.O.S.B.—echoed in porch and hall,
and he had more than one distinguished passage of
arms with a taxi-driver. Jaikie thought he had
forgotten him, till suddenly he heard his hoarse
whisper in his ear, " There's your gentry," and
looked up to see two men entering the hotel.

One was beyond doubt Sigismund Allins, the man
whom Mr. Craw had recognized yesterday in the
Gledmouth motor, the man opposite whom he himself had dined at the Grey Goose Club. He was
dressed in a golfing suit of *crotal* tweeds, and made
an elegant symphony in brown. Jaikie's eye passed
to his companion, who was the more conspicuous
figure. He was short and square, and had a heavy
shaven face and small penetrating eyes which were
not concealed by his large glasses. He wore an
ulster of a type rarely seen on these shores, and a
small green hat pushed back from a broad forehead.
As the light of the porch fell on him Jaikie had a

sudden impression of an enormously vigorous being, who made Allins by his side seem like a wisp of straw.

He had another impression. The two men were talking eagerly in a foreign tongue, and both seemed to be in a state of high excitement. Allins showed it by his twitching lips and nervous hands, the other by his quick purposeful stride and the way he stuck his chin forward. Within the last half-hour they had seen something which had strongly moved them.

This was also the opinion of Grierson, delivered confidentially, as he superintended the moving of some baggage. "They maun hae been doun meetin' the train," he whispered, "and they've gotten either guid news or ill news."

There was no reason why he should stay longer, so Jaikie took his departure, after asking his friend the head-porter to keep an eye on the foreigners. "I've my reasons," he said, "which I'll tell you later. I'll be up some time to-morrow to have another crack with you."

At the lodge-gates he encountered the man called Wilkie returning from the town. "How did ye get on wi' Grierson? Fine? I thocht ye would. Tam's a rale auld-fashioned character, and can be desperate thrawn if ye get the wrang side o' him, but when he's in gude fettle ye'll no find a nicer man. . . . I've been doun at the station. I wanted a word wi' the Knockraw shover."

"Knockraw?"

"Ay. The folk in Knockraw have hired twae cars from us for the month, but they brocht their

ain shover wi' them.   A Frenchie.   Weel, there was
something wrong wi' the clutch o' ane o' them, and
they wrote in about it.   I saw the cawr in the town,
so I went to the station to speak to the man.   He
was meetin' the express."

"Was he meeting any one ? "

"Ay, a young lad cam' off the train, a lang lad in
a blue top-coat.   The shover was in a michty hurry
to get on the road and he wadna stop to speak to
me—said he would come back the morn.   At least,
I think he said that, but his English is ill to follow."

"Did the new arrival speak to any one at the
station ? "

"No a word.   He just banged into the cawr
and off."

Jaikie, having a good deal to think about, walked
slowly back to the Green Tree.   Another Evallonian had arrived to join the Knockraw party.
Allins and his friend had been at the station and
must have seen him, but they had not accosted him.
Was he wrong in his suspicions, and had Allins
nothing to do with the Evallonians ? . . . Yet the
sight of something had put him and his companion
into a state of profound excitement.   The mystery
was getting deeper.

He purchased at the station copies of that day's
View and *Wire* as an offering for Mr. Craw.   He also
ascertained from a porter, whom he had known of
old, that a guest had arrived for Knockraw.   "I
should have cairried his bag, but yon foreign shover
was waitin' for him, and the twae were out o' the
station and into their cawr afore ye could blaw your

nose. Ugh, man! since this damned election sterted Portaway's been a fair penny waddin'. Half the folk that come here the noo should be in a menawgerie."

Mr. Craw was seated by his bedroom fire, writing with great contentment. He announced that he also had been for a walk. Rather shamefacedly he confessed that he had wanted to taste a butter biscuit again, and had made his way to the baker's shop. "They are quite as good as I thought," he said. "I have kept two for you."

He had had an adventure in a small way, for he had seen Mr. Allins. Alone, and wearing the russet clothes which Jaikie had observed at the Hydropathic. He had seen him coming up the Eastgate, and, remembering Jaikie's caution, had retired down an alley, whence he had had a good view of him. There was no doubt on the matter ; it was Sigismund Allins, the member of his secretariat.

Jaikie presented him with the two papers and sat down to reflect. Suddenly he was startled by the sound which a small animal might make in heavy pain. Mr. Craw was reading something in the *Wire* which made him whimper. He finished it, passed a hand over his brow, and let the paper fall to the ground.

On the front page, with inch headlines, was the triumph of Tibbets. " Mr. Craw Speaks to the World ! " was the main heading, and there were a number of juicy subsidiaries. The prophet was unveiled with a vengeance. He preached a mercantile and militant patriotism, a downright, heavy-handed, man-of-the-world, damn-your-eyes, matter-of-fact philosophy. Tibbets had done his work well. Everything that the *Wire* had urged was now fathered on the *Wire's* chief rival. The thing was brilliantly staged—the dim library at Castle Gay, and the robust and bright-eyed sage scintillating among its ancient shadows. Tibbets had behaved well, too. There was not a hint of irony in his style ; he wrote as convert and admirer ; he suggested that the nation had been long in travail, and had at last produced a Man. The quondam sentimentalist and peacemaker stood revealed as the natural leader of the red-bloods and the die-hards.

"What will they think of me ? " the small voice wailed. "Those who have trusted me ? "

What indeed ! thought Jaikie. The field-marshal who flings his baton into the ash-bin and announces that the enemy have all the virtues, the prophet who tells his impassioned votaries that he has been pulling their leg, the priest who parodies his faith's mysteries—of such was Mr. Craw. Jaikie was himself so blankly astonished that he did not trouble to think how, during the last feverish days, that interview could have been given.

He was roused by the injured man getting to his feet. Mr. Craw was no longer plaintive—he was determined, and he was angry.

"There has been infamous treachery somewhere," he announced in a full loud voice. "Have the goodness to order a car. I start at once for Castle Gay, and there I am going to—to—to wring somebody's neck."

CHAPTER XIII

PORTAWAY—RED DAVIE

JAIKIE lifted his head in astonishment. This was a Craw whom he had not met before—a man of purpose, with his hackles up. He was proposing to take that bold course which Jaikie himself had urged at the Back House of the Garroch, to loose the entangling knot by cutting it. But, strangely enough, Jaikie was now averse to that proposal, for he had come to suspect that business was afoot which made it desirable that Mr. Craw should keep at a distance from Castle Gay.

" That's a pretty good score for *you*," he said.

" What do you mean ? It's an outrage. It must be at once repudiated."

" The *Wire* has been hoaxed. You've got them in your hand. They'll have to eat humble pie. But I'm blessed if I know how it happened. Tibbets is no fool, and he would not have printed the stuff unless he believed it to be genuine. Who has been pulling his leg ? It can't have been Dougal—he must have known that it was too dangerous."

" I shall find out at Castle Gay."

" There's no need to go there—at least there's no hurry. Telegraph to the *View* telling them to

announce· that the interview in the *Wire* is bogus.
I'll take it round to the office before it closes."

Mr. Craw was in the mood for action. He at
once drafted a telegram, signing it with the code-
word which he employed in emergencies and which
would secure the instant attention of his editor.
Jaikie took it and departed. " Remember to order
a car," Mr. Craw called after him, but got no
reply.

But when he reached the Post Office Jaikie did
not send the telegram as originally drafted. It was
borne in on him that this bogus interview was a disguised blessing. If it went uncontradicted it would
keep Tibbets quiet ; it had changed that menacing
creature from an enemy to an ally. So on his own
responsibility he altered the telegram to " Do not
repudiate *Wire* interview for the moment," and
signed it with Mr. Craw's code-word. That would
prevent any premature disavowal from Castle Gay.

Jaikie dispatched the wire and walked slowly back.
His mind was busy with a problem which each hour
seemed to develop new ramifications.

There was first the question of Sigismund Allins.
Jaikie was firmly resolved that Allins was a rogue,
and his chief evidence was his own instinct. There
was something fishy about the man's behaviour—
his premature and secret return from holiday, his
presence at the Hydropathic under another name,
his association with the strange foreigners. But
above all he remembered Allins's face and manner of
speech, which had inspired him with profound mis-
trust. A hard and a varied life had made Jaikie a

good impressionist judge of character. He remembered few occasions when he had been wrong.

That morning he had reached a conclusion. Mr. Allins—for a consideration—had brought the Evallonians to Knockraw, and had arranged for the announcement of Mr. Craw's journey abroad. He was a gambler, and probably hard up. Mr. Craw's disappearance, if he was aware of it, must have upset his calculations, but that, after all, was the Evallonians' concern : Allins's task had probably only been to get them into Craw's vicinity. There might be a contingent payment due to him if the Evallonians succeeded in their mission, and in that case it was to his interest to further their efforts. But he could scarcely do that at Castle Gay, for his connivance might leak out. No. It was quite clear that Allins had every reason to be absent during their visit.

Why, then, had he returned ? To advise the Evallonians and earn his contingent payment at a safe distance ? That was intelligible enough, though dangerous. There must be people in Portaway who knew him by sight, and a rumour of his arrival might reach Castle Gay. He had not disguised himself, except by posing as a foreigner, and he was walking about brazenly in the streets. . . . The more Jaikie thought about it, the less reason he could find for Allins's return. It was a risk which no discreet blackguard would take, and he believed Allins to be discreet. No, there must be some overmastering motive which he could not guess at.

His mind turned to the foreigners at the Hydro-

16

pathic. Were they Evallonians, a reserve summoned
to wait in the background ? Jaikie regretted that
his ignorance of foreign tongues had prevented his
identifying their speech. He could think of no
reason for their presence. The business was very
secret, and did not require numbers. The three
plenipotentiaries at Knockraw were abundantly
adequate. . . . They had behaved oddly, too. Allins
and another had visited the station and witnessed
the arrival of a visitor for Knockraw. They had not
spoken to him or to the Knockraw chauffeur, and
the visitor had left in a mighty hurry, as if anxious
to be unobserved. But the sight of him had put
Allins and his friend into a state of considerable
excitement. He remembered their eager talk at
the Hydropathic door.

His reflections came to a sudden halt, for an idea
had struck him, an idea so startling that for the
moment he could not compass it. He needed more
information. The last part of his return journey
was almost a canter.

He found Mr. Craw still fuming over the *Wire*.

" I didn't send your telegram," he said. " As
long as the interview goes unrepudiated it will keep
Tibbets quiet, so I think we'd better let it alone for
a day or two."

Mr. Craw disregarded this act of indiscipline.

" Have you ordered a car ? " he asked crossly.

Jaikie pulled a chair up to the small fire, which
had been lit by his order, and regarded his companion seriously.

" I don't think you should go back to Castle

Gay to-night," he said. " You'll only fall into the thick of that Evallonian mess. Perhaps Barbon and Dougal have got it settled, and it would be a pity to spoil their game. By eleven o'clock to-morrow morning we'll know the position, and I think that you should wait at least till then. There's no need to hurry. You've got the *Wire* in a cleft stick."

Mr. Craw's ire was slightly ebbing.

" I shall not rest," he answered, " till I have run the author to ground and exposed the whole shameful affair. It is the most scandalous breach of the comity of journalism that I have ever heard of."

" I agree. But it won't do you any harm. It will only make the *Wire* look foolish. You don't mean to give them any chance to get back on you through the Evallonian business. Up to now you've won all along the line, for they've had to confess their mistake in their mystery stunt about your disappearance, and soon they'll have to climb down about the interview. Don't spoil your success by being in a hurry."

As I have said, Mr. Craw's first fine rapture of wrath was cooling. He saw the good sense of Jaikie's argument. Truth to tell, he had no desire to face the Evallonians, and he was beginning to see that fortune had indeed delivered his rivals into his hands. He did not answer, but he crumpled the *Wire* and tossed it to Jaikie's side of the fireplace. It was a token of his reluctant submission.

" I want to ask you something," Jaikie continued. " It's about Evallonia."

" I prefer not to discuss that hateful subject."

" I quite understand. But this is really rather important. It's about the Evallonian Republic. What sort of fellows run it ? "

" Men utterly out of tune with the national spirit. Adventurers who owe their place to the injudicious patronage of the Great Powers ! "

" But what kind of adventurers ? Are they the ordinary sort of middle-class republicans that you have, for example, in Germany ? "

" By no means. Very much the contrary. My information is that the present Evallonian Government is honeycombed with Communism. I have evidence that certain of its members have the most sinister relations with Moscow. No doubt they speak fair to foreign Powers, but there is reason to believe that they are only waiting to consolidate their position before setting up an imitation of the Soviet régime. One of their number, Mastrovin, is an avowed Communist, who might turn out a second Bela Kun. That is one of the reasons why Royalism is so living a force in the country. The people realize that it is their only protection against an ultimate anarchy."

" I see." Jaikie tapped his teeth with the nail of his right forefinger, a sure proof that he had got something to think about.

" Have you met any of those fellows ? Mastrovin, for example ? "

" I am glad to say that I have not."

" You know some of the Royalists ? "

" Not personally. I have always in a matter like

this avoided personal contacts. They warp the judgment."

"Who is their leader? I mean, who would sit on the throne if a Royalist revolution succeeded?"

"Prince John, of course."

"What's he like?"

"I never met him. My reports describe him as an exemplary young man, with great personal charm and a high sense of public duty."

"How old?"

"Quite young. Twenty-six or twenty-seven. I have seen his portraits, and they reminded me of our own Prince Charles Edward. He is very fair, for his mother was a Scandinavian Princess."

"I see." Jaikie asked no more questions, for he had got as much information as for the moment he could digest. He picked up the despised *Wire*, straightened it out, and read the famous interview, which before he had only skimmed.

He read it with a solemn face, for he was aware that Mr. Craw's eye was upon him, but he wanted badly to laugh. The thing was magnificent in its way, the idiomatic revelation of a mind at once jovial and cynical. Tibbets could not have invented it all. Where on earth had he got his material?

One passage especially caught his notice.

"*I asked him, a little timidly, if he did not think it rash to run counter to the spirit of the age.*

"*In reply Mr. Craw relapsed smilingly into the homely idiom of the countryside. 'The Spirit of the Age!' he cried. 'That's a thing I wouldn't give a docken for.'*"

Jaikie was a little startled. He knew some one who was in the habit of refusing to give dockens for things he despised. But that some one had never heard of Tibbets or Castle Gay, and was far away in his modest home of Blaweary.

That day the two travellers escaped from the tyranny of ham and eggs. They ate an excellent plain dinner, cooked especially for them by Mrs. Fairweather. Then came the question of how to spend the rest of the evening. Mr. Craw was obviously unsettled, and apparently had no desire to cover foolscap in his bedroom, while the mystery afoot in Portaway made Jaikie anxious to make further explorations in the town. The polling was only a few days off, and there was that ferment in the air which accompanies an election. Jaikie proposed a brief inquisition into the politics of the place, and Mr. Craw consented.

A country town after dark has a more vivid life than a great city, because that life is more concentrated. There is no business quarter to become a sepulchre after business hours, since the domestic and the commercial are intermingled. A shopkeeper puts up his shutters, has his supper upstairs, and presently descends to join a group on the pavement or in a neighbouring bar parlour. The children do not seem to retire early to bed, but continue their games around the lamp-posts. There are still country carts by the kerbs, stray sheep and cattle are still moving countrywards from the market, and long-striding shepherds butt their way through the crowd. There is a pleasant smell of cooking about, and a hum of compact and contented life. Add the excitement of an election, and you have that busy burghal hive which is the basis of all human society —a snug little commune intent on its own affairs, a world which for the moment owes allegiance to no other.

It was a fine evening, setting to a mild frost, when Jaikie and Mr. Craw descended the Eastgate to the cobbled market-place where stood the Town Hall. There it appeared from gigantic blue posters that the Conservative candidate, one Sir John Cowden, was holding forth, assisted by a minor member of the Government. The respectable burghers now entering the door did not promise much amusement, so the two turned up the Callowa into the oldest part of the old town, which in other days had been a nest of Radical weavers. Here their ears were greeted by the bray of a loud-speaker to which the wives by their house-doors were listening, and, having traced it to its lair, they found a beaky young man announcing the great Liberal Rally to be held that night in the new Drill Hall and to be addressed by the candidate, Mr. Orlando Greenstone, assisted by no less a personage than his leader, the celebrated Mr. Foss Jones.

" Let's go there," said Jaikie. " I have never seen Foss Jones. Have you ? "

" No," was the answer, " but he tried several times to make me a peer."

They had to retrace their steps, cross the Callowa bridge, and enter a region of villas, gardens, and ugly new kirks. There could be no doubt about the attraction of Mr. Foss Jones. The road was thronged with others on the same errand as theirs, and when they reached the Drill Hall they found that it was already crowded to its extreme capacity. An excited gentleman, wearing a yellow rosette, was advising the excluded to go to the hall of a neighbouring church. There an overflow meeting would be held, to which Mr. Foss Jones's speech would be relayed, and the great man himself would visit it and say a word.

Jaikie found at his elbow the mechanic from the Hydropathic called Wilkie.

" I'm no gaun to sit like a deaf man listenin' to an ear trumpet," he was announcing. " Hullo, Mr. Galt ! Weel met ! I was sayin' that it's a puir way to spend your time sittin' in a cauld kirk to the rumblin' o' a tin trumpet. What about a drink ? Or if it's poalitics ye're seekin', let's hear what the Socialists has to say. Their man the nicht is in the Masons' Hall. They say he's no much o' a speaker, but he'll hae a lively crowd aboot him. What d'ye say ? . . . Fine, man. We'll a' gang thegither. . . . Pleased to meet ye, Mr. Carlyle. . . . Ony relation o' Jock Carlyle, the horse-doctor ? "

" Not that I'm aware of," said Mr. Craw sourly. He was annoyed at the liberty taken by Jaikie with his surname, though he realized the reason for it.

To reach the Masons' Hall they had to recross the Callowa and penetrate a mesh of narrow streets east of the market square. The Labour party in Portaway made up for their lack of front-bench oratory by their enthusiasm for their local leaders. Jaikie found himself wedged into a back seat in a hall which was meant perhaps to hold five hundred, and at the moment contained not less than eight. On the platform, seen through a mist of tobacco smoke, sat a number of men in their Sunday clothes and wearing red favours, with a large, square, solemn man, one of the foremen at the Quarries, in the chair. On his right was the Labour candidate, a pleasant-faced youth with curly fair hair, who by the path of an enthusiasm for boys' clubs in the slums had drifted from Conservative pastures into the Socialist fold. He was at present engaged in listening with an appreciative grin to the oratorical efforts of various members of his platform, for that evening's meeting seemed to have been arranged on the anthology principle—a number of short speeches, testifying from different angles to the faith.

" We'll now hear Comrade Erchie Robison," the chairman announced. Comrade Robison rose nervously to his feet, to be received with shouts of " Come awa, Erchie ! Oot wi't, man. Rub their noses in't." But there was no violence in Comrade Erchie, who gave them a dull ten minutes, composed mainly of figures which he read from a penny exercise book. He was followed by Comrade Jimmy Macleish, who was likewise received with favour by the audience and exhorted to " pu' up his breeks and gie them hell." But Jimmy, too, was a wet blanket, confining himself to a dirge-like enunciation of Tory misdeeds in various foreign places, the pronunciation of which gave him pain. " Whaur did ye say that

happened ? " said a voice. " Tchemshooershoo,"
said Jimmy. " Man, there couldna be sic a place.
Ye've got a cauld in your heid, Jimmy," was the
verdict. The only exception to this dismal decorum
was a woman, who had a real gift of scolding rhetoric.
Her theme was " huz puir folk," and she announced
that she came from a " Glesca stair-heid." She was
vigorous and abusive, but she had a voice like a saw,
and five minutes of her were a torment to the ear.

Then the candidate rose. He was elegant, he was
wholesome, and he was young ; he had not made
the mistake of dressing down to his part ; in that
audience of grim faces, worn with toil and weather,
he looked as out of place as a flamingo among crows.
His speech, which he delivered with the fluency born
of frequent repetition, was an emotional appeal for
the under-dog. He deprecated bitterness, he repudiated any intent of violence ; such arguments
as he gave were a plea rather for a change of heart
than a change of the social fabric. He was earnest,
he was eloquent, he was transparently honest, and
there was something in his youthful candour which
attracted his hearers, for his periods were punctuated
with loud applause. But from the man on Jaikie's
right they evoked only heartbroken groans.

Jaikie looked at this neighbour and recognized
him. He was a middle-aged man, with a good deal
of hair and beard plentifully streaked with grey.
His features were regular and delicate, and his whole
air was of breeding and cultivation—all but his eyes,
which were like live coals under his shaggy brows.
His name was David Antrobus, a name once famous

in Latin scholarship, till the War suddenly switched
his attention violently on to public affairs. He had
been a militant pacifist, and had twice gone to gaol
for preaching treason. In 1920 he had visited Russia
and had returned a devout votary of Lenin, whose
mission it was to put alcohol into the skim milk of
British Socialism. In Glasgow he was known as
Red Davie, and Jaikie had met him there in Dougal's
company, when he had been acutely interested to
hear a creed of naked nihilism expounded in accents
of the most scholarly precision. He had met him
in Cambridge, too, the preceding term. Mr. Antrobus
had been invited to lecture to a group of young
iconoclasts, and Jaikie, in company with certain
Rugby notables, had attended. There had been a
considerable row, and Jaikie, misliking the manner
of Mr. Antrobus's opponents, had, along with his
friends, entered joyfully into the strife, and had
helped to conduct the speaker safely to his hotel and
next morning to the station.

The man returned Jaikie's glance, and there was
recognition in his eyes. " Mr. Galt, isn't it ? " he
asked. " I am very glad to see you again. Have
you come to spy out the nakedness of the land ? "

" I came to be amused," was the answer. " I
have no politics."

" Amused ! " said Mr. Antrobus. " That is the
right word. This man calls himself a Socialist
candidate, but his stuff is the merest bleating of the
scared bourgeois sheep. Evils, for which the only
remedy is blood and steel and the extreme rigour
of thought, he would cure with a penny bun."

" Are you here to help him ? "

" I am here to break him," was the grim answer.
" My business is to hunt down that type of humbug
and keep it out of Parliament. Answer me. Would
it not terrify you to think that such a thing as that
was fighting *beside you* in the day of battle ? His
place is among our enemies, to be food for our
powder."

Mr. Antrobus would have said more, but his
attention was distracted by the neighbour on his
other side, who asked him a question. He bent his
head deferentially to listen, and over the back of it
Jaikie saw the strong profile and the heavy jaw of
the man whom a few hours before he had observed
with Allins at the Hydropathic door.

There was a short colloquy between the two, and
then Mr. Antrobus inclined again towards Jaikie.
The man was courtesy incarnate, and he seemed to
think that the debt he owed Jaikie for his escape at
Cambridge must be paid by a full confession of faith.
He enlarged on the folly of British Socialism, the
ineptitude and dishonesty of official Labour. " Tory-
ism," he said, " is our enemy—a formidable enemy.
We respect it and some day will slay it. Liberalism
is an antique which we contemptuously kick out of
the road. But Labour is treason, treason to our
own cause, and its leaders will have the reward of
traitors."

Jaikie put his mouth close to his ear : " Who is the
man on your right ? " he asked. " I fancy I have
seen him before."

" Abroad ? "

" Abroad," Jaikie mendaciously agreed.

" It must have been abroad, for this is his first visit to Britain. It would not do to advertise his name, for he is travelling incognito. But to you I can tell it, for I can trust you. He is a very great man, one of the greatest living. Some day soon all the world will ring with his deeds. To me he is an old friend whom I visit several times each year for counsel and inspiration. He is the great Anton Mastrovin. You have heard of him ? "

" Yes. And I must have seen him—perhaps in Vienna. One does not easily forget that face."

" It is the face of a maker of revolutions," said Mr. Antrobus reverentially.

But at that moment the great man rose, having no doubt had enough, and Mr. Antrobus docilely followed him. Jaikie sat tight through the rest of the candidate's speech, and did not squeeze out till the proposing of the resolutions began. But it may be assumed that he did not pay very strict attention to the candidate's ingenious attempt to identify the latest Labour programme with the Sermon on the Mount. He had something more urgent to think about.

CHAPTER XIV

PORTAWAY—ALISON

JAIKIE rose next morning with the light of a stern
purpose in his eye. He had thought a good deal
about his troubles before he fell asleep, and had
come to certain conclusions. . . . But he must go
cannily with Mr. Craw. That gentleman was in an
uncomfortable humour, and at breakfast showed
every sign of being in a bad temper. The publica-
tion of Tibbets's interview had roused a very natural
wrath, and, though he had apparently acquiesced in
Jaikie's refusal to send his telegram or transport
him to Castle Gay, his aspect had been rebellious.
At breakfast he refused to talk of the Labour meeting the night before, except to remark that such
folly made him sick. Jaikie forbore to disclose his
main suspicion. The news of other Evallonians in
the field, Evallonians of a darker hue than those at
Knockraw, would only scare him, and Jaikie preferred an indignant Craw to a panicky one.

Yet it was very necessary to smooth him down, so
after breakfast Jaikie and Woolworth went out into
the street. At a newsagent's he bought a copy of
that morning's *View*, and to his relief observed that
Mr. Craw's article was on the leader page. There it

was, with half-inch headlines—*The Abiding Human Instincts*. That would keep him quiet for a little. He also visited a chemist and purchased two small bottles.

Mr. Craw seized avidly on the paper, and a glimmer of satisfaction returned to his face. Jaikie took advantage of it.

"Mr. Craw," he said with some nervousness, "I found out some queer things yesterday, which I'll tell you when I'm a little more certain about them. But one thing I can tell you now. Your man Allins is a crook."

Mr. Craw raised his head from toothing his own eloquence.

"Stuff and nonsense! What evidence have you?"

"A great deal. Allins has come back mysteriously when he wasn't expected : he has not gone near Castle Gay : he is at the Hydropathic here under an assumed name, passing as a foreigner : and he is spending his time with the very foreigners who are giving you trouble. Isn't that enough?"

Mr. Craw looked perturbed. At the moment he had a healthy dislike of Jaikie, but he believed him to be honest.

"Are you sure of that?"

"Absolutely sure. I suspect a great deal more, but what I'm giving you is rock-bottom fact. . . . Now, it's desperately important that Allins shouldn't recognize you. You can see for yourself how that would put the lid on it. So I don't want you to go much about in the daytime. You can stay

here and write another of your grand articles. I
hope to get money and clothes for you to-day, and
then you can carry out your original plan. . . .
Would you mind if, just for extra security, I touched
up your face a little ? You see, in these clothes
even Allins wouldn't recognize you, especially with
the fine complexion the weather has given you.
But when you get your proper clothes from Castle
Gay it will be different, and we can't afford to run
any risks."

It took a good deal of coaxing for Jaikie to
accomplish his purpose, but the reading of his own
article, and the near prospect of getting his own
garments, had mollified Mr. Craw, and in the end he
submitted.

Jaikie, who as a member of the Cambridge A.D.C.
knew something about making up, did not overdo
it. He slightly deepened Mr. Craw's complexion,
turning it from a weather-beaten red to something
like a gipsy brown, and he took special pains with
the wrists and hands, and the tracts behind the
ears. He darkened his greying eyebrows and the
fringe of hair which enclosed his baldness. But
especially he made the lines deeper from the nose to
the corner of the mouth, and at the extremity of the
eyes. The result was that he did away with the air
of Pickwickian benevolence. Mr. Craw, when he
looked at himself in the mirror, saw a man not more
than forty, a hard man who might have been a
horse-coper or a cattle-dealer, with a good deal of
cynicism in his soul and his temper very ready to
his hand—which was exactly how he felt. Short of

a tropical deluge to wash off the stain, it would not be easy to recognize the bland lineaments which at that moment were confronting the world from the centre of his article in the *View*.

This done, Jaikie proceeded to reconnoitre. He was convinced that Alison would answer his summons and come at eleven o'clock to the Green Tree. He was equally convinced that she would not ask for him, so it was his duty to be ready for her arrival. He found that from the staircase window he had a view of the stable yard and the back door of the inn, and there he set himself to watch for her.

At two minutes before eleven a girl on a pony rode into the yard. He saw her fling her bridle to the solitary stable-boy, and be welcomed by Mrs. Fairweather like a long-lost child. She talked to the hostess for a minute or two, while her eyes ran over the adjacent windows. Then she turned, and with a wave of her hand, walked towards the street.

Jaikie snatched his hat and followed. He saw her moving towards the Eastgate—a trim figure, booted and spurred, wearing a loose grey coat and a grey felt hat with a kestrel's feather. She never looked behind her, but walked with a purposeful air, crossed the Eastgate, and took a left-hand turning towards the Callowa. Then at last she turned her head, saw Jaikie, and waited for him. There was a frank welcome in her eyes. Jaikie, who for the last few days had been trying to picture them in his mind, realized that he had got them all wrong ; they were not bright and hard, but of the

17

profound blue that one finds in water which reflects a spring sky.

" I've brought the money," she said. " Fifty pounds. I got it from Freddy." And she handed over a wad of notes.

" And the clothes ? "

" Mother of Moses, I forgot the clothes ! They can't really matter. What does Mr. Craw want with more clothes ? "

" He is wearing some pretty queer ones at present. And he wants to go to London."

" But he mustn't be allowed to go to London. You said yourself that he was safest under the light —here or hereabouts. London would be horribly dangerous."

" Of course it would. I don't want him to go to London. I'm glad you forgot the clothes."

" Where is he ? "

" Sitting in his room at the Green Tree reading an article he's written in the *View*. He's getting rather difficult to manage."

" You must keep him there—lock him up, if necessary—for I can tell you that things at Castle Gay are in a pretty mess."

She paused to laugh merrily.

" I don't know where to begin. Well, first of all, Dougal—Mr. Crombie—imported a friend of his on Sunday from somewhere in Carrick. His name is Dickson McCunn, and he's the world's darling, but what use Dougal thought he was going to be is beyond me. There was rather a mishap at Knock-raw—your friend Tibbets got locked up as a poacher

—and Count Casimir was in an awful stew, and sent him over to us to be pacified. Mr. McCunn received him, and Tibbets took him for Mr. Craw, and wrote down what he said, and published it in an interview in yesterday's *Wire*. Dougal says that the things he said pretty well knock the bottom out of Mr. Craw's public form."

" So that was it," said Jaikie. " I very nearly guessed that it was Dickson. Mr. Craw didn't like it, but I persuaded him not to get his papers to repudiate it. You see, it rather wipes off Tibbets from our list of enemies."

" Just what I said," replied the girl. " Freddy wanted to wire at once about it, but I stopped him. We can disavow it later when we're out of this mess. . . . Now for the second snag. Count Casimir has also imported an ally, and who do you think it is ? Prince John of Evallonia."

No exclamation could have done justice to Jaikie's emotion. In a flash he saw the explanation he had been fumbling after. But all he said was, " Whatever for ? "

" Heaven knows ! To impress Mr. Craw when they find him. To impress us all. Perhaps to make me fall in love with him. They seem to think I'm rather an important person."

" Have you seen him ? "

" Yes. We all dined at Knockraw last night. The Prince is an agreeable young man, as tall as Robin Charvill, but much slimmer."

" Handsome ? " Jaikie asked with a pang at his heart.

" Extremely. Like an elegant Viking, says Freddy, who doesn't know anything about Vikings. Like the Young Pretender, says Aunt Hatty."

" Have you fallen in love with him ? " The words had not passed his lips before Jaikie repented his audacity.

But the girl only laughed. " Not a bit of it. I'm not attracted by film stars. He's terribly good-looking, but he's as dull as an owl. I can see that he's going to add considerably to our troubles, for he seems quite content to settle down at Knockraw till he can bring his charms to bear on Mr. Craw."

" We must get him shifted out of that," said Jaikie grimly. " Now you must hear my story. First of all, that man Allins is a blackguard."

He recounted briefly the incidents of the past days, dwelling lightly on their travels in the hills, but more fully on the events since their coming to Portaway. The girl listened with widening eyes.

" You see how it is," he concluded. " Allins has double-crossed the people at Knockraw. He arranged for their coming here to see Mr. Craw, and no doubt got paid for it. That in itself was pretty fair disloyalty to his chief. But he has arranged with the Republicans to catch the Royalists at work, and with their Prince there, too. He must have suspected that they would play the Prince as their trump card. No wonder he was excited when he saw who arrived at the station last night. It'll be jam for the Republicans to find their enemies in the act of plotting with a magnate of the British Press. The Royalists will be blown out of the water—and also Mr. Craw. I can tell you the Republicans at the Hydropathic are not innocents, such as you describe the people at Knockraw. They're real hard citizens, and they mean business. They've got a man among them who is the toughest Communist in Europe."

The girl twined her hands. " Jaikie," she said, " things are getting deliciously exciting. What shall we do next ? "

He thrilled at the Christian name.

" There's only you and I that can do anything. The first thing is to get Casimir and his friends away from Knockraw."

" That won't be easy. They're feeling too comfortable. You see, they've made a devout ally of Mr. McCunn. Dougal brought him to Castle Gay because he thought he would talk sense to them— he said he was a typical Briton and would soon convince them that Britain wasn't interested in their plans. Instead of that he has fallen completely under the spell of the Prince. He would talk about nothing else last night coming home—said it was a sin and a shame that such a fine lad should be kept from his rights by a wheen blue-spectacled dominies." She gave a very good imitation of Dickson's robust accents.

" Just what he'd do. He was always desperately romantic. I think Dougal must have taken leave of his senses. What does Dougal say about things ? "

" Chiefly oaths," said the girl. " He argues with Casimir and the Professor, and makes no more impression than a toothpick on a brick wall. You

might say that the situation at Castle Gay was out
of hand. The question is, what are you and I
going to do?"

The assumption of alliance warmed Jaikie's heart.

"I must get somehow to Knockraw," he said.
"It had better be to-morrow morning early. There
are six of the Republicans here, and this election
has brought some queer characters into the town.
You may be certain that they're keeping a pretty
good watch up the water. The first thing to make
sure of is that the Prince does not stir out of doors.
You must get Casimir on the telephone and put the
fear of God into him about that. Pitch it high
enough to scare him. . . . Then you must meet me
at Knockraw to-morrow morning. Say eight o'clock.
I can tell them all I know, and there's a lot they can
tell me that I don't know. But they won't believe
me unless you're there to back me up."

He looked down to find a small dog standing on
its hind legs with its paws on his arm.

"What's that?" Alison asked.

"That's Woolworth—the terrier I bought from
the drover. I told you about him."

The girl bent to fondle the dog's head, upon
which Woolworth laid muddy paws on the skirts
of her coat. "He must be introduced to Tactful
and Pensive," she said. "He seems to belong to
the same school of thought. . . . I had better get
back at once and alarm Knockraw. . . . It's all
right. I usually leave my pony at the Green Tree,
so there's nothing unusual in my going there. But
we'd better not arrive together."

Jaikie, unwilling to leave her side, accompanied her as far as the Eastgate. But just before they reached it, he stopped short and whistled on Woolworth. He had seen Allins advancing towards them, and Allins had seen the girl. Apparently Allins desired to avoid a meeting, for he turned sharply and dived up a side street.

" What is it ? " said Alison, who had been interrupted in the middle of a sentence.

" It's Allins. He saw us both. That's a pity. He and I are bound to have a meeting sooner or later, and I didn't want him to connect me with Castle Gay."

It was significant of Jaikie's state of mind that, though he allowed five minutes to elapse between Alison's entering the stable yard and his own approach to the inn, the first thing he did when he was inside the door was to rush to the staircase window, where he was rewarded by the sight of a slim figure on a black pony leaving the gate, pursued by Mrs. Fairweather's farewells.

As luck would have it, the rain began after luncheon, and there was no temptation for Mr. Craw to go out of doors. A fire was again lit in his bedroom, and Jaikie sought a bookseller's and purchased him a selection of cheap reprints of the English classics, a gift which was received without gratitude.

" I have got fifty pounds for you," he told him. " I saw Miss Westwater this morning."

Mr. Craw showed little interest. The mild satisfaction due to reading and re-reading his own article had ebbed, and he was clearly in a difficult temper.

" But she forgot to bring the clothes. I'm so sorry, Mr. Craw, but I'm afraid you can't go to London to-night."

" I have no intention of going to London to-night," was the cold answer.

Jaikie regarded him curiously. He thought he realized the reason for this change of purpose. The interview had awakened some long-dormant spirit in Mr. Craw. He felt that he was being taken advantage of, that his household gods and his inner personality were being outraged, and he was determined to fight for them. That would have been all to the good four days ago, but now it was the very deuce. Jaikie did not dare to tell him the true story of the interview: the thought of Dickson, innocently masquerading as his august self, would only infuriate him. What he wanted was to get back to Castle Gay, and that at all costs must be prevented. So Jaikie imparted a little judicious information.

" I heard from Miss Westwater that Prince John of Evallonia arrived at Knockraw last night. They all went to dinner there to meet him."

" Good God ! " exclaimed Mr. Craw. He was startled at last out of his dumps. " That is a terrible blunder—a terrible calamity. They won't be able to keep his visit secret. I shall be credited——" His eyes told the kind of unpleasant thing with which he would be credited.

" Cheer up, sir," said Jaikie. " We'll find a way

out. But you see how impossible it is for you to go to Castle Gay. . . . And how important it is that nobody should recognize you here. . . . If all goes well, you can disavow the interview, and the world will think you have been all the time out of the country."

Mr. Craw said nothing. He had started morosely upon the Essays of Addison, and the big glasses adorning his weather-beaten face gave him the air of a pious bookmaker.

Jaikie went out into the rain and made a few calls. He visited the lounge of the Station Hotel in the hope of finding a thirsty Evallonian comforting himself after the drought of the Hydropathic. But he found nobody there except a stray bagman and one or two rainbound golfers. Then he proceeded to the Hydropathic, where he had a few words with the head-porter. The foreigners were all abroad ; they had departed after breakfast in two cars ; whither the deponent did not know. Their habits ? Well, there was always one or two of them on the road. The young man seemed to spend a lot of time in the town, and Wilkie had reported that he had seen him with some queer-looking folk. " He's maybe a poalitician," he added. " There's a heap o' that trash in Portaway the noo."

Jaikie penetrated to the back parts of the establishment, and found Wilkie in the boiler-house, too much occupied to talk.

" Yon was a dreich show last night, Mr. Galt," was all he found time to say. " I've tried a' three pairties and there's no ane to mend the ither. My faither used to say that in the auld days an election in Portaway was one lang, bluidy battalation. This time I don't believe there'll be a single broken heid. Folks nowadays hae lost a' spunk and pith. There's twa-three Communists in the town, and there's plenty of them among the lads at the Quarries. Maybe they'll brichten up things afore the polling-day."

" When is that ? " Jaikie asked, and was told " Friday." " It'll be a big day in Portaway," Wilkie added, " for, forby being the nicht o' the poll, it's the Callowa Club Ball. Fancy dress, nae less. It used to be in the auld Assembly Rooms, but that's a furniture depository noo, so they haud it in the big room at the Station Hotel. I've seen fifty cairriages and pairs in Portaway that nicht, but noo it's a' motors."

Jaikie returned about tea-time, to find that Mr. Craw had fallen asleep over Addison. Mercifully he slept for several hours, and awoke in a better temper, and, having had no tea, with a considerable appetite for dinner. He must be given air and exercise, so, after that meal, the rain having ceased, Jaikie proposed a saunter in the town. Mr. Craw consented. " But I will go to no more political meetings," he said. " I am not interested in this local dog-fight."

It was a fresh night, with a south-west wind drifting cloud galleons up from the Solway. They walked down the Callowa side, along the miniature quays, till they were almost outside the town limits, and could see dimly, beyond the last houses, the wide *machars* which stretched to the salt water and gave Portaway its famous golf course. Presently one of the causes of Mr. Craw's oppression became evident. He had caught a cold. He sneezed repeatedly, and admitted, in reply to Jaikie's anxious inquiries, that he had a rawness in the back of his throat and a congested feeling in his head.

" This won't do," said Jaikie. " I'm going to take you straight home and put you to bed. But first we'll stop at a chemist's and get you a dose of ammoniated quinine. That generally cures my colds, if I take it at the start."

They returned to the foot of the Eastgate, just where it joined the market square, and at the corner found a chemist's shop. The owner was about to put up his shutters, but the place had still the dazzling brightness which is associated with the sale of drugs. Mr. Craw was accommodated with a small beaker of the bitter compound prescribed by Jaikie, and, as he swallowed it with many grimaces, Jaikie saw a face at the street door looking in on him. It was the face of Allins.

Mr. Craw saw it, too, in the middle of his gasping, and, being taken unawares, it is probable that an involuntary recognition entered his eyes before Jaikie could distract his attention. At any rate Jaikie saw on Allins's face, before it disappeared, an unpleasing smile.

He paid for the mixture and hustled Mr. Craw out of the shop. Allins did not appear to be in the immediate neighbourhood. " You saw that ? " he whispered. " I believe he recognized you. We've

got to give him the slip. Very likely he's watching us."

Mr. Craw, nervous and flustered, found himself
hurried up the Eastgate, to the right, to the left, to
the left again—it was like the erratic course of a
bolted rabbit. Twice Jaikie stopped, darted into
the middle of the street, and looked behind. The
third time he did this he took his companion's arm
and dragged him into a run. "The man's following
us," he said.

At all costs the pursuit must be baffled, for till
they had thrown it off it was impossible to return
to their inn. Once again Jaikie stopped to reconnoitre, and once again his report was bad. "I see
his grey hat. He's not above twenty yards behind."

Suddenly they found that the people were thicker
on the pavement. There was some kind of movement towards a close on their left, as if it led to a
meeting. Jaikie resolved to take the chance. Allins
would never think they would go indoors, he argued,
for that would be to enter a trap. He would follow
on past the close mouth, and lose their trail.

He drove Mr. Craw before him into a narrow
passage, which was pretty well crowded. Then
they entered a door, and started to climb a long
stair. The meeting, whatever it was, was at the
top of it. It took them some minutes to get up,
and at the top, at the door of the hall, Jaikie looked
back. . . . To his disgust he saw the hat of Allins
among the throng at the bottom.

It was Jaikie's rule, when cornered at football
or anything else, to play the boldest game, on the

theory that it was what his opponent would least
expect. The hall was not large, and it was very
full, but at the far end was a platform which still
held some vacant seats. In the chair was Red
Davie, now engaged in making introductory remarks. In an instant Jaikie had come to a decision.
It was impossible to prevent Allins in that narrow
hall seeing Mr. Craw at close quarters. But he
must not have speech with him, and he must see
him under circumstances utterly foreign to his past
life. This latter was the essence of true bluff. So
he marched him boldly up the central passage and
ascended the platform, where he saw two seats empty
behind the chairman. He interrupted Red Davie
to shake hands effusively, and to introduce Mr.
Craw. " My friend, Mr. Carlyle," he said. " He's
one of you. Red hot."

Red Davie, in his gentle earnest voice and his
precise scholarly accents, was delivering a reasoned
denunciation of civilized society. He was the
chairman, but he was obviously not the principal
speaker. Jaikie asked in a whisper of a man
behind him who was expected, and was told Alec
Stubber, a name to conjure with. " But his train's
late and he'll no be here for twenty minutes. They'll
be gey sick o' Antrobus or then."

Jaikie looked down on the upturned faces. He
saw Allins standing at the back of the hall near
the door, with his eyes fixed on the platform and
a half-smile on his face. Was that smile one of
recognition or bewilderment? Happily Mr. Craw
was well hidden by the chairman. . . . He saw row

upon row of faces, shaven and bearded, young and
old, but mostly middle-aged. These were the Communists of the Canonry, and very respectable folk
they looked. The Scottish Communist is a much
misunderstood person. When he is a true Caledonian, and not a Pole or an Irishman, he is simply
the lineal descendant of the old Radical. The Scottish Radical was a man who held a set of inviolable
principles on which he was entirely unable to compromise. It did not matter what the principles
were ; the point was that they were like the laws of
Sinai, which could not be added to or subtracted
from. When the Liberal party began to compromise, he joined Labour ; when Labour began to
compromise, by a natural transition he became a
Communist. Temperamentally he has not changed.
He is simply the stuff which in the seventeenth
century made the unyielding Covenanter, and in the
eighteenth the inflexible Jacobite. He is honesty
incarnate, but his mind lacks flexibility.

It was an audience which respected Red Davie,
but could not make much of him, and Red Davie
felt it himself. The crowd had come to hear Alec
Stubber, and was growing a little restless. The
chairman looked repeatedly at his watch, and his
remarks became more and more staccato. . . .
Allins had moved so that he now had a full view of
Mr. Craw, and his eyes never left him.

Then Jaikie had an inspiration. He whispered
fiercely to his neighbour : " Allins is watching you.
There's only one way to put him off the scent.
You've got to speak. . . . Denounce the Labour

party as you've often done in the papers. Point
out that their principles lead logically to Communism. . . . And, for God's sake, speak as broad
as you can. You must. It's the only way."

Mr. Craw would certainly have refused, but he
was given no time. Jaikie plucked the chairman's
elbow. " My friend here," he whispered, " could
carry on for a little. He'd be glad of the chance.
He's from Aberdeen, and a great worker in the
cause."

Red Davie caught at the straw. " Before Comrade Stubber arrives," he said, " and that must be
in a very few minutes, you will have the privilege
of hearing a few words from Comrade Carroll, who
brings to us the fraternal greetings of our Aberdeen comrades. No man in recent years has worked
more assiduously for the triumph of the proletariat
in that unpromising quarter of Scotland. I call on
Comrade Carroll."

He turned round, beamed on Mr. Craw, and sat
down.

It was perhaps the most difficult moment of that
great man's life. Crisis had come upon him red-
handed. He knew himself for one of the worst
speakers in the world, and he—he who had always
had a bodyguard to shield him from rough things—
who was the most famous living defender of the
status quo—was called upon to urge its abolition, to
address as an anarchist a convention of anarchs.
His heart fluttered like a bird, he had a dreadful
void in the pit of his stomach, his legs seemed to
be made of cotton-wool.

Yet Mr. Craw got to his feet. Mr. Craw opened his mouth and sounds came forth. The audience listened.

More—Mr. Craw said the right things. His first sentences were confused and stuttering, and then he picked up some kind of argument. He had often in the *View* proved with unassailable logic that the principles of Socialism were only half-hearted Communism. He proved it now, but with a difference. For by some strange inspiration he remembered in what company he was, and, whereas in the *View* he had made it his complaint against Labour that it was on the logical road to an abyss called Communism, his charge now was that Labour had not the courage of its principles to advance the further stage to the Communist paradise. . . . It was not a good speech, for it was delivered in a strange abstracted voice, as if the speaker were drawing up thoughts from a very deep well. But it was not ill received. Indeed, some of its apophthegms were mildly applauded.

Moreover, it was delivered in the right accent. Jaikie's injunction to " speak broad " was unconsciously followed. For Mr. Craw had not lifted up his voice in public for more than thirty years, not since those student days at Edinburgh, when he had been destined for the ministry and had striven to acquire the arts of oratory. Some chord of memory awoke. He spoke broadly, because in public he had never spoken in any other way. Gone were the refinements of his later days, the clipped vowels, the slurred consonants. The voice which was speaking at Jaikie's ear had the aboriginal plaint of the kingdom of Fife.

Jaikie, amazed, relieved, delighted, watched Allins, and saw the smile fade from his face. This being who stammered a crude Communism in the vernacular was not the man he suspected. He shrugged his shoulders and jostled his way out of the hall.

As he left, another arrived. Jaikie saw a short square man in a bowler hat and a mackintosh enter and push his way up the middle passage. An exclamation from the chairman, and the applause of the meeting, told him that the great Stubber had appeared at last. Mr. Craw, in deference to a tug from Jaikie, sat down, attended by an ovation which was not meant for his efforts.

The two sat out that meeting to its end, and heard many remarkable things from Comrade Stubber, but Jaikie hurried Mr. Craw away before he could be questioned as to the progress of Communism in Aberdeen. He raced him back to the Green Tree, and procured from Mrs. Fairweather a tumbler of hot whisky and water, which he forced him to drink. Then he paid his tribute.

" Mr. Craw," he said, " you did one of the bravest things to-night that I ever heard of. It was our only chance, but there's not one man in a million could have taken it. You're a great man. I offer you my humble congratulations."

Mr. Craw blushed like a boy. " It was rather a dreadful experience," he said, " but it seems to have cured my cold."

CHAPTER XV

DISAPPEARANCE OF MR. CRAW

NEXT morning Jaikie arose at six, and having begged of an early-rising maid a piece of oatcake and two lumps of sugar (a confection to which he was partial), set out on foot for Knockraw. He proposed to make part of his route across country, for he had an idea that the roads in that vicinity, even thus early in the morning, might be under observation.

Mr. Craw descended at half-past eight to find a pencilled message from Jaikie saying that he would be absent till luncheon and begging him to keep indoors. Mr. Craw scarcely regarded it. He had slept like a top, he ate a hearty breakfast, and all the time he kept talking to himself. For he was being keyed up to a great resolution.

A change had come over him in these last days, and he was slowly becoming conscious of its magnitude. At the Back House of the Garroch he had been perplexed and scared, and had felt himself the undeserving sport of Fortune. His one idea had been to hide himself from Fortune's notice till such time as she changed her mind. His temper had been that of the peevish hare.

But the interview in the *Wire* had kindled his wrath—a new experience for one who for so long had been sheltered from small annoyances. And with that kindling had come unrest, a feeling that he himself must act, else all that he had built might crumble away. He felt a sinking of the foundations under him which made passivity mere folly. Even his personality seemed threatened. Till that accursed interview was disowned, the carefully constructed figure which he had hitherto presented to the world was distorted and awry. . . . And at the very moment when he had it in his power to magnify it ! Never, he told himself, had his mind been more fruitful than during the recent days. That article in yesterday's *View* was the best he had written for years.

Following upon this restlessness had come a sudden self-confidence. Last night he had attempted an incredibly difficult thing and brought it off. He marvelled at his own courage. Jaikie (whom at the moment he heartily detested) had admitted that he had been very brave. . . . Not the only occasion, either. He had endured discomfort uncomplainingly—he had assisted to eject a great hulking bully from a public-house. He realized that if any one had prophesied the least of these doings a week ago he would have laughed incredulously. . . . There were unexpected deeps in him. He was a greater man than he had dreamt, and the time had come to show it. Fragments of Jaikie's talk at the Back House of the Garroch returned to his mind as if they had been his own

inspiration. " You can carry things with a high
hand." . . . " Sit down in your own house and be
master there." . . . " If they turn nasty, tell them
to go to the devil." That was precisely what he
must do—send his various enemies with a stout heart
to the devil.

He particularly wanted to send Allins there.
Allins was the second thing that broke his temper.
That a man whom he had petted and favoured and
trusted should go back on him was more than he
could endure. He now believed whole-heartedly
in Jaikie's suspicions. Mr. Craw had a strong sense
of decency, and Allins's behaviour had outraged it
to its core. He had an unregenerate longing to
buffet his former secretary about the face.

His mind was made up. He would leave Portaway forthwith and hurl himself into the strife. . . .
The day of panic was over and that of action had
dawned. . . . But where exactly should he join the
battle-front ? . . . Knockraw was out of the question. . . . Castle Gay ? That was his ultimate
destination, but should it be the first ? Jaikie had
said truly that Barbon and Dougal might have got
things well in train, and, if so, it would be a pity to
spoil their plans. Besides, Castle Gay would be the
objective of his new enemies, that other brand of
Evallonian at which Jaikie had hinted. Better to
avoid Castle Gay till he had learned the exact lie of
the land. . . . The place for him was the Mains.
Mrs. Brisbane-Brown, whom he had always respected,
lived there ; she knew all about his difficulties ; so
did her niece, who was one of Jaikie's allies. The

high-nosed gentility of the Mains seemed in itself a protection. He felt that none of the troubles of a vulgar modern world could penetrate its antique defences.

So with some dregs of timidity still in his heart, but on the whole with a brisk resolution, he left the inn. The wet south-west wind, now grown to half a gale, was blowing up the street. Mr. Craw turned up the collar of his thin raincoat, and, having discarded long ago his malacca cane, bought a hazel stick for a shilling in a tobacconist's shop. This purchase revealed the fact that the total wealth now borne in his purse was five shillings and threepence. He was not certain of his road, but he knew that if he kept up the right bank of the Callowa he would reach in time the village of Starr. So he crossed the bridge, and by way of villas and gas-works came into open country.

Knockraw is seven miles from Portaway as the crow flies, and after the first two miles Jaikie took the route of the crow. It led him by the skirts of great woods on to a high moorish ridge, which had one supreme advantage in that it commanded at a distance large tracts of the highway. But that highway was deserted, except for a solitary Ford van. Jaikie had reached the edge of the Knockraw policies, and the hour was a quarter to eight, before he saw what he expected.

This was a car drawn up in the shelter of a fir wood—an aged car with a disreputable hood, which no doubt belonged to some humble Portaway garage.

What was it doing there so early in the morning ?
It stood in a narrow side-road in which there could
be little traffic, but it stood also at a view-point. . . .
Jaikie skirted the little park till he reached the slope
of Knockraw Hill, and came down on the back of
the house much as the luckless Tibbets had done on
the previous Saturday night.　He observed another
strange thing.　There was a wood-cutter's road up
the hill among the stumps of larches felled in the
War, the kind of road where the ruts are deep and
the middle green grass.　It was not a place where a
sane man would take a car except for urgent reasons.
Yet Jaikie saw a car moving up that road, not a
decayed shandrydan like the other, but a new and
powerful car.　It stopped at a point which commanded the front door and the main entrance to the
house.　It could watch unperceived, for it was not
in view from below, it was far from any of the roads
to the grouse moor, and there were no woodmen at
work.

Jaikie made an inconspicuous entrance, dropping
into the sunk area behind the kitchen, and entering
by the back door.　To an Evallonian footman, who
in his morning garb looked like an Irish setter, he
explained that he was there by appointment ; and
Jaspar, the butler, who came up at that moment,
apparently expected him.　He was led up a stone
stair, divested of a sopping waterproof, and ushered
into the low-ceilinged, white-panelled dining-room.

In that raw morning hour it was a very cheerful
place.　Alison sat on the arm of a chair by the fire,
with her wet riding-boots stretched out to the blaze.

Opposite her stood a young man in knickerbockers, a tall young man, clean-shaven, with a
small head, a large nose, and smooth fair hair.
Prince Odalchini was making coffee at the table,
and the Professor was studying a barograph.
Casimir, who was attired remarkably in very loud
tweeds and white gaiters, came forward to greet
him.

Alison jumped to her feet. " This is Mr. Galt,
sir, that I told you about," she informed the young
man. Jaikie was presented to him, and made the
kind of bow which he thought might be suitable for
royalty. He shook hands with the others, and then
his eyes strayed involuntarily to Alison. The fire
had flushed her cheeks, and he had the dismal feeling
that it would be starkly impossible for anything
under the age of ninety to avoid falling in love
with her.

They sat down to breakfast, Alison on Prince
John's right hand, while Jaikie sat between Casimir
and the Professor. Jaikie was very hungry, and his
anxieties did not prevent him making an excellent
meal, which Casimir thoughtfully did not interrupt
with questions. One only he asked : " I understand
that Mr. Craw is with you ? You have just left
him ? "

Jaikie was a little startled. Alison must have
given this fact away. A moment's reflection assured
him that it did not matter. With the Knockraw
party the time had come to put all their cards on
the table.

" I left him in bed," he said. " He had a difficult

time last night. We fell in with Allins, and he
thought he recognized Mr. Craw. We took refuge
in a Communist meeting, and Allins followed us. I
knew the chairman, and there was nothing for it
but to get him to ask Mr. Craw to speak. And speak
he did. You never heard anything like it. He
belted the Labour party for not being logical and
taking the next step to Communism, and he did it
in the accents of a Fife bailie. That was enough
to make Allins realize that he was on the wrong
scent."

" How splendid ! " Alison cried. " I never
thought . . ."

" No more did he. His nearest friends wouldn't
recognize him now. He scarcely recognizes himself."

Jaikie spoke only once again during the meal.

" Do you know that this place is watched, sir ? "
he asked Casimir.

" Watched ? " three voices exclaimed as one.

" I came on foot across country," said Jaikie,
" for I expected something of the kind. There's an
old Portaway car in the by-road at the south-west
corner of the park, and there's a brand-new car on
the wood-road up on the hill. Good stands both,
for you'd never notice them, and if you asked
questions they'd be ready with a plausible answer.
We're up against some cleverish people. Has Miss
Westwater told you anything ? "

" Only that Mr. Sigismund Allins is a rascal," said
Casimir. " And that is grave news, for he knows
too much."

Jaikie looked at the four men, the kindly fanatical
eyes of Prince Odalchini, the Professor's heavy
honesty, Casimir's alert, clever face, Prince John's
youthful elegance, and decided that these at any
rate were honest people. Foolish, perhaps, but
high-minded. He was a good judge of the other
thing, having in his short life met much of it.

The table was pushed back, the company made
a circle round the fire, and Jaikie was given a
cigarette out of Prince John's case. The others
preferred cigars.

" We are ready to listen, Mr. Galt," said Casimir.

Jaikie began with a question. " It was Allins
who arranged your visit here ? "

Casimir nodded. " He has been in touch with us
for some time. We regarded him as Mr. Craw's
plenipotentiary. He assured us that very little was
needed to secure Mr. Craw's active support."

" You paid him for his help ? "

" We did not call it payment. There was a gift—
no great amount—simply to cover expenses and atone
for a relinquished holiday."

" Well, the first thing I have to tell you is that
somebody else has paid him more—to put a spoke
in your wheel."

" The present Government in Evallonia ! "

" I suppose so. I will tell you all I know, and
you can draw your own conclusions."

Jaikie related the facts of which we are already
aware, beginning with his first sight of Allins in the
car from Gledmouth on the Sunday evening. When
he came to the party of foreigners at the Hydropathic

he could only describe them according to the account
of the head-porter, for he had not yet seen them.
But, such as it was, his description roused the liveliest
interest in his audience.

" A tall man with a red, pointed beard ! " Casimir
cried. " That can only be Dedekind."

" Or Jovian ? " Prince Odalchini interjected.

" No. I know for certain that Jovian is sick
and has gone to Marienbad. It must be Dedekind.
They have used him before for their dirty work. . . .
And the other—the squat one—that is beyond doubt
the Jew Rosenbaum. I thought he was in America.
The round-faced, spectacled man I do not know—
he might be any one of a dozen. But the youngish
man like a horse-breaker—he is assuredly Ricci.
Your Royal Highness will remember him—he
married the rich American wife. The fifth I take
to be one of Calaman's sons. I heard that one was
well thought of in the secret service."

" There's a sixth," said Jaikie, " whom I have
seen myself. I saw him in Allins's company, and
I saw him at a Labour meeting. He's a short, very
powerful fellow with big glasses and an underhung
jaw that sticks forward. I know his name, too.
He's called Mastrovin."

It was a bombshell of the largest size. " Mastrovin ! " each of them exclaimed. It was as if
a flood of dark memories and fears had been unloosed, and every eye was troubled. " Gracious
God ! " Casimir murmured. " And Ricci and Dedekind in conjunction ! Crime and fanaticism have
indeed joined hands." He leaned over to Prince

John. " I fear that we have brought your Royal
Highness very near to your most deadly enemies."

Then he bowed to Jaikie. " You have given us
news of extreme importance, and we are most deeply
your debtors. If you are to help us—and I think
you desire to—it is necessary that you should understand the situation. . . . The present Government
in Evallonia is Republican. We believe that it is
not loved by the people and but ill suited to the
national genius. But it is loved by the Powers of
Europe, especially by Britain. They see in it a
sober, stable, bourgeois government such as those
enjoyed by France and Germany, and in their own
interest the present rulers of Evallonia play up to
them. They are always ready with the shibboleths
of democracy, and at Geneva they speak wonderful
things about peace and loving-kindness. But we,
Mr. Galt, we who are in close touch with the poor
people of Evallonia, know better. We know that
the Government is a camarilla of selfish adventurers.
Already in many secret ways they are oppressing
the poor. They think, most of them, not of Evallonia, but of their own power and their own pockets.
And some think of darker things. There are among
them men who would lead Evallonia into the black
ways of Russia. There is above all this Mastrovin.
He holds no portfolio—he has refused many—but
he is the power in the background. He is the most
subtle and dangerous mind in Europe to-day, and he
is a fanatic who cannot be intimidated or persuaded
or purchased. Why is he here ? Why are Dedekind
and Ricci and Calaman and Rosenbaum here ?

They cannot harm us with the Evallonian people—
that they know well, for every day among the
Evallonian masses disgust with their régime is growing and enthusiasm for our Prince as their deliverer.
. . . They are desperate men, and they must mean
desperate things."

" I daresay they're all that," said Jaikie. " But
what kind of desperate act would profit them?
That's what puzzles me."

" They could kidnap his Royal Highness," Prince
Odalchini put in. " Here—on a foreign shore—far
from his friends."

" I don't think so," said Jaikie. " Britain is
a bad place for that kind of game—our police are
too good. Besides, what would they do with him
if they got him? Kidnapping would be far easier
on the Continent, and if they wanted that they must
have had plenty of chances. . . . Suppose they
meant to do him bodily harm? Could they choose
a worse place than this, where a foreigner is un-
common and conspicuous, and would half a dozen
of their chief people turn up to do the job? It
would be insanity, and they don't strike me as
insane."

" What then is your explanation?" the Professor
asked sombrely.

" They want to discredit his Royal Highness and
his party. You say they can't do that with the
Evallonians. But they can do it with the Powers.
They can do it with Britain. Suppose they publish
to the world details of his Royal Highness and yourselves plotting a revolution on British soil with

Mr. Craw. We're a queer people, and one thing we can't stand is having our country used for foreign intrigues. The news of it would put up the back of Tory and Socialist alike. And the notion that Mr. Craw was in it—well, it would be the end of Mr. Craw and the Craw Press."

"Of course it would," said Alison, who had followed Jaikie's exposition with appreciative nods.

"I'm certain I'm right. They want to compromise you. They and Allins believe that Mr. Craw is at Castle Gay. They know that you are at Knockraw, and they know that what they hoped for has happened, and that his Royal Highness is here. They are waiting to find just the kind of compromising situation they want. And they're desperate men, so they won't stick at much to bring it about. I have no doubt at all that Mastrovin has ways and means of mobilizing some pretty tough elements in Portaway. Remember, too, that the election is on Friday, and the Canonry will be all upside down that day."

"By God, I believe the boy is right," said Casimir, and the Professor acquiesced with a solemn nod.

"I've got it," Jaikie cried. "I believe Friday—the day after to-morrow—is the day they've chosen to act. The countryside, as I say, will be upside down, the police will all be at the polling stations, and there will be a good chance for high-handed proceedings. I can't just guess what these will be, but you may take it that they will be adequate."

"But they won't find Mr. Craw," put in Alison.

"I don't think that that will matter. If they

can get you somehow connected with Castle Gay we'll never be able to persuade people that Mr. Craw was not there, or at any rate was not privy to the meeting. Not after that interview in the *Wire*," and he looked across at Alison. " The world knows his opinions, and will assume Barbon to have his authority. No, Allins has been lucky, and things up to now have turned out rather well for him."

" What do you advise ? " It was Prince John who spoke. He looked at Jaikie as at another young man, who might be more useful than middle-age.

" Well, sir, if we know what they intend—and I think my guess is right—we start with one big advantage. Besides, I may find out a great deal in the next two days. But there's one thing to be done at once. We must shorten our front of defence, and get rid of Knockraw."

" Will you please explain ? " said Casimir.

" You must give up your mission. You must see that it's impossible. You can't do anything with Mr. Craw. Even if he were hot on your side, and not scared to death at the very mention of you, you can do nothing with him now. Your business is to prevent this mission of yours becoming a deadly blow to your cause and setting Britain violently against you. You see that ? "

The silence proved that they did see it.

" May I ask, Mr. Galt," Casimir spoke, " what exactly is your position in this affair ? Are you one of Mr. Craw's journalists, like Mr. Crombie ? "

" No, thank Heaven. I've nothing to do with journalism My position is the same as Miss Westwater's. We like Mr. Craw and we don't like Allins, and we're going to do our best to protect the one and down the other. Our attitude to you is one of benevolent neutrality, but we're for you against the other blighters."

Prince John laughed. " That is candid and fair. Go on, sir. What is your plan ? "

" You must leave Knockraw, and the sooner the better. It's a rotten place to defend. It's as open as a cricket-field. You and your household must clear out. You've no local people indoors, so you should be able to do that unostentatiously. But you mustn't take his Royal Highness with you. You must depart exactly the same party as you arrived. We must take no chances. Nobody knows that he is with you except Allins and his friends, and nobody else must ever know. He can join you in London, where nothing matters."

" And meantime what is to become of him ? "

" You must entrust him to us. Miss Westwater and I will undertake to get him somehow quietly into England—and alone. What do you say, sir ? "

" I will gladly entrust myself to Miss Westwater," said Prince John with a bow.

" Then you must be the first to leave, sir," said Jaikie. " Every hour you spend in this house and in this company increases the danger. I think Castle Gay is the right place for you, for it's not very easy for anybody to get near it. But we'll have to move cautiously. I think that the best place to go first will be the Mains."

Casimir brightened. " I have a high regard for

Mrs. Brisbane-Brown," he announced. " She might be of the utmost service."

" I'll back Aunt Harriet to put anything through," said the loyal Alison.

Jaikie was aware that four pairs of eyes were scrutinising him closely, and small wonder. He had wandered in out of the rain an hour ago, a complete stranger, and here he was asking four men of ripe experience and high position to put their fortunes in his hands. He faced the scrutiny with his serious, gentle eyes, very little perturbed, for he had a purpose now, and, as was his custom, was wholly absorbed in it. They saw his small wedge-shaped countenance, his extreme youthfulness, his untidy hair, his shabby clothes, but, being men of penetration, they saw something else—that sudden shadow which seemed to run over his face, tightening it into a mask of resolution. Every line of Jaikie spoke of a brisk purpose. He looked extraordinarily dependable.

Prince John spoke first.

" I was never much in love with this venture, my dear Casimir, and now I have only one wish— to be well out of it. We shall be well advised if we are guided by Mr. Galt. You and I must clearly separate and not reunite till London. I am the compromising article, but I shall be much less conspicuous alone."

" We go—when ? " said Casimir, looking at Jaikie.

" I should advise to-night—a moonlight flitting, as we say. You can send the keys to the lawyers— say you were called home suddenly—anything. It's

a foul day, so you'd better stop indoors, or if you
go out leave word with your servants to keep a good
watch and let nobody in.   You have two cars, I
think, and they're both hired from Portaway. Leave
them in a Gledmouth garage and catch the night
train to London.   I'll arrange with the Portaway
people to send for them—they're friends of mine."

" And his Royal Highness ? "

" I want him out of this house now. This dirty
weather will help us.   Miss Westwater can arrange
for a groom from the Castle to fetch his kit—he'd
better come in a dogcart, as if he were on an errand
to the servants.   Our first job is to get the Prince
out of Knockraw and safe in the Mains without
any mortal eye seeing him. . . . I'm ready, if you
are, sir."

Jaikie stood up stiffly, for the armchair had been
very deep and his legs were rather cramped, and
the others rose with him.   He asked one more
question : " Was the Prince out of doors yesterday ? " and was told that he had been on the moor
for some rough shooting.   He had worn a different
suit from that which he was now wearing, and a
white mackintosh.   " Good," said Jaikie.   " I want
him now to put on the oldest and dingiest waterproof you can raise.   But you must be sure to have
that white mackintosh sent to Castle Gay."   A
plan was vaguely building itself up in his head.

Jaikie arranged the departure with an eye to the
observation-points on the hill and in the by-road.
The mere exit from Knockraw was not a difficult

problem ; the real trouble would come when they were beyond the policies and in the rough pastures which stretched to the eastern wall of Castle Gay park. Once at that wall they were safe for a time, for there was a gate of which Alison had the key, and inside the park there were Mackillop and his myrmidons to ward off strangers.

Alison had her pony brought round, and set off at a canter down the avenue. Her arrival had been observed, and her going must be not less conspicuous. She rode fast through the drizzle till she reached the steading of Kirnshaw, which is one of the Castle farms. There she left her pony, and returned on foot to a clump of birches at the edge of a broomy common, where she was to meet the others. Her local knowledge could not be dispensed with.

The first part was easy. Jaikie and Prince John emerged from a scullery window and by way of a thicket of laurels reached a fir planting which led to the park boundary. The rain now descended in sheets, and soon they were both comprehensively wet, but it was the right weather for their task. There must be but poor visibility for the watcher on the hill, and the car in the by-road controlled only the direction of Portaway. . . . It was easy, too, to cross the road by which Tibbets had pursued the Knockraw car. It was full of twists and turns, and at this hour as empty of humanity as the moor. After that came half an hour of slinking through patches of furze and down hedgerow ditches, till the clump of birches was reached, where Alison awaited them. So far the Prince had behaved well, and had obeyed Jaikie as a docile novice in a deer forest obeys a masterful stalker.

But with Alison in the party complications began. They had still three-quarters of a mile to cover before they reached the Castle park wall, and, since they were descending a slope, they were more or less in view of the road from Portaway which followed the left bank of the Callowa. Jaikie, who had a sense for landscape like a wild animal's, had this road always in his mind, and sometimes he made them crawl flat for yards, sometimes run hard in cover, sometimes lie on damp earth till some alarm had ceased. The trouble was Prince John, who became suddenly a squire of dames. He wanted to help Alison over every difficulty. He would rise to his full height in crossing a brook that he might give her a hand, he did the same thing in parting the bramble coverts, and he thought it his duty to make polite conversation in spite of Jaikie's warning growl.

The girl, as active as a squirrel, needed no assistance, and was much embarrassed by these attentions. Already Jaikie had forced the Prince's head down into the heather several times when he had raised it to address Alison, and he was just beginning to wonder how his companion was to be sternly reprimanded without *lèse-majesté*, when Alison anticipated him.

" Prince," she said in her clear high voice, " do you mind if I mention that for the present the Age of Chivalry has gone ? "

They crossed the high road when, after a reconnaissance by Jaikie, the coast was pronounced clear, and with some difficulty induced the gate in the park wall to open. Now for a space they were safe, so they restored their circulation by running down a glade of bracken to where the Callowa lay in its hollow. The river was rising, but it could be forded at a shallow, and the three splashed through, Alison going first to escape Prince John's obvious intention of carrying her across. After that they went more warily, for there were points in the neighbourhood from which this section of the park could be commanded. Indeed their route was very much that taken by Jaikie and Dougal on their first visit, and they passed under the very tree in which Alison had been perched. Just before noon they reached the gate in the further wall.

Jaikie, with the help of the bough of an adjoining tree, shinned up, raised his head above the top, and cautiously prospected the highway. Opposite was a low fence, and then a slope of hazels and rhododendrons which was part of the Mains demesne. Once inside that pale they were safe. The road was empty. He gave the word, and Alison and the Prince darted across and in a moment were out of sight.

An instant later a man appeared round the bend of the road. He was a fisherman, for he carried a great salmon-rod and he wore brogues and waders. As he came nearer Jaikie recognized him, and tumbled off the wall. It was Mr. McCunn, who proposed to fish the Bridge pool of the river and was taking the quickest way to it.

Jaikie cut short his greeting, for a car was coming down the road. "Not a word," he whispered. "Let me speak." . . . Then, raising his voice, "It's a grand day for a salmon. . . . What's your fancy for flies ? . . . The water is three feet up already. . . . I saw a big one in the Bridge pool, thirty pounds if he was an ounce, but pretty black. . . ."

So he chattered as the car passed. It was a two-seater, and in it was one man, Allins. He slowed down, and Jaikie's babble must have come clearly to his ear.

"Have you taken leave of your senses, Jaikie ? " the mystified Dickson asked.

"Yes. I'm as daft as a yett in a high wind. D'you know what I've been doing all morning ? Dragging a prince through burns and bogs by the hair of his head. . . . I'm going to watch you fishing for ten minutes and you've got to answer me some questions."

When Alison and Prince John halted in a recess of the hazel thicket, whence ran a rustic path to the upper garden, they found another occupant of that hermitage. This was a small man, very wet and muddy, in a ruinous waterproof, rather weary, and apparently in some alarm. It was a full minute before Alison recognized in the scarecrow the celebrated Mr. Craw.

CHAPTER XVI

ENEMY'S COUNTRY

JAIKIE, being very wet, trotted most of the way back to Portaway. The rudiments of a plan were growing in his mind, and he had a great deal to think about and a great deal to do. . . . The enemy was keeping a close watch, and must have got together a pretty considerable posse to help him. It was a bold thing for Allins himself to be in the neighbourhood of Castle Gay. But then, he reflected, Allins's visits there had not been frequent—he generally took his holiday abroad in the autumn—and, when there, he probably never stirred much outside the park gates. Besides, he would not be easy to identify with the collar of his ulster turned up and a cap pulled over his brows. Only one who, like Jaikie himself, was on the look-out for him, would be likely to recognize him. No, Allins was safe enough.

He reached the Green Tree to find no Mr. Craw or any message from him, and learned from a maid that he had sallied forth about half-past nine. . . . Jaikie sat down and considered, while he ate a luncheon of bread and cheese. Mr. Craw could not be wandering about Portaway—he knew the risk he ran in the town. He must have gone up the water. But where? Had he taken the bit between his teeth and returned to Castle Gay? It seemed the only explanation. Mr. Craw, puffed up with last night's achievement, had discovered a new self-reliance, and proposed to steer his own course.

It was an unforeseen complication, but there was no help for it. He must trust to luck, and go on with his own preparations. After all, for the moment Mr. Craw was not the chief piece on the chess-board.

Jaikie dried the legs of his trousers at Mrs. Fairweather's kitchen fire. Then he took some pains with his toilet. His old flannel suit was shabby but well-cut, and, being a tidy mortal, he wore a neat, if slightly bedraggled, soft collar and tie. This would scarcely do, so, at a neighbouring draper's, he purchased a rather high, hard, white collar and a very vulgar striped tie. At a pawnshop he invested in an imitation-silver watch-chain with a football shield appended, and discarded his own leather guard. His hair was a little too long, and when he had reduced it to further disorder by brushing it straight up, he regarded himself in a mirror and was satisfied. He looked the very image of the third-rate reporter or press-photographer, and he could guarantee an accent to correspond. His get-up was important, since he proposed to make himself ground-bait to attract the enemy.

His business was to find Allins, and he believed that the best covert to draw was the lounge of the

Station Hotel. So, accompanied by the neglected Woolworth, he made his way to that hostelry. The hour was half-past two, and he argued that a gentleman who had lunched droughtily in the Hydropathic might be inclined for a mild stimulant. He sought the retreat of his friend, the head-porter, which had the advantage of possessing a glass window which commanded about three-quarters of the lounge.

To his relief he saw Allins sitting by a small table, and beside him Tibbets. They appeared to be deep in talk, Tibbets especially expounding and gesticulating.

That eminent journalist, after his Sunday's triumph, had made a tour of the Canonry to get material for a general article on the prospects of the election. He had returned to Portaway with a longing for better food than that furnished by country inns, and had lunched heavily in the Station Hotel. While in the enjoyment of coffee and a liqueur, he had found himself next to Allins, and according to his wont had entered into conversation. Tibbets was a communicative soul, and in a little time had told his neighbour all about the *Wire* interview, and, since that neighbour showed a flattering interest, had faithfully recounted every detail of his visit to Castle Gay. He had not mentioned his adventure at Knockraw, for he was an honest man, and regarded complete secrecy on that point as part of the price of the Craw interview.

Jaikie observed the two, and rightly deduced what they were talking about. That was all to the good. It would convince Allins that Mr. Craw was at Castle Gay, and lull any suspicion he might have entertained on the subject. He wished he knew himself where Mr. Craw was. . . . He was reminded of a duty. There was no public telephone in Portaway, and nothing of the kind in the Green Tree, but the head-porter had one in his cubbyhole, and gave him permission to use it. He rang up Castle Gay and asked to speak to Dougal.

When he heard the gruff hallo of his friend, he informed him of Mr. Craw's disappearance. Had he arrived at the Castle ?

" Good God ! " came the answer. " He's not here. What on earth are we to do ? Isn't he somewhere in Portaway ? "

" I don't think so. I believe he's on his way to you. I wish . . ."

At that moment Jaikie was compelled to ring off, for Tibbets was leaving the lounge, and if he remained at the telephone Tibbets would see him. He particularly did not want to see Tibbets, so he subsided on to the floor. When he rose, Tibbets had left the hotel, but Allins was still in the lounge. He might leave at any moment, so there was no time to be lost.

Followed by Woolworth, whom the rain had made to look like a damp white sponge set on four spindly legs, he sauntered into the lounge and sat himself on a couch a yard or two from Allins, the dog squatting docilely beside him. He spoke to Woolworth in a way which was bound to attract the attention of his neighbour. While he looked round, as if for a waiter, he observed that Allins's eye was fixed on him. He hoped that, in spite of his strange collar and tie, Allins would recognize him. He had been seen in company with Alison, he had been seen that very morning outside Castle Gay park : surely these were compromising circumstances which Allins must wish to investigate.

He was right. Allins smiled at him, came over, and sat down beside him on the couch.

" I saw you at the meeting the other night," he said pleasantly. " What do you think of the local Communists ? "

Jaikie was something of an actor. His manner was slightly defensive, and he looked at the speaker with narrowed eyes.

" Very middling." His voice was the sing-song of the Glasgow slums. " My friend wasn't bad. Ye heard him—I saw ye at the back of the hall. But yon Stubber ! " He spat neatly into the adjacent fire. " He was just a flash in the pan. Fine words and no guts. I know the breed ! "

" I didn't hear Stubber—I had to leave early. Your friend, now. He seemed to know a good deal, but he wasn't much of an orator."

" Carroll's his name. Jimmy's red hot. But ye're right. He's no much of a speaker."

Jaikie extracted from a waistcoat pocket a damaged Virginian cigarette, which he lit by striking a match on the seat of his trousers.

" Have a drink," said Allins

" I don't mind if I do."

" What will you have ? "

" A dry Martini. If you had sampled as much

bad whisky as me in these country pubs, you would never want to taste it again."

Two cocktails were brought. "Here's luck," said Allins, and Jaikie swallowed his in two gulps as the best way to have done with it. One of his peculiarities was a dislike of alcohol in every form except beer, a dislike increased by various experiments at Cambridge. Another was that alcohol had curiously little effect on him. It made him sick or sleepy, but not drunk.

"Are you a Communist?" Allins asked.

Jaikie looked sly. "That's asking . . . No, by God, I'm no afraid to confess it. I'm as red as hell. . . . That's my private opinion, but I've to earn my living and I keep it dark."

"What's your profession, if I may ask?"

"I'm a journalist. And with what, d'ye think? The Craw Press. I'm on their Glasgow paper. I'm here to cover the election, but our folk don't want much about it, so I've a lot of time on my hands."

"That's an odd place for a man of your opinions to be."

"Ye may say so. But a chap must live. I'm just biding my time till I can change to something more congenial. But meanwhile I get plenty fun studying the man Craw."

"Do you know him?"

"Never clapped eyes on him. None of us have. But he lives in this neighbourhood, and I've been picking up a lot of information about him these last few days."

Jaikie had the art of watching faces without his

scrutiny being observed, for his own eyes appeared
to be gentle and abstracted. He respected Allins's
address. Allins's manner was at once detached and
ingratiating, and he spoke with a suspicion of a
foreign accent. His eyes were small, sharp, and
observant. He had the high gloss which good living
and regular exercise give, but there were anxious
lines about the corners of his eyes, and something
brutal about the full compressed lips. The man
was formidable, for he was desperately anxious ;
he was in a hole, and would stick at little to get
out of it.

Jaikie's last words seemed to rouse him to a
livelier interest.

" Have another drink," he said.

" I don't mind if I do. Same as before."

Allins ordered a single cocktail. Jaikie sipped it,
and then took the glass in his right hand. As he
spoke he lowered it, and gradually bestowed its
contents on the thick damp fleece of the couchant
Woolworth, who was so wet already that he took
no notice.

" Mr. Craw lives here ? " said Allins. " Of course.
I remember now. His is the big house some miles
up the river."

" You passed it this morning," said Jaikie, greatly
daring. " Yon was you, wasn't it, that I saw in
the two-seater ? I was having a yarn with an old
fisherman body who had got a day's fishing in the
Callowa. I thought that, seeing he was allowed to
fish the water, he could tell me something about
Craw."

" And did he ? "

" Not him. He was only a Glasgow grocer that had got leave from the factor."

" Then what have you found out about Mr. Craw ? "

" The queer thing is that I've found out so little. The man's fair immured, and they won't let people inside the place. I'm grand at getting on with plain folk, and I've made friends with a good few of the people on the estate. It's a daft-like business. They keep the lodge gates locked up like prisons, but there's a dozen places you can get into the park. I've been all round the gardens, and not a soul to object. I could have got in at any one of twenty windows if I had wanted. Oh, I can tell ye, I've had some fun up there. Craw would fire me the morn if he knew what I had been up to."

It was Jaikie's cue to appear a little excited, as if the second cocktail had been too much for him.

" Have another drink ? " said Allins.

" I don't mind if I do. The same . . . No, wait a jiffey. I'll have a lickyure brandy."

As the waitress brought the drink, the head-porter also appeared.

" They're ringin' up frae Castle Gay, Mr. Galt," he said. " Wantin' to know if ye're still in the hotel ? "

" Tell them I've just gone," said Jaikie, and he winked at Allins.

He sipped the brandy and looked mysteriously at his neighbour.

" There's a girl living up thereaways. I don't

know her name, but she wants this dog of mine. She saw him in Portaway the other day, and was mad to buy him. It seems that he's like a wee beast she had herself that died. She offered me four pounds for him, but I wasn't for selling. . . . That was her ringing up just now. She's a determined besom. . . . I wonder who she can be. Craw is believed to be a bachelor, but maybe he has had a wife all the time on the sly."

As Jaikie spoke he decanted the brandy on the back of the sleeping Woolworth. This time he was not so successful. Some of the liqueur got into the little dog's ear, who awoke and violently scratched the place with a paw.

" That beast's got fleas," said Jaikie with a tipsy solemnity.

" What you say about Castle Gay is very strange," said Allins. " Why should a great man, a publicist of European reputation, live in such retirement ? He can have nothing to conceal."

Jaikie assumed an air of awful secrecy.

" I'm not so sure. I'm not—so sure—about that." He thrust his face closer to the other's. " The man is not doing it because he likes it. There must be a reason. . . . I'm going to find out what that reason is. . . . I've maybe found it."

He spoke thickly, but coherently enough. He did not want Allins to think that he was drunk— only excited and voluble.

" Have another drink ? "

" Don't mind if I do. Another b-brandy. It must be the last, all the same, or I'll never get out of this hotel. . . . What was I saying ? Oh, ay ! About Craw. Well, isn't it ridiculous that he should behave like an old ostrich ? Ay, an ostrich. He locks his lodge gates and lets nobody inside his house, but half the pop'lation of the Canonry might get in by the park. . . . What's Friday ? I mean the day after the morn. It's the polling day. The folk up there will all be down at Portaway voting, and they'll make a day of it—ay, and a night of it. . . . Man, it would be a grand joke to explore Castle Gay that night. Ye could hold up Craw in his lair—no harm meant, if ye understand, but just to frighten him, and see how he likes publicity. It's what he's made his millions by, but he's queer and feared of a dose of it himself."

" Why don't you try ? " said Allins.

" Because I must think of my job. There might be a regrettable incident, ye see, and I'm not wanting to be fired. Not yet. . . . Besides . . ."

" Yes ? "

" Besides, that kind of ploy wouldn't get me much forward. I want to find out what Craw's feared of, for he's damned feared of something. And the key to it is not in Castle Gay."

Allins was listening intently, and did not notice the small moan which came from the sleeping Woolworth as something cold splashed in the vicinity of his tail.

" Where ? " he asked.

Jaikie leaned towards him and spoke in a thick whisper.

" Did you ever hear of a place called Knockraw ? "

" No," said Allins.

" Well, it's next door to Castle Gay. And there's some funny folk there. Foreigners. . . . I've nothing against foreigners. Ye're maybe one yourself. Ye speak a wee thing like it. . . . But the Knockraw foreigners are a special kind, and they've got some hold on Craw. I don't yet know what it is, but I'll find out. Never fear, I'll find out. I've been hanging about Knockraw these last days, and if I liked I could tell ye some queer tales."

Jaikie suddenly raised his eyes to the clock on the wall and gave a violent start.

" Govey Dick! It's close on four! Here! I must go. I can't sit havering any longer, for I've some stuff to get off with the post. . . . I'm much obliged to ye. It's been very enjoyable. Ye'll keep your mouth shut about what I've told ye, for I'm not wanting to get into Craw's black books."

He rose slowly to his feet and steadied himself by the table. Allins rose also and held out his hand.

" This has been a very pleasant meeting, Mr. Galt," he said. He had got the name from the head-porter's message. " I wonder if I could persuade you to repeat it quite soon. This very evening, in fact. I am staying with some friends at the Hydropathic. Could you drop in for a light supper about ten o'clock? We are strangers in Scotland, and should like to hear more from you about local politics—and journalism—and Mr. Craw."

" I don't mind if I do. But the Hydropathic's black teetotal."

Odalchini. He in no way drew upon his imagination, for he was speaking to men to whom the three had for years been familiar.

" Is there not a fourth ? " Mastrovin asked.

Jaikie appeared to consider. " Oh, yes. There's a young one. He came the night before last, and was out shooting yesterday." He described elaborately the appearance of Prince John. " He wears a white mackintosh," he added.

Mastrovin nodded.

" Now, will you tell us why you think these people have some hold on Mr. Craw ? "

Jaikie appeared to hesitate. " Well—ye see—I don't just quite like. Ye see, Craw's my employer. . . . If he heard I had been mooching round his house and spying—well, I'd be in the soup, wouldn't I ? "

The alcoholic bravado of the afternoon had evaporated. Jaikie was now the treacherous journalist, nervous about his job.

" You are afraid of offending Mr. Craw," said Mastrovin. " Mr. Galt, I assure you that you have much more reason to be afraid of offending us. . . . Also we will make it worth your while."

Threats again. Jaikie's face grew a shade paler, and his heart began to thump. He appeared to consider anew.

" Well, I'll tell ye. . . . Craw never entertains anybody. His servants tell me that he never has any guests from the neighbourhood inside the door. But the people at Knockraw dined at Castle Gay last Saturday night, and the Castle Gay party dined

at Knockraw on Monday night. That looks queer
to begin with."

The others exchanged glances. They apparently
had had news of these incidents, and Jaikie con-
firmed it. Their previous knowledge also established
Jaikie's accuracy.

" Anything more ? "

" Plenty. The people at Knockraw have brought
their own servants with them. Everybody inside
the house is a foreigner. That looks as if they had
something they wanted to keep quiet. . . . It would
have been far cheaper to get servants in the Canonry,
like other tenants."

Again Mastrovin nodded.

" Anything more ? "

" This," said Jaikie, allowing a smile to wrinkle
his pallor. " These Knockraw foreign servants are
never away from Castle Gay. They spend half
their time crawling about the place. I've seen one
of them right up at the edge of the terrace. I daresay they're all poachers at home, for they're grand
hands at keeping cover. Now, what does that
mean ? " Jaikie seemed to be gaining confidence
and warming to his task. " It means that they're
not friends of Craw. They've got something coming
for him. They're spying on him. . . . I believe
they're up to no good."

Mastrovin bent his brows again.

" That is very interesting and very odd. Can
you tell us more, Mr. Galt ? "

" I can't give ye more facts," said Jaikie briskly,
" but I can give ye my guesses. . . . These Knock-

raw folk want something out of Craw. And they're
going to get it. And they're going to get it soon.
I'll tell ye why I think that. The polling's on
Friday, and on that day there's a holiday at Castle
Gay. Craw's very keen—so they tell me—on his
people exercising what he calls their rights as citizens.
All the outdoor servants and most of the indoor will
be in Portaway, and, if I'm any judge, they'll not be
back till morning. Maybe you don't know what a
Scotch election is like, especially in the Canonry.
There'll be as many drunks in Portaway as on a
Saturday night in the Cowcaddens. The Knockraw
foreigners will have Craw to themselves, for yon
man Barbon, the secretary, is no mortal use."

Jaikie observed with delight that his views roused
every member of the company to the keenest interest, and he could not but believe that he had
somehow given his support to a plan which they
had already matured. It was with an air of covering
his satisfaction that Mastrovin asked, in a voice
which he tried to make uninterested :

" Then you think that the Knockraw people will
visit Castle Gay on Friday night ? "

" They won't need to visit it, for they'll be there
already," said Jaikie.

" What do you mean ? "

" I mean that by this time they've all shifted their
quarters, bag and baggage, to the Castle."

" How the devil do you know that ? " It was
Allins who spoke, and his voice was as sharp as a
dog's bark.

" I found it out from one of the Castle maids. I

can tell ye it's all arranged. The servants have left, but the gentry are shifting over to the Castle. . . . I was at Knockraw this morning, and I saw them packing the guns in their cases. They're done with shooting for the year, unless," he added with a grin, " there's some shooting of a different kind at Castle Gay."

This news produced an impression as great as the most sensitive narrator could have desired. The seven men talked excitedly among themselves—not, to Jaikie's regret, in French.

" It looks as if ye didn't believe me," he said, with irritation in his tone. " Well, all I can say is, send out somebody to Knockraw the morn's morning, and if the place is not all shuttered up and not a chimney smoking, ye can call me the worst kind of liar."

" We accept what you say, Mr. Galt," said Mastrovin, " and we will test it. . . . Now, on another matter. You say that you have explored the park of the Castle very thoroughly, and have seen the Knockraw servants engaged in the same work. . . . We have here a map. As a proof of your good faith, perhaps you will show us the route by which these servants approached the gardens unobserved."

He produced a sheet of the largest-scale Ordnance Survey.

" Fine I can do that," said Jaikie. " In my young days I was a Boy Scout. But I'm awful dry with so much talking. I'll thank ye for some more beer."

His glass was filled, and he drained it at a draught, for he was indeed very thirsty. A space was cleared on the table, and with a pencil he showed how the park could be entered at the Callowa bridge and elsewhere, and what sheltered hollows led right up to the edge of the terrace. He even expounded the plan of the house itself. " There's the front door. . . . A man could get in at any one of these lower windows. They're never shuttered. . . . No, the gardeners' houses are all down by the kitchen garden on the east bank of the Callowa. The chauffeurs and mechanics live on the other side just under the Castle Hill. . . . The keepers ? Mackillop is miles away at the Blae Moss ; one of the under-keepers lodges in Starr, and one lives at the South Lodge. Craw has a very poor notion of guarding his privacy, for all he's so keen on it."

Jaikie yawned heavily—partly in earnest, for he was very weary. He consulted the cheap watch at the end of his recently purchased chain. He was searching for the right note on which to leave, and presently he found it. It was no occasion for ceremony.

" I wasn't much in my bed last night, and it's time I was there now—or I'll be dropping under this table." He got to his feet and made an embarrassed survey of the company.

" I'm much obliged to you gentlemen for your hospitality. We've had a great crack, but for God's sake keep it to yourselves. . . . I've maybe said more than I should have, but it's your blame for leading me on. . . . I want ye to promise that you'll never mention my name. If it came out that I had been spending my time nosing into his private affairs, Craw would fire me like a shot. . . . And he doesn't pay badly."

"You need not worry, Mr. Galt," said Mastrovin. "We are not loquacious people. Let me recommend you to be equally silent—especially in your cups."

"Never fear. I'll take care of that." Jaikie gave an imbecile giggle, bobbed his head to the company, and took his leave. Allins did not offer his hand or trouble to open the door. They had had all that they wanted from this bibulous, babbling little reporter.

At the door of the Hydropathic Jaikie remembered suddenly that they had promised to remunerate him for his confidences. He wished he had collected his fee, for he believed in taking every opportunity of spoiling the Egyptians. But he could do nothing now. He was as one who had escaped from the cave of Polyphemus, and it would be folly to go back for his hat.

At the Green Tree he found a note which had been brought by a boy on a bicycle. "*Dear Jaikie,*" he read, "*set your mind at ease. Mr. Craw is here at the Mains, being lectured by Aunt Harriet. You have made him twice the man he was. Love from Alison.*"

He read this missive at least eight times. Then he put it carefully into his pocket-book, and laid the pocket-book under his pillow. Last night, though that pocket-book contained fifty pounds in Treasury notes, it had lain casually on his dressing-table.

CHAPTER XVII

JAIKIE OPENS HIS COMMUNICATIONS

JAIKIE slept like a log and awoke next morning in high spirits. These were mainly attributable to Alison's letter, which he re-read many times while he dressed. She had called him " Jaikie " on paper ; she had sent him her love : the whole enterprise was a venture of his and Alison's—the others were only lay figures. At breakfast he had some slight uneasiness as to whether he had not been a little too clever. Had he not given too much rein to his ingenuity ? . . . He had prevented Prince John joining the others in their midnight flitting. No doubt it was in a general way desirable to scatter in a flight, but he could not conceal from himself that the Prince might now be safe in the English midlands, whereas he was still in the very heart of danger. Well, he had had a reason for that, which he thought Alison would appreciate. . . . And he had gone out of his way to invite an assault on Castle Gay. He had his reason for that, too, many reasons, but the chief, as he confessed to himself, was the desire for revenge. He had been threatened, and to Jaikie a threat was a challenge.

He spent half an hour in cleansing Woolworth, whose alcoholic flavour the passage of hours had

not diminished. His bedroom had smelt like a
public-house. First he borrowed big scissors from
Mrs. Fairweather, and clipped the little dog's shaggy
fleece and his superabundant beard and whiskers.
Then he washed him, protesting bitterly, with soap
and hot water, and dried him before the kitchen
fire. He made a few alterations in his own get-up.
The stiff collar and flamboyant tie of yesterday were
discarded, and for neckwear he used a very faded
blue scarf, which he tied in the kind of knot affected
by loafers who have no pride in their appearance.
He might meet Allins or one of the Evallonians in
the street, and he had no desire to be recognized.
He looked now, he flattered himself, like a young
artisan in his working clothes, and to complete the
part he invested in an unfashionably shaped cap.

Attended by the shorn and purified Woolworth,
he made for the railway station. Portaway, as has
been explained, is an important main-line station,
but it is also the junction for a tiny single-line
railway which runs down the side of the Callowa
estuary to the decayed burgh of Fallatown. Once
Fallatown was a flourishing port, with a large trade
to the Cumberland shore and the Isle of Man, a
noted smuggling centre, and the spot from which
great men had taken ship in great crises. Now the
ancient royal burgh is little more than a hamlet,
with a slender fishing industry, a little boat-building,
and one small distillery. Jaikie did not propose
to go as far as Fallatown, but to stop at the in-
termediate station of Rinks, where he had some
business with a friend.

He crossed the bridge and reached the station without mischance. The rain of the preceding day had gone, and had left one of those tonic October mornings which are among the delicacies of Scottish weather. There was no frost, the air was bracing and yet mild, the sky was an even blue, the distances as sharp as April. From the bridge Jaikie saw the top of the great Muneraw twenty-five miles distant, with every wrinkle clear on its bald face. The weather gave an edge to his good spirits. He bought a third-class return ticket for Rinks, and walked to the far end of the station, to the small siding where the Fallatown train lay, as if he had not a care in the world.

There he got a bad fright. For among the few people on the little platform was Allins, smoking a cigar outside a first-class carriage.

Jaikie hastily retreated. Why on earth was Allins travelling to Fallatown? More important, how on earth was he to escape his notice at such close quarters? At all costs Allins must not know of his visit to Rinks.

He retreated to the booking-office, and at an adjoining bookstall bought a paper with the notion that he might open it to cover his face. In the booking-office was a large comely woman of about thirty, much encumbered with a family. She carried an infant in one arm, and a gigantic basket in the other, and four children of ages from four to ten clung to her skirts. Apparently she desired to buy a ticket, and found it difficult to get at her purse because of the encumbrance in her arms. " I want

three return tickets to Fallatown," she was telling
the clerk, while she summoned the oldest child to
her aid. "Hector Alexander, see if ye can get
Mither's purse oot o' Mither's pooch. Na, na, ye
gomeril, that's no whaur it bides. Peety me that I
suld hae sic feckless weans. . . . Mind the basket
then. . . . Canny, it's eggs. . . . Gudesakes, ye'll
hae them a' broke."

Hector Alexander showed signs of tears, and
one of the toddlers set up a wail. The mother
cast an agonized look round and caught sight of
Jaikie.

"Can I help ye, mistress?" he said in his friendly
voice. "I'm for Rinks mysel'. It's a sore job
traivellin' wi' a family. Gie me the wean and the
basket. Ye havena muckle time, for the train
starts in three minutes."

The flustered woman took one look at his face,
and handed over the baby. "Thank ye kindly.
Will ye tak' the bairns to the train and I'll get the
tickets? Hector Alexander and Jean and Bessie
and Tommy, you follow the gentleman. I'm sure
I'm awfu' obliged."

So it fell out that Jaikie, with an infant beginning
to squall held resolutely before his face, a basket in
his right hand, and four children attached to different
parts of his jacket, made his way to the Fallatown
train, passing within ten feet of his enemy. The
third-class coach was just behind the engine. Allins
did not spare even a glance for the much-encumbered
youth. Jaikie found a compartment with only one
old woman in it, and carefully deposited the basket

on the floor and the four children on the seats, the while he made strange noises to soothe the infant. The guard was banging the doors when the hustled mother arrived and sat down heavily in a corner. She cuffed Hector Alexander for blowing his nose in a primitive way, and then snatched the now obstreperous babe from Jaikie's arms. " Wheesht, daurlin' ! Mither's got ye noo. . . . Feel in my pooch, Bessie. There's some jujubes for you and Jean and wee Tommy."

The old woman surveyed the scene over the top of her spectacles. Then she looked at Jaikie.

" Ye're a young chiel to be the faither o' sae mony weans."

The mother laughed hilariously. " He's no their faither. He's just a kind freend. . . . Their faither is in the Gledmouth hospital wi' a broken leg. He works in the Quarries, ye ken, and a month yestreen he got a muckle stane on his leg that brak it like a pipe stapple. . . . Thank ye, he's gettin' on fine. He'll be out next week. I'm takin' the weans to see their grannie at the Port."

The infant was quieted, and the two women embarked on a technical discussion of human ailments, while the four children found an absorbing interest in Woolworth. The little dog was deeply offended with his master and showed it by frequent artificial sneezes, but he was not proof against the respectful blandishments of the children. Consequently when he left the carriage at Rinks, he had two of their jujubes sticking in his damp fleece.

Jaikie, with the dog in his arms, sheltered behind

a shed till the train had left the platform. He had
a glimpse of Allins's unconscious profile as he was
borne past. Then he went out to the roadside
clachan which was Rinks, and turned his steps over
the salty pastures to the riverside.

The *machars*, yellowing with autumn, stretched
for miles before him till in the south they ended in
a blue line of sea. The Callowa, forgetting its high
mountain cradle, had become a sinuous trench with
steep mud banks, at the bottom of which—for the
tide was out—lay an almost stagnant stream.
Above the grasses could be seen here and there
the mast of a small vessel, waiting in the trough
for the tide. The place was alive with birds—
curlew and plover and redshank and sandpiper—
and as he jumped the little brackish ditches Jaikie
put up skeins of wild duck. It was a world in
which it was good to be alive, for in the air there
was both the freedom of the hills and the sting
of the sea.

Presently he reached the little colony of huts beside the water. Down in the ditch which was the
Callowa lay three small luggers ; there was an
antiquated slip and a yard full of timber. One of
the huts was a dwelling-house, and before its door,
sitting on a log, was a man in sea-boots and jersey,
busy mending a sail. He looked up as Jaikie
appeared, dropped his task, took the pipe from his
mouth, and grinned broadly. " Whae would hae
thocht to see *you* here ? " was his greeting. " Is
Mr. McCunn wi' ye ? "

" Not this time," said Jaikie, finding a place on

the log. " But he's in this countryside. How's the
world treating you, Mr. Maclellan ? "

Jaikie had come here several times with Dickson,
when the latter, growing weary of hill waters, desired
to fill his lungs with sea air, and appease his appetite
for slaughter by catching the easy salt-water fish.
In Mr. Maclellan's boat they had fished the length
of the Solway, and beyond it far down the English
coast and round the Mull. Once even in a fine April
they had crossed to the Isle of Man and made the
return journey by night.

" No sae bad," Maclellan answered Jaikie's question. " Ye'll see the *Rosabelle's* new pentit. It's
been a fair season for us folk, and the weather has
been mercifu' ! . . . It's ower lown the noo, but
it'll no be long or it changes. The auld folk was
sayin' that this month will gang oot in snaw. When
are you and Mr. McCunn comin' to hae a shot at
the jukes ? The first nip o' frost and there'll be a
walth o' birds on the tideway."

" Mr. McCunn's not much of a shot," said Jaikie,
" and just now he has other things to think about.
. . . What's that ? " he asked suddenly, pointing
towards the sea. On the right of what seemed to be
the Callowa mouth rose the top-gear of a small ship,
a schooner with auxiliary steam.

" That ? " said Maclellan, turning his deep-set,
long-sighted eyes in the direction of Jaikie's finger.
" That's a yatt—a bonny wee yatt. She's lyin' off
Fallatown. What she's doin' there I canna tell,
unless she belongs to some shooting-tenant."

" Has she been there long ? "

21

" Since the day afore yesterday. I was thinkin'
o' takin' the dinghy and gaun down to hae a look
at her."

Jaikie pondered. A yacht at Fallatown at this
season of the year was a portent. Now he
understood the reason of Allins's journey. . . . He
understood something more. The people at the
Hydropathic would not stick at trifles. Kidnapping ? No, there could be no reason for that. They
did not want to put themselves in the wrong. But
it might be that they would desire to leave quietly
and speedily, when their business was done, and
the little ship at Fallatown gave them the means.
. . . Jaikie smiled. It was a pleasure to deal with
people who really meant business. He no longer
felt that he had been too ingenious.

" Is the *Rosabelle* in good trim ? " he said.

" Never better. As ye see, she's new pentit."

" Well, Mr. McCunn wants you to do a job for
him. He's staying up the water at Starr, and he
has a friend with him who wants to get over to
Cumberland to-morrow night. It's a quicker way
than going round by Gledmouth and Carlisle. Could
you put him over to Markhaven—that's where
he wants to go—some time before midnight to-
morrow ? "

Maclellan considered. " High tide's about 9.15.
I could slip doun wi' the ebb. . . . There's no
muckle wind, but what there is is frae the north.
. . . Ay, I could set your freend over if he cam'
here round about eleven—maybe, a wee thing later."

" That's splendid. Mr. McCunn will bring him

down. He wants to see you again. . . . There's just one small thing. Keep the business entirely to yourself. You see, Mr. McCunn's friend has a reason for wanting to get away quietly. . . . I'm not quite sure what it is, but there's some tiresome engagement he wants to cut, and it wouldn't do if the story got about that he had made a moonlight flitting to avoid it. He's rather a big man in his way, I believe. A politician, I think."

Maclellan nodded with profound comprehension. "There's walth o' poaliticians in the Canonry the noo," he observed. "It's a dowg's trade. I don't blame ane o' the puir deevils for takin' the jee. Tell Mr. McCunn I'll never breathe a word o't. . . . Peety there's nae smugglin' nowadays. I wad be a fine hand at it, bidin' here wi' nae wife and nae neebors."

Jaikie spent a pleasant morning. He boarded the *Rosabelle* and renewed his memory of her tiny cabin ; he enjoyed a rat hunt in Woolworth's company ; he helped Maclellan to paint the dinghy : he dined with him at noon on Irish stew. Then he borrowed his bicycle. There was a train to Portaway at 1.30, but it was possible that Allins might travel by it, and Jaikie was taking no needless risks. "Send back the thing when ye're through wi't," Maclellan told him. "I've nae need o't the noo. I thought o' bicycling in to vote the morn, but I'm inclined to bide at hame. I'm seeck o' poalitics."

Going very slow, so that Woolworth might keep up with him, Jaikie managed to avoid Portaway altogether, and joined the Callowa valley three miles above the town. After that he went warily, reconnoitring every turn of the road, till he was inside the Mains avenue. He arrived a few minutes after the hour he had named to Dougal.

At the edge of the lawn Alison was waiting for him.

" Oh, Jaikie," she cried, " isn't this a stupendous lark ! Such a party in the drawing-room ! A real live Pretender to a Throne—and very nice-looking ! Freddy as anxious as a hen, and Dougal as cross as thunder—I've discovered that that's Dougal's way of showing nervousness ! And Mr. Craw ! What have you done with Mr. Craw ? He's as bold as brass, and nobody can manage him except Aunt Hatty. . . . Jaikie, you're very disreputable. I don't like your clothes a bit. Where did you get that horrible scarf ? "

" I was worse yesterday," was all that Jaikie would say. " What I want to know is—have you kept Prince John indoors ? And what about the servants ? They mustn't talk."

" He has never put his head outside since he arrived yesterday—except for an hour after dark last night when I took him for a walk on the hill. The servants have nothing to talk about. We call him John, and pretend he is another Australian cousin like Robin. Freddy sent a groom to Knockraw to pick up his kit."

" How did that go off ? "

" All right. The groom went to the back door. There was a good deal of luggage—enough to fill the dogcart. He said he met a lot of people—a man

in the avenue and several on the road. I suppose
these were the spies ? "

" The groom went straight to Castle Gay ? "

" Yes. Middlemas arranged for getting the things
over here after dark."

" That was lucky. The sight of the luggage
going to the Castle will have helped my reputation
for speaking the truth, when the story gets to the
Hydropathic this morning. You realize that all
this neighbourhood is being watched ? "

" Of course I do. It's a delicious feeling. There's
been some very odd people in cars and on bicycles
along the road, and Mackillop has hunted several
out of the park."

" Mackillop had better stop that," said Jaikie.
" For the next twenty-four hours it would be as
well if the park were open to the public."

" Are you serious ? " Alison looked puzzled.
" Come in at once and explain things. I've had a
lot of trouble keeping our own lot quiet. Mr. Craw
has been rather above himself. That beloved Mr.
McCunn is my great ally. He said, ' I'll take no
responsibility about anything till Jaikie comes. It's
Jaikie that's got the sow by the lug.' "

Mrs. Brisbane-Brown's drawing-room was as bright
and gracious in the October sun as when Jaikie had
visited it a week ago. But then he had entered it
with curiosity and trepidation ; now it seemed too
familiar to give a thought to ; it was merely a background for various human beings with whom he had
urgent business. The coffee cups were still in the
room, and the men were smoking. Prince John

wore the clothes he had worn the day before, and in the clear afternoon light looked more elegant than ever. He was talking to Charvill, who was much about his height, and looking up at them was Dickson McCunn in an ancient suit of knicker-bockers, listening reverently. The hostess sat in her accustomed chair, busy at her usual needlework, and beside her was the anxious face of Mr. Barbon. Dougal was deep in that day's issue of the *View*. But the centre of the company was Mr. Craw. He stood with his back to the fire, his legs a little apart, and his eyes on Mrs. Brisbane-Brown. He seemed to have recovered his balance, for there was no apology or diffidence in his air. Rather it spoke of renewed authority. He had also recovered his familiar nattiness of attire. Gone were the deplor-able garments provided by the Watermeeting inn-keeper and the Portaway draper. He wore a neat grey suit with a white line in it, a grey tie with a pearl pin, and the smartest of tan shoes. His garb was almost festive.

" I am very glad to see you, Mr. Galt," said Mrs. Brisbane-Brown. " You look a little the worse for wear. Have you had luncheon ? . . . Well, you have been giving us all a good deal to think about. It looks as if the situation had rather got out of hand. Perhaps you can clear things up."

Jaikie's mild eyes scanned the party. He saw Dougal hungry for enlightenment, Mr. Barbon fear-ful lest some new horror should be sprung upon him, Charvill prepared to be amused, Prince John smilingly careless as being used to odd adventures,

Dickson puzzled but trustful, Mr. Craw profoundly suspicious. He met their eyes in turn, and then he met Alison's, and the lashes of one of hers drooped over her cheek in a conspirator's wink.

" A week ago," he said slowly, " I was given my instructions. I was told to find Mr. Craw at the Back House of the Garroch and keep him hidden till the Evallonians left Knockraw. I have fulfilled them to the letter. There's not a soul except ourselves knows where Mr. Craw has been. Nobody has recognized him. The world believes that he's living quietly at Castle Gay. . . . And the Knockraw people by this time must be in London. . . ."

Mrs. Brisbane-Brown laughed. " A very good account of your stewardship. . . . On the other side the situation can scarcely be said to have cleared. We have his Royal Highness here in close hiding, and a number of men in Portaway who mean every kind of mischief to him and to Mr. Craw. The question is, what we are to do about it. This state of affairs cannot go on indefinitely."

" It can't," said Jaikie. " It must be cleared up to-morrow night."

" Will you please explain ? "

" It all begins," said Jaikie, " with the man Allins."

" He is shockingly underbred," said Mrs. Brisbane-Brown. " I never understood why Mr. Craw employed him. Poor Freddy can't have been happy with him. . . . You think he is something worse ? "

" I can prove that he is a rogue," said Jaikie calmly, and embarked on his tale.

He dealt first with Allins, recounting his meetings with him, from the Cambridge club to the episode of the previous day. He told the story well, and he purposely made Mr. Craw the hero of it—Mr. Craw's encounter with Allins in the street, Mr. Craw at the Socialist meeting, Mr. Craw as a Communist orator. The hero was made a little self-conscious by the narrative, but he was also flattered. He became slightly pink and shifted his feet.

" What astonishing presence of mind ! " said Mrs. Brisbane-Brown. " I warmly congratulate you."

" I must not be understood to have made a speech in favour of Communism," said Mr. Craw. " It was a speech condemnatory of official Socialism, showing its logical culmination."

" Anyway, it did the trick," said Jaikie. " Allins dropped his suspicions. Mr. Craw's disguise was pretty good in any case. You saw him yourself yesterday."

" I did," said Mrs. Brisbane-Brown. " I thought he was the piano-tuner from Gledmouth, who is a little given to drink."

Mr. Craw frowned. " Will you continue, Mr. Galt ? Detail the suspicions you entertain about Mr. Allins."

" He brought the Evallonians to Knockraw, and was paid for it. We have it on their own testimony. He brought the other Evallonians to Portaway and is being paid for it. And the man is in a sweat of fear in case the plot fails. The price must be pretty big."

" The plot ! What is it ? What evidence have you ? "

" The evidence of my own eyes and ears.   I spent part of yesterday afternoon with Allins, and two hours last night with him and his friends."

Jaikie had an audience which hung on his lips while he told of how he had made himself ground-bait for the predatory fish.   There was a good deal of the actor in him, and he did full justice to his alcoholic babblings of the afternoon, and the grim inquisition of the evening.   He even allowed part of his motive to appear.   " They called me a little rat," he said meditatively.

" You led them to believe that Count Casimir and his friends were now at Castle Gay.   May I ask why ? "   Mr. Craw's voice was harsh with offence.

" Because I wanted the Knockraw people to have plenty of time to get clear."

" For which purpose I am to be sacrificed ? "

" Your interests and theirs are the same.   You must see that.   What they want is to find the Evallonian monarchists and Prince John and you yourself in some close relation, and to publish the fact to the world.   That would give them a big advantage.   It would kill your power to help Casimir, and it would put Britain definitely against him.   Our people would never stand the notion that you and the Evallonians were conspiring on British soil, and the presence of Prince John would put the lid on it. You see that, don't you ? "

" I see that it was desirable to get rid of the Knockraw tenants. . . . But I do not see why I should be exposed to a visit from those Republican miscreants."

" It was the only way to make Casimir's escape
certain. . . . What will happen, Mr. Craw ? The
Republicans think that Casimir and the Prince are
safe at Castle Gay. They won't trouble very much
about them till to-morrow night, when they are
coming to see you, hoping to catch the lot of you
in the very act of conspiracy. They chose Friday
because it is the day of the poll, and the countryside will be in a stir, and they think that your outdoor and indoor servants will be mostly in Portaway.
Well, all you've got to do is to be there to meet them,
and tell them you never heard of any such nonsense,
and send them all to blazes. Then it will be they
who will look the fools, and you won't be troubled
any more from that quarter. We must settle this
business once and for all, and give you some security
for a quiet life."

" It will be a very unpleasant experience for me,"
said Mr. Craw. But there was no panic in his voice,
only irritation. The listeners received the impression that there would be a certain asperity in Mr.
Craw's reception of the Evallonian delegates.

" Of course," Jaikie added, " it will all have to be
stage-managed a little. You can trust me for that."

" What I don't understand," said Mrs. Brisbane-
Brown, " is why his Royal Highness did not accompany the Knockraw party. . . . It sounds shockingly
inhospitable, sir, and I need not tell you how deeply
honoured I am to have you in my house. But I am
thinking of your own interests. You are the most
important personage in this business, and it was imperative to get you out of danger at once. Yet you

are still here, in hiding, only five miles from your bitterest enemies."

Jaikie looked a little embarrassed. "Perhaps I was wrong, but it seemed to me that the best chance of the Prince's safety was to keep him apart from the others. You see, those people at Portaway are not to be trifled with. They have got lines down every-where, and for all I know they may have discovered the flight of Casimir and his friends and followed them. But Casimir doesn't greatly matter as long as the Prince is not with him. There's nothing wrong in three Evallonian gentlemen visiting Scotland; the trouble begins when they get into Mr. Craw's neigh-bourhood, and when they have the Prince in their company. I thought it safer to break up the covey."

"But how is the Prince to get away?"

"I have arranged all that. There's a man, Mac-lellan, down at Rinks—he's a friend of Mr. McCunn. He has a boat, and he'll put the Prince across to Markhaven and never breathe a word about it. My suggestion is that Mr. McCunn and the Prince drive to Rinks to-morrow night, getting there about 11. There's a train leaves Markhaven at 8.15 next morning which gets to London at 4.30. Once in London he is for all practical purposes safe. . . . The difficulty will lie in getting him away from here. There's a man in Portaway will bring a car—a friend of mine; but I may as well tell you that every corner of this place will be pretty well watched. I told the Evallonians that the Prince was now at Castle Gay. We must do something to keep up that pretence."

" To-morrow night is the Callowa Club Ball," said Mrs. Brisbane-Brown, but no one was listening.

" I think Mr. Charvill should transfer himself to the Castle as soon as possible," said Jaikie. " He's about the Prince's height."

" I have three tickets for the Ball," went on the hostess. " I usually take tickets, but I have not been for years. This year I proposed to take Alison and Robin."

" Mr. Charvill must wear the Prince's white waterproof—whatever the weather—and show himself on the terrace. There will be people to see him, and it will divert attention from the Mains."

Mrs. Brisbane-Brown obtained an audience at last, for she raised her voice to a high pitch of authority.

" I have a plan," she said. " His Royal Highness will come with me to the Ball. It is fancy dress, and he can go as Prince Charles Edward—I have the clothes, wig and all. They belonged to my husband, who was something of the Prince's height and figure. . . . There will be no need for special precautions. A car from Portaway will take my niece, my cousin, and myself to the Station Hotel. At a certain hour in the evening the Prince will leave us and motor to Rinks, where Mr. McCunn will see him safely on board. It is all perfectly simple."

" That's a good idea," said Jaikie fervently. He saw the one snag in his plan neatly removed. " I'll arrange about the car. His Royal Highness must lie very close here till to-morrow evening. It might be a good thing if he went to bed. And Mr. Charvill had better get to the Castle and inside that waterproof."

Mr. Craw made one last protest.

" You have cast me for a very unpleasant part." He looked with disfavour at Jaikie, whom he had come to fear, and with an air of appeal at Dougal, whom he regarded more particularly as his hench-man. It was the henchman who replied :

" You'll have nothing to do, Mr. Craw. Simply to sit in your own chair in your own library and watch those foreigners making idiots of themselves. Then you can say what is in your mind, and I hope the Almighty will put some winged words into your mouth."

An hour later Jaikie stood with Dougal on the terrace of the Mains in the fast-gathering twilight. To them appeared Alison, bearing in her arms a reluctant Woolworth.

" Such a thing has never happened before," she declared. " This evil dog of yours has seduced Tactful and Pensive into raiding the chicken run. They have killed three cockerels. . . . Jaikie, you've introduced a touch of crime into this quiet country-side."

" And that's true, Miss Westwater," said Dougal. " I don't know if you realize it, but we're up against something rather bigger than we pretended indoors."

" I want Jaikie to tell me one thing," said the girl. " Why didn't he let Prince John go with the others ? I wondered at the time. Oh, I know the reason he gave, but it wasn't very convincing."

Jaikie grinned. " Haven't you guessed ? I wanted to please Dickson McCunn. Dougal and I owe everything to him, and it's not much we can do in return. He's a great romantic character, and you can see how he's taken up with Prince John. He was telling me that he has been looking up books at the Castle and finds that the Prince is partly descended from Elizabeth of Bohemia and from the Sobieskis. Prince Charlie's mother was a Sobieski. It will be meat and drink to him to be helping the Prince to escape in the middle of the night in a boat on the Solway shore."

The girl laughed softly. " There couldn't be a better reason," she said. . . . " Then about to-morrow night ? Why have you taken such pains to arrange a visit to Castle Gay—telling the enemy that everybody would be there—encouraging them, you might say ? "

" It was the common-sense plan. I had other reasons, too, and I'll tell you them. I want to see those blighters made to look foolish. I want to see it with my own eyes. You know, they called me a rat, and tried to threaten me. . . . Also, I was thinking of Mr. Craw. This last week has made him a new man."

" That is certainly true. He is losing all his shyness. And Aunt Hatty is so good for him. I believe that, if this crisis goes on much longer, he'll propose to her."

" To-morrow night," said Jaikie, " will put the finishing touch to Mr. Craw. If he confronts the Evallonians in his own house and packs them off

with a cursing, he'll have henceforth the heart of an
African lion."

"He'll need it," said Dougal solemnly. "I tell
you we're up against something pretty big. . . . I
have the advantage of knowing a little about the
gentry down at Portaway. My politics have taken
me into some queer places, and I've picked up news
that never gets into the Press. . . . First of all,
Craw is right to some extent about the Evallonian
Republic. It's not what the newspapers make out.
There's a queer gang behind the scenes—a good
deal of graft, a fair amount of crime, and a lump
of Communism of rather a dirty colour. . . . And
these people at the Hydropathic are some of the
worst of them. They gave you false names last
night, but Casimir, so Miss Westwater tells me,
recognized them from your description, and he gave
them their right names. I know something about
Rosenbaum and Dedekind and Ricci, and I know
a whole lot about Mastrovin. They're desperate
folk, and they know that their power is on a razor
edge, so they won't stick at trifles. . . . You may
be right. They may only want to find the Monarchists in a thoroughly compromising position and
publish it to the world. . . . On the other hand,
they may have a darker purpose. Or perhaps they
have two purposes, and if one fails, they will try the
other. It would suit their book to make Casimir
and Craw the laughing-stock of Europe, but it would
suit their book even better to have done with Casimir
and Co. altogether—and especially with Prince John.
. . . To remove them quietly somewhere where they

would be out of action. . . . For I haven't a doubt
that Casimir is right, and that any moment Evallonia may kick the Republicans over the border."

"I thought of that," said Jaikie. "They have a
yacht waiting at Fallatown."

Dougal listened with wide eyes to this fresh piece
of news.

"To-morrow night," he said solemnly, "there's
going to be some sort of a battle. And we must
prepare every detail as carefully as if it were a real
battle. Man, Jaikie!" and he beat his companion's
back, "isn't this like old times?"

"How marvellous!" Alison cried, and the dusk
did not conceal the glow in her eyes. "I'm going
to be in it. Do you think I'm going to that silly
Ball? Not I!"

"You will certainly be in it," Jaikie told her.
"You and I are going to have the busiest evening
of our lives."

CHAPTER XVIII

SOLWAY SANDS

THIS simple tale, which has been compelled to linger in too many sordid by-paths, is to have at last one hour of the idyllic. But an idyll demands a discerning mind, a mind which can savour that quality which we call idyllic, which can realize that Heaven has for a moment brought spirit and matter into exquisite unison. "We receive but what we give," says the poet, "and in our life alone doth Nature live." Such a mind was Mr. McCunn's, such a maker of idylls was the laird of Blaweary. He alone of men perceived the romance into which he had stumbled, and by perceiving created it. *Cogitavit, ergo fuit.*

Prince John did not go to bed on Thursday afternoon as Jaikie had advised. On the contrary he played bridge after dinner till close on midnight, and was with difficulty restrained from convoying Robin Charvill on his road to Castle Gay. But next morning he stayed in bed. It was a mild bright day of late autumn; the pheasants were shouting in the woods; the roads were alive with voters hastening to Portaway; Charvill was to be observed, by those who were meant to observe him, sitting on a seat on

the Castle terrace in the royal white waterproof : and
in the midst of that pleasant bustle of life Prince
John was kept firmly between the sheets at the
Mains, smoking many cigarettes and reading a detective novel provided by Alison.   The cause of this
docility was Dickson, who came over after breakfast and took up position in the sitting-room adjoining the royal bed-chamber.   It was his duty to see
the Prince out of the country, and he was under-
taking it in a business spirit.

Jaikie, his headquarters the Green Tree, spent
a busy morning over transport.   Wilkie, the mechanic at the Hydropathic, was his chief instrument,
and he was also his intelligence officer.   He brought
news of the Evallonians.   Allins had been having a
good many conferences in the town, he reported,
chiefly in a low class of public-house.   He had also
hired two cars for the evening—the cars only, for
his party preferred to find the drivers.   " He's got
the Station Hotel Daimler," said Wilkie, " and
young Macvittie's Bentley.   They'll be for a long
run, nae doot.   Maybe they're leaving the place,
for Tam Grierson tells me they've got a' their bags
packed and have settled their bills. . . . I've got
our Rolls for you.   Ay, and I've got my orders clear
in my mind.   I bring the Mains folk down to the
Ball, and syne I'm at the hotel at ten-thirty to take
the young gentleman doun to Rinks, and back
again to take the leddies home. . . . 'Deed, yes.
I'll haud my tongue, and ye can see for yersel'
I'm speirin' nae questions.   For this day and this
nicht I'm J. Galt's man and naebody else's."   He

laid a confidential and reassuring finger against
his nose.

The one incident of note on that day was Jaikie's
meeting with Tibbets. He ran against him in the
Eastgate, and, on a sudden inspiration, invited him
to the Green Tree and stood him luncheon—Mrs.
Fairweather's plain cooking, far better than the
pretentious fare of the Station Hotel.

" Mr. Tibbets," he said solemnly, when his guest
had stayed his hunger, " you're proud of your profession, aren't you ? "

" You may say so," was the answer.

" And you're jealous of its honour ? I mean
that, while you are always trying to get the better
of other papers, yet if any attack is made on the
Press as a whole, you all stand together like a stone
wall."

" That's so. We're very proud of our solidarity.
You get a Government proposing a dirty deal, and
we'd smash them in twenty-four hours."

" I thought so. You're the most powerful trade
union on earth."

" Just about it."

" Then, listen to me. I'm going to confess something. That walking tour we told you about was
all moonshine. Dougal—he's my friend—is a journalist on one of the Craw papers, and he's been at
Castle Gay for the last week. I'm not a journalist,
but there was rather a mix-up, and I had to lend a
hand. . . . You scored heavily over your interview
with Craw."

" My biggest scoop so far," said Tibbets modestly.

" Well, it was all bogus, you know. You never saw Craw. You saw another man, a friend of mine, who happened to be staying at the Castle. He didn't know he was being interviewed, so he talked freely. . . . You had a big success, because your readers thought Mr. Craw was recanting his opinions, and you emphasized it very respectfully in no less than three leaders. . . . Naturally, Craw's pretty sore."

Tibbets's jaw had fallen and consternation looked out of his eyes.

" He can't repudiate it," he stammered.

" Oh yes, he can. He wasn't in the house at the moment. He's there now, but he wasn't last Sunday."

" Where was he ? "

" He was with me," said Jaikie. " Don't make any mistake. He has a perfectly watertight alibi. He's only got to publish the facts in his own papers to make the *Wire* look particularly foolish."

" And me," said Tibbets in a hollow voice. " They've just raised my screw. Now they'll fire me."

" Probably," said Jaikie coolly. " It will be the hoax of the year, and the *Wire* is sensitive about hoaxes. It has been had lots of times. . . . But you may ask why the thing hasn't been disavowed already ? This is Friday, and your interview appeared last Monday. A telegram to the *View* signed with Craw's private code-word would have done the trick. That telegram was written out, but it wasn't sent. Can you guess why ? "

Tibbets, sunk in gloom, looked far from guessing.

"I stopped it. And the reason was because we want your help. What's more, that telegram need never be sent. The interview can remain unrepudiated and your own reputation untarnished. It has done a good deal of harm to Craw, but he'll say no more about it if——"

"If?" came Tibbets's sharp question.

"If you give us a hand in an altogether different matter. Craw is being bullied by a gang of foreigners—Evallonians—Evallonian Republicans. That would be grand stuff for the *Wire*, wouldn't it? Yes, but not a word must appear about it unless it is absolutely necessary, for, you see, this is a case for your famous solidarity. A portion of the British Press is being threatened, and in defence the rest of it must stand shoulder to shoulder. You're the only representative of the rest on the spot; and I want you to come with me to-night to Castle Gay to see what happens. There may be no need for your help—in which case you must swear that you'll never breathe a word about the business. On the other hand, you may be badly wanted. In Craw's interest it may be necessary to show up a foreign plot to intimidate a British newspaper proprietor, and between the *Wire* and the *View* we ought to make a pretty good effort. What do you say?"

Tibbets looked at Jaikie with eyes in which relief was mingled with disappointment.

"Of course I agree," he said. "I promise that, unless you give me the word, I will wipe anything

I may see or hear clean out of my memory. I
promise that, if you give me the word, I will put my
back into making the highest and holiest row in the
history of the British Press. . . . But, Mr. Galt, I
wish you hadn't brought in that interview as the
price of my help. I needn't tell you I'll be thankful
if it is allowed to stand. It means a lot to me. But,
supposing Craw disowned it straight away, I'd still
be glad to come in on to-night's show. I've got
my professional standards like other people, and
I'm honest about them. If Craw's independence is
threatened by somebody outside our trade, then
I'm out to defend him, though he were doing his
damnedest to break me. Have you got that ? "

" I've got it," said Jaikie, " and I apologize.
You see I'm not a journalist myself."

Dickson McCunn spent the day, as he would have
phrased it, " in waiting." He was both courtier
and business man. Middlemas was left to see to
the packing of the Prince's kit. Dickson's was no
menial task ; it was for him to act for one day as
Chief of Staff to a great man in extremity. He
occupied his leisure in investigating Mrs. Brisbane-
Brown's reference library, where he conned the
history of the royal house of Evallonia. There could
be no doubt of it ; the blood of Stuart and Sobieski
ran in the veins of the young gentleman now engaged
in bed with a detective novel and a box of cigarettes.

He lunched alone with Mrs. Brisbane-Brown.
Alison, it appeared, was at the Castle, to which late
the night before Mr. Craw had also been secretly

conveyed. In the afternoon Dickson fell asleep, and later was given a solitary tea by Middlemas. At the darkening Alison returned, the Prince was got out of bed, and there was a great mustering of the late General's Highland accoutrements. Presently Dickson had the felicity of watching a young man in the costume of Prince Charles Edward (and, if the miniature in the drawing-room was to be trusted, favouring the original in most respects) being instructed by Alison, with the assistance of her gramophone, in the movements of the foursome and the eightsome reels. Dickson sat through the performance in a happy trance. The faded Stuart tartan of the kilt and plaid, the old worn velvet of the doublet, the bright silver of dirk and sword-hilt, the dim blue of the Garter riband, were part of something which he had always dreamed. The wig was impossible, for the head of the late General had been larger than the Prince's, but Dickson applauded its absence. He had always thought of Prince Charlie as wearing his own hair, and that hair not too long.

Mrs. Brisbane-Brown appeared at dinner " *en grande tenue*," as she expressed it, with a magnificent comb of diamonds surmounting her head. But Alison was in her ordinary outdoor clothes. The Ball was not for her, she said, for she had far too much to do. Jaikie was due at the Castle at half-past eight, and she must be there when he arrived. " That woman Cazenove," she observed, " is no manner of use. She has been fluttering round Mr. Craw like a scared hen, and undermining his self-confidence. She is undoing all the good you did him, Aunt Hatty. I have told Bannister to carry her to her bedroom and lock her in if she gets hysterical."

She left before the meal was over, and her adieu to the Prince scandalized Dickson by its informality. " See that you turn up the collar of your ulster, sir, and tie a muffler round your chin. There are several people near the gate who have no business to be there. I shall have some fun dodging them myself."

The car, driven by Wilkie, duly arrived at the stroke of nine, and Mrs. Brisbane-Brown, attended by her nephew, who was muffled, as one would expect in an Australian, against the chills of a Scots October, was packed into it by Middlemas and her maid. Dickson did not show himself. His time was not yet, and he was fortifying himself against it by a pipe and a little hot toddy.

The story of the Ball may be read in the *Canonry Standard and Portaway Advertiser*, where the party from the Mains was incorrectly given as the Honourable Mrs. Brisbane-Brown, the Honourable Alison Westwater, and Mr. John Charvill. The Australian cousin was a huge success, and to this day many a Canonry maiden retains a tender memory of the tall young Chevalier, who danced beautifully—except in the reels, where he needed much guidance—and whose charm of manner and wide knowledge of the world upset all their preconceived notions of the inhabitants of the Antipodes. His aunt introduced him also to several of the neighbouring lairds, who found him not less agreeable than their womenkind. It was a misfortune that he left so early and so

mysteriously. His name was on many virginal pro-
grammes for dances after midnight. Lord Fosterton
wanted to continue his conversation with him about
a new method of rearing partridges which Mr.
Charvill had found in Czecho-Slovakia, and young
Mr. Kennedy of Kenmair, who was in the Diplomatic
Service, and whose memory was haunted by a re-
semblance which he could not define, was anxious
to exchange gossip with him about certain circles in
Vienna with which he appeared to be familiar. As
it was, Mr. Charvill departed like Cinderella, but
long before Cinderella's hour.

At half-past ten Wilkie returned to the Mains and
Dickson's hour had come. He wore a heavy motor-
ing ulster and a soft black hat which belonged to
Barbon. It seemed to him the nearest approach he
could find to the proper headwear. From Bannister
he had borrowed a small revolver, for which he had
only four cartridges. He felt it incongruous—it
should have been a long sword.

At a quarter to eleven he stood on the pavement
outside the Station Hotel, which was empty now,
for the crowd which had watched the guests' arrival
had departed. A tall figure in a greatcoat came
swiftly out. Dickson held the door open while he
entered the car, and then got in beside him. His
great hour had begun.

I wish that for Dickson's sake I could tell of a
hazardous journey, of hostile eyes and sinister faces,
of a harsh challenge, a brush with the enemy, an
escape achieved in the teeth of odds by the subtlety
and valour of the Prince's companion. For such

things Dickson longed, and for such he was prepared. But truth compels me to admit that nothing
of the sort happened. The idyllic is not the epic.
The idyll indeed is an Alexandrian invention, born
in the days when the epic spirit had passed out of
life. But Dickson, whose soul thirsted for epic,
achieved beyond doubt the idyllic.

Prince John was in a cheerful, conversational
mood. He was thankful to be out of what promised
to be a very tiresome entanglement. He wanted to
be back in France, where he was due at a partridge
shoot. He had enjoyed the Ball, and purposed to
take lessons in reel-dancing. "You have pretty
girls in Scotland," he said, "but none to touch Miss
Westwater. In another year I back her to lead
the field. There's a good hotel, you say, at Markhaven, where I can get a few hours' sleep. . . . My
friends by this time are in London, but we do not
propose to meet till Paris. . . . Happily the wind
is slight. I am not the best of sailors."

He conversed pleasantly, but Dickson's answers,
if respectful, were short. He was too busy savour-
ing the situation to talk. He addressed his companion, not as "Sir," but as "Sire."

The car stopped a little beyond the hamlet of
Rinks, and "Wait here," Dickson told Wilkie;
"I'll be back in less than half an hour." He
humped the heavier of the Prince's two cases (which
was all the baggage the Prince proposed to take
with him) and led him, by a road he knew well, over
the benty links and by way of many plank bridges
across the brackish runnels which drained the

marshlands. The moon was high in the heavens, and the whole cup of the estuary brimmed with light. The trench of the Callowa was full, a silver snake in a setting of palest gold, and above it, like a magical bird, brooded the *Rosabelle*. Only the rare calls of sea-fowl broke into the low chuckle and whisper of the ebbing tide.

Maclellan was waiting for them, Maclellan in sea-boots and an ancient greatcoat of frieze.

" Man, I'm glad to see ye, Mr. McCunn," was his greeting. " I'm vexed we're to hae sae little o' ye, but I'm proud to be able to oblige your freend. . . . What did you say his name was ? Mr. Charles ? It's a grand nicht for our job, Mr. Charles. The wind's at our back—what there is o't. It's no muckle the noo, but there'll be mair oot on the Solway. We'll be in Markhaven by ane o' the mornin'."

Dickson's ear caught Maclellan's misapprehension of Charvill. He did not correct it, for the name Maclellan gave the Prince was the name he had long given him in his heart.

Far down the estuary he saw the lights of a ship, and from its funnel a thin fluff of smoke showed against the pale sky.

" That's the yatt that's lyin' off Fallatown," Maclellan said. " She's gettin' up steam. She'll be for off early in the mornin'."

It was the last touch that was needed to complete the picture. There lay the enemy ship, the English frigate, to prevent escape. Under its jaws the Prince must slip through to the sanctuary of France. The place was no longer an inlet on a lowland firth. It was Loch Nanuamh under the dark hills of Moidart —it was some Hebridean bay, with outside the vast shadowy plain of the Atlantic. . . .

They were on the deck of the *Rosabelle* now, and, as the Prince unbuttoned his ulster to get at his cigarettes, Dickson saw the flutter of tartan, the gleam of silver, the corner of a blue riband. In that moment his spirit was enlarged. At last—at long last—his dream had come true. He was not pondering romance, he was living it. . . . He was no more the prosperous trader, the cautious business man, the laird of a few humdrum acres, the plump elder whose seat was the chimney-corner. He was young again, and his place was the open road and the sea-shore and the uncharted world. He was Lochiel, with a price on his head and no home but the heather. . . . He was Montrose in his lonely loyalty. . . . He was Roland in the red twilight of Roncesvalles. . . .

The Prince was saying good-bye.

" I'm very much obliged to you, Mr. McCunn. Some day I hope we may meet again and renew our friendship. Meanwhile, will you wear this as a memento of our pleasant adventure ? "

He took a ring from his finger, a plain gold ring set with an engraved cornelian. Dickson received it blindly. He was to remember later the words which accompanied it, but at the moment he scarcely heard them. He took the Prince's hand, bent low, and kissed it. Happily Maclellan was not looking.

" God bless your Royal Highness," he stam-

mered, " and bring you safe to port. And if you
ever have need of me, a word will bring me across
the world."

He was on the bank now, the mooring rope had
been loosed, and the *Rosabelle* was slipping gently
down the current. Maclellan had begun to hoist the
sail. The Prince stood in the stern and waved his
hand, but Dickson did not respond. His thoughts
were too insurgent for action. His whole soul was
drawn to that patch of dark which was the boat,
momentarily growing smaller, speeding down a path-
way of silver into a golden haze.

" I meant it," he said firmly to himself. " By
God, I meant it. . . . I'm sixty-one years of age on
the 15th of next month, but a man's just as old as
his heart, and mine's young. I've got the ring. . . .
And maybe some day I'll get the word ! "

He took his seat beside Wilkie and amazed him
by his high spirits. All the road to Portaway he
sang what seemed to be Jacobite songs. " *I'll to
Lochiel and Appin and kneel to them*," he crooned.
When they picked up Mrs. Brisbane-Brown at the
hotel, she travelled alone inside the car, for Dickson resumed the outside seat and his melodies.
" *Follow thee, follow thee, wha wadna follow thee !* "
he shouted.

" Ye havena got the tune richt," said the distracted Wilkie.

" Who cares about the tune ? " Dickson cried.
" It's the words that matter. And the words are
great."

The car halted in the street of Starr village.

Presently Dickson joined Mrs. Brisbane-Brown in-side, and the place beside the driver was taken by a bulky stranger.

"A friend of mine," he told the lady. " He'll maybe come in useful at the Castle."

CHAPTER XIX

MR. CRAW IS MASTER IN HIS OWN HOUSE

A LITTLE after ten o'clock the front-door bell of Castle Gay was violently rung. The summons was answered by Bannister, unattended by the customary footmen. He opened upon a strange spectacle. A conventicle stood upon the doorstep, no less than six men, and behind them on the gravel were two large cars, in which other figures could be discerned. It was a fine night with a moon, and the astonished butler was left in no doubt about the strength of the visitors.

An authoritative voice demanded Mr. Craw. Bannister, jostled out of all his traditions, admitted that his master was at home.

"We will speak with him," said the voice.

The butler stammered something about an appointment.

"He will see us," said the voice firmly. "You need announce no names. Take us to him at once." By this time the six were well inside the doorway, and Bannister had retreated nervously into the hall. It was one of the six, not the butler, that shut the door behind them.

Then Bannister seemed to recover himself. He offered to help the leader in removing his coat, for all six wore travelling ulsters. But he was roughly waved aside. "You will stay here, Hannus," the leader said to one of the party, "and if any one attempts to leave blow your whistle. Our friends outside will watch the other doors. Now, you," he turned to Bannister, "take us instantly to Mr. Craw."

The butler was certainly recovering. "Mr. Craw is in the library," he said, in a tone which was wonderfully composed considering the circumstances. "One moment, sir, and I will light the staircase."

He slipped into the cloakroom on the left side of the hall, and in a moment the great staircase was flooded with light. But in his three seconds of absence Bannister had done something more. He had switched on the light in a minute chamber at the base of the tower, which was one of the remnants of the old shell of the Castle. This chamber had the advantage of looking directly upon the park, and a light in it shone like a signal beacon down the Callowa vale.

"Will you follow me, sir?" he said, and five of the visitors, with eyes as wary as colts, ascended the broad carpeted stairs, while the sixth remained on duty below, standing rigid in the centre of the hall as if to avoid an ambush. It was odd behaviour, but not more odd than that shown by the ascending five. Bannister found himself poked in the back by the barrel of a pistol, and, when he looked round, the pistol's owner grinned and nodded, to point his warning that he was not to be trifled with.

Bannister took no notice. He had recovered the impassiveness of a well-trained servant. He behaved as if such visitors and such manners were in no way abnormal, and led them along the upper gallery and flung open the door of the library.

" Gentlemen to see you, sir," he announced, and when the five had crowded in he shut the door behind them. He seemed to be amused and to have urgent business on hand, for he darted down a side staircase towards the lower regions of the house, and as he went he chuckled.

The library was half in dusk. There was a glow from the big fire on the hearth, and one lamp was lit in the central chandelier. The long lines of vellum and morocco on the walls made a dim pattern in the shadows, and the great Flemish tapestry was only a blur. But there was a reading-lamp on the big table, which partly illumined the blue velvet curtains of the six tall narrow windows.

At the table in his accustomed chair sat Mr. Craw, spectacles on nose, and a paper in his hand, and opposite him was the discreet figure of Miss Elena Cazenove, her pencil poised above her note-book. At the end of the table stood Mr. Barbon, with the air of a secretary waiting to supplement or endorse some ukase of his chief. Both men wore dinner jackets. It was a pleasant picture of busy domesticity.

Mr. Craw raised his eyes from the paper at the interruption. He had nerved himself to a great effort, and his heart was beating uncomfortably. But he managed to preserve an air of self-possession.

23

The features of the marble Augustus on the pedestal behind him were not more composed.

"What does this mean?" he said sharply, in a voice to which nervousness gave the proper irritability. "Bannister!" He raised his voice. But the butler had gone, and the five men in ulsters had approached the table.

He took off his spectacles, but he did not rise. "Who on earth are you?" he demanded. The words came out like pistol shots. The voice was a little startled, which in the circumstances was right.

"Our names do not matter." Mastrovin bent his heavy brows upon the comfortable figure in the chair. This was not quite what he had expected. He had hoped to come upon a full conclave, Royalty and Royalists and Craw in the act of conspiring. He had hoped for a dramatic entry, an embarrassed recognition, a profound discomfiture, and he found only an elderly gentleman dictating letters. Instead of a den of foxes he had stumbled upon a kennel of spaniels. He was conscious that he and his companions struck a discordant note in this firelit room. He must make the most of the discord.

"I offer the conventional apologies for our intrusion, Mr. Craw," he said. "But, as you know well, those who play a certain game cannot always preserve the politenesses. We have come to have a few words with you and your guests."

"I shall not require you for the present, Miss Cazenove," said Mr. Craw, and the lady clutched her note-book, and with a wavering snipelike motion left the room.

" Well ? " said Mr. Craw, when the door had closed behind her. He had sat back in his chair and Barbon had moved to his side.

" The guests to whom I refer," Mastrovin continued, " are four Evallonian gentlemen in whom we are interested."

" Evallonian gentlemen ! " exclaimed Mr. Craw. " Barbon, this man must be mad."

" Let me give you their names," said Mastrovin gently. " They are Count Casimir Muresco, of whom all the world has heard ; Prince Odalchini, and Professor Jagon. Last, but by no means least, there is Prince John, the claimant to the Evallonian throne."

Mr. Craw had pulled himself together and had entered on the line of conduct which had already been anxiously rehearsed.

" I have heard of all four," he said. " But what makes you think they are here ? I do not keep foreign notables on the ice in my cellar."

" We have evidence that at this moment they are under your roof. Be well advised, Mr. Craw. You cannot deceive us. We are perfectly informed of all that has been happening here. At this moment every exit from your house is watched. You had better surrender at discretion."

" Barbon," said Mr. Craw in a pained voice, " what in Heaven's name is he talking about ? "

Mr. Barbon was fussy and anxious in the ordinary relations of life, but not for nothing did the blood of a Cromwellian Barebones run in his veins. His war record had proved that he could be cool enough

in certain emergencies.   Now he was rather enjoying himself.

" I'm sure I don't know, sir," he said. " The
first three men are, or were, the shooting tenants
of Knockraw.   I knew Count Casimir slightly, and
they came to dinner last Saturday night, and we
dined with them on Monday.   I heard that they
had now gone home.   I know nothing about Prince
John.   There was nobody of that name with the
Knockraw people when they dined here."

" I see," said Mr. Craw. He turned to Mastrovin.
" Is that information any use to you ? Apparently
you must look for your friends at Knockraw.   I
myself have been away from home and only
returned last night.   I know nothing whatever
about your Evallonians.   I never saw them in
my life."

" I am sorry to be obliged to give you the lie,"
said Mastrovin.   " We have evidence that three of
them came here two days ago.   We know that
Prince John is here—he was seen here this very day.
I warn you, Mr. Craw, that we are difficult people to
trifle with."

" I have no desire to trifle with you."   Mr. Craw's
manner was stately.   " You come here uninvited,
and cross-examine me in my own library.   I have
told you the literal truth.   You, sir, have the air
and speech of a gentleman.   I shall be obliged if
you will now withdraw."

For answer the five men came a little nearer, and
Barbon sat himself on the arm of his chief's chair.
He was beginning to measure the physical prowess

of the visitors. The difficulty lay in what they
might have in their ulster pockets.

Over the fireplace there was a huge coat of arms
in stone, the complete achievement of the house of
Westwater, and above this was a tiny balcony. It
was flush with the wall and scarcely discernible
from below—it was reached by a turret stair from
the old keep, and may once have been a hiding-
place, the Canonry equivalent of a " priest's hole."
At this moment it held Alison and Jaikie. They
had a full view of Mr. Craw's face and of the Evallonian profiles.

" Will you inform us who are the present inmates
of this house ? " Mastrovin asked.

" Let me see," said Mr. Craw. " Apart from
Mr. Barbon, whom you see here, there is Miss Cazenove, who has just gone, and Mr. Crombie, who is
one of my Press assistants. Then there is a young
Australian friend called Charvill. There is also a
country neighbour, Mr. McCunn, but he is out this
evening and will not be home till late. That is all,
I think, Barbon, besides the domestic staff ? "

" Will you kindly have them assembled here ? "

The tone nettled Mr. Craw, in spite of the restraint
he had put upon himself.

" You are insolent, sir," he rapped out. " You
would be justly served if I summoned my servants
and had you kicked out of doors. Who are you to
issue commands ? "

" We happen to be in command," said Mastrovin
with a thrust forward of his heavy chin. " Your
household staff is depleted. Your outdoor staff is

in Portaway and will not return till morning. They
were seen to leave your park gates. We have our
own people inside and outside this house. You will
be wise to obey us."

Mr. Craw, having remembered his part, shrugged
his shoulders. He touched a button on the table,
and Bannister appeared with a suddenness that
suggested that he had been lurking outside the door.

"Have the goodness to ask Mr. Charvill and Mr.
Crombie to come here," he said. "You will find
them, I believe, in the billiard-room."

The billiard-room was at the other end of the
house, but the rapidity with which the two presented
themselves argued a less distant lair. Dougal had
his pipe, and Robin Charvill had his finger in a
novel to mark his place. Mastrovin cast an eye
over their physical proportions, which were not
contemptible. Craw was, of course, useless, but
there were three able-bodied opponents if trouble
came. But he was accustomed to similar situations,
and had no doubt about his power to control them.

"You say this is all your household. Very well.
We will soon test your truthfulness. We are going
to search your house. You four will remain here
till I return, and two of my friends will keep you
company. You "—he turned to Bannister, who
stood discreetly in the background—" will accompany me."

Up in the gallery Jaikie chuckled. "Just what I
hoped," he whispered to Alison. " Bannister knows
what to do. You and I must show them a little
sport." The two slipped out to the turret staircase.

Rosenbaum and Dedekind were the two left behind to guard the prisoners in the library. They had done the same sort of thing before and knew their job, for they took up positions to cover the two doors. Each had his right hand in the pocket of his ulster. The face of the Jew Rosenbaum was heavy and solemn, expressionless as a ship's figurehead, but Dedekind was more human. He shifted his feet, undid the top button of his ulster, for the night was not cold, and the fire was good, and looked as if he would like to talk. But the party of four seemed to be oblivious of their gaolers. Mr. Craw resumed his papers, Barbon was busy making entries in a note-book, Dougal had picked up a weekly journal, and Charvill had returned to his novel. They gave a fine example of British phlegm, and disregarded the intruders as completely as if they had been men come to wind up the clocks.

Meantime Bannister, with the injured air of an abbot who is compelled to reveal to some raiding Goths the treasures of his abbey, conducted Mastrovin, Ricci, and Calaman over the castle. They descended into the hall, where they found the sixth Evallonian at his lonely post : he reported that he had seen and heard no one. They investigated the big apartments on the ground-floor, including the nest of small rooms beyond the dining-hall. Then they made an elaborate survey of the main bedroom floors, both in the ancient central keep and the more modern wings. They found everything in order. They penetrated to Mr. Craw's luxurious chamber, to which he proposed, as we know, to add a private bathroom. They raided the rooms which housed Barbon and Dougal, Charvill and Dickson McCunn, and they satisfied themselves by an inspection of the belongings that the inmates were those whom Bannister named. They entered various bedrooms which were clearly unoccupied. And then they extended their researches to the upper floors.

It was here that their tour became less satisfying. The upper floors of Castle Gay are like a rabbit-warren—clusters of small rooms, tortuous passages on different levels, unexpected staircases, unlooked-for *cul-de-sacs*. It was hard for any stranger to preserve his sense of direction, and to keep tally of all that he saw. The business was complicated by the hidden presence of Alison and Jaikie, and of Tibbets, who had been summoned from his own lair. Also of the beagle pups, Tactful and Pensive.

Alison, who knew every cranny of the house, took command, and Jaikie and Tibbets in their stocking-soles followed. . . . The Evallonians would hear suddenly loud voices at a corridor's end, and on arriving there find no one. Lights would be turned on and as suddenly turned off. There would be a skirl of idiot laughter as they came into a passage, cold and blue in the light of the moon. . . . Also there were dogs, dogs innumerable. A hound would suddenly burst into their midst and disappear. Ricci fell heavily on one of the stairways, because of a dog which swept him off his legs.

The searchers, puffing and bewildered, lost their tempers. Bannister found a pistol clapped to his chest, and turned on Mastrovin a pallid, terror-stricken face.

" What infernal maze is this you have brought us to ? " the voice behind the pistol demanded. " Answer, you fool. There are people here, many people. Who are they ? "

The butler was a figure of panic. " I don't know," he stammered. " You have seen the rooms of the staff. Up here no one sleeps. It is the old part of the house. They say it is haunted."

" Haunted be damned ! " Mastrovin turned suddenly and peered into a long, low attic, empty except for some ancient bedsteads. There was a sound without, and as he moved his head he saw the butt-end of a human form disappearing apparently into the ground. It was Tibbets, who was a little behind the others. The sight quickened Mastrovin's paces. For a little he preceded Bannister, darting with surprising rapidity in the direction of any noise. But all that happened was that he hit his head hard on a beam, and, opening a door hastily, all but cascaded down a steep flight of steps. And his movements were enlivened by echoes of ghostly merriment above, below, before, behind him. . . .

In a secluded corner Alison, Jaikie, and Tibbets were recovering their breath. The girl shook with laughter. " Was there ever such a game of hide-and-seek ? " she panted.

But Jaikie looked grave.

" We mustn't rattle them too much," he said. " They're a queer lot, and if we wake the savage in them they may forget their manners. We don't want anything ugly to happen. They'll give up in a little if we let them alone, and go back to the library."

But it was a full half-hour before Mastrovin left those upper floors, and, with each minute of failure to find what he sought, his fury and his suspicions increased. Alison and her two squires followed the party at a discreet distance, till they saw them enter the library corridor. Jaikie took a glance into the hall below, and observed that the Evallonian sentry was no longer there. He knew that he was now lying gagged and trussed in a corner of the cloak-room. The time had come for Mackillop and his friends to act.

The three squeezed into their little gallery above the fireplace, just as the Evallonians entered the library. Mr. Craw was still writing in apparent unconcern. As a matter of fact he had written his name six hundred and seventy times on sheets of foolscap by way of steadying his nerves. Dougal was smoking and reading the *Spectator*, Barbon was apparently asleep, and Charvill still deep in his novel. As they entered, Rosenbaum and Dedekind moved towards them, and there were some rapid questions and answers.

Something which the leader said woke all five into a sudden vigilance. The slouch and embarrassment disappeared, and their bodies seemed to quicken with a new purpose. The five took a step towards the table, and their movements were soft and lithe as panthers. They were no longer clumsy great-coated foreigners, but beasts of prey.

The sweat stood on Mastrovin's brow, for he was

of a heavy habit of body and had had a wearing time upstairs. But his voice had an edge like ice.

" I have seen your house," he said. " I am not satisfied. There are people hiding in it. You will bring them to me here at once or . . ."

He paused. There was no need to put his threat into words ; it was in every line of his grim face : it was in the sinister bulge of his hand in his ulster pocket.

Mr. Craw showed his manhood by acting according to plan. He was desperately afraid, for he had never in his life looked into such furious eyes. But the challenge had come, and he repeated the speech with which he had intended to meet that challenge.

" This is pure brigandage," he said. " You have not given me your names, but I know very well who you are. You must be aware, Mr. Mastrovin, that you will not further your cause by threatening a British subject in his own house."

The risk in preparing speeches beforehand is that the conditions of their delivery may be far other than the conditions forecast in their preparation. Mr. Craw had assumed that the Evallonians were politicians out to secure a political triumph, and that, when this triumph tarried, they would realize that their audacity had defeated its purpose and left them at his mercy. He had forgotten that he might have to deal with men of primeval impulses, whose fury would deaden their ears to common sense.

At the sound of his name Mastrovin seemed to stiffen, as a runner stiffens before the start. Then

he laughed, and it was not a pleasant sound. He
turned to his followers. " He knows me," he cried.
" He is not as innocent as he pretends. He knows
of us from our enemies. They are here. We are
close to them. Now there will be no mercy."

In a voice that made Mr. Craw jump in his chair
he thundered : " One minute ! I will give you one
minute ! "

He had his pistol out, and little blue barrels
gleamed in the hands of the other four, covering
Barbon, Dougal, and Charvill. Mr. Craw sat stupe-
fied, and his spectacles in the tense hush made a
clatter as they dropped on the table. The gilt
baroque clock on the mantelpiece struck the quarter
to midnight.

In the little gallery the estate mechanician had
that morning arranged a contrivance of bells. There
was a button at Jaikie's elbow, and if he pressed it
bells would ring in the corridor outside and in the
ante-room. There by this time Mackillop and his
men were waiting, in two parties of five, all of them
old soldiers, armed with rifles and shot-guns. At
the sound of the bells they would file in and over-
awe the enemy—ten weapons in ten pairs of resolute
hands.

Jaikie's finger was on the button, but he did not
press it.

For the first time in his life he had to make a
momentous decision. Dougal and he had planned
out every detail of that evening's visit, and believed
that they had foreseen every contingency. But they

had forgotten one. . . . They had forgotten how different these five foreigners below were from themselves. These were men who all their lives had played darkly for dark stakes—who had hunted and been hunted like beasts—to whom murder was an incident in policy—whose natural habitat was the cave and the jungle. He was aware that the atmosphere in the library had changed to something savage and primordial—that human lives hung on a slender hair. A devil had been awakened, a devil who was not political. . . . If Mackillop and his men appeared in the doorway, if the glint of weapons answered those now in the hands of the five, it would be the spark to fire the mine. These men would fight like cornered weasels, oblivious of consequences—as they had often in other lands fought before. No doubt they would be overpowered, but in the meantime—— In that warm and gracious room the Den had been re-created, and in that Den there were only blind passions and blind fears.

He did not press the button, for he knew that it would be to waken Hell.

As it was, Hell was evident enough. His companions felt it. Alison's hand tightened convulsively on his arm, and as for Tibbets behind him— he heard Tibbets's teeth chatter. Down below the four men, covered by the five pistols, knew it. Mr. Craw's face was the colour of clay, and his eyes stared at Mastrovin as if he were mesmerized. Barbon and Charvill had also whitened, and sat like images, and Dougal seemed to be seeking self-com-

mand by sucking in his lips against his clenched
teeth. In a second anything might happen. The
jungle had burst into the flower-garden, and with
it the brutes of the jungle. . . . A small hopeless
sound came from Jaikie's lips which may have been
meant for a prayer.

Suddenly he was aware that Mastrovin's eyes had
turned to the door which led to the ante-room. Had
Mackillop shown himself ?

" Stand ! " Mastrovin cried. " Not another step
on your life ! "

A voice answered the Evallonian's bark, a rich,
bland, assured voice.

" Tut, tut, what's all this fuss about ? " the voice
said. " Put away that pistol, man, or it'll maybe
go off. *Sich* behaviour in a decent man's house ! "

Jaikie was looking down upon the bald head of
Dickson McCunn—Dickson in his best suit of knickerbockers, his eyes still bright with the memory of his
great adventure on the Solway sands, his face ruddy
with the night air and as unperturbed as if he were
selling tea over the counter. There was even a smile
at the corner of his mouth. To Jaikie, sick with fear,
it seemed as if the wholesome human world had
suddenly broken into the Den.

But it was the voice that cracked the spell—that
pleasant, homely, wheedling voice which brought
with it daylight and common sense. Each of the
five felt its influence. Mastrovin's rigour seemed to
relax. He lowered his pistol.

" Who the devil are you ? " he grunted.

"My name's McCunn," came the brisk answer. "Dickson McCunn. I'm stopping in this house, and I come back to find a scene like a demented movie. It looks as if I'm just in time to prevent you gentlemen making fools of yourselves. I heard that there was a lot of queer folk here, so I took the precaution of bringing Johnnie Doig the policeman with me. It was just as well, for Johnnie and me overheard some awful language. Come in, Johnnie. . . . You're wanted."

A remarkable figure entered from the ante-room. It was the Starr policeman, a large man with his tunic imperfectly buttoned, and his boots half-laced, for he had been roused out of his early slumbers and had dressed in a hurry. He carried his helmet in his hand, and his face wore an air of judicial solemnity.

"Johnny and me," said Mr. McCunn, "heard you using language which constitutes an assault in law. Worse than that, you've been guilty of the crime of *hamesucken*. You're foreigners, and maybe no very well acquaint with the law of Scotland, but I can tell you that *hamesucken* is just about the worst offence you can commit, short of taking life. It has been defined as the crime of assaulting a person within his own house. That's what you're busy at now, and many a man has got two years' hard for less. Amn't I right, Johnny?"

"Ye're right, sir," said the policeman. "I've made notes o' the langwidge I heard, and I hae got you gentlemen as witnesses. It's *hamesucken* beyond a doubt." The strange syllables boomed ominously, and their echoes hung in the air like a

thunderstorm. " Gie me the word, sir "—this to
Mr. Craw—" and I'll chairge them." Then to the
five—" Ye'd better hand ower thae pistols, or it'll
be the waur for ye."

For the fraction of a second there was that in
Mastrovin's face which augured resistance. Dickson
saw it, and grinned.

" Listen to reason, man," he cried genially, and
there was a humorous contempt in his voice which
was perhaps its strongest argument. " I know fine
who you are. You're politicians, and you've made
a bad mistake. You're looking for folk that never
were here. You needn't make things worse. If
you try violence, what will happen ? You'll be
defying the law of Scotland and deforcing the police,
and even if you got away from this countryside—
which is not likely—there's not a corner of the globe
that could hide you. You'd be brought to justice,
and where would your politics be then ? I'm speaking as a business man to folk that I assume to be in
possession of their wits. You're in Mr. Craw's hands,
and there's just the one thing you can do—to throw
yourselves on his mercy. If he takes my advice he'll
let you go, provided you leave your pistols behind
you. They're no the things for folk like you to be
trusted with in this quiet countryside."

Jaikie in the gallery gave a happy sigh. The
danger was past. Over the Den had descended the
thick, comfortable blanket of convention and law.
Melodrama had gone out of the air. Mastrovin and
his friends were no longer dangerous, for they had
become comic. He prodded Tibbets. " Down you

get. It's time for you to be on the floor of the house." Things could now proceed according to plan.

Then Mr. Craw rose to the height of a great argument. He rescued his spectacles, rested his elbows on the table, and joined his still tremulous finger-tips. Wisdom and authority radiated from him.

" I am inclined," he said, " to follow Mr. McCunn's advice and let you go. I do not propose to charge you. But, as Mr. McCunn has said, in common decency you must be disarmed. Mr. Barbon, will you kindly collect these gentlemen's weapons."

The five were no longer wolves from the wilds : they were embarrassed political intriguers. Sullenly they dropped their pistols into the waste-paper basket which Barbon presented to them.

Mr. Craw continued :

" I would repeat that what I have told you is the literal truth. Your countrymen were at Knockraw and dined here with Mr. Barbon, but I did not meet them, for I only returned yesterday. As for Prince John, I do not know what you are talking about. Nobody like him has ever been in Castle Gay. You say that he was seen here this very morning. I suggest that your spies may have seen my friend Mr. Charvill, who is spending a few days with me. . . . But I am really not concerned to explain the cause of your blunders. The principal is that you have allowed yourselves to be misled by an ex-servant of mine. I hope you have made his rascality worth his while, for it looks as if he might be out of employment for some little time."

24

Mr. Craw was enjoying himself. His voice grew round and soothing. He almost purred his sentences, for every word he spoke made him feel that he had captured at last an authority of which hitherto he had never been quite certain.

" I am perfectly well informed as to who you are," he went on. " You, sir," addressing Mastrovin, " I have already named, and I congratulate you on your colleagues, Messieurs Dedekind, Rosenbaum, Calaman, and Ricci. They are names not unknown in the political—and criminal—annals of contemporary Europe. . . . You have put yourself in a most compromising position. You come here, at a time when you believe that my staff is depleted, with a following of your own, selected from the riff-raff of Portaway. You were mistaken, of course. My staff was not depleted, but increased. At this moment there are ten of my servants, all of whom served in the War, waiting outside this door, and they are armed. Any attempt at violence by you would have been summarily avenged. As for your ragamuffin following, you may be interested to learn that during the last hour or two they have been collected by my keepers and ducked in the Callowa. By now they will have returned to Portaway wiser and wetter men. . . .

" As for yourselves, you have committed a grave technical offence. I could charge you, and you would be put at once under arrest. Would it be convenient for the Republican Party of Evallonia to have some of its most active members in a British dock and presently in a British gaol ? . . . You are even more completely in my power than you imagine.

You have attempted to coerce an important section of the British Press. That, if published, would seal the doom of your party with British public opinion. I have not only my own people here to report the incident in the various newspapers I control, but Mr. Tibbets of the *Wire* is present on behalf of my chief competitors, and at my request has put himself in a position also to furnish a full account.

"But," said Mr. Craw, moving his chair back from the table and folding his arms, "I do not propose to exact any such revenge. You are free to go as you came. I will neither charge you, nor publish one word of this incident. But a complete record will be prepared of this evening's doings, and I warn you that, if I am ever troubled again in any way by you or your emissaries, that record will be published throughout the world's Press, and you will be made the laughing stock of Europe."

Mr. Craw ceased, pressed his lips, and looked for approbation to Dougal, who nodded friendlily. Mastrovin seemed about to reply, but the nature of his reply will never be known. For Dickson broke in with: "You'd better hurry, gentlemen. You should be at Fallatown within the next three-quarters of an hour, if your yatt is to catch the tide."

This final revelation of knowledge shut Mastrovin's lips. He bowed, and without a word led his friends from the room, after which, through the lines of Mackillop's deeply disappointed minions, they descended to the front door and their cars. Dickson chose to accompany and speed the parting guests.

With their departure Mrs. Brisbane-Brown entered the library from the ante-room, where she had waited under Mr. McCunn's strict orders. Jaikie and Alison, whose heads were very close together in the little balcony, observed her arrival with interest.

"Aunt Hatty has been really anxious," said the girl. "I know that look on her face. I wonder if she's in love with Mr. Craw. I rather think so. . . . Jaikie, that was a horrid strain. I feel all slack and run down. Any moment I expected to see those devils shoot. I wouldn't go through that again for a million pounds."

"No more would Mr. Craw. But it will have made a man of him. He has been under fire, so to speak, and now he'll be as bold as brass."

"He owes it all to you."

"Not to me," Jaikie smiled. "To me he very nearly owed a bullet in his head. To Dickson McCunn. Wasn't he great?"

The girl nodded. "Mr. McCunn goes off in a fury of romance to see a rather dull princeling depart in a boat, because he reminds him of Prince Charlie. And he comes back to step from romance into the most effective kind of realism. He'll never give another thought to what he has just done, though he has saved several lives, but he'll cherish all his days the memory of the parting with Prince John. Was there ever such an extraordinary mixture?"

"We're all like that," was the answer.

"Not you. You've the realism, but not the sentiment."

"I wonder," said Jaikie

Ten minutes later Mr. McCunn was refreshing himself in the library with a whisky-and-soda and sandwiches, for the excitements of the night had quickened his appetite.

" I got the idea," he explained to Dougal, " by remembering what Bismarck said during the Schleswig-Holstein affair—when he was asked in Parliament what he would do if the British Army landed on German soil. He said he would send for the police. . . . I've always thought that a very good remark. . . . If you're faced with folk that are accustomed to shoot it's no good playing the same game, unless you're anxious to get hurt. You want to paralyse them by lapping them in the atmosphere of law and order. Talk business to them. It's whiles a very useful thing to live in a civilized country, and you should take advantage of it.

" Ay," he continued, " I accompanied yon gentry to the door. I thought it my duty to offer them a drink. They refused, though their tongues were hanging out of their mouths. That refusal makes me inclined to think that it will not be very long before Prince John sits on the throne of Evallonia. For it shows that they have no sense of humour, and without humour you cannot run a sweetie-shop, let alone a nation."

CHAPTER XX

NEXT evening the sun, as it declined over the Carrick hills, illumined a small figure plodding up the road which led to Loch Garroch. Very small the figure appeared in that spacious twilight solitude, and behind it, around it, in front of it scampered and sniffed something still smaller. Jaikie and Woolworth were setting out again on their travels, for there was still a week before the University of Cambridge claimed them.

Jaikie had left Castle Gay in a sober and meditative mood. " So that's that," had been his not very profound reflection. Things did happen sometimes, he reminded himself, unexpected things, decisive things, momentous incidents clotted together in a little space of time. Who dare say that the world was dull ? He and Dougal, setting out on an errand as prosaic as Saul's quest of his father's asses, had been suddenly caught up into a breathless crisis, which had stopped only on the near side of tragedy. He had been privileged to witness the discovery by an elderly gentleman of something that might almost be called his soul.

There could be no doubt about Mr. Craw. Surprising developments might be looked for in that hitherto shy prophet. He had always been assured enough in his mind, but he had been only a voice booming from the sanctuary. He had been afraid of the actual world. Now that fear had gone, for there is no stiffer confidence than that which is won by a man, otherwise secure, who discovers that the one thing which he has dreaded need only be faced to be overcome. . . . Much depended upon Mrs. Brisbane-Brown. Jaikie was fairly certain that there would be a marriage between the two, and he approved. They were complementary spirits. The lady's clear, hard, good sense would keep the prophet's feet in safe paths. He would never be timid any more. She would be an antiseptic to his sentimentality. She might make a formidable being out of the phrasing journalist.

Much depended, too, upon Dougal. It was plain that Dougal was now high in the great man's favour. A queer business, thought Jaikie, and yet natural enough. . . . Jaikie had no illusions about how he himself was regarded by Mr. Craw. Hatred was too strong a word, but beyond doubt there was dislike. He had seen the great man's weakness, whereas Dougal had only been the witness of his strength. . . . And Craw and Dougal were alike, too. Both were dogmatists. They might profess different creeds, but they looked on life with the same eyes. Heaven alone knew what the results of the combination would be, but a combination was clearly decreed. Dougal was no more the provincial journalist ; he would soon have the chief say in the direction of the Craw Press.

At the thought Jaikie had a momentary pang. He felt very remote not only from the companion of his week's wanderings but from his ancient friend.

Mr. Craw had behaved handsomely by him. He had summoned him that morning into his presence, and thanked him with a very fair appearance of cordiality. He had had the decency, too, not to attempt to impose on him an obligation of silence as to their joint adventures, thereby showing that he understood at least part of Jaikie's character.

"Mr. Galt," he had said, "I have been much impressed by your remarkable abilities. I am not clear what is the best avenue for their exercise. But I am deeply in your debt, and I shall be glad to give you any assistance in my power."

Jaikie had thanked him, and replied that he had not made up his mind.

"You have no bias, no strong impulse ? "

Jaikie had shaken his head.

"You are still very young," Mr. Craw had said, "but you must not postpone your choice too late. You must find a philosophy of life. I had found mine before I was out of my teens. There is no hope for the drifter."

They had parted amicably, and, as he breasted the hill which led from the Callowa to the Garroch, Jaikie had found himself reflecting on this interview. He realized how oddly detached he was. He was hungry for life, as hungry as Dickson McCunn. He enjoyed every moment, but he knew that his enjoyment came largely from standing a little apart. He

was not a cynic, for there was no sourness in him.
He had a kindliness towards most things, and a
large charity. But he did not take sides. He had
not accepted any mood, or creed, or groove as his
own. *Vix ea nostra voco* was his motto. He was
only a seeker. Dougal wanted to make converts ;
he himself was still occupied in finding out what
was in his heart.

For the first time in his life he had a sense of loneliness. . . . There was no help for it. He must be
honest with himself. He must go on seeking.

At the top of the hill he halted to look down upon
the Garroch glen, with the end of Lower Loch Garroch a pool of gold in the late October sun. There
was a sound behind him, and he turned to see a girl
coming over the crest of the hill. It was Alison,
and she was in a hurry, for she was hatless, and
her cob was in a lather.

She swung herself to the ground with the reins
looped round an arm.

" Oh, Jaikie ! " she cried. " Why did you leave
without saying good-bye ? I only heard by accident
that you had gone, and I've had such a hustle to
catch you up. Why did you do it ? "

" I don't know," said Jaikie. " It seemed difficult to say good-bye to you, so I shirked it." He
spoke penitently, but there was no penitence in his
face. That plain little wedge of countenance was
so lit up that it was almost beautiful.

They sat down on a bank of withered heather
and looked over the Garroch to the western hills.

" What fun we have had ! " Alison sighed. " I

hate to think that it is over. I hate your going away."

Jaikie did not answer. It was difficult for one so sparing of speech to find words equal to that sudden glow in his eyes.

" When are we going to meet again ? " she asked.

" I don't know," he said at last. " But we are going to meet again . . . often . . . always."

He turned, and he saw in her face that comprehension which needs no words.

They sat for a little, and then she rose. " I must go back," she said, " or Aunt Hatty will be dragging the river for me."

They shook hands, quite prosaically. He watched her mount and turn her horse's head to the Callowa, while he turned his own resolutely to the Garroch. He took a few steps and then looked back. The girl had not moved.

" *Dear Jaikie*," she said, and the intervening space did not weaken the tenderness of the words. Then she put her horse into a canter, and the last he saw was a golden head disappearing over the brow of the hill.

He quickened his pace, and strode down into the Garroch valley with his mind in a happy confusion. Years later, when the two monosyllables of his name were famous in other circles than those of Rugby football, he was to remember that evening hour as a crisis in his life. For, as he walked, his thoughts moved towards a new clarity and a profound concentration. . . . He was no longer alone. The seeker had found something infinitely precious. He had a spur now to endeavour, such endeavour as would make the common bustle of life seem stagnant. A force of high velocity had been unloosed on the world.

These were not Jaikie's explicit thoughts ; he only knew that he was happy, and that he was glad to have no companion but Woolworth. He passed the shores of Lower Loch Garroch, and his singing scared the mallards out of the reeds. He came into the wide cup of the Garroch moss, shadowed by its sentinel hills, with the light of the Back House to guide him through the thickening darkness. But he was not conscious of the scene, for he was listening to the songs which youth was crooning in his heart.

Mrs. Catterick knew his step on the gravel, and met him at the door.

" Bide the nicht ? " she cried. " 'Deed ye may, and blithe to see ye ! Ye've gotten rid o' the auld man ? Whae was he ? "

" A gentleman from London. He's safely home now."

" Keep us a'. Just what I jaloused. That's a stick for me to haud ower Erchie's heid. Erchie was here twae days syne, speirin' what had become o' the man he had sae sair mishandled. D'ye ken what I said ? I said he was deid and buried among the tatties in the yaird. No anither word could Erchie get oot o' me, and he gae'd off wi' an anxious hert. I'll keep him anxious. He'll be expectin' the pollis ony day."

Five minutes later Jaikie sat in the best room, while his hostess lit the peat fire.

" Ye've been doun by Castle Gay ? " she gossiped.
" It's a braw bit, and it's a peety the family canna
afford to bide in it.   It's let to somebody—I canna
mind his name.   We're on his lordship's land here,
ye ken.   There's a picture o' Miss Alison.   She
used to come often here, and a hellicat lassie she was,
but rale frank and innerly.   I aye said they wad
hae a sair job makin' a young leddy o' her."

Mrs. Catterick pointed to where above the mantelpiece hung a framed photograph of a girl, whose
face was bordered by two solemn plaits of hair.

" It's a bonny bit face," she said reflectively.
" There's daftness in it, but there's something wise
and kind in her een.   'Deed, Jaikie, when I come
to look at them, they're no unlike your ain."

THE END

PRINTED IN GREAT BRITAIN AT
THE PRESS OF THE PUBLISHERS

NELSON'S NOVELS

Select List of some of the most famous modern novels. These volumes contain as much reading matter as the full-sized novel now issued at 7s. 6d. net.   Set in clear type, and strongly bound.

At 2s. net

ARNOLD, MRS. J. O.	The Merlewood Mystery
BAILEY, H. C.	Beaujeu
BAUM, J. E.	Gold and a Girl
BELL, J. J.	Atlantic Gold
BELL, J. J.	Wee Macgreegor
BELLOC, HILAIRE	The Girondin
BENTLEY, E. C.	Trent's Last Case
BIRMINGHAM, GEORGE A.	The Simpkins Plot
BRUCE, MAJOR GEORGE	The Rainbow of Saba
BUCHAN, JOHN	Mr. Standfast
BUCHAN, JOHN	John Macnab
BUCHAN, JOHN	Witch Wood
BUCHAN, JOHN	The Dancing Floor
BUCHAN, JOHN	Midwinter
BUCHAN, JOHN	The Three Hostages
BUCHAN, JOHN	Greenmantle
BUCHAN, JOHN	Salute to Adventurers
BUCHAN, JOHN	Prester John
BUCHAN, JOHN	Huntingtower
BUCHAN, JOHN	The Path of the King
BUCHAN, JOHN	The Runagates Club
CASTLE, A. AND E.	If Youth but Knew

[*Continued*

NELSON'S NOVELS—*Contd.*

At 2s. net

CHAMBERS, WHITMAN	Don Coyote
CHAMBERS, WHITMAN	Contraband Coast
CONRAD, JOSEPH	Romance
CRAWFORD, F. MARION	Sant' Ilario
CRAWFORD, F. MARION	Dr. Claudius
CRAWFORD, F. MARION	Arethusa
CULLUM, RIDGWELL	The Heart of Unaga
CULLUM, RIDGWELL	The Trail of the Axe
CULLUM, RIDGWELL	The Men who Wrought
CULLUM, RIDGWELL	The Law-breakers
CULLUM, RIDGWELL	The Triumph of John Kars
DE LA PASTURE, MRS. HENRY	The Man from America
DE LA PASTURE, MRS. HENRY	The Tyrant
DE LA PASTURE, MRS. HENRY	The Grey Knight
DE MORGAN, WILLIAM	Joseph Vance
DOYLE, A. CONAN	The Refugees
DRAGO, HARRY SINCLAIR	The Desert Hawk
FERGUSON, W. B. M.	Other Folks' Money
FIELDING, HOWARD	The Confederate
FRIEND, OSCAR J.	Gun Harvest
GOLDEN, HARRY	Unseen Acres
GREY, ZANE	Light of Western Stars
GREY, ZANE	The Lone Star Ranger
GREY, ZANE	The Rainbow Trail
GREY, ZANE	Riders of the Purple Sage

[*Continued*

NELSON'S NOVELS—*Contd.*

At 2s. net

GREY, ZANE	Wildfire
GREY, ZANE	The Border Legion
GREY, ZANE	Desert Gold
GREY, ZANE	Heritage of the Desert
HEWLETT, MAURICE	The Forest Lovers
HOBART, D. B.	The Adventure Trail
HOPE, ANTHONY	Simon Dale
HUTCHINSON, A. S. M.	The Happy Warrior
HUTCHINSON, A. S. M.	Once Aboard the Lugger—
JACOBS, W. W.	The Castaways
JACOBS, W. W.	Ship's Company
KENDALL, OSWALD	The Missing Island
LANCASTER, G. B.	Jim of the Ranges
LOMBARD, CLAIR	The Lumber King
MACNAUGHTAN, S.	The Expensive Miss Du Cane
MACNAUGHTAN, S.	Christina M'Nab
MALET, LUCAS	The Wages of Sin
MARSHALL, IAN	The Strange Case of Vintrix Polbarton
MORTON, WILLIAM	Masquerade
NIVEN, FREDERIC	The Justice of the Peace
NORRIS, W. E.	Matthew Austin
OLLIVANT, ALFRED	The Gentleman
PARKER, SIR GILBERT	Seats of the Mighty
PARKER, SIR GILBERT	Donovan Pasha
PEASE, HOWARD	The Tattooed Man
PERRY, CLAY	The Two Reds of Travoy
PHILLIPS, H. LAWRENCE	A Friendless Millionaire

[*Continued*

NELSON'S NOVELS—*Contd.*

At 2s. net

PRESTON, ARTHUR	Saddle Tramp
PRESTON, ARTHUR	Thunder Island
" Q "	The Splendid Spur
RATH, E. J.	The Stolen Car
RATH, E. J.	The Riddle of the Wilds
RATH, E. J.	The Flying Courtship
RATH, E. J.	Let's Go
ROBERTS, MORLEY	Salt of the Sea
SABATINI, RAFAEL	Sea Hawk
SANDEMAN, F. S.	Riders of the Wild West
SAVILE, FRANK	The Red Wall
SEDGWICK, ANNE DOUGLAS	Franklin Kane
SIDGWICK, MRS. ALFRED	Cousin Ivo
ST. JOHNSTON, COL. T. R.	Pearl of Fortune
TAYLOR, MARY IMLAY	The Man Who Awoke
THYNNE, MOLLY	The Red Dwarf
TWAIN, MARK	Huckleberry Finn
TWAIN, MARK	Tom Sawyer
ULRICH, ROY	Wanda of the White Sage
VANCE, L. J.	The Black Bag
WATSON, H. B. MARRIOTT	The House in the Downs
WEYMAN, STANLEY	The Red Cockade
WEYMAN, STANLEY	A Gentleman of France
WHITE, STEWART E.	Rules of the Game
WILDRIDGE, OSWALD	On the Other Side of the Wall
WILSON, CHERRY	Stormy

THOMAS NELSON AND SONS, Ltd
London, Edinburgh, New York, Toronto, and Paris